Don Quixote de La Mancha
(Part II)

ALONSO FERNÁNDEZ DE AVELLANEDA

Don Quixote de La Mancha (Part II)

Being the spurious continuation of Miguel de Cervantes' Part I

Translation and Edition by

ALBERTA WILSON SERVER
University of Kentucky
and
JOHN ESTEN KELLER
University of Kentucky

Footnotes by
TOM LATHROP

Illustrated by
HAL BARNELL

Juan de la Cuesta
Newark, Delaware

Cover illustration by Hal Barnell
Cover design by Michael Bolan

An imprint of LinguaText, Ltd.
270 Indian Road
Newark, Delaware 19711-5204 USA
(302) 453-8695
Fax: (302) 453-8601
www.JuandelaCuesta.com

MANUFACTURED IN THE UNITED STATES OF AMERICA

ISBN: 978-1-58871-162-5 (PAPERBACK)

This book was originally published in hardback in 1980
with the ISBN 0-936388-01-3, Library of Congress Card No. 80-80491

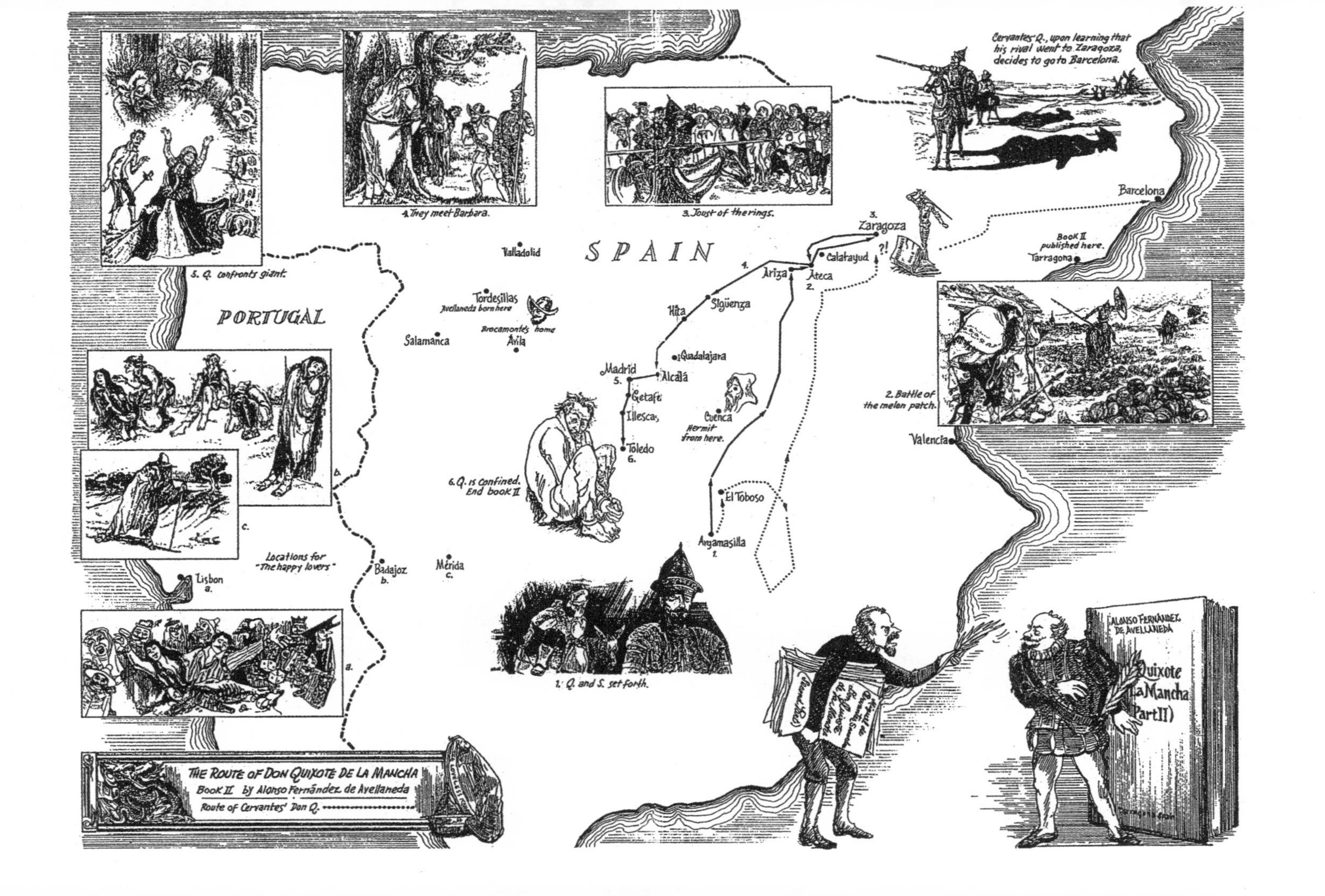
THE ROUTE OF DON QUIXOTE DE LA MANCHA
Book II by Alonso Fernández de Avellaneda
Route of Cervantes' Don Q.
SPAIN
PORTUGAL
5. Q. confronts giant.
4. They meet Barbara.
3. Joust of the rings.
Cervantes Q., upon learning that his rival went to Zaragoza, decides to go to Barcelona.
Barcelona
Book II published here.
Tarragona
3. Zaragoza
?!
Calatayud
Ateca 2.
Ariza
4.
Sigüenza
Hita
Guadalajara
Alcalá
Madrid 5.
Getafe
Illescas
Toledo 6.
Cuenca
Hermit from here.
El Toboso
Argamasilla 1.
2. Battle of the melon patch.
Valencia
Valladolid
Tordesillas
Avellaneda born here
Brocamonte's home
Ávila
Salamanca
6. Q. is confined. End book II
1. Q. and S. set forth.
Locations for "The happy lovers"
Lisbon a.
Badajoz b.
Mérida c.
a.
b.
c.
ALONSO FERNÁNDEZ DE AVELLANEDA
Quixote La Mancha Part II)
(Second Part)

Translators' Introduction

WHEN MIGUEL DE CERVANTES SAAVEDRA saw part I of *El ingenioso hidalgo don Quixote de la Mancha* published in 1605 he could have had no conception of his novel's enormous popularity. When its world-wide success became apparent to him, even though it did not enrich him, since he had sold the publishing rights to a bookseller named Francisco de Robles, his satisfaction and pride must have overcome him. Perhaps it was his hope, perhaps his intent that led him to end Part I with hints of a third sally on the part of Don Quixote and Sancho Panza. Certainly he left his novel open-ended and even printed in its very last line a dare to anyone to attempt to continue the adventures of his characters. And, not content with this, within a few pages of *Don Quixote*'s dénouement, he wrote: "There is only the tradition, handed down in La Mancha, to the effect that in the course of this third expedition he went to Saragossa . . . " The novel actually ends with a series of epitaphs and sonnets to Don Quixote, Sancho, Dulcinea, and Rocinante, said to have been set down by the Academicians of Argamasilla and discovered by an old physician in a leaden box buried in a ruined hermitage. The final paragraph reads: "Such were the verses that could be made out. The others, being worm-eaten, were turned over to an academician that he might decipher their meaning by conjecture. It is reported that he has done so, at the cost of much labor and many sleepless nights, and that it is his purpose to publish them, which leads us to hope that we may be given an account of Don Quixote's third sally."

To many readers Cervantes' Part II excels his Part I through its greater unity, its deepening of character, both of Don Quixote and of Sancho Panza, and because it depends far less upon a series of madcap adventures. Its humor is quite as evident as in Part I, but it is accompanied by a certain winsomeness and a new sympathy for the two adventurers. We suspect that Cervantes began the continuation not long after the completion of his first volume despite the fact that in 1613 he published his *Novelas exemplares* which must have required some length of time to compose and write. Part II appeared in 1615 and its success was as phenomenal as had been that of Part I.

But this continuation of the expeditions of Don Quixote and Sancho Panza was marred for Cervantes by the appearance in 1614 of a rival or spurious set of adventures about Don Quixote written by a person who used the pseudonym Alonso Fernández de Avellaneda, usually known nowadays simply as Avellaneda. And so the dare at the end of Part I was taken, and Cervantes was furious. To this day no one knows the identity of Avellaneda, although some of the best scholars have attempted to recognize him. Whoever he was, he somehow seems to have gotten wind of what Cervantes' Part II contained, perhaps by managing somehow to see Cervantes' own manuscript, for he did far more than send Don Quixote and Sancho off to Saragossa as Cervantes had written was to be their destination. At times he actually reproduced whole lines seen in Cervantes' forthcoming book with many of the same proverbs and all this verbatim. He titled his novel *Segundo tomo del ingenioso hidalgo don Quixote de la Mancha que contiene su tercera salida: y es la quinta parte de sus aventuras* 'Second Volume of the Ingenious Hidalgo Don Quixote of La Mancha which Contains his Third Sally and is the Fifth Part of his Adventures' (Cervantes' own first book was divided into *four* parts). Avellaneda took advantage, then, of the opportunity to continue a story about internationally famous literary characters and to profit from its sale, but apparently an even greater bonus to Cervantes' rival was the chance to vilify, insult and otherwise damage Cervantes himself whom he seems to have hated exceedingly, even though he obviously admired his craftsmanship.

It was Avellaneda's novel that led Cervantes to alter certain parts of his second volume, and, as it will be recalled, to change the itinerary of the adventurers and send them, not to Saragossa for the jousts there, but instead to Barcelona. In fact, he actually gained considerably from his rival's book. He not only refuted the journey to Saragossa, but brought off a considerable *coup* in the way he gave his rival the lie. He actually availed himself of one of Avellaneda's characters, a certain Don Álvaro Tarfe, and brought him to an inn where Don Quixote was lodging. There the knight himself, who by then knew of the spurious adventures by another Don Quixote, confronted him. In Part II, Chapter LXXII, in which this occurs, Don Álvaro is struck by the genuineness of the real Don Quixote and Sancho Panza and is forced to admit that the false one, the one whom he had known, is a poor imitation of the original. Moreover, at Don Quixote's request, Tarfe makes a sworn and notarized statement to the effect that he had before that day never seen the real Don Quixote. Nor was this the only occasion seized upon by Cervantes to lambast the spurious account. In Chapter LIX Sancho and his master talk to two gentlemen who have read the book about the other Don Quixote and Sancho, and they flay it mercilessly to Don Quixote's immense satisfaction. And in Chapter LXI, as Don Quixote enters Barcelona to which Cervantes had deliberately sent him in order to negate Avellaneda's sending him to Saragossa, a man cried out welcome "not to the false, not the ficticious, not the apocryphal one that we read of in mendacious histories that have appeared of late, but the true and legitimate one, the real one that Cid Hamete Benengeli, flower of historians, has portrayed for us."

And that was not all, for in Chapter LXX, after a character named Altisidora had returned to life from her feigned death, she reported that at the gate of hell she had seen about a dozen devils playing a kind of tennis, not with balls, but with books. And after knocking a certain book out of its binding, one devil asked what its title was. The devil who picked up the book said, "This is the *Second Part of the History of Don Quixote de la Mancha*, not written by Cid Hamete, the original author, but by an Aragonese who, according to his own account, is a native of Tordesillas." "Take it away," said the other. "Throw it into the bottomless pit so I shan't have to see it." "Is is as bad as all that?" "It is so bad," said the first devil, "that if I had deliberately set myself to write a worse one, I shouldn't have been able to achieve it."

Avellaneda's contributions to Cervantes' Part II increased still more the excellence of that belated volume, though in a way even Cervantes may not have at first realized. But upon reflection he must have come to understand, even in the heat of his never diminishing fury, that his attacker had actually led him to material he would not have otherise utilized. Out of the substitution of Barcelona for Saragossa emerged, as Cervantes wrote the last sections of Part II, a series of adventures that surely enriched his work more than would have the Saragossan jousts. The journey to and stay in Barcelona provided the opportunity of including some of Part II's most interesting aspects. This should have mollified Cervantes somewhat.

One other amusing ploy that Cervantes used to discredit Avellaneda is the timing of the third sally in Part II. Avellaneda had sent the knight and squire on the road to adventure one full year after they returned from the second sally at the end of Part I. In Part II Cervantes allowed them only a *month's* rest before they slipped away to seek further adventures as knight errant and squire. So the real Don Quixote learned about the false one long before the false one ever went out on the road, and in fact, the real Don Quixote was dead and buried before the false one ever left home.

Though attempts to identify the man behind the pseudonym of Avellaneda have proved fruitless so far, his writing has served to tell us much about the kind of person he was and why he motivated his protagonists and sketched their characteristics as he did at great variance with Cervantes'. He seems to have been a very pious and probably a very narrow-minded individual, whereas Cervantes gives little evidence of his own religiosity, and in fact writes in a vein that is little short of irreligious. Avellaneda, for example, related as one of the long interpolated tales he used (so as to be in conformity with Cervantes' use of this narrative technique in Part I) a famous miracle of the Virgin—which is incidentally one of the most moving verisons of the story. In another he made it very clear that his regard for sin was severe. Moreover, all through his book are elements which lead one to suspect that he was deeply influenced by the movement of the Counter Reformation. These sentiments, however, did not prevent him from writing in a lewd or coarse way or from using rough language not employed by Cervantes. In short, Avellaneda's book can be considered in some of its sequences definitely scatological.

He wrote in Aragonese, or at least filled his work with many elements from that dialect. This in no way kept him from being a fine writer or from having produced a novel which can still be read with profit and entertainment. His syntax is good, his vocabulary rich, and sometimes colloquial, and his erudition very apparent. Given his knowledge of so many books and his hard-shelled conservatism and religiosity, it might be safe to opine that he was an ecclesiastic.

Like Cervantes, Avellaneda subscribed to the tried-and-true classic design of fiction and included the nine elements of the design, rendering each—plot, setting, conflict, characterization, theme, style, effect, point of view and mood or tone—with skill and confidence. He weaves plot skillfully and maintains suspense; his settings, though not described in detail, never fail to give the reader an adequate idea of the milieu through which his characters move; he sustains characterization and creates in Don Quixote and Sancho strong characters who do not follow the patterns Cervantes implanted upon his own; he lays down clearly the outlines of conflict and has the power to catch and hold the reader's attention; theme, which in Avellaneda is multi-faceted, concentrates on the damnation of the novels of chivalry not many of which he had actually read; in style, to be discussed at greater length below, he is to us attractive and expert; his point of view, made evident through Don Quixote himself for the most part, is that of a madman who thinks he is a knight errant or some character he had read about in books; the effect of the novel is powerful and sometimes cruelly so; the mood or tone, severe at times, at times humorous, is evoked throughout.

Possibly the greatest fault of Avellaneda is repetitiveness. He dwells upon the character of Don Quixote as a full-fledged madman capable of engaging in not much beyond bizarre and insane adventures and possessed of a mind so deranged that it never permits him moments of lucidity, for he always thinks he is someone he is not. Cervantes began Part I, it should be recalled, with a hero who saw himself as some personage from literature or history and usually from novels of chivalry—Amadís de Gaula, Beltenebros or Rinaldo de Montalbán, for example—and thereby set a pattern Avellaneda would follow throughout his own book. But Cervantes soon abandoned this sort of insanity and allowed his knight to reveal his psychosis in other ways, thereby strengthening his character and causing his actions to lead to an almost personal emotional attachment for him in the mind of his readers. Cervantes' Don Quixote is somehow loveable, and his purposes which move him through life, though distorted, make him consistently attractive.

In Part I Cervantes utilized the rich lore of Spanish balladry with great effect and reader appeal, for his audience knew and loved ballads. Later, but especially throughout Part II, he abandoned ballads almost entirely. Avellaneda, on the other hand, continued to use ballad lore throughout his work.

Avellaneda sees in insanity something to laugh at and make fun of without the chords of sympathy for the insane which Cervantes knew so well how to touch. Possibly he was simply incapable of understanding the more delicate and still scarcely understood components of madness and therefore could not impart to his Don Quixote the poetic and pathetic qualities Cervantes knew how to share with his readers. One senses in Cervantes a deep-seated tolerance and sympathy for the disordered mind. Even those who do not know this or even that he created one of the most intersting and pathetic madmen in literature in his *novela*, the *Licenciado vidriera*, sense the marvelous characterization of the mad knight. We can laugh at Avellaneda's descriptions of Don Quixote's antics and cavortings, as we laughed with Cervantes in Part I, but we cannot, in the spurious novel become one with Don Quixote.

As for Sancho's character in Avellaneda's hands, he appears as a roughneck, a stupid yokel, a true buffoon who elicits the kind of humor one laughs at in a trained bear. He wields a cruelly satiric sword against Sancho as a member of the great unwashed and a boorish peasant, revealing an innate scorn for such lowly people. How different from Cervantes who made Sancho the hearty, loveable, quasi-ignorant, quasi-wise creature he is to us. In passing, we remark that Avellaneda must have been an urban dweller and this may explain and partially justify his satrire of rustics and the fact that most of the adventures of Don Quixote and Sancho take place in towns or cities. In Cervantes, most occurred in rural areas or even in the wilderness.

We believe that no two people who write about the same characters can possibly create them in similar molds. It is not surprising, then, that the two Don Quixotes and the two Sancho Panzas are as different as they are. Cervantes, aware of human foibles, and with sympathy for the untutored at whom he may poke fun but always in a kindly fashion, with his greatness of heart, his broad experience in life itself—writer, traveler, soldier, government official, husband and father —and perhaps above all his ability to live the part of his characters and feel with them and for them, created the pair we know and love. And yet those who have not read his masterpiece, and they are myriad, alas, see Don Quixote and Sancho much as Avellaneda saw them. Ask most people who Don Quixote is and they are likely to reply simplistically that he was a crazy knight who tilted at windmills. Can we be certain that seventeenth-century Spaniards thought more highly of Part II, because today we hold the opinion that it surpasses Part I? Perhaps the general reading public in Cervantes' time enjoyed Cervantes' knight who fought sheep and had his teeth knocked out by Yanguesan carriers more than the poignancy of that knight's love for the peerless Dulcinea.

How good an author was Avellaneda? Better than most, by far, we believe. Had all trace of both parts of the true *Quixote* been lost and forgotten, Spanish literature could claim with considerable pride that Avellaneda had produced a great novel with memorable characters. It is comparison with the unsurpassable masterpiece the true *Quixote* is that has diminished the false *Quixote*'s worth. But even comparison did not always result unfavorably for Avellaneda. When Alain-René Lesage's translation into French of the spurious novel appeared in 1704, a century after the first publication of Cervantes' Part I, he printed a prologue in which he extolled Avellaneda highly and led Spaniards themselves to consider it as great or even greater than Cervantes' work. Considerable controversy was generated and in it Avellaneda's work did not suffer in repute. Even as late as 1852 in France the translator A. Germond de Lavigne was still hailing Avellaneda as Cervantes' superior in the area of novel writing. But since then the current has changed and today, as we all know, thousands read Cervantes and few Avellaneda. This can be explained by the fact that there have been very few editions of the false *Quixote* published in Spain (but in recent years *two* excellent annotated editions have apeared) and virtually no translations appear. Perhaps the Spanish scholar and critic Menéndez Pelayo best clarifies the cause. "It should not be forgotten that the literary merits of Avellaneda are difficult to perceive for the simple reason that the second apocryphal part cannot be read without our unconsciously remembering the *Quixote* of Cervantes; and that it is a most difficult test for any writer to be balanced at each step against the best novel ever written."

THE PRESENT TRANSLATION

We hope that our translation has not been warped or colored in any way by our knowledge of Cervantes' work, a masterpiece which cannot be bested. And we insist, even in the face of all that has been written in comparison of the two novelists, that Avellaneda produced a lively and fascinating book, shaped, it is true by a man as different from Cervantes as Lope de Vega from Calderón de la Barca, and for this reason worthy of modern study and enjoyment. The false *Quixote* has much to recommend it, and we hope that through our translation, the first in English in almost two centuries, our contemporaries may enjoy reading is as much as we have enjoyed its translation.

We have not produced a perfectly literal translation, for had we done so, how could we have rendered Avellaneda's seventeenth-century parlance into our own? In our opinion, lack of literalness is not a drawback, nor has it damaged our production. To us a good translation should carry over the ideas and imagery of the original tongue into that of the second with as few changes in meaning, concept, and thought as possible. Actually, we have taken very few liberties with the original, but to preserve euphony and avoid monotony we have sometimes translated *dixo*, 'he said,' in various ways. When feasable we have used the most modern and accepted American English. Occasionally, to enhance readability, we have broken up some of Avellaneda's more lengthy sentences into shorter and more easily digestible units.

Little effort has been made to versify Avellaneda's poetry, for such a daring course would have altered meaning.

We can only hope that this modern translation will make an important masterpiece from the past come to life in the present for the English-speaking world. Therefore we have striven to make Avellaneda speak as clearly and as naturally to our own readers as he spoke to his, presenting nothing in our language that was not in essence in his.

JOHN E. KELLER

ALBERTA WILSON SERVER

Publisher's Note

THE DESIGN of this book is based directly on the original Spanish edition of 1614; the look of the title page which you will see when you turn this leaf, the format of the preliminary pages of the book, the style of chapter openings and endings, and certain other details, all derive from the original edition. In order to prepare our design, we went to the Hispanic Society of America in New York, and there, in the Society's rare book section, examined and measured their precious copy of Avellaneda's *Don Quixote*. For this privilege we are indebted to Dr. Theodore Beardsley, Director of the Hispanic Society.

The large decorated capitals beginning each chapter are not from the Tarragona edition of 1614, but rather belong to the original stock of type used in Juan de la Cuesta's seventeenth century Madrid print shop. These woodcuts were graciously provided by Professor Roberto M. Flores of the University of British Columbia.

In one major feature, this edition is quite different from the original edition; the first edition was *not* illustrated, and this one is. Hal Barnell of New York City is the artist who has given both face and figure to the second Don Quixote and Sancho who wandered about Spain. Avellaneda's book has only been illustrated a few times in its publication history, yet Hal has proven that the subject has immense pictorial possibility. In addition to the illustrations, the artist has provided new versions of the decorated letters not contained in Cuesta's original collection; notably K and W, which were not a part of the seventeenth-century Spanish alphabet.

In the early stages of the preparation of this edition, Professor James K. Saddler of our Editorial Board expertly guided the project, and if the edition came out well, we are convinced that it is due in large measure to him.

We also owe special thanks to Professor Joseph R. Jones of the University of Kentucky who was very helpful in providing translations of many of the Latin quotations found in the text.

SECOND
VOLUME OF
THE INGENIOUS HIDALGO
DON QUIXOTE DE LA MANCHA,
which contains his third sally and is the fifth part of his adventures.

Composed by the licenciado Alonso Fernández de Avellaneda, born in the village of Tordesillas.

To the Mayor, Councilmen and Nobles of the Illustrious town of Argamesilla, fortunate native land of the hidalgo Knight Don Quixote de la Mancha.

Duly Licensed, In Tarragona in the establishment of Felipe Roberto, A. D. 1614

To the Mayor, Councilmen and Nobles of the Illustrious town of Argamesilla[1] de la Mancha, Fortunate Native Town of the Hidalgo[2] Knight Don Quixote, Glory of Those Professing Knight-Errantry

ANCIENT IS THE CUSTOM[3] of dedicating books about the excellent qualities and deeds of a famous man to his illustrious homeland, which, like a mother, created him and brought him to light; and even so is the custom of a thousand cities to vie over which should be the native village of a great talent and a serious personage. And since the hidalgo knight Don Quixote de la Mancha is exactly that (for his undeard-of prowess is so well-known through the world), it is proper that that fortunate village which your Lordships rule, his home town and that of his faithful squire Sancho Panza, should so be, and to dedicate to you this Second Part which relates the victories of the one and the good services of the other, no less envied than true. Take then, your Lordships, under your Manchegan protection, this book and the zeal of the one who composed it against a thousand vilifications, for they deserve it, the book for itself, and the author for the danger to which he has exposed himself, placing his work in the arena of the masses, that is to say, in the horns of an indomitable bull, etc.

---

[1] It was never stated *anywhere* in Cervantes' novel that Argamasilla (which Avellaneda always spells Argamesilla) was, in fact, Don Quixote's home town. At the end of Part I, however, we do find burlesque verses about Don Quixote written by certain academicians of Argamasilla (I, 52 [These references are to Cervantes' *Don Quixote*, Part number and Chapter number]), and this has led many to believe that Argamasilla was the right town. At the end of Cervantes' Part II (74), we read that his village was spefically not named "in order that all of those towns of La Mancha might contend among themselves for the right to adopt him and claim him as their own." [All quotations from Cervantes' novel are from the Samuel Putnam translation.] Of course, Cervantes may have declined to name the village in specific reaction to Avellaneda's insisting it was Argamasilla.

[2] *Hidalgo* refers both to a low noble rank (entitling one to be called *Don* as well) and the meaning 'gentlemen'; the double meaning is in force here. English has borrowed this word intact.

[3] This dedication is seemingly "clearly unclear" on purpose; one never really knows what the antecedent of most pronouns is, and this translation tries to preserve the patent incomprehensibility of the original.

Prologue

Since the story of Don Quixote de la Mancha is almost a play, it cannot nor should it fail to have a prologue. therefore, at the beginning of this second part of his exploits there appears this one, less boastful and offensive to its readers than the one Miguel de Cervantes Saavedra placed before his first part, and more humble than the one he wrote for his *Novelas*, satirical rather than exemplary, although quite ingenious.

He will not consider as such the accounts in this story, which is continued as authoritatively as he began it, with a copy of the faithful records which came into his hand (and I say «hand» because he himself admits he has only one,[1] and while we are talking so much about everybody we should say of him: «As an soldier as old in years as he is youthful in courage, he has more tongue than hands»). But let him complain about my work because of the profits I take away from his second part. At least he cannot refuse to admit that we both have one aim, which is to banish the harmful lesson of the inane books of chivalry so commonplace among rustics and idle people. However, we differ in method: he took that of offending me, one so justly praised by the most distant nations, one to whom our nation owes so much because of his having for so many years decorously and richly entertained the theaters of Spain with innumerable stupendous plays, with the artistic strictness the world demands and with the assurance and purity to be expected from a minister of the Holy Office.[2]

---

[1] Cervantes was wounded and maimed in his left hand during the naval battle of Lepanto in the Gulf of Corinth, 1571, when the united Christian fleets defeated the navies of Islam.

[2] No one knows the relationship between Cervantes and Avellaneda; in his own second part to *Don Quixote*, which appeared a year after Avellaneda's, Cervantes seems to get his first knowledge of Avellaneda while writing Chapter 59. Yet, because of this statement in Avellaneda's prologue, some people have believed that Avellaneda was none other than the great playwright Lope de Vega (with whom Cervantes did not get along), and who indeed "richly entertained the theaters of Spain with innumerable stupendous plays," but Avellaneda's many incidences of Aragonese spellings and structures deny this.

My purpose has not been only to bring the stupidities of Sancho to the present comedy, avoiding offending anybody or making a display of learned synonyms (although I could do the latter well but the former poorly); I only say that nobody need be startled that this second part comes from a different author, for there is nothing new about different persons pursuing the same story. How many have spoken of the love affairs of Angélica and what happened to her? Various *Arcadias* have been written, and the *Diana*[3] is not all by one hand. Since Miguel de Cervantes is now as old as the Castle of Cervantes,[4] and is so hard to please because of his years that he is annoyed by everybody and everything, he therefore so lacks friends that when he wished to adorn his books with pompous sonnets he had to attribute them (as he says) to Prester John of the Indies of the Emperor of Trebizond, perhaps not finding a titled person in Spain who would not be offended if his name were mentioned, so many having permitted their names to appear at the beginning of books by the author he backbites—please God may he stop this, now that he has taken refuge in the sanctuary of the Church. Let him be content with his *Galatea* and prose plays, for that is what most of his novelettes are; let him not vex us.

Saint Thomas, in 2, 2, *quaestio* 36, teaches us that envy is sadness because of another's good fortune and prosperity, a doctrine he took from John of Damascus. In book 31, Chapter 31, of the moral exposition he made for the story of Saint Job, Saint Gregory says that the children of this vice are hatred, gossip about and defamation of one's neighbor, joy over his troubles, and regret about his good fortune; and well is this sin called envy: *a non videndo, quia invidua non potest videre bona aliorum.*[5] All are effects as infernal as their cause, so contrary to Christian charity, of which Saint Paul said in 1 Corinthians: 13 : *Charitas patiens est, benigna est: non emulatur, non agit perperam, non inflatur, non est ambitiosa . . . congaudet veritati,* etc.[6] But on this subject he excuses the errors in the First Part

[3] Versions of the story of Angélica appeared in 1586 and 1602, the latter by Lope de Vega; the Italian Sannazaro's *Arcadia* (1504) was revised in Spanish by the same Lope (1598); Jorge de Montemayor's *Diana* was continued by two different authors, both of their works appearing in 1564.

[4] A ruined fortress in Toledo, built in the eleventh century!

[5] From the *Etymologies* of St. Isidore: ". . . from not seeing because the envious man is unable to bear the good of others."

[6] Verses 4-6, which read: "Love is patient; love is kind and envies no one. Love is never boastful, nor conceited, nor rude; never selfish, not quick to take offense. Love keeps no score of wrongs; does not gloat over other men's sins, but delights in the truth." Avellaneda's memory seems imperfect.

by the fact that it was written among people in prison:[7] because of this he could not avoid being smirched by them, nor could he help coming out other than complaining, gossipy, impatient, and short-tempered, as prisoners are. This part varies somewhat from his First Part because my disposition differs from his, and in matters of opinion about anything historical, and as authentic as this is, each can strike out in the direction he pleases. This is truer when one has such a wide field as the multitude of papers I have read to compose this story, not to speak of the equal amount of those I have failed to read.

Let nobody complain because printing of such books is permitted, for this one does not teach lewdness but rather not to be crazy. When so many *Celestinas,* mother and daughter,[8] are now in permitted to roam about the public squares, a Don Quixote and a Sancho Panza may well be allowed into the fields, for they were never known to have any vice: rather, they had the commendable desire to right
injustices done to orphaned girls,
undo wrongs,
etc.

[7] Cervantes suggested in the Prologue to Part I that his work was *of the type* that "might be engendered in a prison," but he never said it was *really* written there. Avellaneda, like innumerable others, has been too narrow in his reading.

[8] *La Celestina* is one of the pinnacles of Spanish literature. Its original version (1499) was written by Fernando de Rojas, and was continued by four different authors; the last version, *The Daughter of la Celestina,* was published in 612.

By Pero Fernández

SONNET

Even though the greatest misdeeds
Require learned and intelligent men,
And I am the most foolish among the stupid,
Willingly and more persistently do I write,

Since for an endless number of days
fame had been hiding in mute books
The most extravagant and headstrong deeds
Ever seen from Illescas to Olias,

I contribute to you, noble readers
The second set of the unlimited inanities
Of the Manchegan nobleman, Don Quixote,

So that you may take warning from his obsession,
For he who tries to run so heedlessly
Cannot have better enjoyment of life.[9]

---

[9] It was common to begin books with prefatory verses; Cervantes' Part I has ten poems at the beginning.

FIFTH
PART OF THE INGENious hidalgo do Quixote de la Mancha and his Knight-Errantry[1]

FIRST CHAPTER, HOW DON QUIXOTE DE LA MANcha returns to his knight-errantry fantasies and certain knights from Granada come to his village of Argamesilla

HE SAGE ALISOLÁN, a modern no less than true historian, says that after the expulsion of the Mohammedan Moors from Aragón (the nation of which he was a descendent) he found among certain historical records written in Arabic[2] the third sally that the invincible hidalgo, Don Quixote de la Mancha, made in order to attend some tournaments being held in the renowned city of Zaragoza.[3]

---

[1] Cervantes' Part I was originally divided into four parts, so Avellaneda's continuation naturally begins with the fifth Part. Modern versions of Cervantes' Part I usually don't show these divisions anymore.

[2] The Arabic historian Alisolán is an imitation of Cervantes' own Arabic historian, Cid Hamete Benengeli, but there are major differences. Here, Alisolán apparently is recounting only what he researched while Cid Hamete is an omniscient wizard author who actually followed every one of Don Quixote's adventures as they were happening; also, whereas Cid Hamete is found virtually everywhere in Cervantes' work, Alisolán's name is mentioned only once.

[3] It is only natural that in Avellaneda's version, Don Quixote should go to Zaragoza, for Cervantes says at the end of Part I (52) that his third sally was to Zaragoza. In Cervantes' Part II, when the "real" Don Quixote learns about a "false" Don Quixote who has gone to Zaragoza, he immediately changes his plan and goes to Barcelona instead, so that there will be no confusion as to who is who (II, 60).

He speaks as follows: After Don Quixote had been taken in a cage to his village by the Priest, the Barber, the lovely Dorotea, and Sancho Panza, his squire,[4] he was placed in a room and chained by the foot with a thick, heavy chain. There, with the not inconsiderable luxury of chicken broth and other substantial restoratives, they slowly brought him back to his right mind. In order not to return to the former fantasies of his fabulous books of knight-errantry, after several days of confinement he began to beg his niece Madalena[5] urgently to get him a good book with which to while away those seven hundred years he expected to remain under that harsh enchantment. On the advice of the Priest, Pedro Pérez, and Master Nicolás, the Barber, she gave him a *Flos Sanctorum* by Villegas and the Gospels and Epistles for the whole year, written in the vernacular, and the *Guide for Sinners*[6] by Fray Luis de Granada. With these lessons, forgetting the chimera of the knights-errant, he was restored to his former judgment and released from imprisonment. After this he began to go to mass, rosary in hand along with the *Hours of Our Lady*. He listened so attentively to the sermons that the inhabitants of the village now thought that he was cured of his seizure and heartily thanked God. Counseled by the Priest, nobody dared say a word to him about the things that had happened because of him. They addressed him not as Don Quixote but as Señor Martín Quijada,[7] which was his right name, but when he wasn't in earshot they had a number of amusing moments talking about him and what they all remembered, such as the affair of rescuing or freeing the galley slaves or the matter of his penitence in the Sierra Morena mountains[8] and all the other things that are related in the first parts of this story.

---

[4] Starting in I, 47, Don Quixote was put in a cage and taken back to his village with the characters named.

[5] Cervantes didn't name the niece until II, 74, where he calls her Antonia Quijada, probably in reaction to Avellaneda's Madalena.

[6] The *Flos Sanctorum* 'The Flower of Saints' was translated by Villegas in 1588; the *Guide for Sinners* was written by Fray Luis de Granada, and published in 1556.

[7] Cervantes doesn't offer a real given name to Don Quixote until Part II, 74, where he is called *Alonso* Quijano, again probably in reaction to Avellaneda's Martín. It should be noted that Martín was a name that was synonymous with craziness at that time. Cervantes also never specified what his hero's real *last* name might have been either, although he listed a number of possibilities : Quijano (II, 74), Quejana (I, 1), Quijada (I, 1) and Quijana (I, 5).

[8] The galley slave adventure is in I, 22, and the penitence in the Sierra Morena begins in I, 23.

As it happened, in the month of August his niece was struck down by one of those fevers called transient by physicians, which last twenty-four hours, and the attack was such that his niece Madalena died within that period of time. The good hidalgo remained alone and disconsolate, but the priest supplied him with a very devout good old Christian woman to keep his house, cook his food, make his bed and serve his other needs, and finally keep the good Priest or the Barber informed of all Don Quixote did or said, in or out of the house, to see if he was returning to his foolish obstinacy about knight-errantry. It so happened that one extremely hot day, after dinner, Sancho Panza came to visit, and, finding him in his room reading the *Flos Sanctorum*, he said "What are you doing, Señor Quijada? How goes everything?"

"Oh, Sancho," said Don Quixote, "Welcome! Sit down here a while; upon my word, I was quite anxious to talk to you."

"What book is that you are reading?" asked Sancho. "Is it about knightly deeds like those in which we were involved so stupidly last year? Be so good as to read a little. Let's see if there is any squire who prospered more than I did, for by the soul of my cloak, that knightly joke cost me more than twenty-six *reales* and my good dapple, stolen from me by Ginesillo,[9] that freelance galley-oarsman, and after all that I'm left neither rook nor king unless the boys make me King of the Roosters[10] for the Carnival parade."

"I am not reading a book of chivalry, for I do not have any," said Don Quixote. "I am reading this *Flos Sanctorum*, which is very good."

"And who was this Flas Sanctorum?"[11] replied Sancho. "Was he a king or one of those giants who turned into windmills a year ago?"

"You are still stupid and uncultured, Sancho," said Don Quixote. "This book deals with the lives of such saints as St. Lawrence who was roasted; St. Bartholomew, who was flayed: St. Catherine, who was thrust on a wheel of knives; and likewise the rest of the saints and martyrs listed for the entire year. Sit down and I'll read you the life of the saint celebrated today, August 20, by the Church; that is, St. Bernard."

"By heaven," said Sancho, "I don't have a taste for knowing about the lives of others; moreover, I should be even more unwilling to let

---

[9] Ginesillo (Ginés de Pasamonte) is the galley slave who stole Sancho's ass after being freed by Don Quixote (the theft is usually placed in I, 22).

[10] The *rey de gallos* 'king of the roosters' was the boy who led a Carnival game in which a rooster was decapitated.

[11] Sancho, not knowing these matters, and also mishearing his master, thinks Don Quixote is referring to a person.

Flos
Sanctorum
BARNELL 80

my skin be taken off or to roast on the grill. But tell me, did they take off St. Bartholomew's skin and roast St. Lawrence after they were dead or as they were dying?"

"Did anyone ever hear such stupidity!" said Don Quixote. "They flayed one alive and roasted the other alive."

"Oh, son of a bitch! How they must have smarted!" said Sancho. "By Jove! I wouldn't be worth a fig for Flas Sanctorum. It's all well and good to recite half a dozen credos on my knees and I could even bear with fasting, provided I ate reasonably well three times a day."

"All the hardships endured by the saints I have told you about, and all the rest this book deals with, were suffered valiantly for the love of God, and thus they gained the kingdom of Heaven," said Don Quixote.

"Upon my word," said Sancho, "a year ago we went through quite a number of misfortunes to gain the miconic kingdom,[12] and we were made monkeys of, but I believe that you probably want us now to become errant saints in order to gain earthly Paradise. But, putting all this aside, read and let's see what is said about the life of St. Bernard."

The good hidalgo read it, and for each page told Sancho some well-pondered things, mingled with axioms of philosophers. All this revealed him as a man of good intellect and clear judgment, had these not been upset by his devotion to the unbridled reading of books of chivalry, the cause of all his derangement.

When Don Quixote had finished reading the life of St. Bernard, he said "How do you like it, Sancho?" Have you ever read about any saint more devoted to Our Lady? More devout in prayer, of more tender tears, and more humble deeds and words?"

"Upon my word," said Sancho, "he was a real saint; from now on I want to take him as my patron saint so that in case I find myself in any trouble (such as that of the fulling mills of long ago or the blanket at the inn)[13] he will help me, since you couldn't leap over the bars of the corral. But do you know, Señor Quijada, I remember that last Sunday Pedro Alonso's son who goes to school took out a book under a tree next to the mill and read to us from it for more than two hours? The book is marvelously beautiful and much larger than that *Flas Santorum*; besides that, at the beginning there is a man in armor, on horseback,

---

[12] Sancho is trying to refer to the Kingdom of Micomicón (I, 19) whose name he doesn't remember accurately. There is also a pun here between miconic and *micos* 'monkeys'.

[13] Sancho here is referring to the fulling mills adventure (I, 20) and when he got blanketed at the inn for Don Quixote's refusal to pay their lodging bill (I, 17).

with an unsheathed sword wider than my hand, and he is striking a cliff such a terrible blow that it is split in half, and through the opening a serpent comes out and he cuts off its head. This, by all that is unholy, is certainly one good book!"

"What's its title?" said Don Quixote. "For if I'm not mistaken I believe Pedro Alonso's boy stole it from me a year ago, and it must be entitled *Don Florisbrán de Candaria,*[14] a very brave knight about whom it deals, as well as other valiant ones such as Admiral de Zuazia, Palmerín de Pomo, Blastodras de la Torre and the giant Maleorte de Bradanca, along with two famous enchantresses, Zuldasa and Dalfádea."

"You're indeed right," said Sancho. "Those two took a knight to the castle of I-don't-know-what."

"Of Azefaros," said Don Quixote.

"Yes, you're right. If I can, I must steal it and bring it here on Sunday for us to read," said Sancho. "Although I don't know how to read, I get much pleasure in hearing about those awful blows and knife-thrusts which split open man and horse."

"Well, Sancho," said Don Quixote, "please bring it to me, but it must be in such a way that neither the Priest nor anyone else will know."

"I promise," said Sancho, "this very night, if I can, I'll surely manage to bring it to you under my cloak. So good-by for now; my wife must be expecting me for supper."

Sancho departed and the good hidalgo was left with his pate boiling with the new refreshment of his vanquished knightly exploits revived in his memory by Sancho. He closed the book and began to walk about the room, weaving in his mind terrible fantastic things, recalling all that which formerly had crazed him. At this moment, vespers sounded; getting his cloak and rosary, he went to attend services with the Mayor, who lived next door. After vespers were over, the councilmen, the Priest, Don Quixote and all the other important people of the village went to the plaza and the group began to talk about whatever most pleased them.

At this point, they saw entering the square from the main street four people of quality, on horseback, with servants and pages and twelve lackeys leading twelve richly saddled horses. On seeing this, those in the plaza waited a bit to find out what all that meant, and then

---

[14] Don Quixote is slightly mistaken, for the volume in question is *Don Philesbián de Candaria* (Anonymous, 1542). It was not among the inventory of Don Quixote's books listed in I, 6, although not all books in the library were mentioned.

the Priest said to Don Quixote, "By the sign of the cross, Señor Quijada, if these people had come here six months ago, you would have thought it one of the strangest and most dangerous adventures you had ever seen or heard of in your books of chivalry. You would have imagined that these gentlemen were probably kidnaping some princess of high rank, and that those now dismounting were four colossal giants, lords of the castle of Bramiforán, the magician."

That's all water under the bridge, Señor Licentiate,"[15] said Don Quixote. "Let's go up and find out who they are, for if I'm not mistaken they must be on their way to Court on important business, because their dress indicates they are people of quality."

They all went up to them and after the usual courteous greetings, the Priest, as the most scholarly, spoke in this way: "Indeed, gentlemen, we very much regret having so many nobles end up in such a small village as this, so lacking in the comforts and hospitality you deserve. There is no inn or lodging which can house so many people and horses as there are here. However, if these gentlemen and I can be of help and you have decided to stay here tonight, we shall try to shelter you as best we can."

One of them, who seemed to be the most important, thanked him, saying in the name of them all: "Gentlemen, we are grateful for the good will you show us without knowing us, and we shall be obliged with very good reason to be grateful and remember your good wishes. We are knights from Granada and we are going to the illustrious city of Zaragoza to some tournaments being held there. Having learned that the tournament's president is a valiant knight, we have resolved to undertake this task in order to gain some renown, impossible to attain otherwise. We intended to get two leagues farther, but since the horses and people are somewhat tired it seemed to us best to spend the night here, even though we might have to sleep on the stone seats of the church if the Priest would permit it."

One of the councilmen who knew more about sowing and about yoking up the mules and oxen of his farm than he did about social graces said to him, "Don't worry a bit about that; we shall give you lodging here for tonight because seven hundred times a year we have companies of bigger braggarts than you and they are not as grateful and well spoken. Upon my word, it costs our Council more than ninety *maravedís*[16] a year."

---

[15] A licentiate is a person who has the equivalent of a Master's degree.

[16] The *maravedí* was an old coin of little worth: there were 272 *maravedís* in a

To stop him from continuing his silly remarks, the Priest said, "Gentlemen, you must be patient. I personally shall see to it that you are lodged, and it will be this way: the two councilmen will take to their homes those two knights with all their servants and horses; I shall take you, and Señor Quijada the other knight. Each will try to entertain his guest as well as his circumstances permit, because, so they say, a guest, whoever he may be, merits being honored; as such, our obligation to serve these knights is the greater, at least so that it not be said that after arriving in a village of couretous people, even though a small one, they had to sleep on the church benches, as this knight says they would do."

Don Quixote said to the knight who fell to his lot and seemed to be the most imporant one: "Certainly, sir, I have been very lucky that you are pleased to make use of my home which, although poor in what is needful for the perfect service of so great a knight, at least will be very rich in good will, which you may accept without further ado."

"Of course, sir," responded the knight. "I consider myself very fortunate to receive a favor from one who speaks such good words with which his actions will surely be in conformity."

After this, as they were taking leave of each other, each one with his guest, they decided to depart fairly early in the morning because of the excessive heat at that season. Don Quixote went home with the knight who fell to his lot; he put the horses in a little stable and ordered his old housekeeper to prepare some fowls and squabs (of which there was quite an abundance in his house) for supper for all those people he brought with him. He also sent a boy to call Sancho Panza, who came very willingly, to help out in any way necessary in the house. While supper was being prepared, the knight and Don Quixote began to stroll about the cool patio. Among other things, Don Quixote asked him what motivated his coming so many leagues for those tournaments, and what his name was.

To this the knight replied that his name was Álvaro Tarfe,[17] and

---

real; this latter coin has been continued (in deflated form) in the modern *duro* (5 pesetas, or about 8 American cents).

[17] Perhaps the most incredible thing Cervantes ever did was to make Avellaneda's Álvaro Tarfe a character in his *own* second part. In Chapter 72, the 'real' Don Quixote happens to meet Álvaro Tarfe, and recognizes him as a person mentioned in the 'other' book. After a discussion with Álvaro Tarfe, Don Quixote convinces him that the 'other' Don Quixote and Sancho (the heroes of the book you are now holding) were imposters, and he has Don Álvaro sign a document, duly witnessed, to that effect. In Avellaneda's book, Álvaro Tarfe plays an important role throughout.

and that he was descended from the ancient line of the Tarfe Moors of Granada, near relatives of the kings and valiant in their own right, as one reads in the histories of the kings of that kingdon of the Abencerrajes, Zegríes, Gomeles and Muzas, who were Christians after the Catholic King Ferdinand conquered the illustrious city of Granada. "Now I am making this journey at the command of an angel in the guise of a woman who is the queen of my will, the object of my desires, the origin of my sighs, the archive of my thoughts, the Paradise of my memories and, lastly, the consummate glory of my life. She, as I say, ordered me to leave for these tournaments, enter them in her name and bring her some of the rich prizes and valuables that will be given as awards to the lucky conquering adventurers. I am going sure and quite certain that I shall not fail to take some to her; since she is accompanying me, as it were, within my heart, the conquering will be sure, the victory certain, the prize safe, and my hardships will attain the glory that for so many long days I have wanted with a burning desire."

"Indeed, Don Álvaro," said Don Quixote, "for many reasons that lady has the greatest obligation to agree to your just pleas. First, because of the hardships for you, making such a long trip in such terrible weather; second, because you are going only at her command, for by so doing, even though things may happen contrary to her desire, you will have fulfilled your obligation as a faithful lover, having done all you could in her behalf. But I beg you to tell me about that lovely lady, her age and name, and those of her noble parents."

"One would need a very great divining art to explain one of the three things you have asked me," responded Don Álvaro. "Passing over the last two, because of the respect I have for her rank, I'll only say that she is sixteen and her beauty is such that all who look at her, even with eyes less passionate than mine, declare that they have not seen, in Granada or in all Andalusia, a more beautiful girl. In addition to the virtues of her soul, she is without any doubt fair as the sun, her cheeks like newly cut roses, her teeth ivory, her lips coral, her neck alabaster, her hands milky, and lastly, she has all the most perfect charms the eye can judge, although in truth she is somewhat small in stature."

"Don Álvaro," answered Don Quixote, "I think that it is certainly just a small blemish, because one of the specifications set by judges for a lady to be considered beautiful is good proportion of body; although it is true that many ladies remedy this defect by adding a think layer of cork to the soles of their Valencian clogs. However, when they are not wearing these, because not everywhere nor at every hour can they be worn, ladies in slippers seem somewhat ugly, because the skirts and silken brocade clothing, cut to the measure of the height they have on their clogs, are so long that they drag two spans' length on the floor. So this is certainly a slight imperfection to your lady."

"On the contrary, sir," said Don Álvaro, "I find that a very great perfection. It is true that Aristotle, in the fourth of his *Ethics*, says that among the attributes of a beautiful woman, as he there describes her, must be that of proportions bordering on large. However, others have had the opposite opinion, because nature, so the philosophers say, does greater miracles in small things than in large ones, and if she made a mistake in the formation of a small body, it would be harder to recognize the error than if it were made in a large body. There is no precious stone that is not small, and the eyes of our body are its smallest parts yet are its loveliest and most beautiful.[18] So in like manner my angel is a miracle by which nature has wished to reveal to us how with her marvelous skill she can gather together in a small space the infinite number of charms she can produce; because beauty, as Cicero says,[19] consists of nothing but a convenient arrangement of the limbs which induce others to look with delight at that body whose harmonizing parts move in a kind of smooth unison."

"I think, Don Álvaro," said Don Quixote, "that you have satisfied with very subtle reasons the objection that I made to the smallness of body of your queen. Let's go in and eat, I beg you, because supper, meager as it is, must be ready. After the meal, I have something of importance to discuss with you as a person who knows how to talk so well on all subjects."

---

[18] Little women are lauded most delightfully in the famous quatrains 1606-17 of Juan Ruiz' *Book of Good Love*.

[19] *De Officiis*, lib. I, xxvii, 98.

CHAP. II. ABOUT THE REMARKS THAT PASSED between Don Álvaro Tarfe and Don Quixote after supper, and how he reveals his love for Dulcinea del Toboso, showing him two ridiculous letters. From all this the knight realizes what Don Quixote is.

FTER DON QUIXOTE had given a fairly good supper to his noble guest, at dessert, when the table was cleared, he listened to the following words from his wise lips: "Certainly, Señor Quijada, I am extremely surprised that during supper I have seen you change somewhat from what you were when I came in. Most of the time I have seen you so absorbed and preoccupied in I know not what fancies that you scarcely answered, and never appropriately, but in a very *ad Ephesios*[1] way, as people say. I have come to suspect that some serious worry troubles you and oppresses your spirit, because I have seen you at times looking at the tablecloth without blinking, your food unchewed, so absent-minded that when I asked you if you were married, you replied, 'Rocinante? Sir, he is the best horse ever bred in Cordova.' Because of this I say that some passion or inner worry torments you. It isn't possible that such an effect should arise from anything else. It may be such that, as I have seen many times in other people, it will kill you, or at least, if it is strong, will make you lose your mind. Therefore, I beg you to be good enough to tell me your feelings, because if the cause be one that I personally can remedy, I shall do so with the fervor that reason and obligation demand. Just as tears, the heart's blood, relieve its tension, ease it and heal it of oppressing melancholy by dissipating it through the springs of the eyes, so, in exactly the same way, sorrow and trouble when confided are relieved somewhat, because the listener, as a dispassionate person, usually gives the sanest and surest advice to help the troubled individual."

Don Quixote then answered, "Don Álvaro, I am grateful for your good will and your desire to demonstrate it, but it is to be expected that those of us who belong to the order of knighthood and have found ourselves in such a multitude of dangers, now with fierce, huge, wild men, now with evil sages or magicians, disenchanting princesses, killing griffins and serpents, rhinoceroses, and fabulous monsters, should get carried away by one of those fancies which are affairs of

---

[1] To speak *ad Ephesios* in Spanish means to say something absurd.

honor and remain preoccupied and absent-minded, sunk in honorable ecstacy, the way you say you have seen me, although I was unaware of it. The truth is that none of these things has taken up my mind at this time, because they are all over for me."

Don Álvaro Tarfe marveled greatly to hear him say he had disenchanted princesses and killed giants, and he began to think him a man somewhat lacking in judgment. So, in order to find out, he said, "Well, can't one learn what now disturbs you?"

Don Quixote said, "It's because of matters that it isn't always lawful for knights-errant to discuss, but seeing that you are who you are, so noble and discreet, and wounded by the same arrow with which the son of Venus has wounded me, I want to reveal my sorrow to you, not so much that you can give me any help, for only that lovely, ungrateful, and very sweet Dulcinea, thief of my will power, can do that, but so that you may understand that I am traveling and have traveled along the royal road of knight-errantry, imitating in deeds and love those valiant early knights-errant who were the light and models for all those who have come after them and have, because of their fine talents, been worthy of professing the holy order of knighthood to which I belong; such as the famous Amadís of Gaul, Belianís of Greece and his son Esplandián, Palmerín de Oliva, Tablante de Ricamonte, the Knight of Phoebus, and his brother Rosicler,[2] with other very valiant princes even of our times, all of whom, since I have imitated them in deeds and exploits, I also follow in love. Consequently, you must know that I am, in love."

Since Don Álvaro was a man of keen perception, he understood at once what his host might be for having said he had imitated those fabulous knights of the books of chivalry. So, astounded by his insane disorder, and so as to comprehend it fully, he said, "I am no little astonished, Señor Quijada, that such a man as you, skinny, wrinkled faced, apparently more than forty-five years old, should be in love, because love is not won except by dint of many harships, bad nights, worse days, a thousand disappointments, jealousy, quarrels, and dangers, because all these and similar things are the roads leading to love. If you are to go over them, you don't look to me like a fit subject to endure two bad nights exposed to dew, rain, and snow, as I know from experience that lovers endure. But tell me, withal, is that woman

[2] All of these are heroes of Spanish books of chivalry, Amadís being the most famous, and the one that most influenced Cervantes' *Don Quixote*. Notice that Esplandián is not Belianís' son, but Amadís'; Don Quixote *should* know better.

you love from this village or is she from another town? If it were possible, I should like very much to see her before I leave, because it's incredible that a man of your good taste should have set his eyes on no less than an Ephesian Diana, a Trojan Polyxena, a Carthaginian Dido, a Roman Lucretia, or a Doralice of Granada."[3]

"In beauty and charm she surpasses all these," responded Don Quixote. "She imitates only the inhuman Medea in fierceness and cruelty, but God grant that with time, which changes all things, and with the news she will have of me and my invincible deeds, she will be mollified and submit to my importunate as well as justifiable pleas. To come to the point, sir, her name is Princess Dulcinea del Toboso (as I am Don Quixote de la Mancha) if you have heard of her, but you must have, since she is so famous for her miracles and celestial qualities."

Don Álvaro wanted to laugh heartily when he heard Princess Dulcinea del Toboso mentioned, but he hid his amusement so that his host might not notice and grow angry. Therefore, he said to him, "Indeed, Señor hidalgo, or rather, knight, I have never in all my born days heard of this princess, nor do I believe that there is one in all La Mancha, unless her surname is Princess, as others are named Marquis.

"Not everybody knows everything," replied Don Quixote, "but before long I'll make her name known not only in Spain, but also in the most distant kingdoms and provinces in the world. She is the one who enraptures my mind, who has me beside myself. Because of her I was long exiled from my home and native province, performing heroic deeds, sending her giants and fierce wild men and knights to kneel at her feet, and despite all that, she reveals herself an African lioness, a Hircanian tigress. To all the letters I write her, filled with love and sweetness, she replies with greatest rudeness and indifference that a princess ever addressed to a knight-errant. I write her longer harangues than those Cataline[4] made to the Roman Senate; more heroic poems than those of Homer and Virgil; more tender things than Petrarch wrote his beloved Laura; more agreeable episodes than Lucan or Ariosto were able to write in their time, and that in our times Lope de Vega wrote for his Filis, Celia, Lucinda, and all the rest he has so

---

[3] The first four are heroines of Antiquity. Diana was the Roman goddess of forests, Polyxena was Paris' sister, sacrificed on Achylles' tomb, Dido was queen of Carthage, and Lucretia stabbed herself after admitting to her husband that she had been raped. The last one is a character in *Orlando Furioso*, a work which influenced both Cervantes' and Avellaneda's *Don Quixote*.

[4] Don Quixote is doubtless referring to Lucius Sergius Catiline, a Roman who endeavored to unite heterogeneous groups into a coherent political force.

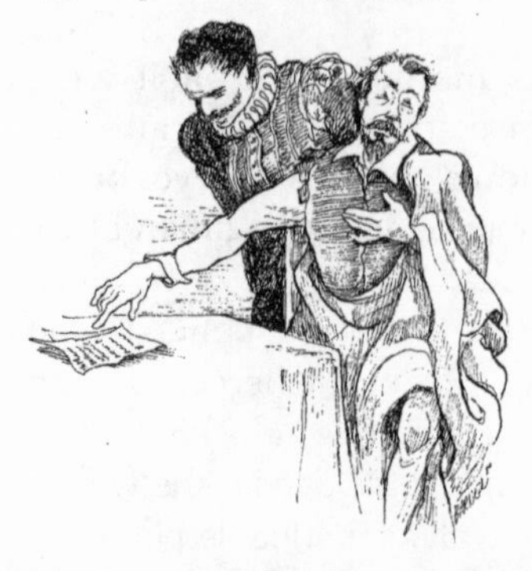

divinely praised. I am like an Amadís in adventures, a Scaevola in seriousness, a Persian Perineo in suffering, an Aeneas in nobility, a Ulysses in astuteness, a Belisario in constancy,[5] and outdoing the fierce Cid in bloodshed. In order that you, Don Álvaro, may see the truth of all that I am saying, I want to get two of those letters I have in that desk over there, one that I sent her recently by my squire, Sancho Panza, and another that she sent me in reply."

He rose to get them and Don Álvaro remained there crossing himself in view of the madness of his host, and he ended up realizing that he was deranged by the inane books of chivalry, thinking them quite authentic and true.

At the noise made as Don Quixote opened the desk, Sancho Panza came in, his belly well-filled with the leftovers from supper. When Don Quixote sat down with the two letters in his hand, he sprawled back in his chair to enjoy a little of the conversation. "Here," said Don Quixote, "you see my squire, Sancho Panza, who will not let me lie with respect to the inhumane sternness of my lady."

"Yes, indeed," said Sancho Panza. "Aldonza Lorenzo, alias Nogales,[6] the real name of the Princess Dulcinea del Toboso, as set down in the first parts of this serious history is a big . . . You can believe what I say, because, on the body of St. Ciruelo, why should my master go about doing so many knightly deeds day and night, undergoing a cruel penance in the Sierra Morena, wearing himself out and not eating, all for a . . . ? But I must hush; that's her business; it's her funeral; the one who errs and corrects himself, commends himself to God; a lone spirit neither sings not weeps; when the partridge sings, it's a sign of rain; and cake will do when there's no bread . . . "

Sancho would have proceeded with his proverbs had Don Quixote not ordered him *imperativo modo* to stop, but nonetheless he answered back, saying, "Would you like to know, Señor Don Tarfe, what the

---

[5] Quintus Mucius Scaevola, a Roman jurist whose life straddled second and first centuries B.C., is probably the one referred to here. Perineo refers to Perianeo of Persia, whom the novelistic hero Belianís de Grecia conquered. Annotators have not identified Belisario.

[6] In I, 25, Lorenzo Corchuelo is listed as Dulcinea 's father and Aldonza Nogales her mother; in the Spanish naming system, the father's last name is given first, and the mother's is second.

disagreeable creature did when I took her that letter which my master wants to read? It was raining, and the filthy thing was in the stable, filling up a garbage basket with a shovel. When I told her that I was bringing a letter from my master (may God give her an infernal bellyache for it!), she took a big shovelful of the manure from where it was deepest and wettest and flung it straight at this sinful face of mine, without saying 'Look out!' In payment for my sins, my beard is thicker than a barber's brush; for more than three days I couldn't get completely rid of the filth she put there."[7]

On hearing this, Don Álvaro clapped his hand to his forehead, saying "Certainly Señor Sancho, your great discretion didn't deserve such an action."

"Don't be astonished, replied Sancho, "for upon my word my master and I, involved because of love for her in adventures or misadventures of last year, more than a few times have suffered some fine drubbings."

"I promise you," said Don Quixote angrily, "that if I arise, Don Señor Shameless Knave, I'll take a stake from that cart and break your ribs and make you remember *per omnia saecula saeculorum.*"[8]

"Amen," responded Sancho.

Don Quixote would have risen to punish him for his impudence had Don Álvaro not held his arm and made him sit down again, making signs to Sancho to be still, which he was for the time being. Don Quixote said, opening the letter, "Here is the letter that this fellow recently took to my lady, and with it her reply, so that you may deduce from them both whether I am right in complaining of her great ingratidude.

"Address on the letter:

To Princess Dulcinea del Tobosoo.

If the vehement love, oh, lovely ingrate! which boils abundantly through the pores of my veins, gave pause that I might take spite against thy lovliness, straightaway it would take revenge of the witless word with which my worriments give thee rankling reproach. Heedest thou, sweet enemy of mine, that I attend not with all my might in nought but righting wrongs to needy people?

---

[7] In Part I, Sancho *never* visited Dulcinea.

[8] "Forever and ever."

Albeit well oft I go enveloped in the blood of brutes, betimes my unsullied mind is exceedingly cheerful and remembers that it is in thrall to one of the greatest women found among queens of high rank. This notwithstanding, that which I now demand of thee is that thou forgiveth me for any excess I may have committed, for ' . . . of love the errors done, worthy are of pardon.'[9] This I beg on bended knee before thy regal respectivity. Thine unto the end of life,

The Knight of the Sad Countenance,
DON QUIXOTE DE LA MANCHA"

"For Heaven's sake," said Don Álvaro, laughing, "this is as elegant a letter as King Sancho of León might have written in his day to Ximena Gómez, at the time he was away from her and she was being consoled by the Cid. But since you are such a courtier, I marvel that you should write so old-fashioned a letter, because those expressions are no longer used in Castile except in plays written for the kings and counts of those golden ages."

"I write in this manner," said Don Quixote, "because since I am imitating in fortitude such ancients as Count Fernán González, Peranzules, Bernardo, and the Cid,[10] I wish also to imitate them in words."

"Well," replied Don Álvaro, "why did you sign yourself the Knight of the Sad Countenance?"

Sancho Panza, who had been listening to the letter, said, "I advised him to do so, and there is nothing truer in the whole letter than that."[11]

"I set myself down as He of the Sad Countenance," added Don Quixote, "not because of what this fool says, but because the absence of my lady Dulcinea made me so sad that I couldn't be comforted. In the same way Amadís called himself Beltenebros, others the Kinght of

---

[9] These are verses taken from the Spanish ballad of Conde Claros, which was to inspire the Cave of Montesinos episode in II, 22-23.

[10] Fernán González (†970) was the founder of Castilian independence and epic verses grew up around his deeds. Rodrigo Díaz de Vivar, the Cid, was Castile's greatest hero of the 11th Century. His deeds are recounted in Castile's only true extant epic, the *Poema de mio Cid* (ca. 1140), which influenced Spanish ballads and drama. Bernardo del Carpio, probably an imaginary Leonese hero, was believed to have lived in the 8th Century. The *Cantar de Bernardo del Carpio*, of Latin vintage, relates his exploits. Peranzules is the hero of 15th Century ballads, notably the one titled *La infanta Sevilla y Peranzules*.

[11] In I, 19, Sancho did invent the name.

Fires, or the Knight of the Images, or of the Burning Sword."[12]

Don Álvaro replied, "And in imitation of whom did you call yourself Don Quixote?"

"In imitation of nobody," said Don Quixote. "Because my name is Quijada I got from it that of Don Quixote the day I was taken into the order of knighthood.[13] But I beg you to listen to the reply that that enemy of my freedom writes me.

"Address:

TO MARTÍN QUIJADA, THE FOOL

> The bearer of this should have been a brother of mine, so that I could have given him the answer in the form of a drubbing with a good club. Don't you know what I am telling you, Señor Quijada? For, on the life of my mother, if you address me again as empress or queen, calling me such jesting names as the Manchegan Princess Dulcinea del Toboso, and similar ones that you usually write, I shall do something to make you remember that my real name is Aldonza Lorenzo or Nogales, on sea and on land.

"Was there ever in the world a knight-errant, no matter how discreet and long-suffering he might be, who could live tolerating such words?"

"Oh, the low-down slut!" said Sancho Panza. "That stuck-up thing should have men to deal with; upon my word, I'd make her pop for her smartness! Even if she is a brawny girl, I'm sure that if I grab her she won't escape from my claws. My master Don Quixote is too easygoing. If he sent her half a dozen kicks in a letter, to be delivered to her belly, upon my word she wouldn't be so argumentative. You must realize, sir, that I know these girls better than I know an egg is worth a penny. If a man speaks politely to them, they give him a slap on the neck and a jab that makes his eyes water. They don't fool with me, because I right off give them a kick harder than that of Friar Hieronymus' mule, more so if I'm wearing new shoes; and the devil take Prester John's mule if he could keep them in line any better!"

Don Álvaro arose laughing and said, "By heaven! If the king of Spain knew that there was this entertainment to be found in this village he would try to have it in his house, even though it cost him a million. Don Quixote, we must get up an hour before daybreak, to avoid the sun, and so, with your permission, I should like to go about retiring."

---

[12] The Knight of the Fires appears in *Don Lisuarte de Grecia*; the Knight of the Images is found in the *Espejo de príncipes*; and the Knight of the Burning sword is Amadís de Grecia.

[13] How can our hero forget that he chose his name (I, 1) some days *before* he was knighted (I, 3)?

Don Quixote consented, and acccordingly Don Álvaro began to undress, and Don Quixote ordered Sancho Panza to take off Don Álvaro's boots and make his bed, which was in the same room. At this point, two of Don Álvaro's pages who had been listening in the doorway came up to carry out these orders, but Sancho Panza did not allow anyone else to perform these services. Don Álvaro was greatly pleased and said to him, while Don Quixote went after some preserved pears, "Pull hard, brother Sancho, and be patient."

"Yes, I will," answered Sancho, "for they are not beasts, and although I am not known as *don*,[14] my father was."

"How's that?" said Don Álvaro. "Did your father have a title?"

"Yes, sir," said Sancho, "but it was tacked on."

"What do you mean, tacked on?" replied Don Álvaro. "Was his name Francisco Don, Juan Don or Diego Don?"

"No, sir," said Sancho. "It was Pedro el Remendón."[15]

The pages and Don Álvaro laughed heartily and he continued asking if Sancho's father was still alive. He replied, "No, sir, more than ten years ago he died of the worst illness you can imagine."

"Of what sickness did he die? asked Don Álvaro.

"Chilblains,"[16] responded Sancho.

"Good God!" said Don Álvaro with a great burst of laughter."Chilblains?! Your father is the first man I ever heard of who died of chilblains, and so I don't believe it."

"Can't everyone die the death that he pleases?" said Sancho. "Well, if my father wanted to die of chilblains, what difference does it make to you?"

In the midst of the laughter of Don Álvaro and his pages, Don Quixote and his old housekeeper entered with a dish of preserved pears and a jug of good white wine. He said, "Don Álvaro, if you can eat a couple of these pears and then take a swig of wine, it will set you on top of the world."

"I am most grateful for your kindness, Señor Don Quixote," responded Don Álvaro. "However I can't accept, because I am not accustomed to eating anything after supper, for it disagrees with me and I

---

[14] *Don* used to be a title of nobility, and Sancho's stock was obviously not noble.

[15] *Remendón* means 'mender of old clothing'.

[16] Chilblains *'sabañón'* is an inflammation of hands and feet due to exposure, and is hardly lethal, but there is a Spanish expression *"comer como un sabañón"* which means, strangely enough, 'to eat greedily'; the suggestion is thus that Sancho's father ate himself to death.

have long experience in the truth of Avicenna's or Galen's maxim, which says that anything fresh on top of undigested food causes illness."[17]

"Well, by my sainted mother!" said Sancho. "Even if that Azucena or Galen, as you call them, told me more Latin expressions than are in the alphabet I would no sooner stop eating than spitting, when food is at hand. By the body of St. Belorge! Not eating is for the castreleons[18] which live on air."

"Well, by the life of my beloved," said Don Álvaro, spearing a pear on the tip of his knife, "you ought to eat this, with Don Quixote's permission."

"Oh, no, by my life, Señor Don Tarfe," responded Sancho. "These sweets, of which there are only a few, disagree with me, although it is true that when there are plenty, they are very good for me." However, he ate it, and then Don Álvaro got into his bed and the pages made up a bed for themselves next to it and retired.

At this point Don Quixote said to Sancho, "Let's go, friend Sancho, to the upstairs room; there we can sleep the short time remaining of the night. There is no need for you to go home now, because your wife must have already retired; besides, I have a little to say to you tonight concerning an important matter."

"By Jove, sir!" said Sancho. "Tonight I am in no condition to give good advice, for I am as round as a ball. The bad thing is that I'll fall asleep right away, since I'm already yawning a lot."

After this, they went upstairs to bed, and when they were in the same bed, Don Quixote said, "Son Sancho, you well know or have read that idleness is the mother and origin of all vices, and an idle man is inclined to think up any evil, and having thought it, puts it into action. As a usual thing, the devil attacks and easily overcomes the slothful because he acts like a hunter who does not fire at birds when they are flying, because it would be both uncertain and difficult, but he waits until they settle down somewhere; seeing them inactive, he fires and kills them. I say this, friend Sancho, because I see that we have been idle for several months and we are not doing our duty, I toward the order of knighthood that I received, and you toward the loyalty of a faithful squire you promised me. I should like, then (so that it won't be said I

---

[17] Avicenna was the 11th Century Arabic philosopher and physician whose most influential work was the *Canon of Medicine*, a great textbook of medical knowledge. Galen was the 2nd Century B.C. Greek physician known as the founder of experimental physiology.

[18] Sancho is referring to chameleons.

received the talent that God gave me in vain and be reprimanded like that fellow in the Gospel, who tied up in his kerchief what his master entrusted to him, and did not try to make a profit from it), for us to return as soon as we possibly can to our military exercise, because in it we shall accomplish two things: first, very great service to God, and the other, help the world, by ridding it of the huge wild men and proud giants who injure with their privileges and wrong the needy knights and afflicted maidens. Thus we shall gain honor and fame for ourselves and our descendants by conserving and increasing that of our ancestors. After this we shall acquire a thousand kingdoms and provinces in the twinkling of an eye, so we'll be rich and enrich our native land."

"Sir, you need not put those warlike ideas in my head because you already know how much they cost me that year, with the loss of my Dapple, may he live to be one hundred; besides this, you never fulfilled what you promised me a thousand times, that within a year I'd be governor of a province, or at least a king, and my wife an admiral and my children princes. I see none of these things accomplished for me (are you listening or asleep?), and my wife is as much Mari-Gutiérrez as she was a year ago, so I don't fancy promises. Besides that, if our priest Pero Pérez finds out that we want to return to our knightly exploits, he'll be sure to put you in chains for six or seven months in *domus Getro*,[19] as they say, as he did before. So I say that I don't want to go with you, and let me sleep, by my life! because my eyes are closing."

"Look Sancho," said Don Quixote, "I don't want you to go like the other time; rather, I want to buy you a donkey much better than the one that Ginesillo stole from you, on which you'll travel like a patriarch. Thus we'll both go better prepared and we'll take money and provisions and a suitcase with our clothes, for I have realized that that is very necessary, so that what happened to us in those accursed enchanted castles won't occur again."[20]

"Well, that way and if my work is paid for every month, I'll go very willingly," responded Sancho.

Hearing his decision, Don Quixote went on saying, "Well, Dulcinea has shown herself so inhuman and cruel, and what's worse, ungrateful for my services, deaf to my prayers, unbelieving of my words, and lastly, opposed to my wishes, that I want to try, by imitating the Knight of Phoebus, who left Claridana, and many more who sought a new

---

[19] 'Jethro's house' refers to jail.

[20] Don Quixote refers here to the troubles he and Sancho had in the inn in I, 17.

love, to see if I'll find in somebody else better faith and greater agreement with my fervent intentions, and also see . . . Are you asleep, Sancho? Hey there, Sancho!"

Upon this, Sancho came to, saying, "I say you're right, sir, for those great wild men are great knaves and it is very right for us to do wrongs to them."

"By heaven," said Don Quixote, "you certainly know what it's all about! Here I am racking my brains telling you what is most important for you and me, after God, and you are sleeping like a dormouse. What I'm saying, Sancho, is, do you understand? . . ."

"Oh, a curse on the slut who bore me!" said Sancho. "Let me sleep, by all that's unholy, for I believe well and truly all that you are saying and intend to say every day of your life."

"A man has enough trouble," said Don Quixote, "when he deals of weighty matters with savages like this one. I want to let him sleep, for I don't want to sleep before putting an end to these honorable contests by winning on the first, second, and third days the most outstanding prizes there are; I want to stay awake, tracing in my mind's eye what later I'll do in reality, like the wise architect who, before beginning his work, has jumbled up in his mind all the rooms, courtyards, capitals for the columns, and windows of the house, in order later to bring them perfectly into being."

In short, the good hidalgo spent what was left of the night, weaving the greatest fantasies in his muddled mind, now talking to knights, now to the judges of the contests, asking them for the prize, and finally greeting with the greatest politeness a richly dressed, very beautiful lady, to whom he presented, from his horse, a rich jewel on the tip of his lance. With these and similar hallucinations he fell asleep at last.

CHAP. III. HOW THE PRIEST AND DON QUIXOTE *bade farewell to those knights and what happened between him and Sancho Panza after they had gone.*

N HOUR before dawn the Priest and the councilmen came knocking at Don Quixote's door. They had come to arouse Don Álvaro, and at their shouts Don Quixote called to Sancho Panza to open up, and he awakened most regretfully. When they had entered Don Álvaro's room, the Priest sat down by his bed and began to question him about how he had gotten along with his host. To this Don Álvaro replied by briefly recounting what had gone on between him, Don Quixote and Sancho Panza that night, and said that if the time of the jousts were not so near at hand, he would have stayed four or five days to enjoy his host's good conversation. However, upon his return he planned to remain longer.

The Priest told him what Don Quixote was and what had happened to him the previous year, which astonished Don Álvaro very much. Changing the subject, they pretended to talk about something else, because they saw Don Quixote enter. At his affable greeting, Don Álvaro got up and ordered the horses and other equipment to be made ready for departure. Meanwhile the Priest and the councilmen went back to offer their guests breakfast, all agreeing to return to Don Quixote's house in order to leave there together.

When they had gone and Don Álvaro was dressed, he drew Don Quixote aside and said, "My dear sir, in a big trunk I have some armor engraved in Milan, which you will be good enough to keep carefully for me in your house until I return. I think I'll not need it in Zaragoza, for I'm sure to have friends there who will supply me with less elegant armor, because this is so elegant that it serves only to draw attention and make me very conspicuous when I wear it."

After saying this, he had it all taken out: breastplate, backplate, gorget, armlets, cuirass, and helmet. When Don Quixote saw these, his flighty mind rejoiced exceedingly and he straight-away made up his mind what he would do with them. Accordingly, he said, "Certainly, sir, this is the smallest way in which I expect to be of service to you, but I trust in God that the time will come when you will be gladder to see me at your side than here in Argamesilla." And he went on asking him, while they were replacing the armor in the trunk, what emblem he planned to wear in the jousts, what livery, what letters or what mottoes. To humor him, Don Álvaro answered all this, not realizing that there was passing through Don Quixote's mind the idea of going to Zaragoza and doing what he did, which will be related in due time.

Upon this Sancho came in, very red and sweaty-faced, saying, "My Señor Don Tarfe, you can now sit down at the table, for breakfast is ready," to which Don Álvaro responded, "Have you a good appetite for breakfast, Sancho?"

"I always have a good appetite, my dear sir," he said, "*Gloria tibi, Domine;*[1] so much so, in fact, that (to tell the truth and shame the devil) I don't remember ever in my life having risen from the table stuffed unless it was a year ago when my uncle, Diego Alonso, steward of the Rosary Guild, appointed me to distribute the charity bread and cheese for the brotherhood; then I had to loosen my belt two notches."

"May God preserve you in that state of health," said Don Álvaro, "for I am envious only of that and your good nature." He ate his breakfast, and then the three knights arrived with their retinue and the Priest, because dawn was breaking. When Don Álvaro saw them he immediately put on his spurs and mounted his horse, after which Don Quixote took Rocinante, saddled and bridled, out of the stable to accompany them. Holding Rocinante by the rein, he said, "Don Álvaro, it would be very difficult to find among the best horses in the whole world one as good as this. There is no Bucephalus, Alfana, Seianus, Babieca, or Pegasus to equal him."[2]

"Indeed," said Don Álvaro, looking at him smiling, "it may be as you say, but he doesn't show it in size, because he's too tall and overly long, besides being very thin. However, the reason he's so bony must be that he is by nature somewhat of an astrologer or philosopher, or because of the long experience he must have of worldly things, for he must have gone through not a few according to the many years he shows he has hidden under the saddle. However that may be, he deserves praise because he shows he is good and docile."

Upon this they all left on horseback and the Priest and Don Quixote accompanied them a quarter of a league from the village. The

---

1 Cervantes' Sancho knew nothing whatsoever about Latin, but Avellaneda's Sancho appears to have a stock of phrases, as this "Glory to God" indicates.

2 Don Quixote knew famous steeds: Bucephalus belonged to Alexander the Great; Babieca was the Cid's famous charger: Ballerophon rode winged Pegasus: Seianus was a famous horse of Roman Antiquity; and Alfana was a horse's name used in Italian and Spanish works before and during Avellaneda's time.

priest went along talking about Don Quixote and his affairs to Don Álvaro, who was much astonished by his strange madness. Yielding to the pleas of the knights, they took leave of each other; and back in Argamesilla, the Priest went home.

After reaching home, the first thing Don Quixote did, after dismounting, was send his housekeeper after Sancho Panza, with orders that when he came he should bring what he had told him he would bring, which was *Florisbián de Candaria*,[3] a book no less foolish than it was irrational.

Sancho came flying, and when they were alone, the room locked from inside, he took out the book from under his jacket and handed it over. Don Quixote received it very joyfully, saying, "Sancho, this is one of the best and truest books in the world, in which there are knights of such great fame and valor that it would be bad luck for the Cid or Bernardo del Carpio to try to wear their shoes!"

Then he placed it on a desk and again repeated at length to Sancho all that he had told him the night before, which he hadn't been able to understand because of his sleepiness. He ended the talk by saying he wanted to go to Zaragoza for the jousts, and that he intended to forget the thankless princess Dulcinea del Toboso, and seek another lady who would better appreciate his services. From there he intended to go to the court of the King of Spain to make himself known by his exploits. "And," added good Don Quixote, "I shall make friends with the grandees, dukes, marquises, and counts who help in the service of his royal person. There I'll see whether one of those lovely ladies around the queen, in love with my stature in contrast to others, will show some sign of true love, now by outward appearances in her person and dress, now by notes or messages sent to the room which the King will doubtless give me in his royal palace. Because of this, envied by many of those knights of the Golden Fleece, they will all try in various ways to put me out of favor with the King. When I discover it, I'll defy and challenge them and kill most of them, and when the King, our Lord, sees my great valor, His Catholic Majesty will be forced to extol me as one of the best knights in Europe."

He said all this with so much spirit, in a ringing voice, raising his eyebrows, his hand on the hilt of the sword which he had not yet removed after going out to accompany Don Álvaro, that he seemed to be already experiencing all that he was saying.

---

[3] This is the work referred to as *Florisbrán* in Chapter 1 (see note 14 of that chapter).

"Consequently, I want you now, my dear Sancho," he continued, "to see some armor that the wise Alquife,[4] my great friend, brought me tonight as I was planning the aforementioned trip to Zaragoza, because he wants me to use it and enter the scheduled jousts and carry off the best prize the judges offer, to the unheard-of fame and glory of my name and that of past knights-errant whom I imitate and even excel."

He opened a large chest in which he had placed the armor and removed it. When Sancho saw the armor, so new and so fine, covered with Milanese insignia and engraving, polished and clean, he doubtless thought it was of silver and said, astounded, "By the life of the founder of the Tower of Babylon, if it were mine I'd convert it all into pieces of eight of the sort that are in circulation now, round as the Host, because just the silver itself, aside from the high relief carving, is worth at the very least, if you tried to sell it on the street, more than ninety billion. Oh, son of a bitch, you tricky things, how you gleam!"

Taking the helmet in his hands he said, "Well, the silver hat is silly! By Pilate's beard, if the brim were wider by four fingers, the King himself could wear it, and I swear that even on the day of the Rosary procession we'll have to put it on the Priest's head, and then he'll go out along these streets, in perfect trim, wearing it and the brocade cape. But tell me, sir, who made this armor? Was it made by that wise Esquife,[5] or did it issue thus from the womb of its mother?"

"Oh, you big fool!" said Don Quixote. "This was made and forged beside the river Lethe, half a league from Charon's boat, by the hands of Vulcan, hell's blacksmith."

"Oh, plague take the blacksmith!" said Sancho. "The devil can go to his forge and sharpen the plow. I'll bet that since he doesn't know me, he'd throw on my virginal beard a big bowlful of that pitch and turpentine he has burning, and it would be a lot worse to get off and even to cure up than the filth Aldonza Lorenzo threw at me recently."

At this, Don Quixote picked up the armor, saying, "Friend Sancho, I want you to see how it looks on me. Help me put it on." No sooner said than done: he put on the gorget, breastplate and backplate, and Sancho said, "By Heaven! These plates look like a work-coat; if they weren't so heavy they'd be very fine for reaping, more so with these gloves." And he picked up the gauntlets.

Don Quixote put on all the pieces and then spoke haughtily to

---

[4] Alquife was a magician from Spanish books of chivalry.

[5] Sancho's mishearing of Alquife.

Sancho in this way, "What do you think, Sancho? Does it look good on me? Don't you marvel at my gallant, fearless appearance?" He said this as he walked about the room, stepping high and grimacing, stamping his heels, raising his voice and making it fuller, graver, and calmer. After this, suddenly such a fancy took place in his mind that, swiftly laying his hand on his sword, he kept approaching Sancho with visible anger, saying, "Wait, accursed dragon, Libyan serpent, hellish basilisk; you'll see from experience the courage of Don Quixote, a second St. George in fortitude. I say you'll see, if I can split in two, with one single blow, not only you but also the ten fiercest giants that the nation of giants ever produced."

Sancho began to run around the room when he saw himself being pursued so threateningly. Getting behind the bed he began to run around it, fleeing from the fury of his master, who was saying as he went slashing right and left about the room, often cutting the curtains, the blankets and the pillows on the bed, "Wait, proud ruffian, because the hour set by the Divine Majesty for you to atone for the evil deeds you have done in the world has now come." All the while he was chasing poor Sancho around the bed, uttering a thousand insulting words, with each one aiming at him a wide-flung slash or stab. If the bed had not been as wide as it was, poor Sancho would have come out in a bad way.

He said, "Don Quixote, in the name of all the wounds of Job, St. Lazarus, St. Francis and especially our Lord Jesus Christ, and by those blessed arrows that the fathers shot at St. Sebastian, have compassion, charity, pity, and mercy on my sinful soul." At all this Don Quixote grew fiercer, saying, "Oh, arrogant one! Do you think now with all your soft words and prayers to appease my just wrath toward you? Return, return the princesses and knights whom you keep illegally in this castle of yours; return the great treasures you have usurped, the maidens you have enchanted, and the enchantress witch, the cause of all these evils."

"Sir, sinner that I am," said Sancho, "I am not a princess nor a knight, nor that noble witch you talk about, but I am the poor black Sancho Panza, your neighbor and former squire, husband of good Mari-Gutiérrez that you have already half-made a widow. Woe to the mother who bore me and to the person who put me here!"

Don Quixote added more angrily, "Bring me, right away, safe and sound, without injury or damage whatsoever, the empress I mention. After that your vile and arrogant self will be at my mercy, if you admit first that you are conquered."

"I'll do that before all the devils," said Sancho. "Open the door for me, and first sheathe your sword, for I'll bring you at once not only all the princesses in the world, but also Annas and Caiaphas[6] themselves, each one whenever you so desire."

Don Quixote very slowly and gravely sheathed his sword; he was fatigued and sweaty from slashing at the poor bed whose blankets and pillows he had turned into a sieve, and if he could have caught up with him, he would have done the same thing to poor Sancho, who came from behind the bed pale, hoarse, and weeping with fear. Kneeling before Don Quixote he said to him, "I acknowledge myself defeated, Sir Knight-errant; promise to pardon me, for I'll be good the rest of my life."

Don Quixote answered him with a Latin verse he knew and often quoted, *Parcere prostratis docuit nobis ira leonis*.[7] Then he said, "Haughty ruffian, even though your arrogance merited no clemency at all, in imitation of those ancient knights and princes whom I imitate and intend to imitate, I pardon you provided that you leave off all evil acts and henceforth be a shelter for the poor and needy, undoing the wrongs and injuries that are so unreasonbly done in the world."

"I swear and promise to do all you tell me," said Sancho. "But tell me, will this matter of undoing wrongs have anything to do with the licentiate Pedro García, curate of El Toboso, who is blind in one eye?[8] Because I shouldn't like to be involved in affairs of our holy Mother Church."

Don Quixote then brought Sancho to his feet saying, "What do you think, friend Sancho? One who does this in a locked room with a lone man like you would do better in a campaign against an army of men, however brave they might be."

"What I think," said Sancho, "is that if you wish to try out these experiments often on me, I'll give up the job."

Don Quixote responded, "Don't you see, Sancho, that it was all pretense, only to make you realize my great courage in combat, skill in overthrowing, and dexterity in attack?"

"Confound the devil who begat my line!" replied Sancho. "Well, then, why were you aiming those colossal slashes at me? Because

---

[6] Annas and Caiaphas were the high priests that Christ was brought to immediately after his arrest (John 18:14-15).

[7] "The wrath of the lion teaches us to pardon the conquered," a medieval Latin verse.

[8] There is an untranslatable pun here, because the word *tuerto* 'wrong' (of Sancho's "undoing wrongs") also means 'blind in one eye'.

when you aimed one, if I hadn't commended myself to glorious St. Anthony, you'd have taken off half my nose, for the wind from the sword went humming past my ears. I wish you had made those attempts not on me but long ago on those shepherds with the two flocks of sheep who knocked out half your molars with stones from their slingshots.[9] But since this is the first time, let it pass, and watch out what you do to me henceforth. Now excuse me, for I'm going to eat."

"Not so, Sancho," said Don Quixote. "Remove my armor and stay to eat dinner with me, so that afterwards we can discuss our departure." Sancho accepted the invitation without hesitation and after dinner Don Quixote sent him to a shoemaker's to bring back two or three large sheepskins from which he made a fine shield[9] with paper board and paste, as big as a spinning wheel for hemp. He also sold two lots and quite a good vineyard and turned everything into cash for the projected journey. He also had a good short lance made with a blade as wide as his hand, and bought Sancho a donkey on which to carry a small suitcase with shirts for himself and Sancho, and the money which amounted to something more than three hundred ducats. Thus did Sancho on his donkey and Don Quixote on Rocinante, according to the new faithful history, make their third and most famous sally from Argamesilla, toward the end of August of God-knows what year, without the Priest or the Barber or anybody else missing them until the day after their departure.

CHAP. IV. HOW DON QUIXOTE DE LA MANCHA AND Sancho Panza, his squire, made a third sally from Argamesilla by night; and of what happened to them on this famous third sally.

HREE HOURS before ruddy Apollo spread his rays over the earth,[1] the good hidalgo Don Quixote and Sancho Panza left their village, the former on his horse Rocinante, wearing all the pieces of armor, the helmet on his head, sitting on his horse gracefully, and Sancho with his saddled donkey on which were two quite large saddlebags and a small suitcase in which they had their underwear.

---

9 The adventure with the flocks of sheep is in I, 18)

10 Many shields of old were made of leather to make them lightweight and easy to wield.

1 This is an obvious imitation of Don Quixote's speech in I, 2, in which he

When they were out of the village, Don Quixote said to Sancho, "Now you realize, my dear Sancho, how favorable everything was for our sally, because, as you see, the moon is shining and the weather is clear. Up to now we haven't encountered anything which could mean bad luck for us; and besides, nobody heard us leave. In short, everything is going according to our wishes."

"That's true," said Sancho, "but I fear that when the priest and the barber miss us they will come with others in search of us, and when they find us, they'll bring us back home, against our wishes, holding us by the collar or in a cage like last year, in which case the fall would be worse than the relapse, by Heaven!"

"Oh, cowardly barber!" said Don Quixote. "I swear on the order of my knighthood that, only because of what you have said, and so that you will understand that there can be no fear whatsoever in my heart, I'm ready to return to the village and challenge to individual combat not only the priest, but also all the priests, vicars, sextons, canons, archdeacons, deans, preceptors, prebendaries, and curates in all the Roman, Greek, and Latin churches, in addition to all the barbers, doctors, surgeons, and veterinarians fighting under the flag of Esculapius, Galen, Hippocrates and Avicenna. Can it be Sancho, that you hold me in such little esteem that you have never seen my courage, the invincible strength of my arm, the extraordinary swiftness of my feet, and the innate vigor of my spirit? I'd dare bet you (and this is a certainty) that if I were split in two and my heart removed, they would find it to be like that of Alexander the Great,

---

imagines how the beginning of his first sally will be recorded when the history of his deeds are published.

said to have been filled with down, an undoubted sign of his great virtue and courage. Consequently, Sancho, in the future don't think you'll surprise me, even though you place before me more tigers than Hircania produces, more lions than Africa has, more serpents than live in Libya, and more armies than Caesar, Hannibal, or Xerxes had. Now let's drop the subject. You will see the truth of it all at those famous jousts in Zaragoza where we're going now. There you will see with your own eyes what I am telling you. However, Sancho, for this it's necessary to put on this shield (better than that from Fez which the brave Moor from Granada requested when he was shouting commands to have the dappled colt of the Vélez family warden saddled for him) some letter or emblem which denotes the passion in the heart of the knight who wears it on his arm. Therefore, at the first village we come across, I want some artist to paint on it two very beautiful maidens enamored of my courage, with the god Cupid above them, shooting an arrow that I receive on my shield as I laugh at him and pay little attention to them; around the edge of the shield will be the inscription THE LOVELESS KNIGHT, and at the top, between me, Cupid, and the ladies, will be this curious though far fetched inscription:

Cupido gets his arrows
From the veins of Peru,
Giving men the *Cu*
And women the *pido.*[2]

"And what are we to do with that *Cu*?" said Sancho. "Is it one of the prizes that we are to get from the jousts?"

"No," answered Don Quixote. "That *Cu* is a crest of two well-rounded feathers which some people are accustomed to wearing on their heads; sometimes they are of gold, sometimes silver, and sometimes of the wood which, when waxed seems transparent in lantern light. Some go so far as to have such feathers form the sign of Aries,

---

[2] This burlesque inscription is obviously quite surrilous in Spanish, and not necessary to footnote in that langauge. Some explanation about the division of *Cúpido* is required in translation, however. *Cu* refers to the female sexual organs here (the word is more appropriately Portuguese than Spanish, but both langauges were widely spoken in the peninsula), and *pido* is the Spanish verb meaning 'I beg [for it].

others that of Capricorn, and still others fortify themselves with the castle of St. Cervantes."[3]

"By heaven," said Sancho, "If I had to wear those feathers, I'd certainly have those gold or silver ones."

"Those trinkets aren't suitable for you because you have a good, ugly, Christian wife," said Don Quixote.

"That doesn't matter," said Sancho, "At night all cats are grey, and if there's no quilt a blanket isn't bad."

"Let's drop the subject," said Don Quijote, "In front of us there's a castle which it would be difficult to find in any country, high or low, or in the states of Milan and Lombardy." He said this because of an inn visible half a league distant.

Sancho responded, "I'm surely glad, because that place you call a castle is an inn. Since the sun is already setting it will be a good thing for us to make our way there so we can spend a very pleasant night and continue our journey tomorrow."

Don Quixote insisted it was a castle, and Sancho that is was an inn. At this point there happened by two men on foot who were surprised at Don Quixote's appearance, in full armor and even with a helmet, considering the extreme heat. They stopped, looking at him, and Don Quixote approached, saying, "Valiant knights, from whom some great ruffian, fighting you contrary to the rules of any order of knighthood, has taken your horses and some lovely maiden that you had with you, the daughter of some prince or lord of these kingdoms, who was to marry a count's son who, although a youth, is a valiant knight in his own right, speak and tell me your trouble, point by point, because you have in your presence the Loveless Knight, if you have never heard of him (but you must have because he is so well-known for his exploits), who swears to you, because of the indifference of the princess Dulcinea del Toboso, the cause of my disaffection, that he will avenge you so well and so much to your satisfaction that you will say it was a lucky day when fortune put in your path one to right the wrongs done you."

The two travelers didn't know what to answer, but, looking at each other, they said, "Sir Knight, we haven't fought with any arrogant ruffian, nor have we had horses or maidens taken from us. However, if you are talking about a fight we had under those trees over there with

---

[3] Avellaneda seems to be insulting Cervantes here, indicating slyly that he is being cuckolded. Since both Aries and Capricorn are associated with horns, and since the Spanish word for 'horned' means 'cuckolded', then seeing the name of Cervantes so nearby in an otherwise unusual context, we can only draw this conclusion.

a certain number of people who caused us a lot of itching around the collars of our doublets and the pleats of our breeches, well, we won a complete victory over that gang, and unless one got away from us in the forest of our patches, all the rest have been killed by the Count of Uñate."[4]

Before Don Quixote could answer, Sancho put in, "Tell us, travelers, that building you see over there, is it an inn or a castle?"

Don Quixote replied, "Whippersnapper, fool! Don't you see from here the high spires, the famous drawbridge and the two very fierce griffins defending the entrance against those who try to enter contrary to the will of the castellan of the castle?"

The travelers said, "If you please, armed knight, that is the inn called 'The Hanged Man's' because a year ago they hanged the innkeeper next to it because he killed a guest and stole everything he had."

"Well, go on then, and curses be with you!" said Don Quixote. "It will turn out to be what I say it is, in spite of everybody.

The travelers were much astonished at the madness of the knight, and Don Quixote said to Sancho, because they were already a musket-shot away from the inn, "Sancho, in order for us to comply fully with the order of chivalry and follow the road taught by the true science of warfare, it is very needful for you to go ahead, reach the castle as if you were a real spy and artfully note the width of the moat, the arrangement of the doors and drawbridges, the fortified towers, platforms, concealed causeways, dikes, counterdikes, trenches, portcullises, sentry boxes, and placement of guardposts; the artillery those inside have; what provisions there are and for how many years; what ammunition; if they have water in the cisterns; and lastly, how many are defending such a great fortress, and what they are like."

"By the body of her who bore me," said Sancho. "This is what wears out my patience with these adventures or misadventures which we go about seeking, in payment for our sins. Here is the inn right in sight, where we can enter without any obstacle at all and eat supper on our money exactly as we please, without any fight or quarrel with anybody. Now you want me to reconnoiter bridges and moats and

[4] The travelers are speaking in jest about their trouble with lice, all of which they have killed by pinching them to death, unless one escaped into the forest of their patched garments. *Uña* 'fingernail' gave rise to the word Uñate, which is a play on the word Oñate; a countship of Oñate was created in 1481 for Don Íñigo Vélez de Guevara. So the battle over the lice was won by pinching or mashing them to death with the *uña* or fingernail.

strange concealed things, or whatever in the devil that list you have given calls them, whereupon the innkeeper, seeing me wandering about measuring the walls of the house, will come out with a club and give me a drubbing, thinking I am going to steal the chickens or something else in the backyard. Come now, by your life! I can be relied upon in whatever happens to us, unless we ourselves start a quarrel."

"It does seem, Sancho, you don't know what is the duty of a good spy," said Don Quixote. "Well, for your information understand that in the first place he must be loyal, because if he is a double spy, informing one side and then the other about what is going on, it is very damaging for the army and merits any punishment whatsoever. In the second place he must be diligent in reporting quickly what he has seen and heard among the opponents, because if the warning arrives late sometimes a whole camp can be lost. The third thing he must be is secretive, so much so that to nobody, be he a good friend or comrade, must he disclose any secret he holds, unless it be to the proper general in person. Therefore, Sancho, go and do as I tell you without arguing, for you well know and have read that one of the reasons the Spaniards are the most feared and esteemed people in the world is because, aside from their valor and fortitude their prompt obedience to their superiors in warfare makes them victorious on almost every occasion. This destroys the enemy; this gives courage to cowards and the timid; finally, because of this kings of Spain have succeeded in becoming the lords of the whole earth, because if the inferiors are obedient to the superiors, with good order and agreement they become firm and stable and with difficulty are broken up and dispersed, as we see easily occurs in the case of many nations because of their lack of obedience, which is the key to every propitious event in war and peace."

"Well, all right," said Sancho. "I don't want to argue any more, for we'd never finish. Follow me gradually; I'm going with my donkey to carry out your command. If there is nothing of what you are talking about, we can stay there, because in truth my insides are already growling from pure hunger."

"God grant you luck in battle, so that you may come out with honor in this enterprise on which you are now setting out, and obtain from the aides-de-camp or generals of some army an honorable profit every day of your life," said Don Quixote. "May my blessing and God's be with you. Be careful not to forget what I have told you about being a good spy."

Sancho then urged on his donkey so hard that he arrived shortly at the inn. When he saw there were no moats, bridges, or spies as his master had said, he laughed heartily to himself, saying, "Doubtless all the fortified towers and moats my master said were at the inn must have been in his head, because I see nothing here but a house with a big yard, and it's undoubtedly an inn, as I said." He went up to the door and asked the innkeeper if there was a place to stay.

Being told there was, he took the suitcase off his donkey and gave it to the innkeeper to take care of until he should ask for it. After this he inquired if there was any supper, and the innkeeper told him there was a very good beef, veal and bacon stew with excellent cabbage, and a roasted rabbit. Good Sancho gave a couple of leaps for joy upon hearing about that blessed stew. He asked at once for barley and straw for his donkey and took his fodder to the stable. While busy giving it to the animal, Don Quixote came up near the inn on his nag, looking the same as already mentioned. The innkeeper and four or five others who were at the door with him marveled greatly at seeing such a phantom and waited to find out what he would do or say. Without speaking a word, he came to within two pikes' distance of the door, gravely looked half-contemptuously at the people who were there and walked around the whole inn, examining it from top to bottom and sometimes measuring the ground from the wall out with his lance. Having gone all around he again took his stand in front of the door and with an arrogant voice, standing up in his stirrups, he began to speak.

"Castellan of this fortress, you knights who are here to defend it with all the soldiers who are inside, sentinels on perpetual guard duty days and nights, winter and summer, with intolerable cold and vexing heat, against enemies who come to assail you and force you to go out on a campaign to try your luck, hand over to me right now and without any argument whatsoever a squire of mine whom you have seized falsely and treacherously and against all the rules of chivalry, without first doing battle with him. I know from experience that he is a person who, if you had done so, would not have hesitated to take on ten of you as a starter. Therefore, I am convinced you took him by treachery, with the power of the enchantment of the old witch you have inside, or by treason. I'm showing too much civility by asking for him in the way I have. I repeat, hand him over to me at once if you wish to remain alive and don't want me to put all of you to the sword and leave no stone of this castle standing."

He went on saying, raising his voice more angrily, "Come now, hand him over immediately, safe and unhurt, together with all the knights, maidens, and squires you hold prisoner with inhuman cruelty in your dark dungeons. If you don't, then come forth, vaunted knights, wearing your heavy armor and your persuasive lances of strong ash-wood, for I'll wait here for all of you."

With this he kept pulling back on the reins; Rocinante was more than anxious to enter the inn because, like Sancho his mouth was watering.

Amazed by the words of Don Quixote and seeing that with lowered lance he was challenging them to fight, calling them chickens and cowards, standing up on his horse, the innkeeper and the rest went up to him and the innkeeper said, "Sir knight, here there is no castle nor fortification, unless it be that of the wine, which is so hearty and strong that it can not only bowl one over but also make one say much more than you said to us. I answer for all of us and tell you that no squire of yours has come here. If you wish lodging, enter, for we'll give you a good supper and a bed that's more than good, and if necessary, there will even be a Galician girl to take off your shoes. Although she's full-breasted, she's cut her teeth years ago and if you don't close your purse don't fear that she will close her arms against you, nor fail to take you in them."

"In the name of the order of knighthood," replied Don Quixote, "if you don't hand over, as I say, the squire and the Galician princess you speak of, you'll die the most abject death that any innkeepers-errant in the world have died."

At the noise Sancho came out saying, "Don Quixote, it's all right for you to come in, for the very instant I entered they all surrendered. Get down, get down! They are all friends; we have become reconciled and they are waiting for us with a very fine beef, bacon and veal stew with turnips and cabbage which is calling out 'Eat me! Eat me!' "

When Don Quixote saw that Sancho was so happy, he said to him, "For Heaven's sake, Sancho, my good friend, tell me if these people have done you any wrong or injury, for I'm here ready to fight, as you see."

"Sir," said Sancho, "nobody in this house has done me any harm; as you can see, both my eyes are whole and strong as I got them at birth. Neither have they cooked up any trouble for me; rather they've cooked up a stew and a rabbit in such a way that Juan de Espera en Dios himself could eat it."[5]

"Well, Sancho," said Don Quixote, "take this shield and hold my stirrups for me to dismount. These people appear to be good-natured, even though paynim.

"I should say paying!" said Sancho. "By paying three reales and a half we'll be dissolute[6] lords of that nice greasy stew."

Upon this Don Quixote got off his horse, which Sancho took to the stable with his donkey. The innkeeper told Don Quixote to remove his armor, for he was in a safe place where, provided he paid for his supper and bed, there would be no quarrel whatsoever. He did not wish to do so, saying that when among pagans one couldn't trust everybody. At this point Sancho arrived, and by dint of earnest pleas managed to have him take off the helmet. After this he set him before a small table covered with a cloth, and told the innkeeper to bring the stew and the roasted rabbit, which was done at once. Don Quixote ate only a very little, for most of the supper was overlooked as he made speeches and grimaces. However, Sancho saved his master from embarrassment, because with a couple of hoistings of his arm he ate up all that was left of the stew and the rabbit, with the help of a generous two quarts of Yepes wine which filled him to capacity.

When the table was cleared, the innkeeper took Don Quixote and Sancho to quite a good room so they could go to bed. After Sancho had removed Don Quixote's armor, he went to give a second ration to Rocinante and his donkey and to water them. While Sancho was engaged in these bestial exercises there arrived a Galician girl who, because she was very polite, was easy about promising and more so about doing. She said to Don Quixote, "A very good evening, Sir Knight. Do you need anything? (Even though we're black, we don't rub off.) Would you like for me to remove your boots or clean your shoes or stay here tonight in case you happen to want something? Good gracious! I think I've seen you here before; even in face and appearance you look like someone I was quite fond of. However, that's water under the bridge; he left me and I left him free as a cuckoo. I do not belong to everybody as do other loose women. I'm a maid, but reserved; a good woman, servant of an honorable innkeeper. A treacherous captain deceived me, taking me away from home under the

[5] Juan Espera en Dios is a charatcter in the Spanish folk tradition who has been around for centuries waiting for Christ's return. His teeth would either be missing or worn out, thus he would require very soft food.

[6] Sancho means 'absolute'.

promise of marriage. He went off to Italy leaving me ruined, as you see; he took away all my clothes and jewels I had taken from my father's house."

Then the girl began to cry and to say, "Woe is me! Alas for me, an orphan and alone, with no help other than that of Heaven! Woe is me! Would that God might send somebody to stab that villain, avenging me for the many wrongs he has done me!"

Since Don Quixote was compassionate by nature, he said when he heard that girl crying, "Of course, beautiful maiden, your piteous troubles have struck my heart in such a way that you have turned to wax what was steel in battle, and so because of the order of chivalry I swear and promise, as a true knight-errant whose duty is to right such wrongs, not to eat bread from a table, nor to dally with the queen, nor to comb my beard and hair, nor to cut my toenails or fingernails, and even not to enter any town,[7] after the jousts in Zaragoza where I'm now going, until I have avenged you on that disloyal knight or captain, and it will be so much to your liking that you will say that God has made you meet a true undoer of affronts. My dear maiden, give me your hand, for I give you mine, as a knight who will fulfill all I say. And tomorrow early, with your veil over your eyes, alone or with your dwarf, mount your fine palfrey and I shall follow you; it might even be that in the royal jousts to which I am now going I shall defend your beauty against everybody and then make you queen of some foreign kingdom or island where you'll marry some powerful prince. Meantime, go to bed, rest on your soft couch and trust in my word, because it will be carried out."

The dissolute girl, seeing herself dismissed in such a fashion, contrary to her hope of sleeping with Don Quixote and getting three or four *reales* from him, became very sad at such a resolute response to such a lengthy harangue, and so she said to him, "Just now, sir, I can't leave home because of a certain difficulty, and if you intend to do anything for me I beg you to be good enough to lend me two *reales* because yesterday as I was washing dishes I broke two Talavera plates and if I don't pay for them my master will give me two dozen heavy blows with a stick."

"Anyone who touches you will be touching the apple of my eye," said Don Quixote, "and I alone am equal to challenging to individual

---

[7] Starting with "not to eat bread" and ending with "not to enter any town," Don Quixote mixes elements from ballads about the Marquis of Mantua and the Cid. In Cervantes' original, Don Quixote was also quite familiar with the ballad of the Marquis of Mantua (I, 5 and 10; II, 25).

combat not only that master of yours but also all masters governing castles and fortresses today. Go on to bed without fear, for this arm will not fail you."

"That's what I thought," said the girl. "See here! Please give me the two *reales* now for I am here ready for whatever you wish."

Don Quixote did not understand what tune the Galician was singing, so he said to her, "Princess, I say not the two *reales* you request, but two hundred ducats which I want to give you right away."

The girl, who knew that one shouldn't bite off more than one can chew, and that a bird in the hand is worth two in the bush, came up to him to embrace him, in order to see if that way she could get the two *reales* she had requested, but Don Quixote got up saying, "I have seen or read of very few knights-errant who, in such critical moments as this in which I find myself, have stooped to any immodesty whatsoever. Therefore, neither will I, imitating them, stoop to it." Thereupon he began to call Sancho, saying, "Sancho, come up here and bring me that suitcase."

Sancho (who had up to then been engaged in a long chat with the innkeeper and the guests, praising his master's outstanding courage, relating his great deeds, since he was so stuffed with the stew he had eaten for supper) came up with the suitcase, and Don Quixote told him: "Sancho, open that suitcase and give this princess two hundred of those ducats we have there, for after having avenged her for a certain wrong done her against her will, she will not only give you that much but many more very costly jewels that a discourteous knight stole in spite of her."

Sancho, hearing the command, responded hotly, "What do you mean? Two hundred ducats! By my parents' bones and even by those of my grandparents, I can't give them any more than I can bump my head against the sky. Look at the smelly wench, daughter of the same kind. Isn't she the one who told me a while ago in the stable that if I wanted to sleep with her and would give her eight *cuartos*, she was there, ready and willing? By Jove! If I grab her by the hair, she'll leap downstairs in one jump!"

When the poor Galician girl saw that Sancho was so angry, she said to him, "Brother, your master has ordered you to give me two *reales*—I neither ask for nor want two hundred ducats, because I see clearly that this gentleman says it to make fun of me."

At this, Don Quixote, amazed by what Sancho was saying, told him, "Do give her more, because tomorrow we'll go with her as far as her land, where we'll be paid in full."

"Now be of good cheer, lady," said Sancho. "Come down here. This way you'll be as much a lady as the bitch that bore you!" Grabbing the suitcase, he pushed the girl down the stairs ahead of him and gave her four *cuartos,* saying, "In the name of the weapons of the giant Goliath, if you tell my master I didn't give you two hundred ducats, I'll slash you more times than there are punch holes on my donkey's saddle!"

"Sir," said the Galician girl, "give me those four *cuartos,* and I'll be very happy."

Sancho gave them to her, saying, "The miserable wretch is well paid for something she didn't work for!"

Here the innkeeper called Sancho to retire on a bed he had made for him of two packsaddles. Sancho did so, using his suitcase for a pillow, and slept very soundly.

CHAP. V. ABOUT THE SUDDEN QUARREL THAT CAME up between our Don Quixote and the innkeeper as he left the inn.

HEN MORNING came, Sancho fed Rocinante and his donkey and had a fair-sized piece of veal (unless it was from its mother, as anything might be expected from this innkeeper's virtue). After this he went to awaken Don Quixote who hadn't been able to close an eye all night long except for a little while at dawn. He had been kept awake by plans for his accursed jousts which made him lose his senses, the more so because that night he had imagined he was defending the beauty of the Galician girl against all foreign and native-born knights and taking her to the kingdom or province where he thought she was a queen or lady.

Don Quixote awoke terrified at Sancho's shouts, saying, "Surrender, valiant knight, and acknowledge that the beauty of the Galician princess is so great that if Polyxena, Portia Albana or Dido[1] were alive they wouldn't be fit to remove her very trim little shoe."

"Sir," said Sancho, "the Galician is very content and well-paid, for I have already given her the two hundred ducats as you ordered; she

---

[1] Portia Albana was Brutus' wife. The others are identified in Chapter 2, note 3.

says she kisses your hand and is at your service, for she is ready and willing to do anything for you."

"Well, Sancho," said Don Quixote, "tell her to have her fine palfrey saddled while I dress and put on my armor so that we can leave."

Sancho went downstairs, and the first thing he did was go to see if breakfast was ready. He saddled Rocinante and put the packsaddle on his donkey, placing at hand the shield and the short, thick lance. Don Quixote came down very slowly, carrying his armor, and told Sancho to put it on him because he wanted to leave at once. Sancho told him to eat breakfast and put on his armor afterwards. Don Quixote absolutely refused to do this, nor did he wish to sit down at the table because he said he could not eat off a tablecloth until he finished a certain adventure he had undertaken. Therefore he ate standing, four bites of bread and a bit of roast mutton; then he mounted his horse and said graciously to the innkeeper and to the other guests who were there, "Warden and knights, think about whether there comes to your mind anything in which I may be of help, for here I am ready and prepared to serve you."

The innkeeper responded, "Sir Knight, we need nothing here except for you or this peasant you have with you to pay for the supper, bed, and barley, and after this leave with no ill feelings."

"Friend," said Don Quixote, "in no book I've read have I seen that when any warden or lord of a fortress has the good fortune to house a knight-errant does he ask for money for the lodging. However, since you put aside the honorable name of warden to make of yourself an innkeeper, I am happy for you to be paid. See how much we owe you."

The innkeeper said they owed him fourteen *reales* and four *cuartos*. "I should quarter you for the shamelessness of the bill if it weren't beneath me, but I don't want to misuse my valor," replied Don Quixote, and turning to Sancho, he ordered him to pay. As he turned around to speak to him, he saw near the innkeeper the Galician girl, broom in hand to sweep the patio. Very courteously he said to her, "Sovereign lady, I am ready to fulfill all that I promised you last night, and you will surely soon be placed in your beautiful kingdom, for it is not right that a king's daughter, such as you, should go about in that way, badly dressed as you are and sweeping the inns of such base people as these. Therefore mount your beautiful palfrey or if, perchance, due to the turn of hostile fortune, you don't have one, climb on this donkey belonging to Sancho Panza, my faithful squire. Come with me to the city of Zaragoza and there, after the jousts, I shall defend your extreme beauty against the whole world by setting up a rich tent in the center of the plaza and next to it a placard, and next to the placard a small but very exquisite platform with a beautiful seat of honor where you will, be dressed in very rich garments. Meanwhile I shall be fighting against many knights who for the sake of winning the approbation of their lady-loves will come there with infinite emblems and devices which will clearly declare the passion in their fiery hearts and the desire to overcome me. However, it will be a difficult (not to say impossible) enterprise for them to attempt to win the prize and honor, for I shall beat them easily, aided by your beauty. And so I say, lady, come with me and leave all else behind."

The innkeeper and the rest of the guests who heard such statements from Don Quixote considered him completely mad and laughed to hear him call his Galician girl a princess, daughter of a king. Nevertheless, the innkeeper turned on his servant girl angrily saying, "Upon my soul, madam shameless whore, I vow I'll make you remember the bargain you've made with this madman, for I'm on to you now. Is this the way you repay me for taking you out of the whorehouse in Alcalá and bringing you here to my house, where you are respected, and buying you that petticoat which cost me sixteen *reales*, and the shoes three and a half? Besides, I was just this day about to buy you a chemise, seeing you don't have a rag left of one. But may I never use a barber's basin again if you don't pay me for everything, and afterwards I'll send you off as you deserve, with a sting (as they say) in your tail to see if you can find anyone who will be as good to you as I have been in this inn. Go on now, curse you, you rascal, and wash the dishes. We'll settle things later." So saying, he raised his hand and gave her a slap and three or four kicks in the ribs, so that she went away stumbling and half-falling.

Oh, good God! You should have seen the inflamed wrath and burning anger that entered into our knight! No asp trodden upon shows greater rage than his when he took hold of his sword, standing tall in the stirrups, and said in a haughty and arrogant tone, "Oh, foolish and base knight! Would you thus strike in the face one of the most beautiful women that can be found in the world? But Heaven will not permit such cowardice and stupidity to remain unpunished."

Hereupon he aimed a terrible blow at the innkeeper, hitting him on the head with all his might in such a way that it would have gone badly with him had Don Quixote not twisted his hand a little. Nonetheless he gave him a good cut on the head. Everybody in the inn became excited and each one took up the weapon he found handiest.

The innkeeper went in the kitchen and brought out a very large three-pronged roasting fork, and his wife a vineyard guard's short lance. Don Quixote turned Rocinante around, shouting, "War! War!"

The inn was on a small hill and a stone's throw away was a quite large meadow, in the center of which Don Quixote took his stand, making his horse prance and holding his naked sword in his hand, because Sancho had the shield and heavy lance. As soon as Sancho saw that the fat was in the fire, he thought that for the second time he was going to be tossed in a blanket; so he struggled out as best he could to calm the people and settle that quarrel. However, the innkeeper, aware of his head-wound, had turned into a lion and was hurriedly demanding his blunderbuss with which he undoubtedly would have killed Don Quixote, had Heaven not saved him for greater perils. The innkeeper's wife and Sancho prevented this, saying that that man was bereft of reason and, since the wound was small, to let him go and the devil take him.

This appeased him, and Sancho, who was not to blame for what had happened, very courteously bade them farewell and went to his master, carrying the shield and heavy lance and leading the donkey by the halter. When he reached Don Quixote he said to him, "Is it possible, sir that for the sake of a working girl worse than the one Pilate, Annas or Caiaphas had, and a rascal to boot, you would be willing to get us involved in such dissension that it almost cost us our skins, because the innkeeper wanted to come with his gun and shoot you? And after that, me, because your silver armor, even if it were lined with velvet, would not have saved you."

"Oh Sancho!" said Don Quixote. "How many people are there

coming? Is it a squadron of cavalry and foot soldiers, or are they coming by regiments? How much artillery, how many armored men with helmets, and how many companies of archers do they have? Are the soldiers old or inexperienced? Are they well-paid? Is there hunger or plague in the army? How many Germans, Rhinelanders, Frenchmen, Spaniards, Italians, and Swiss are there? What are the names of the generals, aides-de-camp, provosts, and campaign captains? Quick, Sancho, tell me, for it's important that, according to the numbers of people we prepare in this big meadow trenches, moats, counter-moats, embankments, platforms, bastions, stockades, catapults and defenses within which we can put cannonballs and fire bombs, firing all our artillery at the same time, and first those that are filled with nails and pellets, because these have a great effect at the first charge and assault."

Sancho replied, "Here there is no breast-plate or leap,[2] as sure as I'm a sinner! There are no Turkish armies, nor mounts, nor droves of donkeys nor bastiones; beasts, yes, for they'll be us if we don't leave right away. Take your shield and lance, because I want to mount my donkey. Since our Lady of Sorrows has delivered us from the sorrows that such well-deserved blows could have caused us at this inn, let's flee from it as from Jonah's whale, because there must be easier adventures to conquer than this, waiting for you out in the world."

"Hush, Sancho," said Don Quixote. "If they see me flee, they will say I am a cowardly chicken."

"Well, by God!" said Sancho. "Even if they call us chickens, capons, or pheasants, this time we've got to go. Get up, Señor Donkey!"

Don Quixote, seeing that Sancho was so determined, did not wish to oppose him any more. Rather, he began to ride along behind him saying, "Of course, Sancho, we were very wrong not to return to the inn and challenge all those traitors and renegades, for that's what they really are, and after that kill them, because it isn't right for such vile, base rabble to live on the face of the earth. If they remain alive, as you see they are, tomorrow they will say that we didn't have the courage to attack them, something I'd as soon die as have people say about me. In fact, Sancho, in this matter of returning we have been extremely befuddled."

"Befuddled, sir?" responded Sancho. "We may be befuddled in the sight of God, but as for this world, we have done as much as our

---

[2] Here Sancho has misunderstood Don Quixote's words "*impetu y assalto*" 'charge and assault', thinking them to be "*peto* [*y*] *salto*" "breastplate [and] leap'.

strength permitted. Consequently, let's travel on before the sun gets any higher; between you and me, you're leaving all those at the inn well-punished."

CHAP. VI. ABOUT THE NO LESS STRANGE THAN DANgerous battle our Knight had with a guard of a melon patch, whom he thought to be Orlando Furioso.[1]

HE GOOD KNIGHT Don Quixote and his squire Sancho Panza, traveled six days on the road to Zaragoza without having anything worthy of note happen to them, except that they were minutely scrutinized in all the villages they passed through, and everywhere Sancho Panza's simple-minded acts and Don Quixote's fantasies caused hearty laughter. In Ariza he took it into his head to personally make a sign and affix it to a post in the plaza, saying that any local or errant knight was lying who said that women deserved to be loved by knights, as he alone would make them confess one by one or ten by ten, although it is their right to be defended and helped in their troubles, as the Order of Chivalry commands, but as for the rest, let men make use of them for procreation under the bond of holy matrimony, without further embellish-

[1] *Orlando Furioso* (1532), a long poem by the Italian writer Ariosto, is loosely based on the French *Song of Roland*.

ment of courtship, because the ingratitude of the princess Dulicnea del Toboso made quite clear that the contrary was great madness. Then he signed at the bottom of the sign: "The Loveless Knight."

Other events as peaceable and stranger than this one occurred in other villages along the way, until he and Sancho arrived near Calatayud, at a village named Ateca, a musket-shot away from that town. The two were going along chatting about what he planned to do in the Zaragoza jousts and how he intended to make a trip to the King's court to make his personal worth be known; then it so happened that he looked around and saw a hut in the center of a melon patch and beside it a man on guard, lance in hand. He halted a bit, staring, and after having some nonsensical reasoning in his mind, he said, "Sancho, stop! If I am not mistaken, this is one of the strangest and never-before-seen adventures you have ever seen or heard of in all your born days: that man you see over there with a lance or javelin in his hand is undoubtedly the lord of Anglante, Orlando Furioso, who as is related in the authentic and true book called *Mirror of Knighthood*,[2] was enchanted by a Moor and taken to guard and defend the entrance to a certain castle, because he was the strongest knight in the universe. The Moor put him under such a spell that in no part of his body except the sole of his foot can he be wounded or killed. This is that furious Roland,[3] who became crazed from rage and anger and tore up trees by the roots because a Moor from Agramante, named Medoro, stole the beautiful Angélica from him. It is even told as a fact (I believe it wholeheartedly because of his strength) that he seized the leg of a mare on which a luckless shepherd was riding, and whirling the horse with his right arm, he threw it two leagues away; he did other strange things like this, which are related extensively and which you can read. So, my dear Sancho, I am resolved not to proceed until I try my luck with him, and if it be such that I conquer and kill him (and it will be because of my personal strength and the swiftness of my horse), then all his glories, victories, and prowess will doubtless be mine, and all the exploits, conquering, giants' deaths, jaw-breaking of lions, and destruction of armies he did all by himself, will be attributed to me alone. If he threw the mare of the shepherd two leagues away, which is told as the truth, everybody will say that he who overcame one who did such a thing, can cer-

---

[2] By Pedro de Reinosa; among its characters are Orlando and Angélica.

[3] Roland (*Roldán*) is the Spanish version of the Italian name Orlando, and this character shows both names in Avellaneda's and Cervantes' novel.

tainly throw another shepherd four leagues away. With this, I shall be famous throughout the world and my name will be feared. Finally, when the King of Spain learns about it, he will send for me and ask me what the battle was like, detail by detail, what blows I gave him, with what cunning I overthrew him, and with what stratagems I avoided his feints so that he thrust at the empty air, and finally, how I killed him by sticking a cheap pin in the sole of his foot. When His Majesty knows all about it and I give you as an eye-witness, I shall undoubtedly be believed. We shall take his head in those saddlebags, and the King will take it and say, looking upon it, 'Ah, Roland, Roland, how does it happen that you, chief of the Twelve Peers of France, have found your equal? Neither your enchantment nor having broken open a huge cliff with only one knife-slash were of any help to you! Oh, Roland, Roland, today how much more splendor and fame does the invincible Manchegan and great Spaniard Don Quixote have.' Therefore, Sancho, don't move from here until I have signed and sealed this frightful adventure by killing the Lord of Anglante and cutting off his head."

Sancho, who had been listening very attentively to his master's speech, answered, saying,"Señor Loveless Knight, I think that we have here, as I see it, no Lord of Argante,[4] because what I see over there is nothing but a man with a lance, guarding his melon patch because many people go by here on the way to the festivals at Zaragoza, they might romp through the melons. So I say that it is my opinion, notwithstanding yours, that we not disturb one guarding his possessions: let him guard them and good luck to him, for that's the way I do with what's mine. Who's telling you to meddle with Giraldo Furioso,[5] or to cut off a poor melon grower's head? Do you want it to be known later and to have the Holy Brotherhood come out after us and harry us and shoot arrows at us and then put us in the galleys for seven hundred years, from which place we'll get out only when the calves of our legs have gray hair. Señor Don Quixote, don't you know that the proverb says: 'He who loves danger will face it whether he wants to or not'? The devil with it! Let's go to the village which is nearby; we'll have supper there at our pleasure and our animals will be fed. Upon my word, if you'd ask Rocinante, whose head is drooping somewhat, whether he'd prefer to go to the

[4] Sancho mishears again; Don Quixote has just referred to Orlando, lord of Anglante, and Sancho repeats it "Argante".

[5] Sancho means Orlando Furioso, of course.

inn or make war with the melon grower, he'd say he would prefer half a peck of barley to one hundred bushels of melon growers. Since this insensitive animal says and begs this of you, and I, in the name of Rocinante and my donkey, implore you earnestly, and in weakened condition, it is right for you to believe us. Remember, too, that many times misfortunes have happened to us because you didn't want to take my advice. What we can do is this: I'll go buy a couple of melons for supper, and if he says he is Gaiteros or Bradamonte[6] or that other demon you mention, I'll be most content for us to rip him open; if he doesn't, let's take him for what he is and be on our way to the royal jousts."

"Oh, Sancho, Sancho," said Don Quixote, "How little you know about adventurous matters! I left my house only in order to win honor and fame, for which we now have at hand an opportunity. You well know that the ancients painted Opportunity with a forelock on the forehead and a completely bald head, giving us to understand that when this lock has passed by there is no way to seize him. Sancho, no matter what you and everybody say, I shall not give up trying this enterprise nor taking into Zaragoza, the day I enter it, the head of this Roland on a pike, with a sign below it reading I CONQUERED THE CONQUEROR. And then bear in mind, Sancho, how much glory will come to me from this! It will cause everybody to do me homage and to surrender to me, so that all the prizes will doubtless be mine. And so, Sancho, commend me to God, because I am going to engage in one of the greatest perils I have seen in all my born days. If, perchance, because the dangers in war are many, I should die in this battle, take me to San Pedro de Cardeña so that in death, sword in hand and seated in a chair like the Cid,[7] I trust that if some Jew should try to touch my beard in mockery, as happened to him, my inert arm will be able to take a hand in this and treat him worse than the Catholic Champion treated the one who did the same thing to him."

Sancho responded, "Oh, sir! I beg you, by Noah's ark, not to talk about dying, for it makes tears as big as my fist roll from my eyes hearing about it, and my heart breaks into little pieces because of my

---

[6] Sancho is referring to Gaiferos and Bradamante: the former is Charlemagne's nephew in the Spanish ballad tradition, and the latter is an Italian woman warrior in Italian epics.

[7] There is a legend to this effect about the dead Cid in San Pedro de Cardeña.

extremely affectionate nature. Unlucky the mother who bore me! If you should die in this battle, what would unhappy Sancho Panza do alone in a strange land, burdened with two animals?"

After this Sancho began to weep in earnest and said, "Woe is me, Señor Don Quixote! I might as well never have known you, and for such a trifle! What will the outraged maidens do? Who will do and undo wrongs? From now on the whole Manchegan nation will be lost; there will be no fruit of knights-errant, for today the flower of them all comes to an end with you. It would have been better if those heartless Yanguesans had killed us a year ago, when they cudgeled us with clubs.[8] Alas, Señor Don Quixote! Poor me! What am I to do without you? Woe is me!"

Don Quixote consoled him, saying, "Sancho, don't cry, because I'm not dead yet; rather, I've heard and read about an infinite number of knights, mainly Amadís de Gaula, who lived many years after having often been in danger of being killed. They came back to their land to die in the house of their parents, surrounded by children and wives. Despite all this, as I have said, if I die you are to do as I say."

"I promise, sir, " said Sancho. "If God takes you, I'll convey your body for burial not only to San Pedro de Sardinia,[9] as you say, but even to Constantinople, even if it costs me what my donkey is worth. Since you are determined to kill that melon grower, give me your blessing here before you leave, and let me kiss your hand. May my blessing and that of St. Christopher be with you."

Don Quixote blessed him very lovingly, and then began to put the spurs to Rocinante, who was so tired he couldn't move. At every step, as he went through the melon patch heading straight for the hut where the guard was, he kept cursing Rocinante who, worn out from hunger, had an appetite for tasting some of the leaves and melons of the green plants, even though he was bridled.

When the melon grower saw that that phantom kept approaching without regard to the damage he was doing to the plants and melons, he began to shout to him to stay out; if he didn't, the devil take him, he'd make him leave the melon patch. Heedless of the words the man was saying to him, Don Quixote continued on his way, and when he was two or three lance-lengths away from him, he began to say, resting his lance on the ground, "Valiant Count Orlando, whose fame and deeds are praised by the renowned and honored Ariosto whose divine

---

[8] Refers to an episode in I, 15.

[9] Sancho refers to San Pedro de Cardeña, of course.

heroic verses give a picture of you, this is the day, invincible knight, when I shall try the strength of my weapons and the keen edge of my sharp sword against you. Today is the day, brave Roland, on which neither your enchantments nor being head of the Twelve Peers, of whose nobility and strength great France boasts, will protect you. You will be conquered and killed by me, if Fortune wills, and your proud head, oh, strong Frenchman, will be taken on this lance to Zaragoza! Today is the day on which I shall enjoy all your exploits and victories; there will be no help for you from Charlemagne's army, nor the courage of your cousin, Renaut de Montauban, nor Montesinos, nor Oliver, nor the magician Maugis with all his spells. Come and face me, for I am one lone Spaniard. I do not come against you like Bernardo del Carpio and King Marsile of Aragon,[10] with a powerful army; I come against you with only my weapons and horse, while you, since you were the one affronted, had some time before going into battle with only ten knights. Answer, don't be mute. Mount your horse or come against me in any way you wish. However, since I understand, from what I have read, that the magician who put you here didn't give you a horse, I'll dismount because I don't want to have any advantage over you in battle."

Hereupon he dismounted. When Sancho saw this, he began to shout, "Attack, master, attack, for I'm here praying in your behalf. I've promised a mass for the blessed souls in Purgatory and another to St. Anthony to protect you and Rocinante."

When the melon grower saw Don Quixote coming at him, lance in hand and protected by a shield, he began to tell him to get out, for if he didn't, he'd stone him to death. As Don Quixote came on, the melon grower threw aside his thick lance and put a stone somewhat larger than an egg in his sling. Drawing his arm back, he let the stone fly like a catapult at Don Quixote, who received it on his shield, which was easily pierced because it was of sheepskin and paper board. Our knight received such a terrible blow on his left arm that it would have been broken had it not been protected by the armlets, but he bore the blow most strongly. As the melon grower saw that he was still persisting in approaching, he placed another and larger stone in the sling and hurled it so straight and with such force that it hit Don Quixote in the middle of the chest; if he had not been wearing the engraved breastplate it undoubtedly would have penetrated his stomach. As it was, thrown by

---

[10] Bernardo is identified in Chapter 2, note 10. King Marsile was the Moorish king of Aragon, Roland's enemy.

a strong arm, it knocked the good hidalgo over backwards and he received such a bad and dangerous fall that with the weight of the armor and the force of the blow he remained half-stunned on the ground. The melon grower, thinking he had killed or crippled him, went running to the village.

Sancho, who saw his master down, believing that the blow from the stone had put an end to Don Quixote and his adventures, went up to him, leading the donkey by the halter, lamenting and saying, "Oh, my poor loveless master! Didn't I tell him that we ought to go to the village without further ado and not raise a fight with this melon grower who is more of a Lutheran than the giant Goliath is? But how did he dare approach him when he was not on his horse when deep in his soul he knew it was God's truth that he could kill him only by sticking a needle or penny-pin in the sole of his foot?"

Thereupon he went to his master and inquired if he was badly hurt; he responded that he wasn't, but that that haughty Orlando had thrown a great boulder at him and knocked him down. He added, "Sancho, give me your hand, because I have come out completely victorious. To accomplish this I needed only to have my enemy flee and not dare to face me; as people say, if your enemy is running away, make a silver bridge for him. So let's let him go, for the time will come when I'll seek him out and to his grief finish the battle which has begun. Only now I feel that this left arm is badly hurt; that furious Orlando must have thrown at me a terrible mace that he had in his hand; if my fine armor had not protected me, I believe that he would have broken my arm."

"Mace?" said Sancho. "I know he didn't have one. But he threw two cobblestones with his sling, and if either one had hit you on the head, upon my word, even with that silver spire[11] or whatever you call it, on your head we would have finished up the task we are supposed to do at the Zaragoza jousts. Give thanks for being alive to a ballad about Count Peranzules that I prayed; it's been proved very efficacious for a pain in the side."

"Give me your hand, Sancho," said Don Quixote. "Let's go rest a while in that hut and then we'll go on since, the village is near.

With this Don Quixote got up and removed Rocinante's bridle, and Sancho took the suitcase and packsaddle off the donkey, putting it all in the hut. Rocinante and the donkey remained absolute lords of the melon patch, from which Sancho took two very good melons which he

[11] Don Quixote's helmet must have had a point on it.

cut with a dull knife he had with him. Then he placed them on the packsaddle so that Don Quixote could eat, but after only a few bites he ordered Sancho to keep them for supper at the inn. No sooner had Sancho eaten half a dozen slices than the melon grower appeared with three well disposed young men, each carrying a fine club.

When they saw the nag and the donkey loose, trampling the plants and eating the melons, they entered the hut blazing with anger, calling them thieves and robbers of other people's property, and accompanying these compliments with half a dozen well-placed blows before the two could arise. To Don Quixote's misfortune he had removed his helmet and he received three or four whacks on the head which left him half-stunned and even somewhat lacerated. Sancho fared worse. Because he wore no corselet, he didn't miss any thumps on his ribs, arms, and head and remained as half-stunned as his master. Without rendering them aid, the men took the nag and the donkey to the village as security for the damage they had done.

When Sancho came to quite a while later and saw the state of affairs and felt his ribs and arms hurting so much that he could scarcely get up, he began to lament to Don Quixote, "Oh, Sir Knight-errant (may he err all the way to the devils in hell!), do you think we've come out well? Is this the triumphant way we are to enter the Zaragoza jousts! What's become of the head of Roland the Enchanted which we are to carry skewered on a lance? May it please St. Apollonius for the devils to skewer him on a spit! I have been telling you seven hundred times we shouldn't get into these meddlesome fights, but go our own way without harming anybody, but there's no avoiding it. Fine then, take those wild pears that have come to you; if we stay here long, please God another half dozen won't come to end the battle that the first ones started! Get up, despite St. Martin's horseshoes! Look, your head is covered with lumps and blood is running down your face, so you are now truly He of the Sad Countenance in payment for your nonsensical acts so deserving of punishment."

Don Quixote, coming to and becoming a little calmer, began to say:

"King Don Sancho, King Don Sancho,
Say not I have told,
That From Zamora under siege
Came forth a traitor bold."[12]

"Curses on the soul of the Antichrist!" said Sancho. "Here we are

[12] The first four verses of the famous ballad about the treason of Bellido Dolfos.

with our hearts in our mouths and you leisurely start on the ballad of King Sancho! Let's leave here, by the grace of all our lineage, and take care of our wounds, for these Barrabases of Gaiteros, or whoever they are, have put us through the mill and have left my arms so I can't raise them to my head."

"Oh, good squire and friend!" responded Don Quixote. "You must know that the traitor who has left me in such a state is Bellido de Olfos, son of Olfos Bellido."

"Oh, curse that Bellido or knave of Olfos,[13] and even the one who got us into this melon patch."

"This traitor, going with me on the road to Zamora, while I was off my horse to go behind some bushes to relieve myself, I say, this Bellido treacherously hurled a javelin at me and got me in this state. Therefore, oh faithful vassal, it's very necessary for you to mount a powerful horse, call yourself Don Diego Ordóñez de Lara, and go to Zamora; when you reach there you will see between the embrasures in the city wall the good old man, Arias Gonzalo, before whom you will issue a challenge to the whole city, towers, foundations, merloned battlements, men, children, and women, and all the other challenges which the son of Bernardo issued to the aforesaid city, and you will kill the sons of Arias Gonzalo, Pedro Arias and the rest."

"By the body of St.Quentin," said Sancho. "If you see what the four melon growers did to us, why the devil do you want us to go to Zamora to challenge a city as important as that one? Do you want five or six million horsemen to come out and put an end to out lives without ever enjoying the prizes at the royal jousts in Zaragoza? Give me your hand; get up and we'll go to the village, which is nearby, so our wounds can be treated and your bleeding stopped."

Don Quixote got up, albeit with quite a little difficulty, and the two left the hut. However, when they didn't see Rocinante or the donkey, the grief Don Quixote showed for him was exceedingly great, and Sancho, going around the hut in search of his donkey, wept as he said, "Alas, donkey of my very soul! What sins have you committed that you should be taken from my sight! My darling donkey, you are the light of my eyes, the reflection of myself; who has taken you from me? Alas my dear donkey, all by yourself with your braying, you could be king of all the donkeys in the world! Where shall I find another man as good as you! Comfort in my work, solace for my troubles, only you under-

---

[13] There is a pun here which is not translatable: "*ese* Bellido *o* vellaco *de Olfos*" 'that Bellido or knave of Olfos.'

stand my thoughts, and I yours as if I were your foster brother! Alas, my dear donkey! I remember that when I went to the stable and you saw the barley being sifted, you brayed and laughed as pleasantly as if you were a person, and you breathed in with a pleasing whistle, answered at the rear by a resonant tone that the barber in my village could never in the world equal on his guitar when he sings the military march at night."

Don Quixote consoled him, saying, "Sancho, don't grieve so much for your donkey. I have lost the best horse in the world, but I'm concealing my sorrow until I find him, because I intend to search the face of the earth."

"Oh, sir," said Sancho, "don't you expect me to grieve, sinner that I am, when they told me in our village that this donkey of mine was a very close relative of that great rhetorical Balaam's ass[14] (may he live a hundred years)? And this has been made very clear by the valor he displayed in this hard-fought battle we've had with the world's most arrogant melon growers."

"Sancho, according to Aristotle nothing whatsoever can be done about the past," said Don Quixote. "Therefore the best thing you can do now is take this suitcase under your arm and carry this packsaddle on your back as far as the village. There we shall find out all we must do in order to find our animals."

"I'll do as you say," said Sancho. picking up the suitcase and telling Don Quixote to throw the packsaddle on him.

"Sancho, see if you can carry it; if you can't, take the suitcase first and then come back for it," replied Don Quixote.

"Yes, I can," said Sancho. "This isn't the first packsaddle I've carried on my back in my life."

He put it on top of him, and, since the crupper came close to his mouth, he told Don Quixote to put it behind his head because it smelled of badly chewed straw.

[14] In Numbers 22:21-35, Balaam's ass saw visions of the angel of the Lord.

CHAP. VII. HOW DON QUIXOTE AND SANCHO PANza reached Ateca, and how a charitable clergyman named Mosen Valentín gave them shelter in his house, making them heartily welcome.

Don Quixote with his shield and Sancho Panza with his packsaddle fitting him like a ring fits a finger set out walking. Upon entering the first street in the village a great crowd of boys began to gather until they reached the plaza, where all those present started to laugh on seeing the arrival of those odd figures. The city officials and six or seven clergymen and other respectable people with them drew near.

Since Don Quixote saw himself in the plaza, hedged in by so many people, all of them laughing, he began to speak: "Illustrious Senate and invincible Roman people, whose city is and has been the head of the universe, consider whather it is just for highwaymen to go out of your city, which your celebrated republic never permitted in former centuries, and for them to steal my precious horse and my faithful squire's donkey on which he carries the prizes and rewards I have won or been able to win in various tourneys and jousts. Consequently, if that former valor has remained in your hearts as pious Romans, hand over, right now, what has been taken from us together with the traitors who, when we were dismounted and not watchful, wounded us as you can see. If you don't, I challenge you all as traitors and sons of others such, and I summon you to come against me one by one in singular combat, or all againt me alone."

Upon hearing such nonsense everybody burst into laughter and a clergyman who seemed more astute came up to them and asked them to be quiet, because he more or less recognized that man's illness and would show him up for what he was, to the entertainment of everybody. After this, in the silence accorded him by the bystanders, he went up to Don Quixote, saying, "Sir Knight, you are surely able to give us a description of those who have injured your head and stolen that horse you mention, because if you make the evildoers known to the illustrious consuls, not only will they punish them, but also all that is found to belong to you will be justly returned."

Don Quixote responded, "It will be difficult to find the one who fought me, because I think he was the valiant Orlando Furioso or at least that traitor Bellido de Olfos."

Everybody laughed, but Sancho, who was burdened with the packsaddle on his back, said, "Why is it necessary to beat about the bush? The one who knocked down my master with a stone is a man who was guarding a melon patch: a callow youth with a long beard and a drooping mustache, God curse him! This fellow stole my master's nag and took my donkey, and I'd rather he'd taken these ears of mine."

The clergyman, Mosen Valentín, was finally sure about what ailed Don Quixote and his squire; so, being a charitable man, he said to Don Quixote, "You and this servant of yours, come with me, Sir Knight, and everything will be done as you wish."

Then he took them to his house and had Don Quixote lie down on a very good bed and sent for the barber to come and treat the lumps on his head, even though the wounds were not serious. When Don Quixote saw the barber ready to treat him, he said, "I take the greatest pleasure, oh, Master Elizebad,[1] in having fallen into your skillful hands, because I know and have read that they are such that, together with the medicines and herbs that you apply to wounds, Avicenna, Averroes and Galen could learn from you. Therefore, oh, wise master, tell me if these deep wounds are mortal. They cannot fail to be, because that furious Orlando injured me with the hugh trunk of an oak tree. Since this is so, I swear to you by the order of chivalry to which I belong that I'll not consent to being treated until I have had full

---

[1] Elizabad is the surgeon in *Amadís de Gaula*, mentioned also in Cervantes' *Don Quixote* (I, 24, 25, 27). Avellaneda misspells his name.

satisfaction and revenge on the one who, treacherously and uninjured, wounded me without waiting like a knight for me to seize my sword."

The clergyman and the barber, hearing Don Quixote speak such words, fully understood he was crazed. Without answering him the clergyman told the barber to treat him and not say a word back, in order not to give him any further reason to talk. After he was doctored, Mosen Valentín ordered that he be allowed to rest, which was done.

Sancho, who had held the light for his master to be treated, was bursting to talk. So, when he was outside the room, he said to Mosen Valentín, "I want you to know that that Girnaldo Furioso[2] struck me; I don't know if it was with the same oak tree he hit my master with or a gold bar. He must have done so, because people say that he is under a spell, and from the way my ribs hurt he must undoubetly have left some devlish fever in them. My trouble is such that throughout my whole body, may God preserve it, he has left nothing intact except, at the very most, a tiny bit of desire to eat. If he had taken this from me, I'd curse all the Rolands, Ordoños, and Claras[3] in the world."

Mosen Valentín, understanding Sancho's appetite, had him given a very good supper while he went to find out who could have taken Don Quixote's horse and Sancho's donkey. When he learned who had attacked them, he ordered that Rocinante and the donkey be rounded up and returned to his house.

When Sancho, who was sitting in the entryway, saw the donkey, he got up from the table and said, embracing him, "Oh, donkey of my soul! You are as welcome as the flowers of May; God grant you and everything on which you set hoof as much joy as your return has caused me. But tell me, how did you get along with that Rodamonte at the siege of Zamora? I hope I'll see him roll down that mount on which Satan tempted our Lord Jesus Christ."

Seeing Sancho so happy about finding his donkey, Mosen Valentín said to him, "Don't worry about anything, Sancho; if your donkey had not appeared I would have given you a jenny just as good if not better, because of my fondness for you."

"That can't be," said Sancho, "because this donkey of mine already knows my disposition and I know his, in such a way that he hardly has

---

[2] Another attempt by Sancho to remember Orlando Furioso.

[3] Claras is Sancho's untraceable mispronunciation of some famous knight, for example, Clarián; there are a number of Ordoños, all kings of León and Asturias (former kingdoms situated in Northern Spain).

started to bray when I understand him, and know if he is asking for barley or straw, or if he wants to drink or wants me to unsaddle him so he can lie down in the stable. In short, I know him better than if I had borne him.

"Well, Sancho, how do you know when the ass wants to rest?" said the clergyman.

"Señor Valentín, I understand asinine language very well," responded Sancho. The clergyman laughed heartily at his reply and ordered very good provisions to be given to him as well as his donkey and Rocinante, because Don Quixote was resting at that time. This was all done very punctually.

After supper two more clergymen, friends of Mosen Valentín, arrived to find out how he was getting along with his guests. He told them, "Gentlemen, gentlemen! They are affording us the most amusement you can imagine here in this house, for the main one, the one who is in bed, imagines himself to be a knight-errant like those of old, Amadís or Phoebus, that the lying books of chivalry call errant. So it is my opinion that because of this madness he intends to go to the jousts in Zaragoza and win many prizes and important rewards. However, we shall enjoy his conversation the days he is convalescing here in my house, and our entertainment will be increased by the innate simplicity of this rustic whom the other calls his faithful squire."

After this they began to chat with Sancho, questioning him in detail about every aspect of Don Quixote. He told them all that had happened the year before, the love for Dulcinea del Toboso, how he used to call himself Don Quixote de la Mancha and now he will be the Loveless Knight when he goes to the jousts in Zaragoza. In this manner Sancho disclosed all that he knew about Don Quixote and they all laughed a great deal over the affair of the galley slaves, the penitence in the Sierra Morena, and his being locked up in a cage. From all this they fully understood Don Quixote's condition and the simplicity with which Sancho followed him, praising his acts.

Sancho and Don Quixote had been at Mosen Valentín's house almost a week when, at the end of this time, Don Quixote thought he was now recovered and it was time to go to Zaragoza to demonstrate his personal valor. One day after dinner he said to Mosen Valentín, "Oh, good sage Lirgando![4] I believe that, since through your great magic I have been brought here to this renowned castle of yours and healed without having deserved it, the time has come for me to leave

---

[4] Refers to Lirgandeo, chronicler of the Knight of Phoebus.

immediately for Zaragoza, with your permission. You know how important it is for my honor and reputation. If fortune favors me (and it will, with you on my side) I intend to present you with one of the best prizes they have, and you will receive it because of the favor you have shown me. I only beg you not to forget me in greater emergencies, because it has been many days since I saw the sage Alquife who is in charge of writing up my exploits. I believe he is intentionally leaving me alone for some toils so that I may learn from them to eat hard bread and stand on my own two feet, as they say. Therefore I want to leave right away. If you will be good enough to send a message with me recommending me to Urganda the Unknown,[5] so that she may treat me if I am wounded in the jousts, you will do me a great favor."

After listening attentively, Mosen Valentín said, "Señor Quijada, you may leave whenever you please, but bear in mind that I am not Lirgando, that lying sage you mention: I am an honorable priest who, moved by compassion on seeing you crazed by your fancies and knightly deeds, has taken you into his house with the purpose of telling and advising you about what is relevant to the situation and warning you, while we are alone and in my house, that you are in mortal sin when you leave your house and estate and that little nephew of yours[6] to go roaming about these roads like a crazy man, making yourself conspicuous and doing so many nonsensical things. I warn you that some time you may do something that will cause you to be arrested, or if they don't recognize your condition, you will be publicly punished, to the public dishonor of your family. Or, if on your campaign you have perhaps killed somebody and there is nobody who can help you or who knows you, the Holy Brotherhood, which doesn't countenance jokes, may catch and hang you; thus you will lose the life of your body and, what is worse, that of your soul. Beside this, you go about scandalizing not only those in your village but also all those who see you like that on the road, in armor. If you don't believe it, remember the day you entered this town; how the boys followed you around the streets as if your were a madman, shouting 'Let's see the man in armor, boys, let's see the man in armor!' I know very well that you have acted as you do, as you say, in imitation of those ancient knights, Amadís and Esplandián, and others invented by books of chivalry, which are as fabulous as they are harmful, which you consider authentic and true, knowing, in all truth, that never in the world were

[5] Urganda the Unknown is a sorceress who is friendly to Amadís.

[6] In Cervantes' *Don Quixote*, there is only a niece and no nephew at all.

there such knights, nor is there any Spanish, French or Italian history—at least an authentic one—which mentions them. They are only fictional compositions published by whimsical people with the object of entertaining idle people who are fond of such lies. By reading them, bad habits are secretly engendered in their spirit, as good habits are engendered in a good spirit. This is why there are so many ignorant people in the world; seeing those big printed books they think, as you do, that they are true, when, as I have said, they are lying compositions. Consequently, Señor Quijada, for the love of God I beg you to come back to your senses. Leave off that madness which has you roaming about, and go back home. Since Sancho tells me you have a fairly good income, spend it in God's service and in doing good for the poor, confessing and taking communion often, hearing mass daily, visiting the sick, reading devout books and conversing with honorable people, above all with the clergy of your village, who will tell you the same thing I'm telling you. If you do this, you will see that you will be loved and respected, not considered a man lacking in judgment, as all those in your village and those who see you roaming about think you are. Also, in the name of all the orders to which I belong I swear that I'll go with you, if you wish, and leave you at the very door of your own house, even if it's forty leagues[7] from here. I'll even pay all the expenses along the way, so you can see I am more solicitous about your honor and the good of your soul than you are yourself. Cease those vain adventures or, better said, misadventures, for you are now an older man. Don't let it be said that you are going back to your childhood ruining yourself and this good rustic who follows you and has as soft a brain as you have."

Sancho, sitting on his beloved donkey's packsaddle, very attentive to all Mosen Valentín's speech, said, "Certainly, Señor Licentiate, your Reverence is very right. I tell my master, and the priest of my area has told him, just what you are telling him, and one can't do anything with him; we have to go on about the world seeking injustices. Last year and this we have never found anyone who hasn't shaken the dust from our ribs, and each day we have been in danger of losing our skin because of the outrageous acts my master commits on the road, calling inns 'castles' and some men 'Gaiteros,' others 'Guirnaldos,' others 'Bermudos,' others 'Rodamontes,' may the devil take them all! The strange

---

[7] A Spanish league is 5872.7 meters, so 40 leagues is 223 kms. The real distance is about 450 kms., although it cannot be expected that everyone will know all distances accurately.

thing is that they are melon growers or muleteers or travelers. Just to show you: the other day at an inn, he openly called a Galician maid-servent a Galician princess, and she was a swindling devil who offered me, in exchange for four *cuartos*, the physical charms inherited from her mother. Because of her he beat up the innkeeper and we thought we'd be in an accursed fight; believe me, may Saint Barbara, patron against thunder and lightening, be my witness that if I'm lying about what I'm telling, may I be without this packsaddle at the hour of my death. My head is split for having preached this advice to him, but you can't do anything with him for he wants me to follow him even against my will. This is why he has bought me this good donkey of mine, and every month gives me nine *reales* and my food for my work. Let my wife look out after herself, as I do, for she has such good quarters."

Don Quixote had been pensive while Mosen Valentín and Sancho Panza were talking, but now, as one who awakens, he began to speak in this way: "Put aside inaction, Señor Archbishop Turpin! I am most astonished that you, belonging to that illustrious house of Emperor Charlemagne, called 'the Great' because of his excellence, and being related to the Twelve Peers of noble France, should be so faint-hearted and cowardly that you would flee from arduous and difficult things and evade dangers, without which it is impossible to win true honor. Great things were never acquired without great difficulties and risks; if I face the present and future ones I do so only magnanimously for the sake of obtaining honor for myself and all my successors. This is just, for he who does not look for his own honor will look out badly for God's. So, Sancho, get me my armor and my horse at once and let's leave for Zaragoza. If I had known about the cowardice and faint-heartedness there was in this house, I never would have stayed in it. Let's leave immediately so that we won't be contaminated."

Sancho went at once to saddle Rocinante and put the packsaddle on his Dapple. The good clergyman, seeing that Don Quixote was so resolute and stubborn, did not try to reason any further; rather, he continued listening to all that he said as Sancho put on each piece of the coat of mail. He made most amusing remarks, stringing together a thousand beginnings of old ballads in a confused and disconnected manner.

Upon mounting his horse he said, " 'Now Calaínos is riding, Calaínos the prince—' "[8] and then, holding his lance and shield, he turned to Mosen Valentín and said haughtily, "Illustrious knight, I am very

---

[8] The first two verses of a version of the ballad about Calaínos.

grateful for the favor you have shown me and my squire in this imperial castle of yours. Therefore think whether I can be of any help in avenging you for any affront done you by some fierce giant, for here is that Mucius Scaevola without terror who, intending to kill Porsena[9] who was besieging Rome, bravely put his naked arm on the fiery brasier, by this act proving great strength and courage as well as his stoicism. Be assured that I shall avenge you on your enemies to your complete satisfaction and you will say it was a lucky hour when you took me into your house."

After this he commended him to God and without waiting for a reply spurred Rocinante. When he reached the plaza and the boys saw him, they began to shout: "Come see the man in armor! Come see the man in armor!" Followed by them he went on at a half-gallop until he was out of the village, leaving all who saw him marveling.

Good Sancho put the packsaddle on his donkey, mounted and said, "Señor Valentín, I don't offer you fights as my master has because I know more about being beaten than I do about fighting, but I am very grateful for the service you have done us; may you do as much many more years. The name of my village is Argamesilla; when I'm there I'll be prepared to serve you in any way I can, and my wife Mari-Gutiérrez will kiss your hand in sign of agreement to do the same."

"God keep you, brother Sancho," said Mosen Valentín. "Bear in mind that I beg you to come by here when your master returns home; you and he will be welcomed, so don't fail to do so."

Sancho responded, "I promise. God be with you, and if it please our lady Saint Águeda, patron saint of nursing mothers, may you live as many years as Father Abraham."

Thereupon he began to urge on his donkey, and as he passed through the plaza the city fathers and everybody there surrounded him to pass a few jokes with him. When he saw them gathered together he said, "Gentlemen, my master is going to Zaragoza for some jousts and royal tourneys; if we kill a gross of those huge giants or Fierablases,[10] for people say that there are many there, I promise to

---

[9] Caius Mucius Scaevola was the 6th Century B.C. Roman hero (different from Quintus Mucius Scaevola, mentioned in note 5 of Chapter 2); Lars Porsena was the Etruscan king who conquered Rome when Scaevola was defending it.

[10] Sancho is referring to Fierabras, a fabled Saracen giant sung about in a French epic poem dealing with the period of Charlemagne. In the epic, Fierabras sacks Rome and steals what remains of the fluid used to embalm Christ. Don Quixote, in Part I (10), makes a batch of Fierabras' balm which he claims is a cure-all.

bring you one of those rich prizes we'll win and half a dozen pickled giants, because you have been good enough to return Rocinante and Dapple to us. If my master gets to be king, or at least emperor (and he will, because he is so brave), and because of him I find myself Pope or monarch of some church, we promise to make all of you in this village at least canons of Toledo."

At Sancho's statement everybody burst out laughing, and when the boys at the back saw that the jurists and the clergy were making fun of Sancho mounted on his donkey, they began to whistle at him and throw cucumbers and eggplants and all who were there were unable to restrain their zeal.

Consequently Sancho had to dismount in a hurry and beat his donkey with a stick to get out of the village. He came across Don Quixote, who was awaiting him and said, "What's the matter, Sancho? What have you done? What's kept you?"

Sancho responded, "Oh curses on the heel bones of Job's wife! Why did you come away and leave me in the hands of the coppersmiths of Sodom? I give you my word, as true as I'll be archbishop of that city as you promised me last year, that after you left, six or seven of those scribes and Pharisees grabbed me and took me to the druggist's; there they poured into me a dose of melted lead that has me dropping hot birdshot through the back door without being able to rest a minute."

"Don't worry about anything," said Don Quixote. "The time will come when we shall be well avenged for all the insults done us in this village because they didn't know us well. But now let's be on our way to Zaragoza. That's the important thing because there you will hear and see marvelous things."

CHAP. VIII. ABOUT HOW THE GOOD HIDALGO, DON Quixote arrived at the city of Zaragoza and the strange adventure with a man being flogged which befell him as he entered.

HE GOOD Don Quixote and Sancho managed to travel so well that at eleven the next day they found themselves a mile from Zaragoza. They met many people walking and riding along the road, coming from the jousts which had taken place there. Since Don Quixote delayed a week in Ateca recovering from his beating, the jousts were held without being honored by his presence as he desired. When he found out about this from the travelers on the road, he was practically desperate and went along cursing his fate. He blamed his rival, the wise enchanter, saying that he had caused the jousts to be held so hastily in order to take from him the honor and glory it was necessary to win , and give the victory due him to the one he maliciously favored. In consequence he was so peevish and melancholy that he wouldn't speak to anybody along the road until he arrived near the Aljafería.[1]

There, since several people came up to look closely at him and find out who he was and why he was entering the city dressed in full armor, he addressed them in a loud voice: "Tell me, gentlemen, how many days ago did the jousts in this city, which I was not able to attend, end? This is what causes the despair which my face reveals, but the reason was that I was busy with a certain adventure and encounter with the furious Roland (would that I had never come across him!). But I shouldn't be Bernardo del Carpio if, not having the good fortune to take part in them, I didn't challenge all the enamored knights in this city and thus be able to gain the honor which I couldn't win because of not being at the famous festivals. Tomorrow will be the day for the challenge. Unlucky be the one hit by my lance or caught by the edge of my sword! By this means I intend to appease my wrath and the anger with which I come to this city. If there is any one of you here or any enamored persons in this strong castle of yours, I challenge them at once as cowards and traitors, and I shall make them confess it aloud on this plain. Let the magistrate, which people say this village has, come out with all the

[1] The Aljafería is the Moorish castle of the 11th Century, later used as the residence of the kings of Aragon. It still stands.

jurists and knights. They are both cowardly and faint-hearted, for one lone knight is challenging them and they are not coming forward like good knights to do battle with me. Because I know that they are such that they won't dare await me on the field, I'm entering the city at once, where I shall put up my placards on all the squares and street corners. The jousts have been held on such short notice because of fear of me and envy of my taking the prize and honors. Come forward, rascally inhabitants of Zaragoza, come forward! I shall make you confess your stupidity and lack of courtesy."

As he was saying this he was making his horse turn and rear so that all of the more than fifty who had gathered to look at him marveled and didn't know what to make of it. Some said, "I swear! This man has gone crazy and is a lunatic!" Others said, "No, but he's a great knave. I'll bet that if the law gets him he'll remember it as long as he lives."

While he was making Rocinante, who would have preferred half a peck of barley, jump around, Sancho said to all those who were discussing his master, "Gentlemen, you needn't talk about my master, because he is one of the best knights to be found in my village. With my own eyes I have seen him do so many extraordinary things in La Mancha and the Sierra Morena that if one were to relate them the giant Goliath's pen would be needed to tell all of them. It is true that not always do the adventures turn out as we should like, because four or five times we got our ribs roughly drubbed. But let them take the consequences: I give you my word that my master has sworn that when we come across them again, provided we catch them alone and sleeping, tied hand and foot, we'll skin them and make a fine shield out of them for my master."

Everybody began to laugh at this, and one of them asked Sancho where he was from, to which he responded, "Gentlemen, speaking with due respect for an honorable man, I am a native of my village which, begging your pardon, is named Argamesilla de la Mancha."

"By Heaven," said another, "I thought that your village had another name, since you mentioned it so politely, but what sort of place is Argamesilla that I have never heard of it?"

"Oh, by the body of the midwife who delivered me!" said Sancho. "It is a village much better than this Zaragoza. It is true that it doesn't have as many towers as this, because in my village there is only one.

Nor does it have around it a great earthen wall like this. But it does have houses, although not many, with fine backyards, each of which will hold two thousand head of cattle. We have a very fine blacksmith who sharpens our plows so well that we thank God for him a thousand times. When we left this time, the councilmen were planning to send him to El Toboso, since there is none in that village. In my village we also have a church; although it's small it has a very lovely high altar and another to Our Lady of the Rosary with a virgin two yards high with a great rosary surrounding her and the Lord's Prayer in gold letters as fat as my fist. It is true we have no clock but the priest has vowed that next Holy Year we'll arrange for a very fine organ."

Here Sancho tried to go to his master who was surrounded by an equal number of people, but one of them seized him by the arm and said, "Friend, tell us what that knight calls himself, so that we may know his name."

"Gentlemen, to tell you the truth," said Sancho, "his name is Don Quixote de la Mancha, and a year ago he called himself He of the Sad Countenance, when he was doing penance in the Sierra Morena, as you must already know about around here. Now he calls himself the Loveless Knight, and my name is Sancho Panza, his faithful squire, an honest man according to the people in my village. My wife is Mari-Gutiérrez and she is so good and honorable that all by herself she can keep a whole community satisfied."

So saying, he got off the donkey, leaving all those present laughing, and made his way to where his master was surrounded by more than one hundred people. Most of them were knights who had come out to enjoy the fresh air and, seeing such a large group of people with a man in armor in their midst, they rode up to see what it was all about.

Seeing them, Don Quixote, the butt of his lance resting on the ground, began to address them: "Valiant princes, and Greek knights whose name and fame is spread from pole to pole, from the Arctic to the Antarctic, from East to West, from North to South, from the blond German to the austere Scythian, in whose great empire of Greece there flourished not only that great Emperor Trebacio and Don Belianís de Grecia, but also the two valiant but never-conquered brothers, the Knight of Phoebus and Rosicler: you already know about our stubborn siege of the famous city of Troy for so many years, and how many skirmishes we have had with these Trojans and my rival Hector whom, because I am Achilles, your captain-general, I have never been able to catch alone so that I may fight him hand-to-hand and, despite his entire strong city, make him give up Helen, taken from us by force.

Oh, brave heroes! You should now take my advice (if you want us to have complete victory over these Trojans and put an end to all of them with fire and blood, without having a single one escape except Aeneas who, as Heaven ordains because he carried his father Anchises on his shoulders out of the fire is to go with certain men and ships to Carthage and thence to Italy to populate that fertile province with all those noble people he will have in his company), which is for us to make a safeguard, a big bronze horse, put in it all the armed men we can and leave it in their field alone with Sinon,[2] whom most of you know, tied hand and foot. We shall pretend to withdraw from the siege so that when they come out of the city and are informed by Sinon and deceived by his pretended tears, at his urging they will take our big horse inside with the intention of sacrificing it to their gods. They will undoubtedly do this by tearing down a section of their city wall in order to get it through. At midnight, after they have all settled down, the armed knights inside the pregnant belly of the horse will come out confidently and in safety will set fire to the whole city. Then we shall certainly come to the rescue unexpectedly to increase the fierce fire, raising our cries to Heaven in time with the flames which will consume towers, capitals of the columns, turrets and balconies as we call out, 'Fire! Fire! Troy is burning and Helen with it!' "

Hereupon he spurred Rocinante, leaving everyone astonished at his strange madness. Sancho also began to urge on his donkey and went after his master who, after entering through the Portillo Gate began to rein in has nag and go very slowly along the street, looking most attentively at the streets and windows. Sancho went along behind him, leading the donkey and waiting to see at which inn his master would stop, because at every inn-sign he saw Rocinante stop and refuse to go on. However, Don Quixote spurred him until he went on much against his will, which Sancho regretted like death because he was really suffering from weariness and hunger.

It so happened that as Don Quixote was going up the street, giving everybody who saw him looking as he did plenty to talk about, the law was bringing in a man riding on a donkey. His back was naked from the waist up, there was a rope about his neck, and he was being given two hundred lashes for being a thief. Three or four constables and notaries were accompanying him, with more than two hundred boys following them. At the sight of this spectacle our knight stopped his

---

[2] Sinon was the Greek spy who persuaded the Trojans to bring the wooden horse inside of Troy.

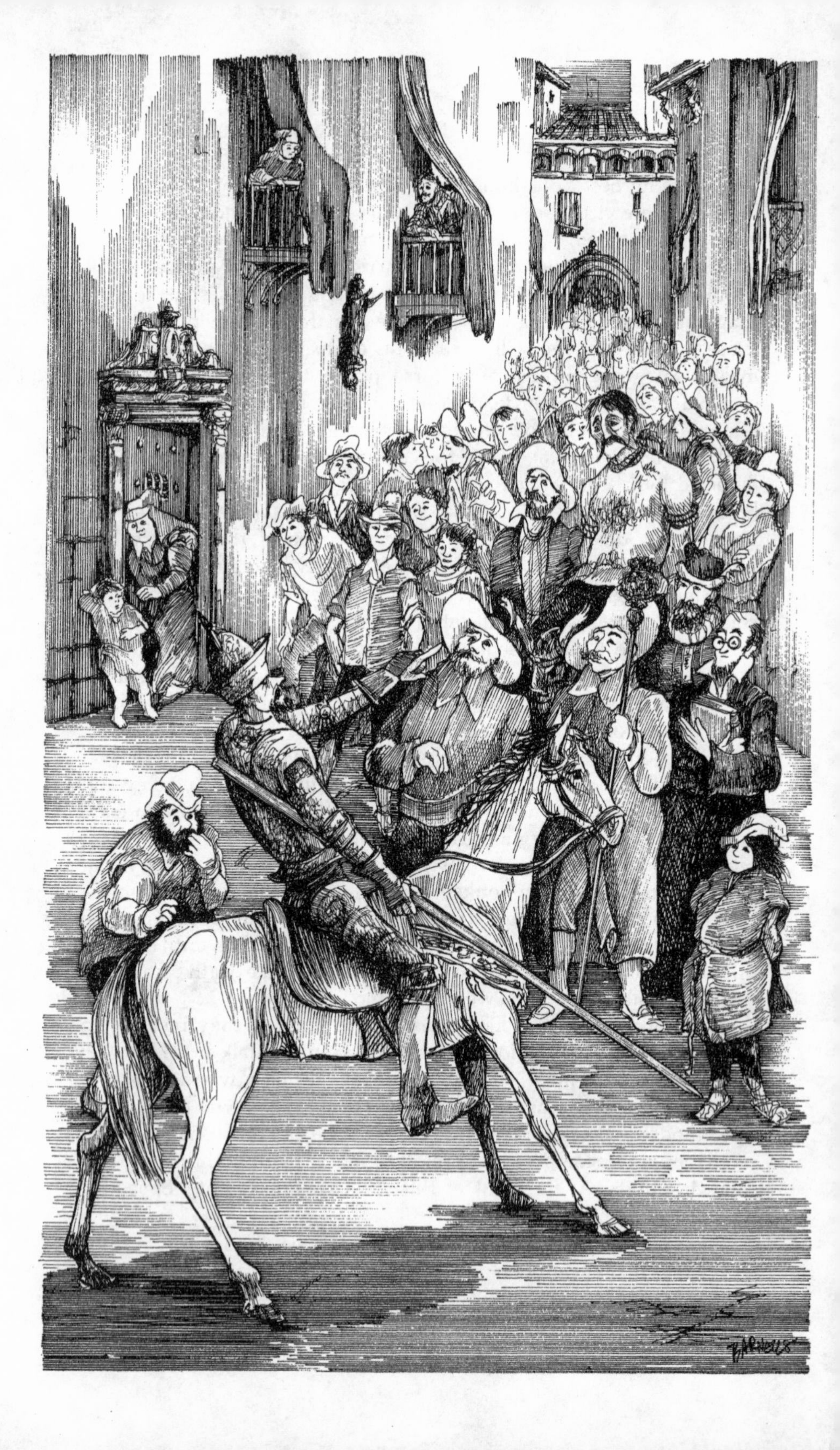

nag, took his stand in the middle of the street and, with lowered lance and proud bearing began to speak loudly in this way:

"Oh, infamous and bold knights, unworthy of this name! Let this knight go free at once, safe and sound. You have arrested him illegally and treacherously, using base unheard-of strategems and plots to catch him unawares. He was asleep beside a clear spring, in the shade of some leafy alders, because of sorrow probably caused by the absence or sternness of his lady. Then you knaves and scoundrels noiselessly took away his horse, sword, lance and other weapons, stripped him of his fine clothing, and are taking him tied hand and foot to your strong castle to put him among the other knights and princesses you are holding unjustly in the dark as well as damp dungeons. Consequently, hand over his weapons at once and let him mount his powerful horse, for he is one who will, within a short time, report your vile, gigantic rabble. Turn him loose, turn him loose quickly, or all of you together attack me alone, as is your custom, and I shall make you and whoever is sending you with him understand that you are all infamous and base rabble."

Upon hearing such words spoken by a man with sword and lance, those who were leading the man being lashed did not know what to reply. However, one of the notaries on horseback, noting that they were halted in the middle of the street and that that man was not allowing the law to take its course, spurred his nag, went up to Don Quixote, seized Rocinante's rein and said, "What the devil are you saying, limb of Satan? Get to one side! Are you crazy?"

Oh, great God! Would that I could paint the burning wrath which at this point took possession of our knight's heart! Stepping back a little he launched forth with his lance at the poor notary in such a way that had he not fallen over the nag's rear Don Quixote would surely have hidden the rusty iron of the lance in his stomach, but this caused our knight to miss his mark.

The constables and other ministers of the law who were there, seeing such an unexpected turn of affairs and suspecting that that man was a relative of the man they were flogging and that he wanted to take him away from them by force, began to shout, "To the aid of the law! To the aid of the law!" The people who were there, not few in number, and some on horseback who came up at the noise tried earnestly to help the law apprehend Don Quixote. Seeing all those people coming at him with unsheathed swords, he began to shout, "War! War! At them, Santiago, Saint Denis![3] Close in! Attack! Death to them!"

[3] The usual call to battle in Spain involved invoking St. James (Santiago—Spain's national patron saint); but invoking the French St. Denis is unheard of.

After his shouts he threw the lance at a constable with such force that if it had not happened to pass under his left arm he would have fared ill.

Then he let the shield fall on the ground, took hold of the sword and brandished it among them all with such bravery and anger that if the horse, which could scarcely move because of weariness and hunger, had helped him he might not have fared as badly as he did. But since there were many people and the cry they continued giving was always, "To the aid of the law," more and more arrived and an infinite number of swordsmen fell upon Don Quixote. Because of this and Rocinante's slowness, together with our knight's fatigue, all of them were able in a little while to take away his sword. Removing it from his hand, they took him off Rocinante and, to his grief, tied his hands behind his back; gripped firmly by five or six constables he was dragged off to jail.

Seeing himself taken along in that manner, he cried out, saying, "Oh, wise Alquife! Oh, my astute Urganda! Now is the time for you to show yourself before this false sorcerer, if you are true friends." At this he tried as hard as he could to break loose, but in vain. The man being flogged went on with his parade, and our knight was taken to jail along the very streets on which he had started out. They put his feet in the stocks and handcuffed him after having taken away all his armor.

At this point one of the jailer's sons came close to him to tell the constable to put a chain about his body. Hearing this, Don Quixote raised high his handcuffed hands and hit the poor lad such a terrible blow on the head that it made quite a wound, his new hat offering no protection. He would have continued with another blow if the boy's father, who was present, had not raised his hand and given him half a dozen punches in the face, making the blood stream from his nose and mouth, all of which left our poor knight, who couldn't clean himself up, transformed into an altar painting of sorrows.

There is no historian, no matter how diligent he may be, who can manage to relate all the things Don Quixote said and did while he was in the stocks. Good Sancho, who had been present at all that had happened, began to weep bitterly when he saw his master being taken away like that and leading his donkey by the halter he followed along the same road, without saying he was the servant. He denounced his luck and the hour he had met Don Quixote, saying, "Oh, I curse him who wishes me ill and takes no pity on me in such an awful bind! Who in the devil ordered me to go back to this man when I went through so many misfortunes the other time, now being beaten, now tossed in a blanket, and at other times in danger of being caught by the Holy Brotherhood, who would have strung me up at the crossroads so that later I'd be neither king nor rook? Poor me! What shall I do? I've a mind to go away in despair to those worlds, through those distant Indies, plunge into those seas between mountains and valleys, eating the birds of the sky and the beasts of the land, doing great penance and becoming another Friar Juan Guarismas,[4] walking on all fours like a wild bear, until a seventy-year-old child should say to me, 'Arise, Sancho, for Don Quixote is now out of jail.' "

Uttering these doleful ditties and tearing at his thick beard, Sancho reached the door of the jail in which he saw his master placed. He remained leaning against a wall, holding his donkey by the halter, to see how the affair would end. From time to time he wept, especially when he heard those coming down from the jail tell all the passers-by that they meant to take the man in armor out to be flogged. Some said he deserved the gallows for his boldness; others, moved by greater charity, condemned him to only two hundred lashes and the galleys for the short time he had obstructed the course of justice with his fine talk. Others said, "I shouldn't like to be in his hide, even if he gives as the excuse for his insolence that he was drunk or crazy."

Sancho felt he would die, hearing all this, but he stayed quiet as a saint. It so happened that the two peace-officers, the jailer, and his son went together to the judge, to whom they presented the case in such a poor light that the judge ordered that at that very moment and without further information they should take Don Quixote through the streets in public punishment and return him to jail until they could legally find out the truth about the crime.

When the peace-officers were on their way back to carry out the aforesaid quick verdict, the flogged man had just returned on his donkey to the jail door, accompanied by boys, as is usually the case. As soon as he saw him, one of the peace-officers said to the executioner, in Sancho's sight, "Hey! Take that man off and don't return the donkey, because right away you'll have to take for a ride along the same streets that half-crazy man who tried to obstruct the law in the performance of its duty. The chief magistrate of the city orders this to be done as an introduction to the galleys and floggings that await him."

Infinite sadness filled poor Sancho's heart when he heard such

---

[4] Sancho is referring to Fra Joan Garí, the Catalan priest who did penance by walking on all fours until he learned from a talking infant that God had pardoned him.

words from the peace-officer, the more so as he saw that everything was being prepared to take his master out for public punishment, and that all the people at the jail door were saying, "The poor knight in armor well deserves the lashes that await him, because he was so stupid that he meddled with the law, without any reason, and as if that were not enough he brained the jailer's son."

These remarks and similar ones had Sancho crazy, not knowing what to do or say. Therefore he did nothing but listen and ask questions here and there. Everywhere he heard bad news about his master's affairs; as a matter of fact they were already starting to unchain him from the stocks in order to take him out for public punishment.

CHAP. IX. HOW A VERY STRANGE ADVENTURE FREED *Don Quixote from the jail and the public punishment to which he was condemned.*

HILE POOR Sancho was shedding bitter tears and waiting, all eyes, to see his master, naked from the waist up and riding his donkey so that he could be given the two hundred lashes promised him as a gift, there rode by seven or eight of the most important knights in the city. When they saw so many people at the jail door at such an unusual hour (for it was after four o'clock) they inquired about the occasion for the gathering. A youth told them what that knight in armor, who they said was going to be brought down to be flogged through the streets, had done and said inside and outside the city and in the jail and how, in the middle of the street he had tried to take a flogged man from the law.

All this astonished them, the more so when they learned that not a man or woman in the city knew him. After this lad, another came up and told them what Don Quixote had said to a troop of knights before entering the city, and he gave their names. At this they laughed heartily, but they wondered why nobody could tell them the reason for his being armed with shield and lance. As Fate would have it, Sancho came up to listen to what was being said about his master. Looking closely at the knights, he recognized Don Álvaro Tarfe among them. Although the jousts had been over for six days, he had not departed because he was waiting for a ring-lancing contest[1] which he and some of the leading knights in the city had ordered for the next Sunday.

When he saw him, Sancho dropped the donkey's halter and, kneeling in the middle of the street in front of the knights, cap in hand and weeping bitterly, he began to speak: "Oh, Señor Don Álvaro Tarfe! In the name of the gospel of Saint Luke, have pity on me and my master Don Quixote, who is in this jail. They want to take him out to be flogged at the very least, if Saint Anthony and you do not prevent it. They say here that he has done I don't know what against the law, without any reason and illegally, and because of it they want to put him in the galleys for thirty or forty years."

Don Álvaro Tarfe recognized Sancho Panza at once and suspected what it could all be about. So, astonished to see him, he said, "Oh, Sancho, what is this? You say your master is the one for whom this caravan is being prepared? However, one can expect anything from his madness and vain fantasy as well as your stupidity, yet I can't quite believe it, even though you assert it with the vehemence you showed as you told me about it."

"He is the one, sir, sinner that I am!" said Sancho. "Go in there and visit him in my stead; tell him that I kiss his hands, and if they plan to take him out on that puny donkey they took in now, he mustn't mount it because I have Dapple saddled and ready for him here; on him he can ride like a patriarch. As he already knows, Dapple walks so smoothly that anyone riding him can carry a cup of wine without spilling a drop."

---

[1] This contest was to test the accuracy of a knight's lance while the knight was charging on a galloping horse; as the knight rode by he would try to spear and remove a suspended ring.

Don Álvaro Tarfe, laughing at what simple Sancho had told him, ordered him not to leave until he came out again. Speaking to two of the aforesaid knights, he entered the jail with them, where they found the good hidalgo Don Quixote being unchained so he could be taken out for public punishment. When Don Álvaro saw him in such a sorry state, face and hands covered with blood and wearing handcuffs, he said to him, "What does this mean, Señor Quijada? What sort of adventure or misadventure has this one been? Now do you think that it is good to have friends at court? Well, this time I shall be such a one to you, as you will see from experience. But tell me, what sort of misfortune has this been?"

Don Quixote looked him in the face and then recognized him. With a humorless laugh he said, "Oh, my lord Don Álvaro! You are welcome. I am very much astounded by the strange adventure you have gone through. In God's name, tell me at once by what means you entered this impregnable castle where I have been held prisoner with all these princes, knights, maidens, and squires in this harsh prison where we have been such a long time. In what way did you kill the two fierce giants at the door, who had their arms raised with two fine steel maces, in order to prevent the entrance of those who, in spite of them, tried to enter? How or by what luck did you kill that exceedingly fierce griffin in the first patio of the castle? In its talons it catches up a man in full armor carries him up on high, and there tears him to bits. Of course I envy such an outstanding exploit, since by your hands we shall all be freed. That wise enchanter, my rival, will be most cruelly killed and the sorceress, his wife, who has caused the world so many ills, must at once be flogged mercilessly and put to public shame."

Don Álvaro said, "They would undoubtedly have put you to public shame if your good fortune, or better said, if God, who settles all things smoothly, had not arranged my arrival. However that may be, I have killed all those giants you mentioned and given the desired freedom to the knights who accompany you, so now since I have been your liberator, it is your duty to obey me as required by the gratitude you owe me and stay in this room alone and handcuffed until I order differently. This is necessary for the successful outcome of my happy adventure."

My lord Don Álvaro," said Don Quixote, "You will be punctiliously obeyed. For the sake of doing you a new service I wish to permit you henceforth to have me as a companion, something I never expected to do with any knight in the world. However, one who has brought to a full and happy conclusion such a dangerous feat as this justly merits my friendship and company so that he may see in me, as in a mirror, what I have done and intend to do in all the kingdoms, islands, and peninsulas in the world until I win the immense empire of Trebizond.[2] There I shall marry a beautiful queen of England and with many tears, promises and pleadings, beget two sons by her. The first will be called He of the Flaming Sword[3] because he will be born with the sign of a burning sword on his breast. The other one will be named Mazimbruno of Trebizond because he will have on his right side a dark steel-colored sign indicative of the terrible blows he will strike in this world with his mace."

They all burst into hearty laughter; but Don Álvaro, hiding his amusement, sent them all out, requesting one of the two knights who had come with him to remain there so nobody would harm Don Quixote while he and the other knight, a very close relative of the Chief Justice, went to negotiate his freedom, which would be easy to obtain because his madness had been so publicly evident.

When they left the jail they mounted their horses and Don Álvaro told one of his pages to take Sancho Panza, whom he already knew, to his lodging and without delay feed him very well and not let him take one step out until his return.

Sancho clamored, "My lord Don Álvaro, bear in mind that my Dapple is as melancholy over not seeing his good friend and faithful companion Rocinante as I was over no longer seeing my master Don Quixote on these streets. Consequently, ask the Pharisees who arrested my master to account for the noble Rocinante because they took him off when the poor thing had said not a single bad word to anybody during the quarrel. Also get news—for they'll tell you—of my master's famous lance and fine shield which, by my faith, cost us thirteen *reales* to have oil-painted by an old painter who had a great wart on his back and lived on I don't know which street in Ariza. My master would send me to the plague if I didn't account for them."

"Go Sancho," said Don Álvaro. "Eat, rest, and don't worry about the rest, for everything will turn out all right."

Sancho left with the page, pulling gently on the halter of his donkey, and when they reached the house they put the donkey in the stable with sufficient food. They gave Sancho a meal as good in quantity as the thousand simple remarks that Sancho made to the pages

---

2 A medieval empire in Northern Asia Minor in the area of the Black Sea; it collapsed in 1461.

3 Epithet of Amadís of Greece.

and people in the house were funny, for he told them all that had happened to him and his master along the road: about the innkeeper as well as the melon grower and the affair in Ateca, all of which was later related to Don Álvaro.

Meanwhile Don Álvaro and the other knight were with the Chief Justice, informing him about Don Quixote's condition and all that had happened to him, about the flogged man as well as about the jailer and the others at the jail. The judge was very glad to send a porter immediately to give the jailer and the constables his order to turn that prisoner over to Don Álvaro, free and at no cost, together with the horse and everything else they had taken from him. All this was done as ordered.

Don Álvaro went to the jail where they again put armor on Don Quixote, now free of his fetters, and handed over the shield, which caused them to laugh heartily when they saw the inscription THE LOVELESS KNIGHT and the figures of Cupid and the ladies. Waiting until nightfall so that he wouldn't be seen, they had a page take Don Quixote, riding Rocinante, to an inn. There the knights, Don Álvaro's friends, were happy to eat supper with him, and after supper they made Sancho Panza recount all that had happened to them along the road. When Sancho said that he had deceived his master by not wishing to give the Galician girl two hundred ducats but only four *cuartos*, Don Quixote went into a rage, saying, "Oh, base villain of a base race! It's very clear that you are not a noble *caballero*, because you gave four *cuartos* to a princess like that one whom you so unjustly make out to be a servant at an inn. I swear, by the order of knighthood I received, that the first province, island, or peninsula will be hers in spite of you and any other scoundrels like you in the world."

All those knights were astonished by Don Quixote's fury, and Sancho, seeing that his master was angry, responded, "Oh, to blazes with it and Saint Susanna's old men! Didn't you know by that servant's physiolgomy[4] and rags that she wasn't a princess or an admiral's wife? And I'll tell you more. I swear that if it hadn't been for me a dealer in old rags would have taken her to turn her into wrapping paper, and the filthy thing doesn't thank me for it now. Well, upon my word, if I

---

[4] Sancho's version of physiognomy.

hadn't been afraid of her my punches would have made her remember Sancho Panza, the flower of all the squires-errant there have ever been in the world. But let it go, for even if she once gave me a slap in the face and a couple of kicks in the back, I did eat up a fine piece of cheese that she had hidden on the kitchen shelf."

Don Álvaro arose, laughing at what Sancho Panza had said, and so did the rest. He ordered Don Quixote to be taken to a comfortable room where they made up a decent bed for him, and where he remained resting and convalescing for two or three days. The pages took Sancho to their room and carried on a most witty conversation with him.

CHAP. X. HOW DON ÁLVARO TARFE INVITED CERtain friends of his to dinner in order to decide on the livery to be worn at the ring-lancing contest.

N THE MORNING Don Álvaro entered Don Quixote's room and said, sitting down in a chair next to his bed, "How are you getting along in this place, my lord Don Quixote, flower of Manchegan chivalry? Is there any new adventure in which we friends can help you? In this kingdom there are many very dangerous ones daily for knights-errant, and recently, in the jousts that were held here many brawny giants and colossal wild men came from different provinces and there were some knights here who were given quite a bit to think about. You were needed here to give such people the punishment they deserve for their evil deeds. However, you may come across them out in the world and make them pay for what they did last year and this."

"My lord Don Álvaro," responded Don Quixote, "I regret and have exceedingly regretted not being at those royal jousts. Had I been in them I believe that neither would the giants have left laughing nor would any of the knights have carried off the precious jewels they took because I was absent. However, I suspect that *nondum sunt completa peccata Amorraeorum*.[1] I mean, the number of their sins are probably not completed yet and God probably plans that when that happens I'll punish them."

Don Álvaro said, "Well, Don Quixote, you must know that for the day after tomorrow, which is Sunday, we have arranged a famous ring-lancing contest among the knights of this city and myself, in which there will be very rich and important prizes. The judges will be the same as those for the jousts: that is, three of the most outstanding knights in this kingdom, one named by the sovereign and two appointed by the Knight Commander. There will also be present many very lovely *Infantas*, princesses, and ladies-in-waiting of rare beauty, turning into a heaven the balconies and windows of the famous Calle del Coso, where you will find two thousand adventures from which to choose. We are all to go into it in livery, and as we enter from the street we'll fly and flash our colors and ribbons with our titles, or display laughable and amusing sayings written on our shield-tablets. If you are so disposed and have strength enough to enter I volunteer to accompany you and outfit you so that you may remain as a participant in our good fortune and so that this city and kingdom may understand that I have a friend who is such a good knight that he alone can win all the prizes in the contest."

Sitting down on the bed. Don Quixote said, "I am very pleased about it so that you may see with your own eyes the things that you have heard about my strength. Although it is true, as the Latin proverb says, that self praise lacks force,[2] nevertheless I can and will say about myself what I am saying because it is so widely known."

---

[1] Don Quixote is trying to quote from Genesis 15:16: "necdum enim completae sunt Amorrhaeorum" 'for the Amorites will not be ripe for punishment till then.'

[2] "Laus in ore proprio viliscet" 'Praise in one's own mouth debases.' A similar proverb is seen in I, 16.

"That's what I believe," said Don Álvaro. "However, stay quietly in bed and rest. So that you may do so more comfortably, we'll put the table in front of it and some of the knights in my team and I will dine with you. After dinner we'll discuss what is to be done, all of us being guided by the judicious advice of one like you who has so much experience in similar games."

Don Álvaro left and the good hidalgo remained with his mind filled with fantasies; unable to rest, he got up and began to dress, earnestly picturing himself in his grim contest. So strong was his imagination that he remained looking at the floor without blinking, with his breeches half on. Then, in a little while he attacked the wall holding his arm out straight and giving a little run and saying, "At the first attempt I have carried off the ring on my lance; therefore, your Excellencies, most upright judges, order that I be given the first prize since it is rightly due me despite the envy of adventurers and spectators present."

At this loud shouting a page and Sancho Panza came upstairs; entering the room they found Don Quixote with his breeches down, talking to the judges and looking at the ceiling. Since his shirt was a little short in front, it didn't fail to reveal a bit of ugliness. When Sancho Panza saw this he said, "Cover your etcetera, loveless sir! Sinner that I am! There are no judges here intending to take you prisoner again or give you two hundred lashes or take you out to be shamed, even though you are only too well uncovering your shame with no reason, you can be sure!"

Don Quixote looked around, and as he lifted the breeches to put them on with his back turned he bent over slightly and revealed from the rear what he had revealed from the front as well as something more repulsive. Sancho, who saw it, told him, "Confounded be my breeches, sir! It's worse than it was before; what you are doing is trying to salute us with all the unmentionable things God has given you."

The page laughed quite a bit and Don Quixote, composing himself as best he could, turned to him and said, "I say that I am very pleased, sir knight, that thy battle be carried on as thou seest fit, on foot or on horseback, with weapons or without them; thou wilt find me ready for anything. Although I am sure of victory, nevertheless I am extremely joyful about doing battle with a renowned knight and before so many people who will see with their own eyes the bravery of so loveless a person as am I."

The page replied, "Sir Knight, there is nobody here trying to do battle with your lordship, and if we are to have one it will be two hours from now with a genteel turkey that is going to be our guest at table."

"That knight you call Turkey, is he from this kingdom or is he a foreigner?" replied Don Quixote. "For nothing in the world would I wish him to be a relative or servant of lord Don Álvaro."

At this Sancho interrupted, saying, "By the life of the ropemaker who made the noose with which Judas hanged himself! With all the books you've read and the Latin words or lists of things you've studied, you still don't understand. Come downstairs and you'll see the kitchen filled with roasting-spits, two or three pots half as big as the water-jars we use in El Toboso, so much mutton stew, meatballs and meatpies that it all looks like an earthly paradise. Upon my word, if you asked me to produce some pre-breakfast saliva I couldn't do it because I have in my body three cups of Malvasía wine, as they call it in this region. It's well-named, because it means 'bad-empty'[3] and a cup is 'bad' when it's 'empty' of it. It's better than Yepes wine, which you already well know. This gentleman gave me a little loaf of white bread weighing about two and a half pounds, so that the drink wouldn't hurt me, and the lame cook gave me two necks which I'm not sure weren't from ostriches, and so they must have been because I chewed my own hands going after them. With all of this I put the wine to bed instantly and braced up my stomach. Sir, I think that these are the true adventures because I run across them in the kitchen, pantry, and a'pot-to-carry cellar, or whatever you call it, and these are much to my taste. I would overlook the salary you give every month if we could stay here and not go about seeking melon growers to make the sign of the cross over our spines. Believe me, this is the sensible thing, for there's the lame cook who seems to adore me and every time I go in to see him, which is often, he fills me a big plate of lean meat, and as soon as he does, I stuff it in like one sucks an egg. He only laughs when he sees how wholeheartedly, and with what good grace I eat, for which God be thanked a thousand times. It's true that last night one of these pages or purges, or whatever they are, told me to suck up a bowl of soup he was carrying, because next to God it was the best thing to put life in me. Not realizing the trickery, I grabbed it with both hands and to do it justice took three or four slurps which I shouldn't have because the big . . . (and consider it said) of a page had put the bowl on the coals, and so it went running down through my stomach making as much liquid as I swallowed pour from my eyes. The cook and this fancy-pants pipsqueak roared with laughter until their jaws were like to breaking, but I give you my word that they won't play such a trick on me again, because the cook gave me a fine slice of melon and, because I had learned my lesson before, I

---

[3] *Mal(a)* means 'bad' and *vacía* means 'empty'.

touched it bit by bit, cautiously, to see if it was burning hot."

"Oh, you big fool!" said Don Quixote. "Would a slice of melon be hot? That makes it clear that you are gluttonously greedy and that your main interest is not in seeking the true honor of knights-errant, but instead, like Epicurus, in stuffing your paunch."

"I do so because I am what I am,[4] said Sancho. At this point they heard Don Álvaro coming to dine with five or six of the renowned knights who were to be in the ring-lancing contest. They had been invited in order to decide on the livery each was to wear and to enjoy Don Quixote as though he were a private performance, so they went straight up to his room and, finding him half-dressed and looking as has been told, they laughed heartily. However, Don Álvaro scolded him for getting up against orders and commanded him to go to bed again and at once, because otherwise they would not dine. Only because of their insistence did he do so. After this the table was set and the food brought and all of them kept calling Don Quixote a sovereign prince. During the conversation they exchanged witty stories and they all asked him strange questions about his adventures, which he answered very gravely and calmly, often forgetting to eat because of relating what he planned to do in Constantinople and Trebizond, now with such and such a princess, again with such and such a giant. He used such extraordinary names that at each one the guests gave a thousand retches of suppressed laughter. Had it not been for Don Álvaro, who was always standing up for Don Quixote and endorsing his ideas with prudent cunning and deceit, he would really have been angered at times.

Nevertheless, he told them that it was unworthy of brave knights to laugh without reason at things that happen every day to knights-errant such as he. Don Álvaro said to them, "It does seem that you are inexperienced and don't know, as I do, the courage of Don Quixote de la Mancha. If you do not know who he is, ask those gentlemen who were flogging that soldier along the streets the other day. They will tell you what he did and said in their presence, in defense of the flogged man, with the aim of a true knight-errant: undoing the wrong that was being done."

With this conversation the meal ended; the table was cleared and they began to discuss the livery for each one in the ring-lancing contest, and the emblems and devices they would display. Then one said, "What

---

[4] A pun is implied here between *"henchir la panza"* 'stuffing your paunch' and *"hago en esto como quien soy"* 'I do so because of what I am (i.e., Panza).

livery will Don Quixote wear? Let's not leave the best gambler without cards. I think he should wear green, the color of young barley, which means hope, and he has that of obtaining[5] and winning all the prizes in the contest."

Another said he didn't agree; instead, as he calls himself the Loveless Knight he should wear purple, with some thorny emblem that would nettle the ladies. Another knight said, "Rather, because he is loveless he should wear a white livery as a sign of his great chastity; it is no small thing for a knight with so many talents to have no love affair, unless he has ceased to make love because there is nobody in the world who deserves him."

The last knight responded, "Well, gentlemen, my avowal is that because Don Quixote is a man who has killed and continues to kill to many giants and wild men, making widows of their wives, he should appear in black livery. In that way he will make it apparent to all who intend to fight him that their fate is black indeed."

"Now," said Don Álvaro. "With your permission I shall now give my opinion, and it has to be be unique, like Don Quixote himself. I think that he should wear no livery at all, but rather, as a true knight-errant, it is right for him to appear in the arena in full armor and fully-armed. In order that he have what is appropriate, I shall make him a gift of what he has, which is the famous set from Milan that I left in his care in Argamesilla. It is as honorable in his possession as it is idle in mine. Because it is somewhat tarnished by road dust and the blood of various giants he has spilled in different battles, I shall have it cleaned and polished so that he may make a more briliant appearance. The device he has on the face of his sheild is suitable, because nobody in Zaragoza has seen it and he has carried the shield the whole way from Ariza, where it was painted, wrapped in a cloth so that it wouldn't lose its lustre, would be like new and look fine, serving as inspiration to his own heavy lance, which he will bear with it; likewise the bearing of his handsome figure, and the swiftness of his famous Rocinante will suffice to make everyone understand that his grace is the illustrious knight-errant who, the other day, came out openly for the honor of that honorable flogged man, and the one who had the adventure with the melon grower, and all the rest that many do not know about."

Everyone said that what Don Álvaro thought was proper. Don Quixote fully agreed and said, "What Don Álvaro has said is truly important, because it often happens that some fierce giant or colos-

---

[5] The pun here is between *alcazal* 'young barley' and *alcanzar* 'obtaining'.

sal wild man, king of some foreign land, will come to such festivities and issue impolite challenges against the honor of the king or princes of the city. In order to discourage such arrogance it is well for me to be in full armor and fully armed. I am a thousand times obliged to Don Álvaro for his generosity in doing me the honor of giving me what I came to return on this occasion and in this place. I assure you that with this equipment I shall not let the sly traitor, a certain enormous giant who goes about the world doing great harm, boast that in this famous kingdom of Aragón there is nobody who dares do battle with him."

With sudden and unexpected rage he leaped from the bed and went from the bedroom to the parlor, short shirt and all, seized the sword which he had in that room, and before all the spectators had time to collect their wits and stop him he began to shout, "Well, here I am, oh, haughty giant! Neither arrogant words nor valorous deeds are of any use against me!" Slashing six or seven times at the tapestries on the walls, he said, "Oh, miserable king, if king you be! The time has come when God is finally tired of your evil acts!"

The knights withdrew to one side, believing that Don Quixote would start after them also, thinking them wild men from beyond the island of Maleandrítica. However, even with the visible desire to laugh that Don Álvaro and the others had as they looked upon the infernal sight offered by the Manchegan, he seized Don Quixote's arm and said, "Listen to me, flower of La Mancha's knighthood, sheathe your sword and go back to bed, for the giant has fled downstairs, not daring to wait for the edge of your cutting sword."

"That's what I believe," said Don Quixote. "These men and similar ones are often more afraid of shouts and words than they are of deeds. Because of regard for you I didn't try to follow him; but let him live, for it will be to his greater harm. However, I guarantee that he will be careful not to come up against me again."

Hereupon, because he was so skinny and weak, he was left with his sides heaving so hard he could scarcely catch his breath. Leaving him in bed with orders that he not move from it until the day of the contest, Don Álvaro ordered Sancho to come upstairs and stay with his master. He and the other knights took their leave, saying they were going to see other friends of theirs from Granada, lodging at the inn of a certain renowned knight, to find out how they

meant to appear in the contest. They did go, in fact, to do this and to inform many important people about Don Quixote's bent toward the extraordinary and how they planned to amuse themselves and give everybody at the plaza something at which to laugh.

CHAP. XI. HOW DON ÁLVARO TARFE AND OTHER *knights from Zaragoza and Granada took part in the ring-lancing contest on the Calle del Coso, and what happened to Don Quixote there.*

OR THREE DAYS Don Quixote was forcibly kept in bed by dint of pleas and guards, for he always had the latter in Sancho Panza and some of Don Álvaro's pages and two knights from among his friends. Some of those were from Granada as well as from Zaragoza, and all of whom shared in some sprightly tales, because at times Don Quixote thought he was riding to the contest; he argued with the judges, quarreled with giants from different regions, and did a thousand other absurdities because he was hopelessly crazy, and Sancho Panza helped it all along with his inanities and incurable foolishness. The only good thing about it was that Don Quixote had excellent lodging and food, for he was beautifully well served in the presence of Don Álvaro who always ate lunch and dinner with him, accompanied each time by different knights.

In due course Sunday arrived, when those knights who were to take part in the contest for the diversion of everyone made ready and adorned themselves as best they could with their rich livery. They all took to the entrance into the Calle del Coso only shields or white cards on which were written the inscriptions each one had in mind as most appropriate, with the aim of enlivening the festival.

However, I do not wish to pass over in silence what was on two richly and curiously detailed triumphal arches which were at either end of the street. The first one, at the entrance as we came from the plaza, was entirely sky-blue damask; in the center, at the top, was Charles V, most invincible emperor and most glorious grandfather of our great Catholic monarch Philip Hermengildo III, in Roman style armor, with a laurel wreath on his head and his general's staff in his right hand. Occupying the highest part of the arch were two Latin verses:

Frena quod imperii longo moderaris ab evo,
Austria, non hominis, numinis extat opus.[1]

His right foot was on a golden orb with an inscription reading:

Alexander ruled his half,
But our Caesar truly
Ruled all of his three parts.

His left foot was on three or four conquered Turks, with an inscription reading:

Qui oves amat, in lupos saevit.[2]

At the base of the arch on the right, on a small pedestal against the column of the arch itself, was the famous Duke of Alba, Don Fernández Álvaro de Toledo, in armor and with his general's staff in his right hand. At his foot was Fame, with a trumpet as she is depicted, on which was written:

A solis ortu usque ad occasum[3]

At the base of the left-hand column of the arch, on a small pedestal, was Don Antonio Leiva,[4] in armor and with a general's staff, like the Duke, and he had this inscription above his head:

If I served my king well,
He also rewarded my affection well
By giving to my *Don* a *Señor*.[5]

The second arch was all of embroidered white damask; at the top was Philip II, very richly dressed, and at his feet was this famous epigram by the excellent poet, Lope de Vega Carpio,[6] officer of the Holy Office:

---

[1] "The fact that you have been holding the reins of the empire for a long time, oh, Austria! is not the work of a man but a god."

[2] "He who loves sheep is merciless with wolves."

[3] "From the rising to the setting sun."

[4] The famous general of Charles I of Spain.

[5] *Don* can mean 'talents' as well as being a title; *señor* is also a title meaning 'lord'. Therefore, this verse can mean: "by giving me a title owing to my talents" or "by a lord giving me the title of *Don*."

[6] This is the same Lope de Vega, the prolific playwright, mentioned earlier.

Philippo Regi, Cesari invictissimo,
omnium maximo Regum triumphatori,
orbis utrisque et maris felicissimo,
catholici Charoli successori,
totius Hispaniae principi dignissimo,
Ecclesiae Christi et fidei deffensori,
Fama, praecingens tempora alma, lauro,
hoc simulacrum dedicat ex auro[7]

To his right was the very Christian and unique prodigy, Don Philip III, our king and lord, completely clothed in cloth-of-gold, with two verses near him which said in Latin:

Nulla est virtutis species quae, maxime Princeps,
Non colat ingenium nobilitate tuum.[8]

At the left was the most invincible prince Don Juan of Austria, in full armor, the general's staff in his hand, his right foot upon the wheel of Fortune, with Fortune herself nailing the wheel fast with a hammer and nail, and this inscription:

The renowned merit,
Which raised you upon my wheel
Like a nail now holds it fast.

There were many more curious enigmas and cryptograms on the arches, but they are omitted to avoid prolixity and because they are not relevant to our intention. I shall say only that the day on which the ring-lancing contest was to be held, the Calle del Coso was richly decorated. All its balconies and windows were adorned with beautifully embroidered tapestries and brocades and were occupied by an infinite number of angels, each with the hope of receiving from her lover's hand, or from the hand of one of those adventurous knights, the prize he had won.

The nobility of the kingdom and the city came to the festival: Viceroy, Chief Justice, deputies, councilmen, and all the other titled people and knights, each one occupying the position which was his right.

---

[7] "Fame dedicates this golden image encircling his illustrious brow with laurel to Philip the King, unconquered Caesar, greatest of all kings, most fortunate ruler of both worlds and the sea, successor of Charles the Catholic, most worthy prince of all Hispania, defender of Christ's Church and of the Faith."

[8] "There is no kind of virtue which your mind, great Prince, does not nobly cultivate."

There also came the judges for the contest, closely attended and splendidly dressed. They were, as we have said, a titled man and two knights in their robes, and they took their places on a rather low, elaborately constructed platform. Upon their arrival the bugles and trumpets began to ring out, and at their sound the knights who were to take part in the contest began to enter, two by two, along the wide street.

The first two were handsome youths in identical livery, there being no difference either between their horses or their costumes, which were of green and white satin with plumes in their bonnets. One bonnet had at the top a hand holding an exquisite salt-shaker sprinkling salt on those feathers from which this inscription floated out on the wind:

> In my soul the divine sun
> Pours down rays, inflaming me,
> As would the sun of grace.

The other knight, recently married to a very beautiful lady, had himself painted on the shield, leading her by the hand as though he were her squire, and the inscription was as follows:

> I rejoice in her, and there is left in me,
> Because she is so rare and lovely,
> Only the fear of losing her.

Behind them came two more, dressed in richly embroidered damask; they wore this uniform because they were both young men in love and jealous. One had painted on his shield an extremely ferocious lioness clothed in a sheep-skin, and he himself was depicted kneeling in front of her, with this inscription:

> Only when she wears a lamb-skin
> Does she reward me with words,
> But in deeds she is a lioness.

The other one had a portrait of his lady on a black field; cap off, he was asking for her hand and she was disdainfully refusing. For this reason he had come to the contest. Because he was a beardless youth, he came out wearing a false white beard, a disguise which quite surprised all the people who knew him, but he reassured them with this inscription on his shield:

Loving and so unloved,
I think I am reaching my dotage,
and so I give proof of it.

Two more entered after these two. They were handsome young men wearing completely different liveries. One was clothed in elaborately embroidered cloth-of-silver and rode a white horse as swift as the wind. On the equally white field of his shield was the portrait of his lady leaning over to help up a dead man who was already in his shroud and had this inscription in the form of a cross on his breast:

Only the sight of her killed me;
But by her divine hand
I win new life and glory.

The second one was a newly-married young man, wealthy by his inheritance but a great spendthrift, so extravagant that he was always in debt and there was no merchant or official to whom he didn't owe money. He made requests in one place; in another he cheated; elsewhere he committed fraud; now he pawned his most valuable gold chain, then his best tapestry. In consequence, after his father was gone he was so burdened with debts that he was obliged to wear nothing but baize, making the excuse that he was in mourning and sorrow for his father. In order to satisfy the gossip of the common people, he had a nun painted on the black field of his shield. She was also clothed in black, darker than that of the shield, and the inscription was:

Since poverty is blessed,
Let mine cover me well:
Give me baize and bid me go.[9]

Thirty or forty knights entered behind these two, two by two, also wearing elaborate and costly liveries. They likewise had very witty and highly ingenious inscriptions, emblems, and devices which I shall not relate so as not to turn into a book of verse what is only a chronicle of the fanciful deeds of Don Quixote. Therefore, we shall only mention his own entrance, which was in the rear guard of all the adventurers, at the side of Don Álvaro Tarfe because the judges had arranged for the entrance to be this way.

Don Álvaro was on a fine dapple-gray Cordovan horse, with rich trappings. He was dressed in cloth-of-gold embroidered with intertwined lilies and roses, and on the white field of his shield he had

[9] The pun is on *vayeta* 'baize' and *vaya* 'go'.

painted the image of Don Quixote and the adventure of the flogged man, very lifelike, with this inscription:

> I bring the one who will become,
> Because of his absurdities,
> The Prince of Lunatics.

All those who knew about the doings of Don Quixote laughed heartily. He made his appearance in full armor, wearing his helmet. Proud of bearing, he entered on Rocinante. Tied by a string to the tip of his lance stretched out a big parchment and written on it in Gothic letters was AVE MARIA. Above the devices and paintings on his shield he had added this tercet in explanation of the parchment hanging from the lance:

> I am much better than Garcilaso
> Because I took away from the cruel Turk
> The *ave* which honors him.[10]

The crowd was much astonished to see that man in armor ready to take part in the ring-lancing contest. Although they did not know the reason for the parchment on the lance, no sooner did they see his figure, Rocinante's skinniness, and the large shield covered with paintings and figures done by a roguish hand, than they all laughed and whistled at him. This sight did not cause such wonder in the people of quality because everybody in this class had learned from don Álvaro Tarfe and the rest of his friends who Don Quixote was, about the strange mania, and the objective in having him appear in the plaza, which was to add to the fun with an absurd adventure. It is not unusual on such festive occasions for the knights to bring lunatics into the plaza, dressed up and adorned, wearing fanciful headdresses, and have them do tricks, tilt, joust, and carry off prizes, as has been seen sometimes in big cities and in Zaragoza itself.

Then, with the motive of making merry in the plaza all those knights went before their ladies to offer them the customary courtesy. One made his trained horse kneel before the mistress of his freedom; another made his horse leap and buck with much agility; still another made his prance about. In short, everyone did all he could to present a good appearance. Only Don Quixote's horse went peacefully and tamely.

---

[10] In some of the versions of this story, Garcilaso de la Vega (this is not the poet of the same name) was doing battle in Moorish Granada, and he tore off a sign which read 'Ave Maria' from the tail of a Moorish soldier's horse.

When Don Quixote and Don Álvaro came up even with the balcony where the judges were, both rendered the due courtesy for the titled person and the others. One of them, who seemed to be the wittiest, leaned over the platform railing and spoke to Don Quixote in this way, in a loud voice and to the laughter of the spectators: "Famous prince, mirror and flower of knight-errantry, I and all this city are extremely grateful to you for considering honoring us with your valiant self. It is true that some of these knights are sad because they are quite certain that in this contest you will win the most precious prizes. However, even though you may merit and win them all, I have decided to give you only the finest one, so that these princes and knights will be better satisfied."

Very calmly and gravely Don Quixote responded, "Certainly, illustrious judge, more upright than Rodamonte,[11] model of judges, I am so grieved over not being at the jousts just over that I am ready to burst. The reason was that I was busy in I know not what adventure of little importance. However, since I couldn't prove my personal worth in previous jousts, because of my absence, I want you to see with your own eyes in this contest, which is pure pastime for my excessive courage, whether what you have heard about me and my talents is as reliable and true as that of Amadís and the former knights who won so much honor throughout the world. However, my courage will be made clearly manifest, because just this morning as the fiery lover of shy Daphne peeped over the balconies of our horizon, I crowned myself with the *ave* of the fortress of God; that is to say, the one that the angel Gabriel brought to the Virgin, as is shown by the writing on my shield, having taken it from a lawless Turk who had it hanging from the tail of an arrogant Frisian horse on which he passed in front of my balcony, irritating my Christian patience. But he found in me another Manchegan Garcilaso, more courageous and older than the first, who avenged such insolence."

Whereupon the judge who was talking to Don Quixote took his parchment and shield and showed them to the other two judges and the rest of the knights who were with them; then, after having examined them and had a good laugh, he gave them back. Having taken his beloved objects, Don Quixote went ahead strutting and looking empty-headedly on all sides. When he reached the end of the street where the others who were to take part in the contest were standing, the

---

[11] Don Quixote means Radamanto (Rhadamanthus), a mythological judge in hell, also seen in II, 39.

flageolets and trumpets began to sound as a signal that the first knights were ready to begin the run.

The judges had ruled that after every round, prizes would be given to the four knights who had performed best. Consequently, after the first round, four prizes were given, although only one knight carried off the ring on his lance. This was Don Álvaro Tarfe, who chose to be among the first to compete, and who, by order of the judges, told Don Quixote he was to run with the last, because that worked out best. Those knights who had won the prizes took them to their ladies. Don Álvaro, the object of his passion being in Granada, gave his prize, beautifully embroidered perfumed gloves, to a quite lovely girl, the sister of a titled person in that kingdom, and she received it with great courtesy and appreciation.

There was a second round and prizes were given to four more, two of whom had lanced the ring. These, like the first, presented them to their ladies. In this way very few, or no knights, failed to present prizes to the lady each looked upon most favorably.

It was now getting late and Don Quixote was importuning Don Álvaro to let him take his turn; if not, in spite of all the judges in Europe, he would do so. Advised of his madness, the judges made a sign to Don Álvaro to let him take two turns, and so he led Don Quixote to a position in the middle of the street, in front of the ring, to await the sound of the trumpets. When he heard them, our knight set out alone, his shield on his left arm, hurriedly spurring Rocinante who, despite the way he was being urged on, was running at a little more than a half-gallop. But he was so unfortunate that when he reached the ring, he placed the lance about two spans above it, over the cord. As he finished the run he lowered the lance in great haste, looking at it very carefully to see whether he had the ring on it. All this aroused visible laughter, the more so when they saw that, not finding the ring, he began very angrily to head his horse back to the starting-point, where Don Álvaro was. With a straight face, Don Álvaro said, "My lord Don Quixote, take a second run at it immediately so that your horse won't get cooled off, for although you didn't get the ring, it was a terrific thrust since it went only half a yard over it."

Without answering a word, Don Quixote pulled Rocinante around and began to run, with Don Álvaro following him at a half-gallop, to the laughter of those watching. Don Quixote came up to the ring a second time and because of his anger and embarrassment he missed it by a half yard beneath. However, seeing how poorly his companion

had performed, Don Álvaro stood up in his stirrups, reached out as far as he could, seized the ring and, coming up very craftily to Don Quixote, put it on the tip of his lance. He was able to do this unnoticed because after making the thrust Don Quixote was carrying the lance over his shoulder in a courtesy gesture. Don Álvaro said to him, "Oh, my lord Don Quixote, pride of La Mancha, victory! Victory! If I am not mistaken, you have the ring on your lance."

Don Quixote, thinking that he had not hit it—which was the truth—looked up and said, "I was just feeling amazed that I had missed twice, but Rocinante—God wish him ill—was to blame for the first pass, because he didn't run as fast as I wanted him to."

"Everything was well done," said Don Álvaro. So now let's go to the judges and you can ask for what is rightfully yours."

The good hidalgo was so puffed up and vain that the street couldn't hold him. Taking his stand in front of the judges and holding up his lance with the ring on it, he said, "Consider what this lance with the ring hanging from it claims, and observe that it in itself demands the prize so justly due me."

The judge who had spoken to him on his entrance to the plaza had a page bring two dozen large leather suspenders probably worth half a *real*. First calling all the knights to hear what he said to Don Quixote, he picked up the suspenders and tied them on the heavy lance, saying in a ringing voice, "I, a second King Ferdinand, by my own hand give you, the invincible knight-errant, flower of knightly chivalry, this renowned prize, ribbons made from the skin of the Phoenix and brought from India, so that you, a loveless knight, may give them to the lady you deem the least loved of all who are on those balconies. In addition to that, I command you and Don Álvaro Tarfe, under pain of my disfavor, to have supper with me in my own house tonight, together with your squire who is, I know, most faithful and worthy of serving a person of your talents."

Then flageolets rang out and Don Quixote went along looking at the balconies and windows. On a rather low one he saw an honest old woman who surely knew more about rue and verbena[12] than she did about receiving prizes. She was with two highly made-up girls of the kind one finds in Zaragoza. Up came our knight to her and put the suspenders on the window-sill with his lance, saying in a loud voice that all could hear, "Most wise Urganda the Unknown, this good knight whom you have always favored so highly on all occasions begs you to pardon his boldness and accept these foreign ribbons made, I am told, from the Phoenix itself, and hold them in esteem, because they are worth a city."

When the two women heard such words from that man in armor and saw that everybody was laughing at his presentation of the leather suspenders to an old woman past sixty, such as the one who accompanied them, they were embarrassed and half-laughing, they slammed the window shut in his face, closing and locking it from the inside without saying a word to him.

Don Quixote was somewhat abashed at the action, but Sancho Panza, who from the start of the jousts had been with two kitchen boys to see the contest and the prizes his master was to win, upon seeing that he was giving the suspenders to that old woman who hadn't wished to accept them, but instead had closed the window, spoke up saying, "By the body of the one who bore that harlot of an old woman, belonging to the times of Mari-Castaña, wife of the great Jew and most whoring old man of the two who were after Saint Susanna! Is she thus to shut the window on one of the best knights in my whole village and refuse to accept the suspenders given her? May they do her no good since she's no good. But who can this person be who my master says is named Urganda? And if she is that one, she ill deserves

---

[12] Both of these are supposed to be aphrodisiacs.

those suspenders which are so big and strong that they surely must be of dog-skin. Upon my word, if I can pick up half a brick I'll make them open up even if they don't want to."

Turning to Don Quixote he said to him, "Throw them over here, since they don't want or deserve them. I'll put them away and we'll save them for ourselves; besides, I need some for my breeches like I need bread to eat, because the ones I now have are full of knots in front. Let's have a look at them, I say, for by God! they'll serve this better use."

Don Quixote lowered the lance, saying, "Here, Sancho, take these valuable ribbons and put them in our suitcase until it's time to use them." Sancho took them, saying, "By the body of Barrabas, look at what that old witch didn't want! But you can believe that I won't let anyone get them out of my claws for less than twenty *maravedís*, even though they may not be worth that, because at least they're made of rabbit-skin, or trout-skin, or the devil knows what."

Ten or twelve persons came up to see the priceless suspenders which that peasant held in his hand. It so happened that among those people gathered together there was a poorly dressed boy, no less light on his feet than he was light-fingered. With the greatest swiftness he seized the aforementioned suspenders and, relying on the rabbit's weapons, in a few jumps he was out of the Calle del Coso. Don Quixote did not see this; if he had, the biggest slice left of the boy would have been his ear. However, good Sancho Panza, who thought he was safe from such an unexpected occurence, began to shout, "Stop him, gentlemen, stop him, sinner that I am! He has stolen from me the best prize in the tourney."

However, when the poor fellow saw that hope of overtaking the boy was lost, he began to weep bitterly, tear his thick beard and wring his hands, saying, "Oh, unhappy mother who bore me! Oh, bitter day for me on which I have lost such lovely suspenders, the best in all Lombardy! Woe is me! What shall I do, and what shall I tell my master about the prize he entrusted to me? What excuse shall I have to evade his knightly anger so that he won't dust my ribs with a knotty oak tree? If I tell him I've lost them, he'll think me a witless squire; if I tell him a rascal stole them from me, he'll be so angry that immediately he'll challenge to open battle not only the rascal who stole them, but also all the rascals to be found in all rascaldom. I'd rather have died than endure such great sorrow! I tell you that I'd very willingly kill myself if I weren't afraid I'd hurt myself; stop, let's get busy. I have in mind going to Don Álvaro's lame cook right away and borrowing two *cuartos* to buy a rope to hang myself; later I'll give him back double the amount. If I happen to find a tree from which my feet can touch the ground I'll throw the rope over the lowest branch and wait until some kindly man passes by, and I'll beg him tearfully to be benevolent and charitable enough to help me hang myself, for the love of God, because I am a poor man, orphaned of father and mother. And so, that's the end. Christ be with you, Don Quixote de la Mancha. You are the bravest knight of all wanderers created by the cold North Wind. Remain in peace also, my darling Rocinante, and remember me, as I remembered you every time I went to put out your feed. Remember too, that day on which, as I thoughtlessly passed next to your rear gate, I said, 'Friend Rocinante, how are you?' You, who still couldn't speak the Spanish language, answered me with a couple of pairs of castanet-claps, firing a harquebus-shot through the garbage-port so accurately that if I hadn't taken it between my snout and my nostrils I don't know what would have become of me. So then, my beloved nag, may the blessing of all the nags of Roncesvalles[13] be with you; if you knew the tribulation in which I have been placed, I am sure you would send me relief for my great sorrow. Now cheer up; I am going, as I say, to tell the cook about my misfortune and I hope to get some help from him. For better never than late, for the early bird catches the worm; finally, strike over there, overcoat, on the lightning bolt's house, for a bird in the bush is worth two in the hand . . ."[14] And he went off stringing together in this fashion more than forty nonsensical proverbs.

[13] Roncesvalles (Fr. Roncevaux) is the Spanish town in the Pyrenees where Roland was killed.

[14] Sancho has indeed garbled a couple of these proverbs badly. The next-to-last one is actually a confused mixture of *two* Spanish proverbs, both of which have no English equivalents: "Strike over there, lightning bolt ('rayo'), on Tamayo's house,' and 'Strike over there, lightning bolt, and not on my overcoat ('sayo')."

CHAP. XII. HOW DON QUIXOTE AND DON ÁLVARO *Tarfe were supper-guests of the judge who invited them at the contest, and the strange and unexpected adventure which befell our valiant knight in the drawing-room.*

HEN THE ring-lancing contest was over and the knights, two by two, had run the courses before the entire city, they left their posts to go home because night was falling. To do likewise, Don Álvaro grasped Don Quixote's hand, saying, "My lord Don Quixote, let's take a little walk along these streets until it's time to go have supper with the gentleman, a very liberal judge, who as you know, has invited us for supper tonight."

"We'll go wherever you wish," said Don Quixote, and since there was no way to make him give his shield and lance to a page to take home, as Don Álvaro wished, he went along taking all this equipment with him. They arrived in plenty of time at the noble house of the host who had invited them for supper. In the entryway, one of his pages took Don Quixote's lance and shield, and they dismounted and immediately went up to the apartment of Don Carlos, as the judge was named. He and other knights, friends he had also invited, arose to go and embrace Don Quixote. When this was done, they said, "Welcome, Sir Knight-Errant, we hope you have the health we all desire, and, for better relief from your recent toil we also want you to remove your armor. You are in a safe place and among friends who wish to serve you and learn from your expertise good military tactics, which I believe we badly need, seeing how poorly our knights performed in the contest. If you had not made up for their mistakes the festival would have turned out to be quite a fiasco."

Don Quixote answered, "Don Carlos, for two reasons it is not my custom to remove my armor anywhere I go, among friends or enemies. First, because a man becomes accustomed to it by always wearing it; as the philosophers say: '*Ab assubetis non fit passio*,'[1] for habit, as you know, changes things into what is natural, so that no task is burdensome. Second, because a man does not know whom to trust nor what may happen, because the events of war are varied. I remember having read in the authentic book about the exploits of Don Belianís of Greece that he and another knight, both in full armor, got lost in the

[1] "What you are accustomed to does not hurt you."

woods and came out into a certain meadow where they found ten or twelve savages roasting a deer. By signs they were invited to partake of it. Quite destitute and hungry, and seeing the humaneness of those barbarians, the knights dismounted and removed the bridles from the horses so that they could graze, but they wouldn't take off their helmets; instead they raised the visors slightly. Sitting on the grass, they were eating a leg of the deer which the savages placed before them. But they had scarcely taken half a dozen bites when, after conferring among themselves in a language the newcomers did not understand, two of the savages slipped up very softly from behind and struck them such a blow on the head with clubs that, had they not had their helmets on, they would doubtless have sustained a fatal injury from those barbarians. As it was, they fell to the ground stunned, and amid a great clamor the savages set about removing their armor, but as they didn't know how to do that task, they only rolled them about here and there over the meadow. As luck would have it, after the wind had refreshed them a little and they saw the sad state of affairs, they got up very swiftly, took hold of their fine swords and began to go after the savages as though they were in an enemy's camp. With each backward slash they made two savages out of one since they were naked."

Don Quixote told this with such anger that he too took hold of his sword and went on saying, "Cutting here, slashing there, here they split one down to his breast, there they left another on one foot like a crane, until they killed most of them." Don Carlos made him sheathe his sword, laughing with the knights at the anger Don Quixote felt about the savages, whom he seemed to have before him.

Taking him by the hand they led him into another room, where they found the supper tables set. Don Carlos looked around and said to one of his pages, "Go in a jiffy to Don Álvaro's lodging—you know where—and call Don Quixote's squire, Sancho Panza. Tell him that his master orders him to come with you at once, because he is also invited. Don't fail to bring him with you."

The page got his cloak and went after him immediately. He found him in the kitchen with the cook, to whom he was very gloomily relating the misfortune of having his fine suspenders stolen, and said "Señor Sancho, come with me right away, because Señor Don Quixote sends for you, seeing that my lord Don Carlos won't sit down at the table until he sees you in the room."

"Señor page, you can tell those gentlemen that I am very grateful, and that I am not at home, and that's why I am not going, and because

I'm roaming about the plaza in search of a ceratin important business matter which has gone astray," responded Sancho very coolly. "But if God is good enough to enlighten me so that I find it, I'll give my word that I'll go at once."

Not so," said the page. "You must come with me, for that's what they've ordered, because you are also invited to supper."

"I must have been talking about tomorrow," replied Sancho. "That being the case, I'll go right away and very willingly. Upon my word, you catch me at a time when I am not ill-disposed, because it's been more than three hours since anything has entered my body except a little plateful of cold meat and a roll which the cook here gave me, God bless him! He put the soul back in my body. But let's go; I don't want to be missing nor to be thought negligent."

After he said this they both left, first bidding the cook farewell. They arrived in the room where supper was already in progress, Don Carlos at the head of the table, Don Quixote at his side, and the rest of the knights seated around the table, and there must have been more than twenty of them. Sancho went up to his master, took off his cap with both hands, and bowed deeply, saying, "A good evening to you both, and may God keep you in His holy glory."

"Oh, Sancho, you are very welcome," said Don Carlos. "But what is this about God keeping us in His holy glory? We are not yet dead, unless these knights are from hunger, since the supper is meager. Even if it is, my great goodwill will be a substitute."

"My lord, since there is no glory for me except when the table is set, I consider it great when I see so many plates filled with ostriches and meat and preserved sweets that I am drooling with satisfaction," said Sancho.

Don Álvaro Tarfe then took a melon from the table and gave it to Sancho, saying "Sancho, taste this melon and if it's good, I'll give you its weight in meat from this plate." He gave him a knife to cut the sample slice, and Sancho said that it hadn't gone well with him when he cut melons in the melon patch at Ateca, so with his permission he would split it as he did in his region. So saying, he dropped it at once on the floor, then picked up the four pieces into which it had broken, saying, "Here it is, cut with one blow without bothering with a knife to slice it."

"Sancho, upon my word you are a curious fellow," said Don Carlos. "I am pleased by your sagacity, for you do at one stroke what others don't do with eight. Here—in my stead you must eat this capon." He said this as he gave him an excellent one that was on a plate. "People tell me that God has given you a special talent for this."

"May the Holy Trinity repay you when you leave this world," replied Sancho, taking the capon, which was already carved, and stuffing it away as quick as a wink. When the pages saw how efficient his teeth were they took it into their heads to empty all the dishes they could reach on the table into his cap. With all this Sancho soon turned into a Jew's harp,[2] but Don Carlos picked up a big dish of meatballs, saying "Sancho, would you dare eat two dozen meatballs if they were well cooked?"

"I don't know what meatballs are, but I do know about granaries,[3] for we have them in my village; but you don't eat *them*; but rather only the wheat that's inside once it's been kneaded."

"They are only little balls of meat," said Don Carlos, handing him the plate, which Sancho took. One by one, as if he were eating a bunch of grapes, he put them between his breast and his back, to the great surprise of those who saw his excellent capacity."

When he finished them he said, "Oh, son of a bitch, you treacherous things! How good you tasted! By heaven, you might be the little balls with which the children in limbo play. I vow that if I return to my village I'll sow at least half a peck of them in a garden I have near my house, because I know they are not grown in all Argamesilla. It may even be that if it's a good year the aldermen will set the price at eight *maravedís* a pound. If that's what happens, they will not be heard nor seen."[4]

Sancho said this as candidly as if in truth they really could be sown. Aware that they were all laughing, he said, "I see only one difficulty in sowing these, and that is that by nature I'm so fond of them that I'd eat them before they could ripen, unless my wife put up a scarecrow so I wouldn't get to them, and even God's aid wouldn't be needed."

"According to that, you are married, Sancho?" said Don Carlos.

Sancho answered, "If it please you, sir, I am, and to my wife, and she is very grateful for your kindness to me."

Everybody laughed at the reply and Don Carlos inquired again if she was pretty, to which he reponded, "By Saint Ciruelo, is she pretty! It's true, if I remember rightly, that along about this season she is

---

[2] A Jew's harp is quite round and wide at the bottom, and that is what Sancho looks like in this scene.

[3] There is a confusion here between *albóndigas* 'meatballs' and *'alhóndigas* 'granaries'.

[4] That is, they will soon disappear.

probably fifty-three years old. Her face is a little dark from going in the sun and she lacks three upper teeth and two lower molars, but in spite of all that there is no Aristotle who could equal her, except that when she gets her hands on two or three *cuartos* she deposits them immediately at the house of Juan Pérez, a tavern-keeper in my village; she carries them away later in the form of vine-juice, in a big pitcher we have, lipless because of her constantly putting her own lips to it."

"Your wife is a good drinker, and you always have a good appetite; you make a good married couple," said Don Carlos. At this, reaching over to a big plate on which there were six creamed chicken breasts,[5] he said, "Sancho, have you any empty corner left for these? After what you've eaten you surely haven't any appetite for them."

"I'm most grateful to you," said Sancho, reaching out and taking them. "Rely on me to eat them, to serve God and his mother." Stepping aside, he ate up four with such haste and pleasure that his beard gave proof of it, because it was not a little whitewashed by the sauce. He put the other two that were left in his bosom, intending to keep them for the next day.[6]

When supper was over and the tables cleared, they all sat down around the room, Don Álvaro Tarfe and Don Quixote on the left of Don Carlos, who made Sancho Panza sit at his feet. At this time Don Álvaro was talking to Don Quixote, making him say a thousand absurd things, although he had been silent during supper, partly because of the fancies he was turning over in his mind concerning what vengeance would be best to take on the wise Urganda who had so publicly discountenanced him by closing the window without accepting the fine suspenders he was presenting to her.

As Don Carlos was talking to Sancho and the other knights were chatting with each other, two very fine musicians entered with their instruments as well as a handsome young clog dancer they brought with them. The musicians sang many songs and played many tunes and the young man expertly clogged and tumbled. Meanwhile Don Carlos leaned over and asked Sancho, so that everybody could hear him, if he would dare do some tumbling, as the young man was doing.

---

[5] This dish, called *manjar blanco* 'white food' in the original, and therefore not translatable as such, consists of breast of chicken, rice flour, milk, and sugar, according to Rodríguez Marín.

[6] In Part II, 62, when Don Antonio Moreno first talks to Sancho, he says that he has heard that Sancho is very fond of creamed chicken breasts and meatballs—referring to this episode in Avellaneda—and Sancho denies that he is a glutton, saying that he is more cleanly than greedy.

Yawning and crossing himself with his thumb in his mouth because he was being overcome by drowsiness after the heavy supper, he replied, "By Jove, sir! I'd tumble down right now in a fine fashion on two or three packsaddles. This devlish man can't possibly have any insides or entrails, for he leaps so lightly; to see if he is hollow inside we need only to put a lighted candle in his behind and he will serve as a lantern."

Here Don Carlos called a page and whispered to him, "Go tell the secretary it's time now." It must be noted that Don Álvaro Tarfe, Don Carlos, and the secretary had contrived to bring to the room that night one of the figures, taller than three yards, that are brought out for the Corpus Christi Day parade in Zaragoza. Even though they are so tall, using a certain harness one man can carry a figure on his shoulders. Well, the people now being in the room, as I have said, after the secretary had received Don Carlos' message, he entered with the giant into one end of the room, which had been intentionally darkened. High above the door through which he had come in, and next to the ceiling was a small window like a skylight which was even with the head of the giant because they were of the same height. Through this window, and sheltered by it, the secretary was to speak without being seen, for after bringing in and setting in place the aforesaid giant which he carried on his shoulders, he went in again to take his post at the window already mentioned.

At the first sight of the giant they all pretended to be excited, taking hold of their swords, but Don Quixote arose, saying, "Rest easy; this isn't anything, and only I know what it can be, for such adventures as these used to occur daily in the houses of the ancient emperors. Everybody sit down, I say, and we shall see what the giant wants; whatever it is, he will be given a reply."

They all sat down. The secretary, a very ingenious man, well coached on what he was to do, began to speak in a loud voice when he saw that everybody had settled down: "Which one of you here is the Loveless Knight?" All were silent, but Don Quixote answered in a very calm voice, saying, "Arrogant and colossal giant, I am the one you seek."

Speaking from above, with his head inside the hollow giant's head, the secretary said, "I thank the immortal gods, especially great Mars, god of war, that at the end of such a long road and so many difficulties I have found in this city what I have been seeking so diligently for a thousand days, and that is the Loveless Knight. Princes and knights who have gathered together in this royal palace of yours, know that I,

if you have never heard of me, am Bramidán de Tajayunque,[7] king of Cyprus; I won this kingdom by myself, taking it away from its legitimate lord and taking it over since I deserved it more than he did. When there came to my ears, in this aforesaid kingdom of mine, news of the unheard-of exploits and strange adventures of Prince Don Quixote de la Mancha, otherwise called He of the Sad Countenance or The Loveless One, I regretted that to make my glory lesser, there was, on the face of the earth, one whose valor and strength equaled mine; therefore I have left my kingdom. I have passed through many other foreign ones to the grief of their rulers, seeking, inquiring, and asking, to the astonishment and fear of all who saw me, where, or in what kingdom or province the aforesaid knight, so famous throughout the world, could be. It is true, and I can't deny it, that wherever I have gone, nothing is discussed or talked about today in the plazas, temples, streets, bake-shops, taverns, and stables except Don Quixote de la Mancha. Well, as I say, stimulated by envy of so many of your exploits oh, great Don Quixote! I have come seeking you for only two reasons: first, to do battle with you, take off your head and carry it to Cyprus to place it at the door of my royal palace, thus making myself lord of all the victories you have had over so many giants and wild men, so that the world will fully understand that I am unique, unrivaled, and the only one who deserves to be praised, esteemed, honored and renowned in all the kingdoms in the universe because I am braver, more valiant and of greater fame than you, all those before you, and those who will come after you. Consequently, if you want to refuse the travail of entering into battle with me, command that your head be given me with no delay and with no excuse, so that I may carry it on my lance, then you may go your own way. The second reason I come is that I have also heard that Don Carlos, owner of this strong castle, has a fifteen-year-old sister of rare beauty and charm, whom I desire; so it is my will that, together with your head, she be given me immediately, so that I may take her to Cyprus and have her as a mistress as long as I please, for she will be highly honored by this. If he won't do this, I challenge and defy him and the whole kingdom of Aragon with him, and all the Aragonese, Catalonians, and Valencians under his rule to face me on foot or on horseback. At the door of this great palace I have my very heavy, enchanted armor in a cart drawn by six pairs of very strong Palestinian oxen; my lance is the lateen yard of a ship; my helmet is the size of the capital on the belfry of the great temple of

---

[7] In Spanish, *taja* means 'he cleaves' and *yunque* means 'anvil'.

Saint Sophia in Constantinople, and my shield is as big as a mill wheel. So then, Loveless Knight, reply at once to all this, because I am in a hurry and have much to do and am needed in my kingdom."

After this the giant was silent and all who knew about the plot feigned innocence as best they could, waiting to see what Don Quixote would reply to the giant. Arising from his seat, he knelt in front of Don Carlos, saying, "Sovereign emperor Trebacio of Greece,[8] since you have accepted me in your empire as a son, if Your Majesty will be pleased to give me permission to speak for everybody and especially for you and this very noble kingdom, I shall answer this diabolical beast, so that in this way I may later give him the better punishment his grave insults and sacrilegious words deserve."

Don Carlos, biting his lips to hold back his laughter and pretending as best he could, threw his arms about Don Quixote's neck and raised him up, saying, "Sovereign Prince of La Mancha, this is not only my cause, but also yours. However, I have become so afraid of the giant Bramidán de Tajayunque that my heart is ready to leap out of my body, and so I say that if you see fit it will be all right to grant him the two things he asks of us, so that we may be freed of the universal ruin which threatens us: you will give him your head, and for my part I am ready, not willing but obliged, to give him my lovely sister Lucretia and let him go to the devil before he does greater harm. Although this is my opinion, I leave the solution of the affair to you. Therefore, dear Prince, bearing this in mind, whatever answer you choose to give him will be the wisest one."

When Sancho, greatly terrified by the giant, heard what Don Carlos told his master he was all eyes and said, "Come now, my lord Don Quixote, in the name of the fifteen saints, to whom Miguel Aguileldo, sacristan of Argamesilla, is very devoted, I beg you to do what Señor Don Carlos says. Why do you want to fight this giant? They say he can split an anvil larger than that of the blacksmith in our village, and serious authors relate that's why he is named Tajayunque. Besides, according to what he says (and I believe him, because such a great and honest man will not say one thing when he means another) that he has a shield the size of a mill wheel. If this is so, the devil take him! Let's send him off once and for all with what he wants; let's not waste any more time on him and give the devil something to laugh at."

Don Quixote gave him a terrible kick in the rear, saying, "Oh, base

---

[8] In the romance of the *Knight of Phoebus*, Trebacio is the father of Phoebus and Rosicler.

and foolish peasant stuffed with garlic since the cradle! Who tells you to meddle in something that is none of your business and doesn't concern you?" Going to the center of the room and facing the giant, he spoke gravely to him in this manner: "Haughty giant Bramidán de Tajayunque, I have listened attentively to your arrogant words giving me to understand what your insane and extravagant desires are. You would already have paid for them had it not been for the respect due the emperor and princes who are here, and because I want to give you publicly and before the whole world, the punishment you deserve, so that it may serve as an example to others like you who dare attempt henceforth such foolish, crazy things. So now, in answer to your demands, I say that I accept your offer to do battle and set as the time tomorrow after dinner, and as the place the wide plaza in this city, called El Pilar because of the sacred temple and fortunate sanctuary which is the very felicitous repository of the divine pillar from which the most blessed Virgin spoke to and consoled her nephew, and the great patron of our Spain, the apostle James, while he was alive. You may appear in this plaza in whatever armor you wish, certain that if you have a mill wheel for a shield, I have a shield from Fez which gives no odds to the Wheel of Fortune itself. In exchange for the head you request of me, I vow and promise not to eat bread from a table nor dally with the queen (in short, I swear all the oaths usually sworn at such critical moments by the true knights-errant you will find listed in the history which relates the bitter mourning over the luckless Baldwin) until I cut off your head and place it over the door of this great palace of my lord and father, the emperor."[9]

"Oh, immortal gods!" said the secretary in a deep, loud voice. "How can you permit one lone man to insult me thus without your wrath making him into meatballs at once? I swear by the order of secretary I received not to eat bread from the floor nor trifle with the queen of spades, hearts, clubs, or diamonds, nor sleep on the point of my sword until I take such bloody vengeance on Prince Don Quixote de La Mancha so that his arms will remain hanging from his shoulders, his legs and thighs will remain fastened to his hips, his head will be swimming, and his mouth, in spite of everybody already born or to be born, will stay beneath his nose."

Sancho, bewildered by the rush of threats and execrations, got up from the floor where he was sitting, placed himself between Don Quixote and the giant and very courteously said to the latter, first removing

---

[9] Baldwin is a character in the ballad about the Marquis of Mantua. This ballad inspires much of the action in I, 5.

his cap with both hands, "Oh, lord Bramidán de Parteyunques,[10] no! In the name of the passion that God suffered, do not do so much harm to my master, who is an honest man and doesn't want to go into battle with you because he isn't built to fight with Comeyunques.[11] Bring him half a dozen melon growers, for upon my word, he can deal with them in a fine fashion. Besides, it's necessary to have Señor Saint Roque's help, because he is the patron saint of pestilence."

The giant, without heeding what Sancho was saying, took out a glove made of two kidskins which he had already had made for that purpose and said, throwing it at Don Quixote, "Cowardly knight, pick up my small, narrow glove as a sign and pledge that tomorrow I'll await you in the plaza you name, after dinner." With this, he backed out through the door by which he had entered.

Don Quixote picked up the glove, which was clearly three palms wide, and gave it to Sancho saying, "Take this glove of Bramidán's and keep it until after dinner tomorrow, for you will see marvels."

Sancho took it and said, crossing himself, "The devil bless you, Balandrán de Tragayunques,[12] or whatever your name is, what huge hands you have! Oh, whoreson, traitor, or rascal, I hope there's a slap in the face waiting for you! In truth, sir, you will have a hard time getting along with this devil. He's so big and terrifying; remember he has sworn to make meatballs out of you like those we ate tonight. But before that time arrives make him some creamed chicken breasts like those we also had for supper. They taste good to me, and I still have two of them in my bosom for a snack."

Hereupon Don Carlos arose from his chair, ordering torches lighted to accompany the knights to their homes. Because it was late, he took leave of them and of Don Quixote and Don Álvaro, who grasped Don Quixote's hand and took him, with Sancho Panza, to his house, where the good hidalgo spent one of the worst nights he had ever had thinking about the dangerous battle he was to have the next day with that mammoth giant whom he believed to be the true King of Cyprus, for he had said so himself.

Here ends the fifth part of the Ingenious Hidalgo,

Don Quixote de la Mancha

---

[10] Sancho remembers the semantics of the name Tajayunque, for *Parteyunques* means 'he splits anvils'.

[11] "He *eats* anvils.".

[12] *Balandrán* is based on *balandrón* 'braggart'—the *-án* coming from the final syllable of Bramidán; Tragayunques means 'he swallows anvils.'

SIXTH PART
OF THE INGENIOUS
Hidalgo, Don Quixote de La Mancha

CHAP. XIII. HOW DON QUIXOTE LEFT ZARAGOZA IN order to go to the court of the Catholic King of Spain to do battle with the King of Cyprus.

HE SCHEMES in the disordered mind of the loveless Manchegan so tormented his faulty judgment and wakeful rest that at early dawn, just as his eyes were closing to get a little rest, the absurd phantoms dreamed up in his common sense sounded the alarm through all parts of his body, the disturbance coinciding with a dream he had that Bramidán had treacherously entered that castle to kill him, with more safety for himself by catching him unprepared. He got up in a great fury to go after him as if he really knew the giant was in the house. Strongly apprehensive and wrathful about this, he kept saying, "Wait, traitor; schemes, stratagems, lies and enchantments will not avail to get you out of my hands."

So saying, he put on his helmet, breastplate and backplate, took up the shield and lance and went about looking everywhere. He then went to the parlor, where he saw light coming through the door of the small room. Because dawn was breaking and the little window was half-open, the first clear daylight was coming through it. Blind with rage he entered this room, and as misfortune would have it, it was the one in which the dejected Sancho was sleeping. As he had gone to bed late and tired, he had fallen asleep with his head half-covered, leaving beside it the big glove that Don Quixote himself had given to his care, and which was the pledge for the challenge that the King of Cyprus, Tajayunque, had issued to him the night before.

Upon seeing the glove, Don Quixote took it in his head that it was the mate of the one he had given Sancho to keep, and that the man sleeping was the giant himself who, exhausted from entering the castle by way of the window, had stretched out to rest until he could find the opportunity to carry out safely his intention of killing Don Quixote. Therefore, with this illusion, he didn't hesitate to give him a terrible blow in the ribs with the lance, saying, "This is the way renegades and traitors pay for the schemes they plot. Die, base Tajayunque, for that is the best thing one can do when he has enemies such as you have in me and sleeps heedlessly."

Sancho awoke, half dazed by the shouts and blows, and no sooner did he sit up in bed in order to arise and see who was saying good morning to him when Don Quixote, who had tossed aside the lance, gave him a big punch in the nose saying, "There's no need to get up, traitor, for you'll die here."

Sancho began to yell, leaping from the bed as best he could; going into the parlor he said, "What are you doing, sir?" I haven't sneaked

into the castle nor am I anyone but your squire Sancho."

"You are nobody but Bramidán, traitor!" said Don Quixote. "That's very evident from the glove that I have found on you, the mate of the one you threw in my face yesterday when you made the challenge."

Both were in only their undershirts, because Don Quixote, with his vivid imagination working when he arose, put on only helmet, breastplate and backplate, as has been said, forgetting about the parts that for a thousand reasons demand better care in covering up. Sancho also came out in an undershirt, not as pure as his mother was the day she was born. The room was rather dark; what with this and his unappeased anger Don Quixote didn't recognize Sancho, but insisted that he was going to kill him, and he was as stubborn about it as Sancho was about invoking saints to help him, yelling, and begging for help.

The house was so disturbed by the shouts of both of them, which were many, that it could well have been called an insane asylum, because the main characters who were making merry were crazy. Some servants in their undershirts came out of their rooms to quell the disturbance and to see who had started it, but their appearance only put wood on the fire, because when Don Quixote saw them all in the same uniform, he took it into his head that they were giants who had come there, again by some art of enchantment, to help the bewitched Bramidán.

Imagining this, he began to thrust the lance about in all directions with such poor aim that here he knocked one down, over there he brained another, and all were at his mercy because they had come out unarmed, so it was like Judgment Day to hear the cries and curses of the wounded. The worst thing about it was that in order to protect himself against them he closed Sancho's door behind him and stood with a lance at the servants' room, saying, "Oh vile scoundrels! Let's see if all of you together will win the famous door of this impregnable bulwark from me."

Sancho cried out to high heaven, calling Don Álvaro who, suspecting what could be the matter, opened the windows of his room and taking his sword in hand, wearing a long damask garment, he came out in his bedroom slippers into the parlor. Astounded by the figures he saw and the fear and weeping of three or four of his pages, and by seeing Don Quixote fiercely gesturing with the glove in his hand, he placed himself at Sancho's side, and set about pacifying that tragedy, saying, "Hurrah, Señor Don Quixote, death to the knaves!

Sancho and I are here, ready to give our lives in your service and in defense of your honor and in vengeance for your affronts. However, so that we can do everything as we wish, tell us right now what has been done to you and by whom. By everything that I can swear to, I swear to take exemplary vengeance on your opponents and immediately."

"Who else can my opponents be, said Don Quixote, "except the colossal wild men, the insolent giants, whose occupation is to go about the world doing wrongs, concocting outrages, offending princesses, insulting high-born duennas, and lastly, other treacheries like the one plotted against my person and valor tonight by the insolent Bramidán de Tajayunque. By the art of enchantment, and accompanied by those scoundrels you see over there, he entered this strong castle surreptitiously to kill me by treachery, fearing that I would kill him this evening in the Plaza del Pilar if he came out for the appointed fight. But as he has failed in his intentions, because I was secretly warned by the wise Lirgando, in whose castle in Ateca I was, and from whose hands I received the health and strength that Orlando Furioso had taken from me by a thousand uncommonly large wounds. I learned that he had secretly entered this fortress to catch me unawares and to be safe and without worry. But my alertness caught him in the act, and with this glove, adornment for his hands and mate of the one Sancho has. Because of this my own hands were duly fast and diligent about putting an end to him, and I should have done so quickly if you, accompanied by Sancho, had not come out to restrain my rage. But I owe the highest esteem and satisfaction to you both: to one, for great favors, and to the other for most faithful service."

"You certainly paid me, and in a very fine fashion," said Sancho. "May God do as much for you and your bones. What do mine owe you, sir, that they should have received a severe drubbing at dawn? I am neither Bramidán nor Parteyunques; yet all my limbs are certainly screaming to high heaven, tired of being clubbed, now in castles, then along roads, and again in melon patches."

"My complaint, son Sancho," said Don Quixote, "is that it could be possible that the lawless Bramidán has just now mauled you. Oh, you dog, you vile, base person of a despicable race, to think that you have laid hands on my most faithful squire! On all twelve signs of the zodiac I swear that you will pay for it without delay."

At this point he was going to repeat the attack on the pages with infernal fury, but since they were on their way downstairs and Don

Álvaro restrained him, his blows missed their target. So, because of this and the impatience of Sancho, who was cursing thirty thousand devils, seeing that after his master had given him a good beating he was blaming it on Bramidán, Don Quixote came up humbly to Don Álvaro to say, "In such apparent peril, such an arduous affair, such grave danger, and so strange an event, tell me what you think is best for me to do, because I shall follow your advice to the letter

"The consideration of such an extraordinary matter must be done more slowly," said Don Álvaro. "So, until the required time, until we know for sure about the decision this bad giant has made whether or not to go to the plaza, I think you should retire to your chambers and not appear in public, in order to assure your safety. As for the rest, I shall take the necessary steps to seek him out and lie in wait for him, and Sancho in his turn will do the same. You should be quite content about having driven him away, making him leave the glove in your possession; this way it will be a perpetual witness of his cowardice as well as of the strength of your arm."

The advice seemed good to Don Quixote and without replying he entered his room, where he took off his armor again and went to bed very satisfied with the victory he had attained. Don Álvaro closed the door to keep him in. Sure that he couldn't get out, he called the pages, who were no little bewildered by the annoying jest, and consoled them as best he could, reminding them that there was no need to pay attention to the things a crazy man did, but to avoid him and what he did. He ordered those who were least injured and could do so, to get dressed and accompany him when he left the house.

This done, Don Álvaro went into his room to get dressed and told Sancho to bring his clothes from the room in which he had slept, because he wanted him to keep him company and entertain him while he was dressing, and Sancho could do the same.

However, Sancho was so fearful that he said, "You'll pardon me, but by the gums and bones of my Dapple, I vow that as long as I live I won't enter that room again nor get the clothes I have there, even if I have to go naked. Our father Adam was a better man, and that's what he did. Body of my breeches! After what happened to me there do you want my master to turn into a Roland when I go in again and, thinking that Parteyunques has come back again in my body, finish by drubbing me on my right side as he did on my left, in order to level my blood? It was a pretty jest! I'll bet you four to one that you wouldn't take my place in bed and undergo from my master what I have suffered. I'm doing quite well enough in not leaving the house immediately and abandoning him, but I don't want to lose what I have won by my good lance (or by my master's bad lance, may God give him a bad one!), and this is the governorship of the first peninsula he conquers, which he offered me so many days ago."

Don Álvaro laughed a long while over his simplicity and fear. Entering the room himself he threw out the clothes and Sancho, taking them under his arm, entered Don Álvaro's room with him. However, he kept saying so many foolish things all this time that although they were inside for more than an hour and a half, it seemed to Don Álvaro only a moment.

As soon as he finished dressing and left the room, intending to go to Don Carlos' home to relate the adventure which had occurred and to laugh about it, taking the opportunity to get new amusement from Don Quixote's mania in the matter of his ill-will toward Bramidán, he saw Don Carlos' secretary, who had authored the first jest, coming up the stairs of his house.

He was coming with a message from his master on a very different subject: to discuss a trip to Court which had suddenly been offered him by letters he had just received by messenger. The trip concerned the arrangement of Don Carlos' sister's marriage to a titled member of the legislature, a kinsman of his.

Don Álvaro was happy at the news because his friend was so pleased, and also because it offered him the best companionship he could desire for his return to Court, which he intended to do later. After talking over this affair and related things, he said, "The most troublesome thing I find about taking my departure is not knowing how to get rid of Don Quixote, because if we go with him it is impossible to travel with the necessary haste. At every step he will think up adventures and stories that will require many days to be laughed over and calmed, like the one that has just occurred to him, the wittiest in the world, which moved me to laughter as much as it did others to tears."

He related it at length, and the secretary crossed himself at the absurdity, but that very account gave him occasion to say, "Rather, if you see fit, it is important for us to order that such an odd fellow, who fancies himself a king, be taken by our cleverness into Court to liven it up; we shall all have to manage it."

"I should be very glad for him to go there," said Don Álvaro, "if he went by a different road and not with us, and made the trip with Sancho in his own way, so that when we arrive, or a few days later, we shall run across him and make him known."

"A plan has just come to me to make everything come out as we would like, the more so since he now has this fancy that Bramidán has taken to his heels through fear," said the secretary. "To carry it out, let me disguise myself in the clothing of a negro, and as Bramidán's servant, enter the house in front of everybody to give him a message from Bramidán, challenging him to present himself in Court within forty days, under penalty of being considered a coward, to carry out the postponed battle and challenge, mindful of the fact that this place is not safe for him because of Don Quixote's many friends, protectors, and followers."

The scheme seemed so clever to Don Álvaro that he praised the secretary and begged him to go to his room right away to put on whatever disguise seemed best. He did so in a jiffy because he found conveniently at hand all he could desire for the effect. When he was disguised and had come into the parlor, Don Álvaro called all his servants and sent one of them to get Sancho out of the kitchen, where he was already saying good morning to his insides with what had been given him by the lame cook, sympathetic partly because of the pitiful way in which he had described the beating his master had given him because, through an illusion by the devil, he had come upon him in his bed, thinking he was Bramidán.

After Sancho had come upstairs and taken his place beside them, unaware of the secret plans, they were all astonished to see that man dressed in a black velvet outfit, with dun-colored breeches, a bonnet much adorned with cameos and feathers, his neck laden with chains and jewels, gilded sheath and sword, a large collar, his face sooty and his hands likewise, with fingers covered with jeweled and plain rings. In short, he looked like one of those black kings painted on altarpieces depicting the Adoration.

Don Álvaro said, "Now, that there are witnesses, and such reliable ones, noble messenger, you may say who you are and what you want."

The secretary replied, "I seek the invincible Manchegan prince, Don Quixote, for whom I have an important message, and I know he is lodged in this great palace."

"Yes, he is here," added Don Álvaro. "You may speak to him in this room." And immediately opening the door to Don Quixote's apartment, he entered with all the others, saying, "Señor Don Quixote, here is a messenger from I don't know which prince." When this was said Don Quixote looked up and, seeing the black man, inquired what message he brought and from whom, saying all this in a harsh voice.

The secretary answered, "Are you perchance the Loveless Knight?"

"I am that very one," replied Don Quixote. "What do you want?"

Then the secretary said very ostentatiously, "Loveless Knight, Bramidán de Tajayunque, most powerful King of Cyprus and my lord, sent me to inform you, prince, that a certain adventure came up yesterday here, in the Court of the King of Spain, in which he is compelled to take part at once. He is glad of it partly because the challenge gets you out into the largest plaza in Europe, where you will have fewer protectors than you would have in this city. Therefore he challenges and charges you to appear there, in full armor, and within forty days. He wishes to prove in that plaza whether all the things the world publishes and says about you are true, for their opinion of you will be confirmed by the courage you show by not being absent on such an urgent occasion and just challenge. If you do not appear, your cowardice and the low esteem that you deserve because of this will be published throughout the kingdoms and provinces of the earth. You are being offered the opportunity of increasing your fame, which I do not believe you will, by fighting a prince of the strength my king has, and in a place where, if you come out victorious, the nobility of Spain will be witnesses to how you become, by the force of your sword, legitimate king and lord of the illustrious and pleasant kingdom of Cyprus, in which you will be able to make a faithful squire I am told you have, by name of Sancho Panza, governor of Famagusta or Belgrade,[1] its two chief cities. He is suited to rule because of his good disposition and squire-like vigilance, for the fertile trees which bear savory meatballs and creamed chicken breasts grow there."

Sancho, who had been listening to the messenger with his mouth watering upon hearing meatballs and creamed chicken mentioned, said to him, "Tell me, Señor Negro, (may God grant him as much happiness as he is black in the face!) are those two blessed cities of Buen Grado and Fambre Ajusta[2] located beyond Seville and Barcelona, or on this other side toward Rome and Constantinople? I would give one of my eyes if we could depart for them right away."

"Are you perchance the squire of the Loveless Knight?" said the secretary.

Then, standing up very straight, strutting and twirling his mustache, Sancho said in an arrogant voice, thinking himself already gover-

---

[1] Famagusta is a city in Eastern Cyprus and Belgrade is the capital of modern Yugoslavia.

[2] Sancho's corruption *Buen Grado* means 'good pleasure' and *Fambre Ajusta* means 'hunger reconciles'.

nor of Cyprus, "Proud and extraordinary squire, I am the one about whom you inquire, as can clearly be seen from my philonasality."

Here Don Álvaro's endurance in containing himself became exhausted and he had to turn his face saying, "Oh, my dear Don Carlos, what a comedy you are missing!" He concealed his laughter at all that as best he could and the secretary continued, "Answer me without more ado, Loveless Knight, for I must overtake my lord, the giant, who is now hurrying to Madrid."

"He has been given the answer by my hand," said Don Quixote, "so that it should not have to go by mail. But tell him that he can be certain that I shall come within the prescribed time, for I shall have the same hands and courage there that I had here in the early morning. But one who has recently had his life at stake does well to delay the fight forty days so he can have that much more time to live. Go in peace and be thankful that you are a messenger and therefore have safe conduct according to good laws in all nations, however antagonistic they may be, for if you were not, you would pay for your master's treachery and the bad treatment he gave my squire when he caught him sleeping."

Half-laughing, the secretary took his leave. As he reached the door Sancho called to him, "Oh, black lord! By the blows my master says yours gave me, which I don't believe, tell me if the governor of those cities, which I shall be, is dissolute[3] lord of those meatballs, as he says."

"Yes, brother," answered the secretary.

"Well, be off and God go with you," said Sancho. "We shall soon be there, my master and I, with Mari-Gutiérrez, who is my wife as God and everybody knows."

"You do well to take her, for the wife of the one who rules the earth must rule the women of Cyprus," said the secretary.

"By heaven!" said Sancho. "My wife probably doesn't know any more about governing than my Dapple. Besides, if I begin to entertain myself with those meatballs I won't remember any more about the governorship than if I were not born for it."

The secretary returned to Don Álvaro's room where he undressed, washed, and dressed again in his own clothes without being seen by the servants, because their master had cleverly entertained them with Sancho and Don Quixote, who talked about the message and made a thousand foolish remarks, speeches and schemes concerning it, until it seemed to Don Álvaro that the secretary had had time enough to do what we have said he did and to go back to Don Carlos' house and tell him all about it, as he in fact had already done.

[3] Sancho means 'absolute' (again).

From this day on Sancho kept nagging his master to go to Cyprus, and every morning he arose with this petition until Don Quixote told him that he could not go there until he had killed the great Tajayunque, king of that kingdom, in public battle in the great plaza in Madrid.

Don Álvaro went to consult with Don Carlos and to discuss the departure as well as Don Quixote's absurd acts and his determination concerning the message of the negro who was Tajayunque's squire. Having agreed that in two days they would both leave with the other knights from Granada, friends of theirs, he went home to spur along Don Quixote's departure so he could get rid of him.

Back at home he spoke to Don Quixote who was hurrying his trip so diligently that there was little need for Don Álvaro to show his own diligence to send him off because, after seeing him, Don Quixote said, "My reputation, Don Álvaro, does not permit me to stay longer than one more day in this city, but I must leave right away to spy on my haughty opponent. You will pardon me if I have shown my gratitude for past favors by so few courtesies, but be assured that because of them you will have in me Greek fire[4] for your enemies, a bolt of lightning for your rivals, and a thousand Hercules, Hectors, and Achilles in this invincible arm to punish the insults done to you only in the minds of those who try to harm you, even though they be the same giants who founded the Tower of Babel if they should be resuscitated just for that occasion." Turning to Sancho he said, "Go on, Sancho; saddle Rocinante quickly, for you have as much at stake as I in making this affair brief, because of the fortunate governorship which you expect."

"Indeed I do expect it," said Sancho. "However, downstairs a very good meal is waiting for us, and it isn't right for it to go to waste nor to insult the lame cook, my good friend, by not eating it. He told me a while ago that he has prepared it in my honor with the greatest elegance and neatness that can be imagined from all the pictures in the shops and stores, done by all the painters of the New World. Upon my word, because of it I have offered to take him to Cyprus and make him king of cooks and governor of cooking pans, because he knows more about dishes than Plato or Pluto, or whatever the devil the apothecaries call him."

---

[4] This was an unextinguishable flame made of pitch and suplhur used as a weapon, particularly by the Byzantine Greeks at the siege of Constantinople.

Don Álvaro highly praised Sancho's opinion; accordingly he had the tables set as Sancho wished, for if they waited for Don Quixote to express his opinion, they would never get to eat, which they all did together with pleasure and without delay. The cook gave them a very good meal, for he had been fore-warned to do so because Don Álvaro was expecting new and important guests. When Don Carlos went to visit him afterwards he stayed with them because he found them discussing their departure, the news of which was spreading.

When he had finished eating, Sancho saddled Rocinante and put the armor on his master, who immediately mounted with lance and shield and left the house at incredible speed, sent off by Don Álvaro with the hope of seeing him at Court, where he had offered to be, without fail, his second in the combat.

Sancho also saddled his donkey, at Don Álvaro's command throwing into the saddlebags the plentiful leftover bread and meat, wrapped in a towel. He said goodby, uttering a thousand hurrahs, silly remarks, and promises about his governorship of Cyprus, his master and servants. After this he loaded Dapple with the saddlebags and the suitcase and with his stocky hindquarters, driving him on, as he said, in search of his master Don Quixote and to overtake the arrogant Bramidán.

CHAP. XIV. ABOUT THE SUDDEN QUARREL SANCHO *Panza had with a maimed soldier who, returning from Flanders, was going to Castile accompanied by a poor hermit.*

SANCHO WAS UNABLE to overtake his master, no matter how hard he tried, until he reached the exit from the city. There he found him standing in front of the Aljafería, so insulted by the catcalls of the boys following him that he did not dare to continue waiting for Sancho, but he did so in the place mentioned, safe from them in the company of a poor soldier and a venerable hermit, on their way to Castile. It was to these persons that Sancho found him talking.

Both were on foot and began walking on, seeing that Don Quixote did so as soon as Sancho arrived. He was much surprised to see his master chatting with the soldier, inquiring where he was from.

He gathered, from what the soldier said, that he was coming from serving His Majesty in Flanders where he had met with a certain misfortune which forced him to leave the encampment without permission. At the border of Flanders and the kingdom of France, certain schemers had relieved him of his valise and taken the papers and money he had.

"How many were there?" asked Don Quixote.

"Four, and they had firearms!" he responded.

Hearing the reply, Sancho broke in saying, "Oh, whoreson, traitors! How many arms of fire did they have? I'll bet they were phantoms from the other world, if they weren't souls out of purgatory, for you say that they had arms of fire."

The soldier looked again at Sancho, who was streched out on his donkey, and seeing his thick beard and stupid face, he thought him some ignorant peasant from the nearby villages and not Don Quixote's servant, so he said to him, "Who tells this common peasant to stick his spoon into something that is none of his business? By God, I swear that if I choose to, I can hit him on the back as many times as he has porcupine quills in his beard. He probably doesn't know that I've beaten up more peasants than I have swallowed gulps of water since the day I was born."

Sancho, hearing what the soldier said, whipped his donkey and launched out against him, intending to run him over, saying, "You are the porcupine and the turpentine and the eater of porcupine and the swallower of turpentine!"

The soldier, who had nothing to do with jokes, attacked, sword in hand. Before the hermit and Don Quixote could prevent it, he hit Sancho on the back half a dozen times and, seizing him by the leg, pulled him off the donkey and would have proceeded to kick him if Don Quixote had not gotten between them. Striking the soldier with the tip of his lance, he said, "Stop! Be respectful, if only because I am present and this is my servant."

The soldier composed himself and said, "Pardon, Sir Knight, I did not realize that this peasant belonged to you."

Sancho had already risen and picked up a good-sized rock from the ground and he began to shout, "Get away from in front of me, my lord Don Quixote, and stand aside and leave me alone with him, for with the first stone I throw at him I'll make him remember the great whore who bore him."

The hermit seized Sancho but couldn't hold him becasue of Sancho's fury. But once his rage was checked a little he said, "By my smock, Señor Don Quixote! Don't I leave you to your adventures without hindering you? Well then, if that's so, why don't you leave me to those God sends me? How do you expect me to learn how to overcome giants? Although this rogue isn't one, you well know that the barber learns his trade on the beard of the humble man."

The hermit said, "Brother, for pity's sake let's have no more of this. Put down that stone." Sancho replied that he wouldn't unless the wild man declared himself conquered.

The hermit went up to the soldier, saying, "Soldier, this peasant is half-witted, as you have been able to deduce from hs words. Let's have no more trouble, for the love of God."

"I say, sir, that I want to be his friend, because your Reverence and this worthy knight so order," said the soldier.

They all went up to Sancho and the hermit said, "This soldier now admits that he is vanquished, as you wish. All that is needed now is for your to be friends and shake hands.

Sancho replied, "But first I want , and it is my will, oh, extraordinary giant, or soldier, or what the devil you are, that since you have admitted being conquered by me you will go to my village and present yourself to my noble wife and beautiful lady, Mari-Gutiérrez, wife of the governor-to-be of Cyprus and all its meatballs, whom you doubtless already know by reputation. Kneeling before her, tell her for me how I overcame you in open battle, and if you happen to have any thick iron chain at hand or in your pocket, put it around your neck so that you look like Ginesillo de Pasamonte and the other galley-slaves that my master, the Loveless One, when God willed him to be He of the Sad Countenance, sent to Dulcinea del Toboso, whose right name is Aldonza Lorenzo, daughter of Aldonza Nogales and Lorenzo Corchuelo." When he had said this he turned to Don Quixote, saying "What do you think, Señor Don Quixote? Aren't adventures to be done this way? Do you think I'm hitting the nail on the head!"

"Sancho," said Don Quixote, "I think that one who associates with good people will become one of them and whoever goes around with lions is taught to roar."

"That's so,"said Sancho, "But one who goes about with donkeys doesn't learn to bray; otherwise, days ago I could have been choirmaster of such acolytes, judging by the time I've spent with them. However, here's my hand, devil take it; shake it very happily and vaingloriously, soldier, and let's be friends *usque ad mortuum*.[1] As for the trip to El Toboso[2] to meet my wife, I give you permission to postpone it."

Embracing him, Sancho took out of the saddlebags a piece of cold mutton he had there with the leftovers and gave it to him. With a roll he had put away in his pocket, the soldier reinforced his weak stomach. Then Sancho climbed on his donkey and they all began to travel along slowly. Don Quixote said to Sancho, "I have been reflecting, son Sancho, on what I have just now seen you do; from this I conclude that with a few adventures such as these you will be able to graduate with honors as a knight-errant."

"By the body of Aristotle!" said Sancho, "I swear to you by the order of squire-errant which I received the day when my bones were blanket-tossed in view of all heaven and the very respectable Mari Tormes,[3] that if you give me two or three dozen lessons daily on what I must do, I promise that within twenty years I'll turn out as good a knight-errant as there is from the Zocodover to the Alcaná[4] in the imperial city of Toledo."

The soldier and the hermit began to comprehend the nature of the companions with whom they were journeying. Finally, Don Quixote

---

[1] "To the death."

[2] Sancho means *Argamasilla*, of course, but Dulcinea (and her town of El Toboso) is still in the front of his mind.

[3] Maritornes is an Asturian wench who appears a number of times in Cervantes' *Don Quixote*, Part I, starting with Chapter 16. Sancho doesn't remember the exact pronunciation of her name.

[4] Zocodover is a square and Alcaná is a street, both in Toledo.

invited them to supper that night and two other nights that they traveled together, until they drew near to Ateca. As night was falling, he said to them, "Gentlemen, Sancho, my faithful squire, and I are compelled to lodge tonight at the home of a clergyman friend. Come with us, for he is such a kind man and so polite that he will do us all the courtesy of receiving us and lodging us."

Because both of them had lean purses it was not difficult to make them accept, so they went on together toward the village. Before reaching it, Don Quixote asked the hermit his name; he responded that he was friar Esteban, a native of Cuenca, and he had been forced to go to Rome on business. Now he was on his way home where he would be welcomed and might have an opportunity to repay him for his kindness on this journey.

When the soldier was asked his name, he said it was Antonio de Bracamonte; he was from the city of Ávila and related to illustrious people there. After this they arrived together at the village and went directly to the house of Mosen Valentín. When they reached his door Sancho dismounted from his donkey and, going into the entryway, began to call out, "Oh, Mosen What's-your-name! Here are your former guests returning to give you credit and honor, as you begged us to do when we were going to the royal jousts in Zaragoza."

The housekeeper came out with an oil lamp in her hand and upon recognizing Sancho she went running into the house, saying, "Come out, sir; here is our friend Sancho Panza." The clergyman came out holding a candle which he gave to the housekeeper when he saw Don Quixote and Sancho, already dismounted. He went up to Don Quixote and said, embracing him, "You are most welcome, model of knight-errantry, and so is your good and faithful squire, Sancho Panza."

Don Quixote embraced him also, saying "I think, honored licentiate, that it would be a great crime if I did not come to rest and receive hospitatlity in your house when I am passing through this village with this revered man and this excellent soldier, who have been such good company for me."

To this Mosen Valentín reponded by saying, "Although I do not know these gentlemen except to serve them, the fact that they are with you is enough to cause me to do anything I can for them." Turning to Sancho he said, "Well, Sancho, how are things with you?"

Sancho responded, "I'm well and ready to serve you. But is your chestnut mule well? Some very reliable people in Zaragoza told me that she had been very sick with sciatica and colic of the colon, as a result of the great choleric heat she flew into with the doctor's stallion;

and because of it she couldn't swallow a bite of bread."

Mosen Valentín laughed very heartily and replied, "Her indisposition and passion have already disappeared and now she is in the best of health and at your disposal, grateful for your concern." After this he said to the guests, "Come into my home, all of you, and while you rest, supper will be prepared." They all entered and good Mosen Valentín had a very good supper cooked and entertained his friends with much affection and goodwill.

Sancho served at the table and never cleared out the barn, so to speak, because he continually had his mouth full. Mosen Valentín said to him, "What became of the prize, brother Sancho, that you promised to bring me from the jousts at Zaragoza? Is this the way honest men keep their word?"

"I promise you that if we had killed that great giant of a king of Cyprus, Bramidán, I would have brought you as good a one as any giants in the world have had," said Sancho. "However, I believe that before many days we'll reach Cyprus, which can't be very far away now, and after we kill him, leave it to me."

"What giant is that?" asked Mosen Valentín. "Or what Cyprus? Is it some mishap like the adventure with the Moorish melongrower whom you formerly called Bellido de Olfos."

Don Quixote took the lead to answer him, and he related point by point what had happened to them in Zaragoza with the giant in the house of Don Carlos, judge of the ring-lancing contest where he had won in the public plaza some suspenders made from the phoneix bird's skin, and what had happened to him afterward at dawn where his friend, Don Álvaro Tarfe, was staying, and where this same Bramidán had by magic entered surreptitiously to kill treacherously all who were there. Thus he would evade the necessity of appearing for the challenge he had issued for the afternoon of the same day, in the Plaza del Pilar, where the giant feared he would be left vanquished. "But he did leave vanquished, if not from the aforesaid plaza, at least from Don Álvaro's dwelling, where I gave him a thousand blows and thrusts with the lance."

"He gave them to my ribs, by the body of my breeches!" said Sancho. "And they were good ones!"

"Sancho, it was the giant," replied Don Quixote. "Since he couldn't take vengeance on the donkey he settled for the packsaddle."[5]

---

[5] There is a Spanish saying: "He who can't hit the donkey hits his packsaddle," meaning that since the giant couldn't take vengeance on Don Quixote, he took it out on Sancho instead.

"It's true he couldn't reach the donkey because it was in the stable," added Sancho. "However, would to God that when I was beaten by the giant, or you, or the harlot who bore you both, I had had the packsaddle on my back as I did when we came from the melon patch, thoroughly cudgeled, to this very same blessed and priestly house, I, orphaned of my Dapple, you, of Rocinante."

Everybody applauded Sancho's simple remarks and Mosen Valentín, since he already knew Don Quixote's nature, understood what it was all about and told the hermit and the soldier, "I'll stake my life that some jolly knights invented this giant in order to have some fun with Don Quixote."

Sancho, who was behind his chair, heard this and said, "No, sir, don't believe it. I myself, with these eyes I got from my mother at birth, saw him enter through Don Carlos' parlor. Besides, five or six oxen pull the cart holding his armor, and his shield is a huge mill wheel, according to what he says himself. It is impossible to think that such a great personage should lie. On the world maps one reads that every day he eats six or seven bushels of barley."

With this the soldier and the hermit fully realized that Don Quixote's mind was unstable and that Sancho was by nature a simpleton. Mosen Valentín, seeing them looking very attentively at Don Quixote, told the soldier to please state his native region and name, with the objective of avoiding the wild fancies and delusions he feared from Don Quixote if they continued to give an opportunity.

The soldier, who was as discreet and noble as he was accustomed to the military, immediately recognized the target his courteous host was aiming at with the question and said, "My dear sir, I am from the city of Ávila, known and famous throughout Spain for the important persons who have honored and honor her now in letters, virtue, nobility, and arms, for she has had illustrious sons in all these fields. I come now from Flanders where I was led by the honorable tendencies I inherited from my parents which I did not wish to allow to deteriorate, but instead I myself wanted to increase what valor and inclination to war they passed on to me with my first milk. Even though you see me ragged as I am, I belong to the Bracamonte family, so well-known in Ávila that there is nobody who doesn't know that it is related to the best people who bring it fame."

"Were you perchance in Flanders at the time of the siege of Ostend?" said Mosen Valentín.

"Sir, I was there from the day on which it began until the day on which the fortress surrendered," said the soldier. "I could still show you two bullet wounds on my thighs, and this left shoulder half toasted by a fire-bomb thrown by the enemy on four or five of us courageous Spanish soldiers who were trying to make the first assault on the wall. It is quite lucky that we were not finished off."

When supper was over Mosen Valentín ordered the table cleared. After this he and Don Quixote, who began to taste the honey of battle and assault, very appealing subjects to his nature, begged the soldier to tell them something about that stubborn siege. He did so in a fascinating way because he conversed with the same wit in Latin as in Spanish.

Before beginning he ordered a short black cloak to be spread out on the table and a little piece of chalk brought; then he drew on the cloak the plan of the fortress of Ostend, showing quite accurately the position of its fortified towers, which greatly pleased Mosen Valentín because he was a curious man. After this he recited the names of the generals, aides-de-camp, and captains who were at the siege and the number of people who died there, their rank, including the enemy's as well as ours, but which we are not going to set down here because it is not relevant.

We shall relate here only what history recounts at this point about Sancho Panza, which is this: when he had listened very attentively to what the soldier said about Ostend, how very strong it was, how so many aides-de-camp and an infinite number of soldiers had been killed, and how conquering it had cost so much bloodshed, he burst out as nonsensically as usual, saying, "By the body of my maker! Is it possible that there wasn't in all Flanders some knight-errant to thrust his lance through the flanks of that big scoundrel Ostend and split him wide open, so that he wouldn't dare cause such great butchery of our people?"

They all burst into laughter and Don Quixote said to him, "But don't you see, big dunce, that Ostend is a great city in Flanders, located on the seacoast?"

"I must have been talking about tomorrow," said Sancho. "By heaven! I thought it was another huge giant like the king of Cyprus we are going to Court to seek and where we'll run across him unless by some magical means he flees because of fear of us. For days all our affairs have been under such a spell that I'm afraid that some time the bread in our hands, the drink at our lips, and every one of the filthy things in the trunk in which Nature deposited it will be enchanted."

Mosen Valentín interrupted the conversation by rising from the table because he thought it was getting late and if he gave time for the questions and answers of master and squire it would take a thousand evenings. Therefore he said, "Gentlemen, all of you are tired and I think it is time to retire. Señor Don Quixote already knows, from the other time, the room in which he is to sleep; this gentleman and the holy man, since they are traveling companions, will not find it amiss to occupy the same bed. I am obliged to request this because I lack enough beds. Sancho can take this candle and go to remove his master's armor, then go up to his attic. So now let's all go to sleep."

Sancho lighted the way for his master, and the soldier and the hermit followed Mosen Valentín, who paced the parlor hand-in-hand with them a short time, telling them all that had happened to him the other time with Don Quixote. They were surprised, but not as much as if they had not seen how he acted between Zaragoza and this place, getting them into a thousand predicaments with his acts and outrageous words.

With all this in mind they agreed to make every effort next morning to endeavor to find out if they could persuade him to cease that vain and crazy way in which he was behaving, and to urge him with suitable Christian words to do what was best for him: to give up trips and adventures, to return to his village and to his home, and not be willing to die like an animal in some ditch, valley, or field, brained or beaten.

Everybody rested quite comfortably that night, and when morning came they hastened to the business of persuading Don Quixote, but every effort was in vain. Instead, their admonitions gave him a reason to arise earlier (for they caught him in bed so that they could talk to him more calmly) and urgently order Sancho, as he did, to saddle Rocinante, because he wished to depart without eating breakfast.

When Mosen Valentín saw that it was a waste of time to give him advice, he had to keep still. By giving breakfast to everybody he gave Don Quixote the opportunity to do as he wished, which was to leave his house, with his companions, as he did, after all had been bidden farewell most courteously by the honorable clergyman and his housekeeper.

They set out on the road to Madrid, but had gone scarcely three leagues when the sun, which was shining with full force, began to bother them so much that the hermit, who was the most fatigued and the oldest, said, "Gentlemen, since it is excessively hot, as you note, and we have only two short leagues to cover to finish our planned day's journey, I think we could, even should, take a siesta until three or four in the afternoon. Over there, off the road, at the foot of those cool willows there is a lovely spring, if I remember rightly. Later, when the sun has set, we shall go on our way."

All were pleased by the suggestion, so they directed their steps that way. When they came near the aforementioned trees they saw sitting in the shade, two canons from the Sepulcro of Calatayud[6] and an official from the same city. They had just sat down there with the same idea of waiting for the sun's heat to pass. The two came up and the hermit said, greeting them very politely, "With your permission, sirs, these gentlemen and I will sit down in this cool spot to take a little siesta until the severe heat moderates." They replied with signs of pleasure that they would be very happy to have such good company the four or five hours they expected to be there.

One of them, surprised to see that man in armor, whispered to the hermit, asking what he was, to which he replied that he did not know any more than that near Zaragoza he had run into him and that peasant, his servant, a very stupid man. He supposed he had gone mad reading books of chivalry. Because of that madness, so he was informed, he had been roaming about like that for a year, thinking he was one of the knights-errant of old one reads about in such books. If he wanted to have a little fun with him, he should sit down over there and bring up a few chivalric topics and he would hear marvelous things.

At this point Don Quixote and Sancho, who had been removing Rocinante's bridle and Dapple's packsaddle, came up to them. After they had all exchanged greetings, one of the canons told Don Quixote to remove his armor because he was so hot and he was in a secure spot where they were all friends. Don Quixote responded that they should pardon him, for he could never remove it except to go to bed: this was required by the rules of his profession. Then he seated himself gravely and they, seeing his determination, did not try to insist any more. So, after they had discussed for a while whatever pleased him, Don Quixote said, "I think, gentlemen , that since we must stay here four or five hours we should spend the siesta with the entertainment of some good story on any subject you like."

Here Sancho sat down, saying, "If this is the case, I'll tell you some choice tales, for I know some of the finest ones you could ask for. Now listen, for I'm beginning. 'Once upon a time there was, all's well, let evil go away, let good come, in spite of so-and-so. Once upon a time there was a male mushroom and a female mushroom who were going to look for kings under the sea.' "

---

[6] The collegiate church of the Holy Sepulchre in Calatayud, founded in the 12th Centrury. Calatayud is about 50 miles southwest of Zaragoza.

"Fool, stop that," said Don Quixote. "Señor Bracamonte here will kindly start the stories with one worthy of his cleverness, about Flanders or any place he sees fit." The soldier responded that he did not wish to argue or make any excuses, because he desired to do as they wished and at the same time give occasion for one of those gentlemen to tell something strange to make up for anything in the following tragic event.

CHAP. XV. HOW THE SOLDIER ANTONIO DE BRACAmonte begins his story about the hopeless rich man.

In Flanders, in the duchy of Brabant, in a city named Louvain, at the main university of those provinces, there was a young gentleman named Monsieur de Japelin, about twenty-five years old, a good student in both types of law, civil and theological. He was endowed so plentifully with the goods that people call fortune, that there were few in the city who could equal him in wealth.

"At the death of his father and mother the young man remained absolute master of everything. Consequently, with freedom and prodigality (wings which take thriftless young people on a flight, only to dash them down with dangerous omens of an unhappy end) he began to slacken in his studies and get involved with others of his age and endowments in a thousand kinds of vice, never missing an opportunity to attend banquets and drunken parties, very customary in those regions.

"It so happened, then, that while he was engaged in these practices he chanced to go one Sunday in Lent to the temple of the Dominican fathers to hear a sermon preached by a priest eminent in doctrine and in spirit. There God touched the heart of the licentious and negligent listener with the preacher's forceful and virtuous words. He left the church so changed that he began to think about leaving the world with all its vanity and pomp and entering the famous and austere order of the Preaching Friars.

"With this intention he turned over his house and his entire fortune to a relative of his to manage during the few days he planned to be absent on business, with the proviso that he give a faithful accounting upon request. After this he went to Santo Domingo and talked to the priest in charge of the Preaching Friars, unburdening his heart. In short, seeing that he was a man of outstanding qualities and known to everybody because of them, it was easy for him to obtain the habit at once, as in fact happened in the aforesaid monastery.

"He lived there for ten months, very satisfied and showing signs of being an exemplary priest, but our universal adversary (who wanders around like a raging lion, endeavoring to find somebody to swallow up, as the Scriptures say, I don't know where)[1] brought to that university, to the detriment of his conscience, two friends of his who had been away from Louvain for several months. They were no little given to vice and even dubious about religion, a plague which because of our sins has spread over those states and into the neighboring ones.

"When they heard that their friend Japelin had become a Dominican monk they regretted it deeply and proposed going to the monastery to persuade him as urgently as possible to leave the road on which he had started to travel and return to his studies. They did what they had decided to do; that very afternoon they went to see him. Having secured permission from the Prior (because the strictness of keeping the novitiates withdrawn from the world during the year of their novitiate is not observed there as it is in our Spain), they embraced him lovingly and after having said a thousand different pleasant things, the one who must have been the more licentious began to speak to him as follows: 'I am surprised, Monsieur de Japelin, to see that you, so cautious and discreet, a gentleman whom the whole city is watching, have given up your studies, contrary to the hope we all had of seeing you an outstanding university professor before may years, famous not only

[1] In I Peter 5:8: "Your enemy, the devil, like a prowling lion, prowls round looking for someone to devour.

in Louvain but in all the universities in Flanders and even in those of the whole world because of your rare ability. Your admirable intellect and apt memory indicated clearly that you would attain this and everything to which you aspired. What increases the wonderment is that, contrary to the expectation of the entire city and even contrary to your own reputation and that of your relatives, you have chosen to put on a monk's habit as if you were a man lacking in wealth, as if you were a simple, unpretentious person and therefore obliged to make such a profession of poverty. Don't you know, sir, that the most precious thing man has is freedom, and that it is worth more, as the poet says, than the gold in Araby? Well then, why do you want to lose it so easily and be subject to, and slave of, one less endowed and beneath you who will command you tomorrow with kicks. Even the letters and documents we friends write for your consolation will have to pass through his hands before reaching yours. Think it over well, sir, and remember that your father, may he rest in peace, couldn't even bear to see pictures of monks. Therefore, my dear friend, I beg you, by the law of the friendship I owe you, to change your mind and give up this folly, or rather, blindness, and return to your estate; God knows what condition it is in because you aren't there. Go back to your studies. Because you are so outstanding and rich, if you like you can marry one of the beautiful wealthy ladies of this land. In this way you may very well be saved and gladden your relatives who, already considering you dead in life, are very sad because of what you have done. Sir, I do not want to tell you any more to look into your heart; I know that if you do you will realize that I am telling you the truth, as a friend who desires your well-being. Since you entered here no more than ten months ago, you have time to correct the mistake you have started and please those of us who love you. Please us by your departure, for I promise you, on my honor, that you will not regret taking my advice, as time will tell.'

"The young monk, greatly confused and melancholy, gazed at the floor and remained silent to all that the devil's minister was saying to him. At last, because he was weak and not well-grounded on matters of perfection and the mortification of his appetites, the frivolous words and foul advice given him by that false friend and true enemy of his welfare convinced him. So, he responded, 'I certainly realize, my dear sir, that all you have said is very true. I am already so regretful about what I have done that more than a week ago I would have left this monastery, except for the gossip and my own reputation. Nevertheless I have decided to follow the counsel and opinion of one who so disppassionately and earnestly tells me what is right for me. In short, I am determined to ask for my clothes this very day and return to my house and estate, for I realize now what they mean to me. There is nothing for you to do except leave and expect me for supper at your inn tonight, sure that I won't fail to be at the supper. However, I beg you to keep this decision of mine secret.' Embracing him with visible joy at the good news, they took their leave.

"The deluded young man went straight to the Prior's cell and told him to order his secular clothing returned immediately, because it was important for his standing to return to his house and estate. Besides this, he could not bear the hardships of the order: to wear wool, not eat meat, get up for matins every night, and do the other things that are practiced. In addition to this, he lied to him about having promised to marry a lady and said he was forced to keep his word by marrying her, obliged by his conscience and the fact that he had received pledges of her honor.

"The Prior was not a little astonished when he heard what the novice was telling him and he replied, filled with amazement, 'I am surprised, Monsieur de Japelin, at your indiscretion and that the spiritual exercises in which you have taken part for ten months as a monk and the good counsel I have always given you as a father have been of so little benefit to you. Don't you remember, son, having heard me say many times that you must be on guard, especially during this year of the novitiate, because the devil would wage cruel war against you at this time, trying with all his astuteness and strong persuasion, as he has now done, to make you leave the order and return to the fleshpots of Egypt,[2] because that's what this thing of returning to the confusion of the world is? He knows that there he can more easily deceive you and make you fall into grave sin in which you will lose not only the life of your body but also, what is worse, the life of your soul. Also remember, son, that you have heard me say that up to now nobody who has taken off the habit he once put on as a monk has come to a good end, because it is God's righteous judgment that if one called to a divine vocation in His service later in his life leaves it, God himself will leave him at his death. This is what he told such people through his prophet: *Vocavi, et rerenuistis ego; quoque in interitu vestro ridebo.*[3] It is true

---

[2] Exodus 15:3.

[3] Proverbs 1:24 and 26: "But because you refused to listen when I called . . . I in turn will laugh at your doom."

that I myself have seen a thousand of these trials and, may it please God, as I beg him, not to carry out his divine justice on your ingratitude and hasty decision. I fear it because I see you so deceived by the devil, for the excuses you are giving me clearly show that they are not forged in any blacksmith's shop other than the infernal one in which he lives. Observe that you need not be surprised if at first you find the hardships you mention in the order, because, as the philosopher says, all beginnings, especially those of arduous tasks, are difficult. After the children of Israel crossed the Red Sea with dry feet they sent certain spies to reconnoiter the land of promise toward which they were traveling. The spies returned with a huge bunch of grapes, so large that it could only be carried on a stick on the shoulders of two strong soldiers, and they said, 'Friends, this is the fruit produced by the land that we are going to conquer, but know that the men who defend it are as tall as pine trees,'[4] which meant that at the start the conquest of that extremely fertile land was difficult, its inhabitants being giants. That is what has happened to you, my son, at the beginning of your conversion; God has permitted you to notice the present hardships with which he intends to test your perseverence, with the aim of obliging you to turn only to him to ask for help in coming out victorious. However, I see that you have surrendered to your enemies at the first encounter, letting them tie your hands without turning to the one who has very generous hands ready to help you. Your coming to ask me for your clothes with such blind determination originates from this. In the name of the passion Christ suffered for you, I beg you, beloved Japelin, to do one thing for me which is refrain for three or four days and pray to God during that time; for my part, I promise to do the same with all the monks in this house. You will see that His Majesty will show you mercy, making you come out victorious in this infernal temptation.'

"All these reasonings put forth by the holy Prior to the uneasy novice did not suffice to turn him from his intention. Instead, he said to him, 'There is no more give or take about this matter, my dear father, for I am resolved to do what I said; I have thought about it and considered it all very carefully.'

"In fact he did leave the monastery that night and, as planned, went straight to the inn where his two friends were expecting him for

---

[4] Based on Numbers 13: 27-29: "We made our way into the land to which you sent us. It is flowing with milk and honey, and here is the fruit it grows; but its inhabitants are sturdy . . . "

supper. They gave him a sumptuous banquet and repeatedly toasted each other very contentedly. After this Japelin again took possession of his estate and began once more to follow blindly his companions' way of life, going with them day and night, and there was not in the entire city a banquet or festival at which the three dissolute young men were not to be found.

"It so happened that he went one day to a distantly related gentleman to talk over something to which he had given a great deal of thought. This man had an extremely beautiful, prudent, and rich niece. Japelin asked for her hand in marriage, remembering that before he became a monk he had already courted her on many occasions, with demonstrations of affection, at a convent of nuns to which she had been entrusted. When the gentleman saw what a good marriage this would be for his niece, because Japelin was her equal in every way, he was as pleased as she was and promised her to him.

"It had not been a full month since she, too, had been taken by this same uncle from the nunnery in which, as has been said, she was entrusted to the care of the abbess, a cousin of hers. She had not consented to becoming a nun as her parents had wished and tried to bring about when they were alive, by having her brought up in the cloister from childhood.

"In fact, these two, newly released from their convent and monastery, did get married with great festivities and universal rejoicing. They had been married three years when she conceived, and her husband was beside himself with joy when he learned she was pregnant. There was no gift in the world too good for his wife; he cherished her and showed her great respect and consideration, treating her with incredible vigilance and a thousand endearments.

"When she had been pregnant six months, it happened that an uncle of this gentleman died; he was governor of a village named Cambray, within the confines of Flanders. When the nephew learned about it he left for the court at Brussels, where very reluctantly (considering his talents and his uncle's good service) they gave him that governorship which he went at once to claim, planning to return later to get his household and possessions.

"Before his departure, he took leave of his wife, to the great sadness of both, and he said to her, 'My dear lady, I am going to settle the affairs of my deceased uncle, the governor, and collect the estate which I have inherited upon his death. This is something that I cannot postpone, as you know. From there I intend to go to Brussels to apply for his post and ask Their Majesties to be kind enough to grant it because of my uncle's good service; I believe this will be easy to obtain. What I beg you to do is take care of yourself during this absence and as soon as you give birth let me know so that I may attend the baptism, which I shall not fail to do. I believe the sight of you will give me as much joy as the sight of the son or daughter you will bear.'

"She promised to do as he said, and kissing her a thousand times he told her goodby, shedding loving tears, and departed for Cambray. There and in Brussels his claim (which has been mentioned) was settled much to his satisfaction; his business delayed his return home some three months. Before he could get back, the lady was seized with labor pains; as soon as she felt them she sent a courier to her husband, urging him to come because at the time of writing, everything pointed to the fact that the day of the birth had arrived. Japelin delayed mounting his horse and starting on his way home no longer than it took him to read the longed-for letter.

"On the road near the city of Louvain he met a Spanish soldier and, catching up with him, he inquired where he was going. After the soldier replied that he was going to Antwerp to have a good time with some friends who had sent for him, and that he belonged to the garrison in the castle at Cambray, Japelin kept on questioning him as they went along and asked him all sorts of things about how the soldiers spent their time at the castle. The soldier answered everything prudently because he was quite experienced even if he was a youth.

"As they were reaching the city gates, Japelin said, 'Soldier, if you don't have to go any farther tonight you may, if you like, come home with me where I'll give you lodging. Although it may not be as good as your valor merits, you will at least have the good wishes of this servant of yours, owner of a fair house and enough income to keep it up with the necessary furnishings and luxury you will see in it. You must realize that I am very fond of the Spanish nation, and the fact that you are from there, together with your natural gifts, oblige me to show this generosity; you will rest and in the morning you can resume your journey more comfortably because it will have been preceded by a reasonably restful night.'

"The soldier replied that he was quite grateful to him for the offer and for the kindness with which it was made, and he thanked him a thousand times. He would be exceeding the bounds of courtesy his ancestry professed if he refused to accept the invitation, so he resolved to stay in Louvain that night even though by doing so he might lose the advantage of his day's journey.

"Chatting like this they reached the much-desired door of Japelin's house, from which a maid-servant happened to come out. When she saw him she went running back up the stairs without saying a word to him, clapping her hands with joy and saying in surprise, 'Monsieur de Japelin, monsieur de Japelin!' With this she descended again to her master with the same signs of satisfaction, saying, 'Good news, sir, good news! This evening my mistress bore a son as lovely as a thousand flowers.'

"At the news he dismounted and as swiftly as the wind and went up the stairs in two bounds, and because of his joy did not take the time to show the soldier the customary civilities. Once in the room he saw his wife in bed and going up to her he greeted her and kissed her many times, saying, 'My love, thank heaven a million times for the favor it has now shown us by giving us a son who, since he will inherit our wealth, may be the staff of our old age, the consolation for our troubles, and joy in all our afflictions.' Upon this he sat down in a chair by the head of the bed, still holding her hand, and the two of them chatted, now about the trip and successful outcome of his business affairs, now about the happy birth, and household matters.

"At nightfall he ordered a table to be placed next to the bed because he wanted to have supper with his wife. Then he immediately had the soldier summoned to join them both at supper, which he did most courteously. However, his eyes did not show due modesty when he looked at the lady, because from the moment he saw her he thought she was the loveliest creature he had seen in all Flanders. (And she actually was, according to what I was told by those who related the story to me, and they were people who knew her.)

"An abundant supper was brought but the Spaniard, who had feasted his eyes on the beauty of the new mother and the charming way in which she was sitting up in bed with her bosom somewhat exposed (because in this respect Flemish women are freer than our Spanish women), ate very little, and that with visible uneasiness.

"When supper was over and the table cleared Japelin ordered his page to bring his clavichord,[5] which he played extremely well, for in those days it was as common for gentlemen and ladies to play this instrument as it is in Spain today to play the harp or vihuela.[6] When it

---

[5] The clavichord is a 'portable harpsichord'; it was about 12" by 42" in size and had a range of about four and a half octaves.

[6] The *vihuela* is a smaller predecessor to the modern guitar.

was brought and tuned he began to play and sing the following verses very melodiously. He himself was the author, for he had, as has been said, a fine mind and was versed in all kinds of knowledge:

Instrument, glorify
  The fact that changeable time
  Cannot alter my happiness
  Nor make me miserable with its forces,
  For today, rejoicing,
  A beautiful angel has given me a beautiful son.

Fortune raised me
  To the most stable part of her wheel;
  And although she is like the moon,
  My luck commands her to be still
  And hold it steady,
  And show her power in my favor.

And so, my dear lady,
  Don't fear that she will ever change our happiness,
  Because this day
  Heaven itself chooses to multiply us;
  For that is the meaning of our joining
  Two into one in order to better love each other.

There is no doubt I was lucky
  When two friends advised me
  Not to become a monk;
  For the pleasures I enjoy are witnesses
  To the fact that their sad fate
  In life pairs them with death.

It is right, since I am rich,
  For me to live happily, eat, and enjoy myself,
  And for the iniquitous miser
  Always to fear me and never be my equal,
  For in peace and in war I can
  Honor the most noble on this earth.

For me to live without anxieties
  For yet a thousand years, free of worries,
  Is right, since my surplus
  Is envied by many of the most prominent people,
  Seeing that my income is
  More than ten thousand a year at least.

And above all this,
  My arm, my fortune, and lucky star
  Today poured forth all they had left
  By giving me a son by a beautiful goddess;
  Because of them, I, noble and young,
  Enjoy a thousand congratulations and joys.

"The music ended with the song and the Spaniard's uneasiness began to increase by the minute, because of having heard the very soft tones issuing from the throat of the rich Flemish man who possessed the angel for whom he was afire.

"When the song came to an end, a page entered at his master's order, to remove the clavichord, for it was already late and time to allow the soldier to rest. So he could do so, Japelin then ordered another servant to take one of the candlesticks from the table and light his way to the first room of the quarters where his valet usually slept, which was next to the room where the lady was in bed. He also gave him orders for the housekeeper to have a good breakfast prepared for that fine soldier so that he could leave Louvain at daybreak and make the day's journey without halting, since his saddlebag would be packed and he would leave after breakfasting.

"Most grateful for this thoughtfulness and for the kindness and hospitality shown by the gentleman and his wife, the soldier took leave with a thousand cordial remarks. Once he was in bed in his room the recollection of the beautiful angel he adored was like a battery of artillery firing on him until he was completely beside himself. He reproached himself for his boldness, picturing the impossibility of the affair to which he aspired, and tried to put out of his mind such an idea as the one which was destroying his tranquility.

"A short time after the soldier had retired the gentleman did likewise, taking leave of his wife with mutual display of love one could expect after such a long absence, with due decorum because of the recent birth. In order not to be tempted to the contrary Japelin went into another room, beyond the one where the new mother was.

"The page who took the soldier off to bed and, thinking that he was tired, said that for the sake of not obliging him to spend a bad night he would go to another room to sleep with other servants. Thus the soldier could rest without fear of his return, and he could do so better alone; for the same reason his master also had a separate bed and had retired in an inner room.

"With this he went away, leaving the lovesick Spaniard more agitated by his last remarks, because, hearing that the lady was sleeping alone and so near him, unaccompanied in the room, gave rise to the diabolical decision he made, an offense against God, disloyalty to his ancestry, and an affront to the honorable hospitality shown him by his noble host, because the passionate fire of raging lust in which he burned was rushing him into such action.

"Accordingly, he resolved to leave his bed and go to the lady's without being heard, sure that she, for the sake of her honor, and in order not to cause her husband grief and upset the house, would be silent. She might even become so fond of him that when her husband went away she would allow him free entrance and entertain him. Although he meditated on the danger to his life he was running if she should happen to scream (as was right), for the husband would undoubtedly come out and they would kill each other, all of which would be followed by exceptional scandal and serious trouble, still his great obsession blinded him to all these obstacles.

"Consequently he arose at midnight, in his undershirt, entered the lady's room and, coming up to her barefooted so he could not be heard, he remained standing a short time, not quite making up his mind, but he decided to go to his room and get his sword. He unsheathed it and went back very softly to the Flemish woman's bed; laying down the sword, he stretched out his hand and put it very gently under the sheets, then laid it on the lady's breast. She awakened at once, startled. Seizing his hand, and thinking that it was her husband (for she could not imagine anyone else in the world daring to do such a thing) she said to him, 'Is it possible, my dear lord, that as prudent a man as you should leave his room and bed at this hour to come to mine, knowing that I bore a child last night and therefore am unable to respond to what you have in mind? By my life, sir, have a little forbearance. Since I am so truly yours, and you are my husband and lord, there will be time after I am in my normal condition for me to respond to whatever you wish, for I owe it to you by wifely laws.'

"She had not finished these modest words when the soldier kissed her on the face without saying a word. She said to him, still thinking he was her husband, 'I am well aware, sir, that you are quite ashamed of what you plan to do, for this is the reason you don't dare answer one word. I also realize that such an intention as this comes from the very great love you have for me, and because of the continence due to such a long absence. If it were not so, you would not have left your bed to come to mine, knowing you would find me in the condition you do find me.'

"Upon hearing these words and deducing from them the lady's misapprehension, he quietly lifted the bedcovers and got into the bed, where he satiated his unmanageable appetite, because when she realized his determination she did not wish to cross him so as not to anger him, for she thought him her husband although she was not a little amazed when he did not speak.

"The act completed, he arose without saying anything, picked up his sword as silently as he could and returned to his room and bed, quite grief-stricken over what he had done. Since guilt is followed by repentance and sin by shame and worry, he was at once so overwhelmed by his evil that he cursed his lack of reasoning and patience, and his accursed decision, thinking about the crime he had committed and the danger he was in if the husband happened to arise before he did.

"The lady was also assailed by her thoughts; it worried her that the one who had been with her had not said a word, whether it could have been her husband or not. But she decided it must have been he and that shame over having done so indecent a thing at a time when she was not ready for such jokes, must have made him keep his mouth shut. In view of all this, she planned (and she should not have) in her heart to give him a loving scolding next morning for what he had done, condemning his lack of continence.

"When the first light of dawn was barely visible, the soldier arose; he had not been able to close his eyes because of his remorse at what he had done. The lady was still sleeping, so he asked the first servants he ran across to open the door and make his excuses to their master for not accepting the breakfast and provisions which had been prepared, because his haste to get started on the day's journey did not allow him time to delay, nor did his obligations permit him to increase the many he already owed that household. Although the servants insisted, attempting to put into his saddlebag what they had prepared for breakfast, there was no way to make him consent. He said it was not his nature to go laden down and they must excuse him; besides, a league away there was a famous hostelry where he planned to stop and eat breakfast. Hereupon he took leave of them and left the place."

CHAP. XVI. IN WHICH BRACAMONTE FINISHES THE story of the hopeless rich man.

HE CANONS and city officials listened attentively to that story and Don Quixote did also, although from time to time he gave signs of wanting to say something in contradiction to the bad advice the students gave Japelin when he was a novice. He wanted to praise the good choice he had made in marrying a beautiful woman, and especially to praise his courage in having aspired to take up the science of war in pursuit of his uncle's governorship, but each time the venerable hermit beside him interrupted him.

However, as he was not at Sancho's side, he could not prevent him from bursting out when he heard about the rascality of the soldier, especially about his lack of guts in not taking the provisions the servants had prepared for his future needs. Therefore he said, with amusing anger, "I swear by God and this cross that the great knave deserved more blows than my Dapple has hairs, and that if I had him here I'd chew him up alive. Where did the great son of a bitch learn not to take what was given him, although it's true that it is not prohibited, I don't mean for soldiers and kings, but not even knights-errant themselves, who are the best in the world? Upon my soul, I believe he is more likely to burn in Hell for that sin than for all the stabs he has given Lutherans and Moors. However, I am not surprised that the conceited fellow was so inconsiderate and thought it over so little if, as you say, he came from Cambray, because I swear by the age of the giant Goliath that that must be the worst country in the world. According to what people say, in the streets and plazas, children and adults, men and women, do not gather up bread and wine nor anything of the sort, but cheesecloth,[1] and because of this they are constantly moaning, which is a sign it must be very bad and must cause cramps in all who eat it."

The canons and Bracamonte laughed at these silly remarks but Don Quixote did not. He said with a gloominess and sorrow worthy of his honorable earnestness, "Stop weeping, Sancho, my son, over the soldier's carelessness and lack of prudence, and whether the moaning you mention comes from the accursed fibers gathered in Cambray or not. Shed bloody tears for the offense and wrong done that noble princess, and for the offense and stain which fell on the famous Japelin's honor through intention or lack of consideration or, most likely, the wickedness of that soldier, a dishonor to our Spain, and a disgrace to the entire military profession which so many nobles, I among them, try to improve at the cost of the noble blood in our veins. However, if I run across him, as I hope to do, I shall let the treacherous blood out of his veins."

"You are free from this responsibility," said Bracamonte, "as you will see if you are patient enough to listen to the rest of the story." They all begged Don Quixote to restrain his justifiable anger, and asked Sancho to be quiet and not try to ascertain what he would hear about. Both promised this very faithfully with a few oaths, and Bracamonte took up the thread of his story.

"When the soldier had left hastily and filled with fear and shame, as related before, the noble, carefree Japelin came out of his room at the hour when the bustle of the household announced it was time to get up. He went up to his wife's bed to say good morning and, concerned to find out what sort of night she had had, he assured her that because of his pleasure at being in his own bed and having an heir, he had scarcely been able to rest.

"His wife laughed at the excuses he was offering, and when he took her white hand she laughingly pretended to be angry and pulled her arm away, saying, 'Certainly, my dear lord, you know how to pretend prettily, and that tongue of yours is going very fast when last night

[1] There is a play on words here based on *Cambray* (the old spelling of the French town Cambrai), which in Spanish is also a fine linen fabric. Cheesecloth, of course, is at the opposite end of the scale.

you were so mute to me. Go away, God bless you, and don't speak to me all day at least, for I'll certainly need that much time to get over my very justifiable anger with you. Even after that, you'll have to beg my pardon, and it won't be granted easily.'

"Japelin laughed at this coolness and, thinking it was funny, kissed her on the face in spite of her, and said, 'By my life, lady, tell me what I have done to anger you; I'll be very glad to find out, although I more or less suspect that it must be because you imagined I slept with somebody here, thus wronging you. And may I die in sin if I have ever even in thought been unfaithful, so get that wild idea out of your head, I beg you, for it offends me not a little.'

"She said again, 'You certainly know how to conceal and deny now what you should rightly have denied your appetite before, acting so inconsiderately, for otherwise a man as prudent and discreet as you are would not have done what your inordinate desire demanded against all reason. I am quite ashamed that you are not more so about coming to my bed last night to lie with me when you were aware of my condition. I regret very much that my justifiable pleading carried so little weight with you that it did not oblige you to return to your bed and not get into mine with the affectionate excesses of our wedding-night. And, making matters worse, you left me without saying a word, although I attribute your silence to the deserved embarrassment caused by your boldness. I am aware, sir, that you will say it arose from your excessive love for me, and although it may seem reason enough to you, I do not accept it. You should have considered the time and my indisposition and have respected and endured such an obstacle; the world wouldn't have been lost had you been continent seven or eight days longer, at the most. But let this pass, for my great love forgives you and hopes for a change in the future.'

"It is impossible to picture how amazed Japelin was when he heard his wife say such words so earnestly and in such detail. As he had a keen mind he immediately suspected all that could have happened, imagining (which was the truth) that the Spanish soldier must have slept alone because of the heedlessness of the guardian page he thought would be in the room with him and not leave him alone. Hence, given the opportunity, which is the mother of grave wickedness, he must have committed that crime in cunning silence. Therefore, dissembling as best he could, he said to the lady, 'Let's say no more, my love, by the life of your loved ones. The intemperance about which you complain originated in my excessive love for you, but on my word as a gentleman, I promise to reform and even to avenge you completely for it all.' Turning aside and boiling with rage he muttered, 'Oh, base and treacherous soldier! By holy heaven I swear not to return home without seeking you all over the world and tearing you to pieces when I find you.'

"After this, concealing his rage with notable cunning, he took leave of his wife, pretending to have important business to attend to. Then he called aside a servant, telling him, 'Without saying anything, saddle the Spanish sorrel for me, for I have to leave shortly.' While the horse was being saddled he finished dressing, went into the room where he kept an assortment of weapons and took out a large javelin. The lady saw it and asked him suspiciously what he intended to do with the javelin.

" 'I want to send it to a neighbor of ours who asked yesterday to borrow it,' he said.

" 'What neighbor of ours can that be who doesn't have any weapons in his house and needs to come to ours for them?' she replied. 'In truth, my love, if you won't take it amiss, you must tell me what it's about.'

"He responded that it was none of her affair but that she would know all about it in a few hours. After this he left the room, a changed expression on his face, heaving sighs, and went downstairs where he began walking about in front of the stable, waiting for the horse to be saddled.

"During the time the servant took to do this, he kept saying to himself in furious despair, 'Oh, perverse and base Spaniard! How badly you have paid me for the good turn I did you by giving you lodging, which I should not have done! Wait, traitor, adulterer at the cost of my deluded wire's innocence! I swear, on her life and that of my son, and mine, that your perfidy will cost you yours. Fly, infamous man, take to your heels, for I shall make my horse's feet equal the intent with which I set out in search of you with the determination of not returning to my native land until I find you, even though you hide in the innermost recesses of the Sicilian Etna itself.'

"No sooner had he said these words than the servant, who had heard them all when he was in the stable, brought out the horse, which Japelin mounted, swift as the wind, saying that everybody should stay and nobody accompany him, because he needed no companionship on the short trip on which he was going. Taking the javelin he left home a madman, spurring the horse and heading him along the road in the direction he thought the soldier was going, leaving the servants in his house bewildered by his fury and the sudden trip which took him away. From what the one who saddled the horse said he had heard, they concluded that he was going in pursuit of the soldier because he had stolen something from the house or because he had said some immodest words to his wife, and that because he was so jealous and noble he intended to take vengeance on the one the mere thought of whom offended him.

"The gentleman, in short, rode after the soldier with such skill that he overtook him within an hour. He pulled down his hat before he came even with him so that he wouldn't be recognized. In the middle of a valley, without the soldier's suspecting it or there being any witnesses who could report the circumstances of his violent death, the strong and offended Japelin, without giving him time to take a hand to defend himself from the sudden attack, plunged the broad blade or sharp iron of the Milanese javelin into his back as swiftly as he could, without saying a word, so that it projected more than two spans in front, in view of the lascivious eyes which had been set on Japelin's very chaste wife. The wretched Spaniard fell to the ground at once."

"Oh, may God and good Saint John wish him well!" said Don Quixote. "That fellow certainly was a fine gentleman; in truth he can thank his excellent diligence for getting ahead of me in taking vengeance for that crime. If he hadn't, I vow by the victory I expect to win soon over the King of Cyprus, that I should have taken such unheard-of revenge that it would have thrown terror in the very noses of the wretched and heinous sodomites burned up by God."

"Well, upon my word, sir, if you didn't do it," said Sancho, "I should have hastened to do my duty, and if that business of Sodom and Gorroma which you mention had failed, I should have drowned him in a flood of phlegm like that of Noah's time."

"But the tragedy doesn't end with this," said Bracamonte. "Nor does the vengeance taken on the soldier by Japelin, because later, after what has been told, he dismounted, pulled the javelin out of the corpse and stabbed it again five or six times, hacking its head to pieces. All was done with inexplicable cruelty; he justly paid with the death of his two lives[2] (as may be supposed), and with so bitter an end, for the small pleasure of his unbridled appetite. The soldier remained there, trampled in his own blood, food for birds and beasts, as an example to bold decisions.

"Somewhat consoled by the vengeance he had taken on his offender, as described, the gentleman slowly returned home. In the

---

[2] His body *and* his soul.

time that he was away, as ill luck would have it, his wife questioned a page about him, because it was after ten o'clock and she did not see him, nor did she know where he was. The indiscreet page answered her at once, saying, 'Madam, my master rode off, javelin in hand, more than two hours ago, without any attendant, and we can't imagine where he went or why. I only know that he was pale and sighing somewhat as he gazed heavenward.'

"As they were talking thus a stableboy, a servant, and the wetnurse came up, and the stableboy said, 'My lady, you must know that something is terribly wrong, because my master kept walking up and down in front of the stable-door the whole time I was saddling the horse. He was sighing and complaining about that Spanish soldier who slept last night in the valet's room and bed, calling him (although I believe he thought nobody heard him) perverse, and a base traitor and adulterer who had cost his deceived wife her innocence. After this he swore on his life, your life, and that of his son, that he would follow him until he overtook him and tore him to pieces, but I never heard him complain about you; rather, from what he said it seems to me he was excusing you. After this, when I led the horse out he mounted and left home in a flash to search for him,'

"When the noble Flemish woman heard the last words of this suspicious news she fell in a mortal swoon onto the pillow from the arms of the servant who had gotten her up and seated her on the bed. She came to in a little while and began to weep bitterly, suspecting (as was true) that the one who had come to her bed the night before had been, without a doubt, the Spanish soldier, with whom she had committed adultery, thinking he was her spouse. At this point she began to berate her fortune, saying, 'Traiterous, perverse, and adulterous person that I am! How shall I be able to look at my noble, beloved husband when I have taken from him in one instant the honor he had because of his own valor and as an inheritance of his natural nobility? Oh, blind and foolish woman! How is it possible you didn't recognize that the one who was getting into your bed was not your husband, but some treacherous person like the false Spaniard! Unhappy one that I am! With what countenance shall I dare face my dear Japelin, for without a doubt he will not believe me even though I swear a thousand times that I am innocent, because I allowed other feet to violate his honorable marriage bed? Sweet husband of mine, henceforth you can justly complain about me and refuse me the loving kindness you used to show me in return for the great love I always declared I had for you: I shall be hateful in your eyes (since I have belied my faithfulness, even though I am guiltless as heaven knows), abhorrent to your ears, insipid to your taste, irritating to your pleasure, and finally, useless for everything which is to your advantage. Return quickly, my dear lord, if perchance you have gone to kill the adulterous Spaniard, and pierce this unwittingly disloyal breast with the same javelin with which you punished him. Since I was an accomplice in the adultery, it is just for me to be his equal in death. Come, I say, and, secure in the knowledge that your guilty wife will not resist you, take full vengeance for my lack of prudence. However, it is not right for me to wait for you to come and take revenge or punish me with the point of the javelin; it is fitting for me to avenge you, so that you may say that you are avenged for my perfidy as well as for the offense done.'

"So saying, the despairing lady (in this state because of passion, anger, and shame) leaped from the bed, tearing her blond, well-dressed braids, her pure cheeks shining with a heavy flood of tiny dewdrops falling from her clouded eyes. She put on a skirt and began to pace the room with such faltering steps, accompanied by sighs, sobs, and laments over what had happened, that all those in the house could not console her; instead, her sorrow moved them to such pity that they were all in need of consolation.

"Well, as I say, with things in this state, they disturbed, the husband absent, the adulterer dead, and she beside herself, she went out into the patio in full view of everybody. After repeating anew the lamentations already mentioned, she threw herself head first into a deep well which was in the center of the patio, without any of those present being able to help her. Her head was crushed into two thousand pieces, so that when her body reached the bottom—a very different place from the one I should like my body to be in at the hour of my death—her soul had already been freed from it. The cries and screams of the household increased the new and mournful spectacle; in the confusion some hurried to look in the well, others went clamoring into the street, and with all this, everything was in an uproar. In an instant the house was filled with sorrowing people, all busy either consoling the household or throwing in ropes and cords, although in vain, thinking they could help one no longer able to be helped.

"In the midst of this general disturbance the unfortunate Japelin happened to reach home. Not knowing the misfortune that had just occurred there, and marveling at seeing so many people gathered in the patio, some standing on the curbstone of the well, others around it, and all weeping, he rode in with the bloodstained javelin in his hand. When he asked what was the matter, the servants came up wringing their hands and clawing at their faces, saying, 'Alas, master, the greatest misfortune anyone alive has ever seen has just occurred, for the mistress, we don't know why, lamenting about that accursed Spaniard who slept in the house last night, and saying she was deceived and adulterous and uttering words which would have moved a rock to pity, and tearing out her hair in handfuls, threw herself into this deep well before we could prevent it, where she was broken into pieces before reaching the bottom.'

Hearing such news, the gentleman remained stunned, not saying a word for a long time; then, a little later, having recovered he threw himself from the horse, and casting himself on the ground, began to mourn bitterly, sighing and tearing his beard with incredible sorrow, saying, in the presence of everybody, 'Alas, my darling wife! What is this? Why did you abandon me? How could you leave me, alone, unavenged, and not take me with you? Alas, my dear wife and my love! How were you to blame if that hated Spaniard deceived you, pretending to be your beloved husband? He alone was to blame, but he has already paid the penalty. Alas, my dearly beloved! How can I live a whole day without seeing you? Where have you gone, my beloved lady? If you had just waited until I returned from avenging you, as I now return, and had killed yourself then, I would have accompanied you in death as I have done in life. Woe is me! What shall I do? Unhappy one that I am! Where shall I go or what decision shall I make? But I have already made up my mind.'

"Saying this, he got up furiously, took hold of his sword and said, 'I swear in the name of the true God that anyone who tries to prevent me from doing what I am going to do will feel the edge of my sharp sword, whoever he may be.' Thereupon he went to the curbstone of the well, uttering a great cry of lamentation, and said, 'Oh, my dear wife! If you despaired for no reason and your spirit is where I cannot accompany you unless I imitate you by dying, it will be right and just, since I loved and desired you in life, for me not to try to be eternally where you are not; therefore don't fear, my darling sweetheart, that I shall tarry in joining you.'

"Since there were quite a few people there, among them many of the city's gentlemen and nobles, they heard what he said. Lest there be some disaster they went up to him in an attempt to console him. Lying on his breast on the curbstone of the well he listened; a little later, turning his head he saw the wetnurse crying bitterly with the child in her arms. Going up to her, with diabolic fury he snatched him from her, seizing him by the swaddling band, and hit him three or four times against the curbstone, breaking his head and arms into two thousand pieces. This despairing decision caused incredible pity and fright in everybody, although nobody dared approach him, fearing his diabolical fury. Thereupon he began to beat his head, saying, 'The son of such an unfortunate father and unhappy mother should not live; neither should the memory of a man like me.'

"So saying, he began to call his wife and say, 'My lady and my love, if you are not in heaven, neither do I desire heaven or paradise, for I shall be most comforted wherever you are, and it is impossible for the punishment of hell to affect me if I am with you, because my happiness is only to be found where you are. I am coming, my lady, wait, wait!' Hereupon, with nobody able to restrain him, he threw himself headfirst into the well, also breaking his head into a thousand pieces, his lifeless body falling upon that of his unfortunate wife.

"Again the weeping of all those present was renewed, again cries were raised to heaven and the house and street were filled with people all marveling at such an event. At the news the governor of the city came at once, learned about the sad event and had the bodies taken out of the well and carried, with the bishop's approval, to a forest near the city, where they were burned and the ashes thrown into a brook which flowed nearby."

Sancho spoke up saying, "In truth, Master Bracamonte needs to wet his gullet, because he has dried it out so much recounting the life and death, obsequies, and end of the life-span of the whole Flemish family of that gentleman destined to come to an unhappy end. I renounce vengeance to him, and my spirit to Saint Peter."

"Sancho is not wrong," said one of the canons. "The sad end of all the main characters in that tragedy is very much to be feared, but the principal actors could expect nothing better (morally speaking), since they had given up the religious orders which they had started to join. As the Prior told the courtier so plainly when he wished to leave the convent, it is a wonder if those who leave it end up well."

"To tell the truth, if Señor Japelin's life had ended as well as the way he honorably put an end to that of the adulterous soldier, I would give half the kingdom of Cyprus which I am to conquer to be in his shoes, because if I died, not in despair, as he did, but in some battle, I would be in the greatest glory; after all, *un bel morir toda la vida honora*,"[2] said Don Quixote.

---

[3] A Hispanified version of Petrarch's line: "A beautiful death honors the whole life."

Sancho tried to start out on another story and the canons and his master prevented it, saying he could tell it later because now it was necessary to show respect for the religious habit of that venerable hermit by giving him the first turn. In consequence, they begged him to consent and tell them something less melancholy than the previous story and not put the souls of all the characters in hell, as happened in the other story, because it had saddened them very much, although they all praised the diligent soldier for his good presentation of the tale and the propriety and modesty he had shown in dealing with matters which in themselves were rather shameful.

The hermit tried to decline, but, seeing it was in vain, and requiring that no one break the thread of his story, began the following one, entirely different from the one just told, especially the ending.

CHAP. XVII. IN WHICH THE HERMIT BEGINS HIS STORY *about the happy lovers.*[1]

NEAR THE walls of one of the outstanding cities in Spain, there is a convent of nuns of a certain order, in which there was one, among others, who was so religious that she was no less known for her modesty and virtues than she was for her rare beauty. Her name was Luisa, and her virtue kept on increasing daily until she became so famous because of her prayers, penitence, and reclusion that when she was twenty-five years old the nuns of the convent, by common consent, chose her as their Mother Super-

[1] Avellaneda here begins one of the most detailed and interesting versions of the story of the runaway nun. King Alfonso X, in his *Cantigas de Santa María* includes five miracles having to do with nuns who forsook their convents or attempted to.

ior. She set such an example and was so prudent in the management of this office that all who knew her and had dealings with her considered her an angel from heaven.

"It so happened one afternoon that a rich, gallant, and discreet young man named Don Gregorio was in the locutory talking to a relative of his when the Prioress came in. He knew her well because as children they had been raised together and had even been innocently in love with each other, since their parents lived in neighboring houses.

"When he saw her he arose, hat in hand, asking about her health and begging her to accept the attentions he enjoyed doing in her service. She said to him, 'Don Gregorio, you are most welcome. Let's hear the latest news from your lips, since we already know your worth from the works of mercy you show us.'

" 'No such thing,' he replied, 'can be shown to *you* by one who was born only to serve, even though it be only the dogs of this blessed house, nor do I have any news to give, because it can't be news to you that the reason for my frequent visits is the obligation I owe my cousin. I am here today because a relative is sending you a note requesting you to give her I don't know what sort of sugar figures in exchange for eight yards of an excellent goat's-hair or striped woolen cloth she is sending you.'

" 'That's all right with me,' said the Prioress. 'However, you will still have to do me a work of mercy: after finishing with Doña Catalina, please take this note to my sister for me; you know which convent, because I have only one sister, a nun. I am expecting some silk flowers for the festival which I am arranging in honor of the Virgin; I must stipulate that you order them brought to me this afternoon, with the answer. Because the errand is so justifiable, and since you have been, from the cradle, a gentleman on whom I could rely, I dare be this bold with you.'

" 'You may send me on affairs of greater importance, my lady,' responded the gentleman. 'I do not lack the wit to recognize my obligations nor will I fail, as long as I live, to take pleasure in carrying them out, because I have a better recollection than you can recall to me of the childish playthings and the signs I gave of being the very devoted servant to one of your singular merit.'

"The Prioress laughed and, half abashed by the potential of such words, took her leave at once, saying she did so in order not to hinder the good conversation and so that he might have time to do the favor requested, as she was awaiting the answer. She had no sooner gone when Don Gregorio, most desirous of showing his goodwill by the haste with which he hurried to do what she had ordered, likewise bade his cousin goodby.

"He went to the convent where the Prioress' sister was, and there kept entering his mind memories of her singular beauty, courteous speech, prudence, and the gravity and decorum of her manners, together with the tactful way she had given him occasion to visit her, by having him serve her in that trifle. These continuous thoughts inspired him with growing affection, which reached such an extreme that he planned, on his return with the reply, to reveal to her, and very clearly, his invincible desire to serve her.

"With this desire he reached the visitor's window at the sister's convent; he called her, gave her the note, and told her to hurry up with the answer, offering to do anything he could. Doña Inés (this was the name of the Prioress' sister) thanked him for his words, gave him the desired reply and gave his page the unusual silk flowers requested, arranged in a large, brightly colored willow basket.

"Don Gregorio returned at once, highly satisfied, to face the discreet Prioress. Upon reaching the visitor's window of her convent and calling her, at her command he went into the same locutory in which he had talked to her. He was quite daft with the joy he felt in his soul for the opportunity she was giving him to explain his desire in the course of their chat, which he intended to prolong for this reason, as one who had already fallen in love with her.

"The recently infatuated young man had no sooner entered the locutory when the Prioress went to it, saying, 'Upon my word, Don Gregorio, you perform the office of collector faithfully, for within an hour I have the flowers I wanted, a reply from my sister, and your presence. I come to thank you, as I should, for your extraordinary diligence.'

"He responded, 'My dear lady, that's why the proverb says: set the table for a bad youth and send him to do the collecting.'

" 'It's well said,' she replied. 'However, that proverb doesn't fit the case (in my opinion) because neither do I think you are bad nor is there any table set in this locutory, nor is it time to eat unless you are telling me it is (for your words indicate that) so that I may serve you a piece of candy or some other sweet trifle. If that is the object of the proverb, I'll gladly hasten to do my duty.'

" 'You don't see the point,' responded Don Gregorio. 'Putting aside candy or other sweets, I'll easily prove that everything the proverb says is found and verified in this locutory.'

" 'How will you prove you are a bad young man?' answered Doña Luisa.

" 'That is the easiest thing to prove,' he said. 'All that is of little value for a given purpose is bad; since I am of so little valuable use for your service, which is what I most desire and upon which I have set my sights, it clearly follows that I am of little worth; and if I am of no value, how much goodness can there be in me unless you give some to me since you are one who is very richly endowed with goodness and with perfection?'

"The prioress said, 'You have become a great rhetorician, so much so that none of us here can answer you because, in short, we are just ordinary, homespun women. Nonetheless, I shall not stop urging you to prove to me how what you said applies, about how you left the table set when you went to take the note to my sister as I requested, since that apparently has proved to me that you are a bad young man.'

" 'My dear lady, that also will not be very hard to prove, because where one sees the happiness of guests and the contentment and pleasure of idle youths, together with the crowd of poor people who flock to the door, it is said that the table is already set and that there is a banquet. I deduce the same thing from the joy I felt when I was rewarded by seeing your magnanimous presence, for I saw in that beautiful sight, worthy of full respect, a most splendid table covered with dainty dishes to please every taste, for I thought it then and I think it now the finest I have ever seen. I see the virtue that glows in you as comforting bread for my weakened courage, accompanied by the salt of your charms and the wine of your smiling friendliness, but I am daunted by the knife of sternness with which I expect your modesty will deal with my boldness, unless that extraordinary beauty, the unquestionable cause, excuses it.'

"Having said this, he kept looking at her without blinking, and a few tears fell from his amorous eyes. They were well seen and better noted by Doña Luisa, whose heart was moved quite a bit although, hiding and concealing the confusion all this caused her as well as she could, she replied (with a merry look), 'From your prudence and discretion Don Gregorio, I never would have thought that, having known me so many years, you could have judged me to be so ignorant that I wouldn't be aware of the double meaning of your words, the pretense in your reasoning, and the falseness of the arguments with which you have tried to test the strength of my imperfect endowments. However, for the time being, let the gallantry pass (for that is what I consider all you have said). Since you have in this house a cousin possessing the charms Doña Catalina has, who very much wishes to please you, you need not pretend any longer. If you do, you will get for your trouble only the burning pitch of desires difficult to extinguish when once aroused, because their very impossibility ordinarily serves as an incentive on which they feed, for if the object is continually present it stirs one more effectively than if it were absent, until the desire is as strong as yours shows it is, when it struggles against things impossible for us nuns. In such wise (for you, as a discreet person, will understand me) I think I have satisfied your words and signs of desire far more than enough, and so with goodwill I bid you farewell. However, I shall not dismiss any request from you for help, but on more reasonable and less impossible matters. If so, you may come a thousand and one times to test the truth of my gratitude. When the tasks of my office keep me occupied, there will be pleasant nuns who are not too busy to come in my place to assist and entertain you.'

"Don Gregorio had been listening to this ambiguous farewell speech with strange uncertainty, staring all the while at the one who was making it. When there was nothing more to hear he responded that he was very grateful for her kindness to him, but any favor, no matter how small, was more than enough; that he understood that he was to be left that way, with the wound caused by the sight of her white coif and lovely face (rich tablecloths on the table which her charms had set for his pleasure); that he thought his life, which was in her hands, would be very short if she did not give him some help to keep on living. After this speech from him the Prioress took her leave, telling him to control himself and to trust time and the frequent visits which she again permitted.

"Don Gregorio returned home so enamored of Doña Luisa that he could not find tranquility by any means; he went to bed supperless, and spent most of the night bemoaning his fortune and the unhappy hour in which he had seen that beautiful angel of a Prioress. As soon as she left him, she too went to her cell in the same anxious state. There she began to turn over in her heart Don Gregorio's clever phrases, the tears he had shed in her presence because of love for her, the great affection he showed, and the danger he thought his life was in if she did not grant him any favor. The fact that he was such an outstanding, excellent man, her friend from childhood, helped the devil (for what is told women once, the devil tells them ten times when they are alone) to get enough wood with which to light, as he did, the lascivious fire in which the chaste heart of the careless Prioress began to burn. The fire was so fierce that she spent the night in the same state of uneasiness as

Don Gregorio, ever thinking up some way to declare her own amorous intentions.

"When morning came she went downstairs to the visitor's window, still anxious, called a trusty messenger and told her, 'Go at once to the house of Don Gregorio, Doña Catalina's cousin, and tell him for me that I send greetings and beg him to be good enough to come here this afternoon, for I have something of importance to discuss.'

"The messenger went immediately and one can imagine Don Gregorio's pleasure on receiving the message as he was sitting on the bed, not planning to get up so soon. He said to the woman, 'Present my compliments to the Prioress and tell her that you found me in bed where I should have remained many days if she had not ordered otherwise, because the ailment with which I left her presence yesterday afternoon distressed me with incredible violence last night. However, with this message I now have the necessary strength to keep the appointment, as I shall at two o'clock on the dot, to find out what she desires.'

"The messenger left and the gentleman-lover remained completely astounded by that news for which he did not know the reason. On the one hand, he thought about the sternness with which she had dismissed him the day before; on the other hand, the fact that she had sent for him so hurriedly (as the messenger had told him) to discuss an important matter, assured or promised him some act of mercy. With intense desire he waited to find out the reason for the visit, and when the hour arrived he went very punctually to the convent, gave his name at the visitor's window and when the reply came for him to go into the locutory, he entered.

"He waited there for the Prioress to appear, and every minute of her delay seemed a century. However, in a short time she came out smiling and showing signs of great friendliness and said to him, not without inner confusion, 'The one who sent for you with such solicitude right after dawn does not dislike you as you believe, Don Gregorio. The signs of the indisposition with which you left last night caused me such great concern that, fearing it arose from the fatigue you suffered going and coming from my sister's convent on my account, I thought it was also my duty to find out, first, about your health; second, to make you forget your past melancholy this afternoon. It was caused by my thoughtlessness, which I must have shown when you took the opportunity during our conversation to say those affectionate and well-considered words with which you intended to give me to understand, by those feigned tears, that recollections of me kept you awake and my few charms made you fall in love. However, your plan has not turned out badly, if you meant to have me send for you; indeed it has been succussful. If that was the motivation for that pretense, now that you have me before you, tell me frankly what you solicit. My natural modesty gives you full permission to do so because (as they say) what is heard cannot offend. I am doing this because you told me when you said goodby that I would be the cause of your early death, and I thought I should not give occasion for everybody to consider me a murderess of one who, possessing so many talents, is worthy of living out the years my good wishes beg God to grant him, trusting that we of this house will lose nothing if one who is such a benefactor should have a very long life.'

"Bold and courteous again, Don Gregorio answered, 'My dear lady, the kindness you have shown me today and are showing me now has been so great, and I am so undeserving, that I think that even though the years of my life be as many as noble and religious desires promise, I couldn't repay the tiniest part of it, however much I devoted them to the service of this community. Since I cannot pay wih equivalent wealth I shall at least pay with what is accepted between circumspect persons, that is, conspicuous gratitude and confession of a perpetual sense of obligation. Nonetheless, I want you to know (and heaven knows how true it is) that if you had not sent the message as quickly as you did, and with it the hope of a visit with you, I would no longer have hope or life at the present hour, so disturbed was I by the loving passion your charms aroused in me. Henceforward, I mean to take care of my life, if only to have something to use in the service of one who knows so well how to make me feel alive when I least expect it. So that I may fully comprehend that you will continue to do this, I want to ask you boldly for another mercy, trusting what you have just said, that you have an interest in my life.'

" 'Let's see what it is,' said the Prioress. 'Your petition will make it easy to judge whether or not it will be right to grant it. Tell me.'

" 'Lady, I ask for nothing, because I should not like to have the same thing happen to me as last night when I caused you distress,' he replied.

" 'Doubtless, if you find it hard to say it must be something as important as gold,' said she.

"Don Gregorio responded, 'It is only a silver hand (that's what your very white hands are) that I may kiss through this grating.

" 'Don Gregorio, even though it is bold on your part, I shall not fail to be as frank and generous, for I promised to be,' said the Prioress.

Taking her hand out of a neat glove, she put it through the grating and Don Gregorio, mad with joy, kissed it, doing and saying a thousand amorous quips and loving things.

" 'Now you must be satisfied,' she said to him.

"The new lover replied, 'I am so much so that I am out of my mind, for this gives me new life, new vigor, new joy, and above all, new trust that daily my hopes will come closer to fruition. So I can say that my entire existence is in your hand in which, just as I place my eyes on it, so do I place now and shall place, as long as I live, my desires and memories.'

"Doña Luisa said, 'Well, Don Gregorio, it is no longer a time for pretence nor for you not to know that if you love me as earnestly as you fancy you are showing me no disrespect. If I have concealed my feelings up to now, it was done only by combatting my will; I was forced to do so, being a woman and a nun, and head of all the nuns in this solemn community, and because I wanted to find out whether perseverance confirmed the signs of the love you began to show me with words and tears. Since my naiveté obliges me to believe what is so hard to verify, I'll say I am most happy to have you visit me daily, I even beg you to do so, varying the hour for greater secrecy. Observe that I am doing even more by confessing I am blindly in love, than by admitting you here after that, for we women feel that the most unthinkable thing to do is to admit our love to one who with that confession usually gains courage to condemn us to perpetual scorn and despairing jealousy. Please God that may not happen to me! You will be free to talk to me without hindrance because my position as Prioress allows me liberty and removes any restrictions, and you may be sure that if you persevere I intend to create greater services for you. This is enough for now, so leave, for I am extremely confused by my decision and feel I am not strong enough to resist greater importunities. Put off anything else for another day.'

"Thereupon the two took leave of each other, as much in love as the rest of the true story will reveal. Then the messages and the love letters began to flow; the visits to increase; they sent each other gifts and presents so frequently that it was already causing quite a bit of notice. However, as all were aware of the Prioress' authority they did not pay as much attention to it as they should.

"This behavior lasted more than six months, until one day when they were talking in the locutory Don Gregorio began to curse the grating which prevented him from enjoying the best pleasure he could enjoy and which he desired. She was of the same mind, because she was so passionately in love with the young man and so different from the way she had been. She came to write love letters and tender words to the point where even Don Gregorio was startled to see her like that, so it was she herself who started her own ruin.

"That same afternoon she said to him, 'Is it possible, sir, that you, demonstrating your love for me as you do, are so faint-hearted and timorous that you don't find a way to enter some hidden place by night where we can both enjoy the sweet fruit of our love without worry? Are you not aware that I am the Prioress and have freedom to do this with due secrecy? For my part, and if you are so disposed, I have a plan worked out which suits my desire and is aided by your cowardice; you could even, if this were not so great, get me out of here and take me wherever it pleases you, for I am alive and ready to follow your wish in every way.'

"Don Gregorio was surprised by this decision and responded, 'My dearest, I have already told you many times that I am prepared for anything that would entertain and please you. Therefore, since you are instructing me what I must do, the affair will be arranged this way: I shall get two horses from my father's house and at the same time collect all the money I can, and at midnight I shall come to that part of the convent which you think best and most secret. When you come out you will ride one horse and I the other, and so we will go together as fast as possible to some foreign kingdom where we will not be known and can live as long as we like. Since you have the keys to the money, silver, and safe deposits of the convent, you will be able to gather up the largest amount of valuables you can so that we shall be assured of never finding ourselves in need.'

" 'That seems to me the right thing to do,' she replied. Immediately they agreed that they should leave at one o'clock the next Sunday night, after matins, at which hour the suitor would be sure to be waiting with the horses at the church door. Since she kept the house keys with her at night she could easily open the sacristy and come out through it into the appointed place at the main entrance to the church. The plan was to travel ten or twelve leagues that night as fast as they could, so that when they were missed it would be hard to find them. They took leave of each other with this understanding and Don Gregorio's promise to send her some carefully acquired ladies' dresses, well wrapped as if they were draperies, for her to wear when she left. After this, the Prioress began systematically arranging for her departure, sewing into an underskirt all the gold coins she could collect, quite a few in number; in a purse she put another large quantity of silver money so that she could have it closer at hand. In all, money and jewels, she took out of the convent more than a thousand ducats.

"Don Gregorio made similar arrangements. He had counterfeit duplicate keys made for certain chests belonging to has father, and he too removed more than a thousand ducats, not counting a large amount of money he borrowed from friends. With the security they had that he was an only son and had an estate which brought in an annuity of more than three thousand, it was easy to find people to lend him the money.

"On the appointed Sunday, at midnight, the hour of universal silence, because of the security offered by early sleep, which is the profoundest, Don Gregorio went downstairs with the packed suitcase he was going to take and made his way to the stable where he saddled two of the best horses. Without being heard he left home and went to the convent, where he waited at the church door for his beloved Doña Luisa to come out.

"When matins were over she returned to her cell, took off her habit and put on the secular clothing sent her by Don Gregorio and which she had in a chest, as has been said. She placed her nun's clothing on a table and left there a long letter explaining that her love for Don Gregorio gave her reason to go away with him (as she was doing). As a final touch she left a lighted candle by her prayer-book and rosary, to which she had always been most devoted and with which all her life she had been attached to the Virgin, our Lady. After this, she picked up a big bunch of keys, for the whole house and church, and left the cell as quietly as possible; going through the cloister she went down to the sacristy, opened it noiselessly, and came out into the main part of the church, still holding the keys.

"To leave she would have to pass in front of an altar to the most Blessed Virgin, to whose image she was especially devoted and whose festivals she observed with the greatest solemnity and devotion she could. Going up to it, she knelt, saying with special inner tenderness and visible lonliness because she was bidding it farewell, depriving herself of the sight of the object she loved best in this life, 'Mother of God, most pure Virgin, heaven knows and you know how much I regret being out of your sight, but my eyes are so blinded by the youth who is taking me away that I am powerless to resist the passionate love which leads me on, and so I am going to follow it without heeding the troubles and harm that threaten me. Nevertheless, I do not want to undertake the journey without commending myself to you, Lady, as I commend to you with the greatest earnestness these nuns who have been up to now in my care. Take charge of them now, charitable Mother, for they are your daughters whom I, a bad stepmother, am leaving and abandoning. Protect them, I beseech you, most holy Virgin, by your angelic purity which is like an all-merciful spring, since you are the Mother of the source of them all, I mean, Christ, our God and Lord. I beg you again, return in my place and look after these servants of yours who remain here more careful about their integrity and salvation than I, for I am rushing headlong after something which will cause me to lose both qualities if you, Lady, do not take pity on me. But I am confident that you will for you are bound by your ineffable and natural piety and by the devotion with which I always said your most blessed rosary.'

"After she had made this short prayer and bowed low before the image she opened the postern gate of the church and then went back to leave the keys in front of the Virgin's altar, after which she went out into the street, closing the door behind her. No sooner was she outside when Don Gregorio, who had been waiting and watching with sharp eyes, came to meet her. He lifted her up and (after holding her a short time in his loving arms, making some improper moves since there was no fear of being seen) set her on the horse he considered the more gentle. They immediately set off at such a pace that daybreak found them six or seven leagues away from where they had started out. In the first village they came upon they provided themselves with the necessary food, intending not to enter a town unless it was night, for they meant to hide from the many people who doubtless would go in search of them.

"In short, gentlemen, that woman had taken the veil and promised God that she would be chaste, and had remained so up to that time, giving visible proof of virtue. That woman lost it for the sake of sensual, passing pleasure, going swiftly along the rough road of her lewdness, forgotten by God, by those of her profession, and forgetting the respect she owed herself. (His Divine Majesty had permitted this to happen because of His secret knowledge and for the sake of showing His omnipotence, which He shows, as the Church clearly states by pardoning great sinners for the gravest sins and also for the sake of demonstrating how much the intercession of the most Holy Virgin, his Mother, is worth, and with how much earnestness she uses it in favor of those who are devoted to her most holy rosary.) But it is no wonder she should do this, having turned God's hand loose, for, as Saint Augustine says, one should be more frightened by the sins that one, abandoned by His divine mercy, fails to commit than by those he does commit. The demons, enemies of our salvation, proclaim, says David, that they gain courage from this to pursue the man who reaches such wretchedness, confidently expecting to overcome him with all sorts of vices: *Deus dereliquit eum: persequimini et comprehendite eum, quia non est qui eripiat.*[2]

"The heedless lovers traveled several days with the fear and dread rightly to be expected by anyone in God's disfavor, not halting until they reached the great city of Lisbon, capital of the illustrious kingdom of Portugal. There Don Gregorio had a marriage document forged and rented a house, buying chairs, tapestries, bureaus, beds, and a dais with pillows for his lady, with all the other equipment needed to furnish an honest home, also buying a black man and woman for servants. After this he ordered regalia and jewels for his adornment and that of his lovely Doña Luisa.

"For many days they spent their life in that city attending everything their blinded senses desired, provided it was amusing, dissolute, or ostentatious. The beautiful stranger (as the Portuguese called her) was present at every festival and play given in Lisbon. By day Don Gregorio also rode about the streets, now dressed in one fine outfit, now riding a different horse and wearing another outfit, and taking his pleasure with that poor apostate of a nun, without any scruples of conscience, totally forgetful of God and without a trace of fear of His divine justice, because, as the Holy Spirit says through the mouth of Solomon, what the wicked man fears least at the height of his evil is God.[3]

---

[2] Psalms 70:11: "God has forsaken him. after him! Seize him; no one will rescue him."

[3] Ecclesiastes 8:13.

"The blind lovers remained in Lisbon two years, spending them in the most riotous and joyous living imaginable, for there were always parties, banquets, festivals and, above all, gambling games to which Don Gregorio devoted himself with no moderation whatsoever.

CHAP. XVIII. IN WHICH THE HERMIT RELATES THE *downfall of the happy lovers in Lisbon, due to the lack of moderation in their social life.*

T IS INEVITABLE that when one takes out without putting in (as the proverb says) nothing will be left. I say this, gentlemen, because Don Gregorio's profligacy and gambling and Doña Luisa's finery and parties so hastily exhausted the money they had brought from their land and since they received no income from anywhere or in any way, at the end of two years they both began to realize they were becoming poverty-stricken. This came on so hurriedly that soon they were forced to sell the hangings and even many or all of the household treasures, after which he sold his three or four horses. However, the sale was of little benefit because, anxious to win or piqued by the loss, he took the money and went to a gambling-house where he lost it all and in addition he even lost a fine short cloak he was wearing. He had to wait until nightfall to return home, so that his acquaintances might not see him (as they did) going capeless along the street.

"When he appeared, mournful, abashed, poor, and capeless, before his Luisa who was waiting for him, quite destitute, the sad lady did not have the courage to scold him for his lack of consideration, fearing she would give him cause to leave her or do something vicious. Instead, she consoled him and insisted they sell the Negroes, which they did. However, the money they got for them was soon all used up, partly because of expenses and partly because of Don Gregorio's excessive gambling (perhaps by divine permission, to bring them to their senses by means of their need). Finally they found themselves without a piece of jewelry to pawn or an article to sell.

"In consequence, the owner of the house, realizing the danger he ran of not collecting from his renters, gave notice he would have the law on them if they did not give him some creditable security. It was impossible to find one, so that gallant young man had to auction off his Luisa's dresses. When the young man saw her weeping, ill-clothed, abashed, and half-desperate, he said to her one day, 'Now, my love, you see the state of affairs and how impossible it is for us to live in this city without attracting considerable attention and being ashamed, because we are so well-known by the most important people whom I haven't the face to ask for help. We have been very thoughtless in spending so immoderately what we brought from our country, without considering what could happen later, but what's done is done. I think that what we should do to forestall greater trouble, since we are in such a predicament, is to leave Lisbon one night, unseen, and end up in the first city in Castile, which is Badajoz.[1] There they don't know us nor have they seen our extravagance and ostentation, as did the people in Lisbon, so we shall get along better and less expensively, because you are so skilled in needlework that it will be easy for you to earn enough for us to live on moderately, now by teaching girls how to embroider, now by sewing for other people.'

"The gloomy lady replied very tearfully and emotionally that he could do what he pleased with her, because she was ready now to follow him in every way without any opposition. They left great Lisbon, as you can imagine, traveling on foot, with no provisions or clothes except what they carried on their backs, Don Gregorio going swordless and coatless because he had gambled away his cape. What he regretted most was that he was unable to take his Doña Luisa away on horseback, for the road was so rough that her delicate feet were torn and pierced because she was wearing the poorest sort of shoes. In short, she was obliged to ask for alms at the doors of the houses in the towns they passed through, as he did also, with the soles of his feet covered with blisters.

---

[1] Badajoz is indeed the first city as you enter Spain from Lisbon on the way to Madrid, but it is in *Extremadura*, not Castile.

"In several days they reached Badajoz, footsore, and there their extreme poverty forced them to go to the poorhouse. They were so poor that they would have spent the night of their arrival supperless if some of the compassionate paupers had not shared the crumbs they had begged that day. Now it was time for the sorrowful Doña Luisa, another prodigal child, to weep and consider the abundance she had had in the convent of which she had been Prioress; now was the time to repent having left it so thoughtlessly with Don Gregorio, to thus gravely offend God and dishonor both their families, finally, now was the time to sob over the loss of the irretrievable jewel of virginity.

"In fact, the unhappy lady spent the night lamenting her misfortune with such unusual emotion that the despondent Don Gregorio did not dare speak to her. Instead, very abashed and melancholy, he listened to her from a corner in the same room. If he said anything it also consisted of mournful words of regret for the hardships he was suffering and expected to suffer, with no hope of being able to return to his home in his lifetime, where he was a rich and pampered first-born son. At the thought of this and of the sorrow of his parents, relatives, and friends, from time to time he heaved such a pitiful sigh from the depths of his grieving soul that it would have moved a stone to compassion. He cursed his lack of prudence, his blind determination, his reckless love and infernal pleasure, and lastly, the first sight of the one who had been the whole cause of such a fatal beginning and dangerous end to the life of his body and soul.

"When morning came after a night spent engaged in such regrets, there entered the poorhouse a young gentleman whose turn it was to verify how many people had come in and slept there that week, because that city, to avoid an influx of vagabonds, had the wise ruling that administrators should visit the migrants weekly and find out their needs. When he came to Doña Luisa and saw she was young and beautiful, even though poorly dressed, he asked where she was from. Showing signs of shame, she replied that she came from Toledo; he inquired if she knew such-and-such important people in that city; the lady answered at once that she did not because she had left there a long time ago. While they were talking Don Gregorio joined them saying, 'My dear sir, this woman is a native of Valladolid, and she is my wife.'

" 'Well, why does she have to lie?' said the gentleman. 'Show me the marriage document; if you are not husband and wife you will be severely punished.' Don Gregorio took out his forged document and showed it to him and the gentleman was satisfied and asked them where they were going, because they could stay there only one day. Don Gregorio replied that they came to that city to settle down and live there.

" 'Well, what is your profession?' asked the administrator. He responded that he had no profession, but that his wife was an excellent seamstress and wished to teach needlecraft to girls if there was any opportunity to do so. 'So, she is to support you,' said the gentleman. 'You will both have a hard time. Nevertheless, in the name of God's love, I shall take you to my house and feed you until I find some opportunity for you and your wife, who seems an honest woman, to live in this region.'

"After this he ordered a page to take them to his house. They were very grateful, and on the way they asked about the resources of the one who was being so kind to them. The page replied that he was a rich youth and so charitable that he gave out alms nearly every day, and so they could be sure he would find them a place to live and if necessary even pay the rent. This was news that made them both visibly happy.

"After he left the poorhouse the gentleman did find them a fairly good dwelling where some seamstresses lived, and he had a good bed and some household articles rented for them, and went to pay the rental for everything else that his guests, who could not pay, were to use. This task accomplished, he went to his home at noon, where he had them fed well, and after eating, he himself took them to the place he had secured for them. They expressed great gratitude for this and for the eight-*real* piece he gave them as an alm; thus they spent the night quite comfortably.

"In the morning Doña Luisa began to inquire of the neighbors about getting needlework to do, because she knew nobody in the city. They told her, 'We who are natives and work exquisitely with our hands, so people say, are starving to death; imagine what you'll do, lady, when you came here just yesterday. In truth, my dear lady, you have come to a very tight-fisted place to earn a living, as experience will teach you.'

" 'In spite of all that, for two or three days I'll give you sufficient work for you to earn at least enough for bread,' said one.

"She thanked her and began embroidering on a bit of work placed in her hands, while Don Gregorio remained in bed thinking that he could endure hunger better that way than he could walking around. That same morning, after visiting the poorhouse the gentleman arrived to find out about the strangers. Finding Don Gregorio in bed he said to him, 'What's the matter, my good man? Where is your wife?'

" 'I am getting along all right up to now,' he responded. 'My wife, about whom you inquire, is at the neighbor's. I beg you not to be surprised at not finding me up; the reason for it is that I don't have even tattered shoes.'

" 'That's probably not so much the cause as laziness is,' said the gentleman. Turning his back he went out to see Doña Luisa and, sitting down on a stool near her, he began to look intently at her hands and face. Noting her features and her modesty, he thought her the most beautiful woman and the most deserving to be loved that he had ever seen in his life. He fell in love right away, for it is impossible not to love that which presents itself clothed in goodness, beauty, or refinement. Overcome by her endowments and showing signs of affection he asked her name and the reason she had left her native land. Without raising her head she replied with some confusion that her name was Doña Luisa and that both she and her husband had fled on horseback from Valladolid because of a certain misfortune which had happened to him (something she hated to confess, and in order not to do so she had said at first that they were from Toledo), and they had stopped in Lisbon, where they remained two years, in which time they had spent the considerable amount of money they had brought with them.

" 'Doña Luisa,' said the gentleman, 'I certainly deeply regret seeing you working for someone as undeserving of you as that great knave of a husband of yours. I see on the one hand your beauty and discretion, and on the other hand I think that he will use up and spend the little you will earn here. In consideration of all that, if you are willing to do what I ask, I give you my word as a gentleman that I'll assist you and befriend you both as much as I can, for I cannot deny that my eyes have looked favorably on you, so much so that my eyes looking into yours are so enamored that I live only with the intention of serving and pleasing you as much as I can. Therefore, I beg of you to demand of me anything you please and it will be my pleasure to do it promptly. My faithful desires want no reward other than to be noticed by you, because with that glory I shall be in the greatest glory I could wish for. Most lovely stranger, don't miss the opportunity Fate offers for your happiness through my fortunate solicitude. Take note that your show of favor to me is something that won't harm you.'

" 'I couldn't be more grateful for the assistance you offer me so nobly when I haven't done anything for you and don't deserve it,' she responded. 'But I am a married woman and with my husband here I should be gravely at fault and in danger if I offended him. Because of this, and mainly because of my duty to God and myself, I beg you to stop courting me. But in any other matter, feel free to ask, and you will see my due gratitude.'

" 'Think it over well, lady,' said the young man. 'I'll see to it that your husband doesn't know or suspect. Use this doubloon for supper tonight; the amount will be double in the future if you would care to use it to give me pleasure, which I shall not have until you give me the answer I want tomorrow. I can be happy only if that reply is what my promise deserves and your beauty foretokens.'

"Driven by necessity, which is a powerful weapon to break down the weak parapets of feminine modesty, Doña Luisa took the doubloon, thanking him very much and giving him quite a little hope of her acceptance of him, because the one who receives is always under great obligation. After this the administrator arose and called aside the oldest woman living in the house and said to her, 'If you succeed in getting Doña Luisa to agree to my pleas and accept my offer I promise on my honor to give you a skirt of fine material, aside from other special things. Therefore, plead with her and persuade her as earnestly as you can. If you are successful in this undertaking come flying to my house with the news, for you will immediately get the reward offered.' The astute go-between assured him that she would do this with a fervor that would give results. Having heard this answer, the gentleman went up to the unprepared lady, took her hand and kissed it without her being able to prevent it, and then left. After his departure, the solicitous old woman skillfully began to win over the perplexed lady, because she knew more about charms of this sort than she did about the psalms of David. She importuned Doña Luisa so much that she was finally convinced and replied that if the affair were kept secret she would try to serve that gentleman as best she could, provided that he would in his turn do all that he had offered to do for her. The old woman was pleased with the answer and took it upon herself to handle the matter impartially and to the complete satifaction of both parties, as the results would show.

"Doña Luisa went into her room, for it was dinner time, and there she told Don Gregorio, point by point, all that had gone on between her and the gentleman. He replied that considering the extreme need and the impossibility of remedying it in any other way she should consent to do his will. He gave full permission and would even provide the place, on condition that she secure all she could in money as well as in jewels and always feign fear and suspicion and charge him to keep the affair secret.

"At this time the old woman was already running to earn her rewards from the enamored gentleman. When she had them and he had agreed that she should arrange with Doña Luisa for them to meet the following night, wherever and however she wished. The whole affair was settled in this way: Don Gregorio, pretending to leave the city, gave her the opportunity to allow the gentleman to enter her own house. He slept with her that night and others, giving her money and whatever she needed for food and wearing apparel. Both she and her husband were able to dress reasonably well on this.

"The affair became public and scandalized the town. Seeing the lady's ostentation, Don Gregorio's magnanimity, and the familiarity with which she treated the gentleman, their going in and out of each other's houses (for the desire and need of the husband made everything easy) caused everybody to realize that the woman from out of town had set up an amusement shop. She gave further occasion for gossip by bedecking herself, sitting at the window, and taking pleasure in being seen and visited, all with Don Gregorio's consent. He was no longer concerned about prospering at the cost of the chastity vowed (but profaned scandalously) of the bedazzled nun, with whom three more rich young men of the city began to be smitten. The lady received their presents, love letters and messages without noting that she was paying for them at the cost of her honor.

"The affair came to an end one night when they all met in the street; because of jealousy, such a serious quarrel arose that the son of an important citizen was killed. On circumstantial evidence the law arrested everybody involved in the fight, depositing Doña Luisa in a lawyer's house. At the end of the month the case lasted they were unable to verify who was the murderer, so they let them all out on bail, letting them have the city for a jail.

"Don Gregorio was the one who got off worst, because he was the last to be released and was sentenced to perpetual exile from Badajoz and its region; he would have been taken through the streets in public punishment except for the diligence of his friend, the administrator, who helped him with money. Upon seeing him free, he gave him a sum that was sufficient to get him out of the city and to Mérida,[2] where he advised him to stay and have a good time a couple of months, until the matter of the exile was negotiated, and he offered to look after Doña Luisa as if she were his own sister. Don Gregorio very willingly accepted the arrangement because he saw it as an open door to what he intended to do, which was to leave Doña Luisa, of whom he was already tired, and he repented his folly in taking on such an annoying burden. He feared that if he continued leading such a life he would find himself riding on some donkey along the public streets of some town, or on some gallows if his crime were discovered. However, he hid all this from her and bade her farewell, advising her to be modest and chaste, and to try industriously to have his exile lifted, or, if this could not be managed, to follow him to Mérida, where he would wait for her. This conversation was held in front of the administrator, who was already looking forward to his absence as much as the lady was, who wished to have more freedom for her dissolute behavior. In fact, everybody wanted the same thing but for different reasons. Don Gregorio received more than five hundred *reales* from his friend and, very well-dressed, left Badajoz on foot for Mérida, a city not far distant."

"By heaven," said Sancho. "That business of idle talkers and that other matter I don't dare mention because of its bad odor,[3] demonstrate very well what a great pig and idle talker Don Gregorio was, who left the nun among so many crows or demons. It will be well, my lord Don Quixote, to undo the wrongs of that poor lady; by doing so we should accomplish the fourteen works of mercy. I'll say more: if you wish to go there immediately I'll accompany you very willingly, even though I know I'll lose or delay taking over the governorship of the great island or kingdom of Cyprus, which comes down to me in a

---

[2] Mérida is a city about fifty miles to the east of Badajoz, famous for its splendid Roman ruins.

[3] The untranslatable puns are *badajos* 'idle talkers' for Badajoz, and the unmentioned *mierda* 'feces' for Mérida.

direct line by virtue of your promise and by the death of the proud Tajayunque, its king, which you will bring about and whose glove I am keeping safely in this suitcase."

Sancho's advice did not sound bad to Don Quixote. Because of it his pate was already beginning to boil so hard that if the audience, very anxious to hear the end of the story, had not pacified him with proper words he would have cast aside everything to leave there at once, leaving them without entertainment. However, when the soldier Bracamonte told him that after they heard where that lady was and how she was getting along, he promised to accompany him on that holy enterprise (for with no very clear information about her affairs and doings he did not think it wise to make the journey, because she might already be elsewhere when they reached Badajoz) Don Quixote calmed down and paid great attention, obliging his squire to do likewise.

They all thanked him and then begged the discreet hermit to continue such an astonishing story, sure that although it was long it would not bore them, so he continued.

CHAP. XIX. ABOUT WHAT HAPPENED TO THE HAPPY lovers on the way back to their beloved home.

DON GREGORIO did not go to Mérida as he had promised the gentleman and Doña Luisa, but went to Madrid, where any luckless man can easily conceal himself and disguise his identity in the bedlam of the Court. Being such a man, with all his nobility, he ended up in the service of a gentleman wearing the robes of a military order. He changed his name and gave no more thought to his lady than if he had never seen her. She paid him back in the same coin; she spent the first day of his absence in new pleasures and in swindling everybody she could, having money as her goal. However, recognizing their own interests, they all began to call a halt, spreading the news about the low morals and free ways of the newcomer. Because of this she found herself without go-betweens and noted, above all, that the administrator occasionally treated her badly because of her ingratitude and dissoluteness, so she realized the danger in which her body and soul were.

"She also soon noticed that although Don Gregorio had been gone so many days he had never written to her, which he could easily have done in Mérida, which was nearby, and he had the obligation to do so because of his duty to her unless, in short, he had changed his mind as women do, and left her, as she thought he doubtless had. She now began to think intently about her bad situation and God began to work secretly in her conscience, making her see how that man was willing to leave her to be an example for penitents, and how powerful was the divine intercession of his blessed chosen Mother, who has the obligation of showing divine pity to those devoting themselves to her most holy rosary with frequent, effective, and docile fidelity. As a result, her spirit became inflamed with love and the fear of God, and she began to melt in tears, grief-stricken over the offenses committed against His Majesty, confused because she did not know how nor in whom to find help or counsel, for she was so burdened with follies.

"Several of her lovers noticed her tears, and wishing to dry them, asked the reason very solicitously, very much wanting to know about it, but it was in vain. The self-confessed guilty lady was already aspiring to superior consolation and so, dismissing them as best she could (which was not easy because the assaults of the lovestruck are even more spirited in the pursuit of what they have once gained in love and tried to leave, if they see it indifferent to or in disdain of them). Enlightened by God, she proposed to return to her city, present herself secretly to a gentleman who was a relative of hers, and reveal to him the whole course of her life so that he might help her to go incognito to Rome and there, at His Holiness' feet, find some way to return to her convent or to any other of the same order, with the objective of having some place where she could atone, as she desired, for the infernal life she had led up to then.

"With this thought, commending herself sincerely to Most Holy Mary, mother of charity and fount of mercy, collecting all the money she had and getting all she could for her dresses and jewels, she dressed herself in a pilgrim's garb—hat, cloak, staff, a heavy rosary about her neck, sandals on her feet. Covered with this penitent apparel, her face muffled, one very dark night she left Badajoz by the road leading to her home, accompanied only by sighs, tears, and the desire for salvation. She avoided the highways as much as possible and almost always managed to travel at night, when she went into the least noisy inns to get what food she needed, after which she went out into the countryside.

"She did not fail to have trouble and harassment from impudent people on the road, but she won them all over by her modesty and rebuffs, and especially by the holy determination which omnipotent grace had caused her to take, of never again offending her God, although she knew she might lose her life a thousand times in a million torments. She also endured hunger, thirst, and cold, because it was the very cold season; also because of this the rains and streams bothered her. Until she got through these miseries, she joined the poorest people she could find, to whom she later gave ample alms. She traveled short distances daily because of weariness and the weather; this was the reason she spent such a long time on the road, for it took her more than four months to reach her home. During this time she visited several religious sanctuaries which appealed to her. Heaven now chose to take pity on her and put an end to her lengthy journey; at last her city came into view. Before entering it she recognized the belfry of her convent and knelt on the ground with an emotion that no tongue, oh discreet gentlemen, could succeed in describing. She dissolved in tears and decided at once to stay there in the countryside until nightfall and then enter at midnight, for greater safety.

"This she did. When it was time she began to walk hesitantly toward the house of the relative to whom she intended to appeal. But on passing in front of her convent (I do not know whether necessity obliged her to do so as much as did affection and the desire to see its walls; it must have been neither, but rather an inspiration from God to bring her trip to the happy end which will be described) just as it was striking eleven, and coming even with the same postern gate of the church door, she saw it was open.

"Amazed at such a thing, she began to say to herself, 'Lord bless me! Is this carelessness due to the nuns or to the sacristan whose duty it is to lock up the church? Is it possible they left the gate open? But can it be that thieves have stolen the altar hangings and altar cloths or the Virgin's crown, which must be of silver, if I am not mistaken? By my life, I must approach quietly (even though I am risking my life by this, for if I do lose it, I'll be losing it in an auspicious spot), to see if there is anybody inside, and give warning in case this has been carelessness on the part of the one in charge of locking up.'

"Hereupon, she very carefully stuck her head in and listened a while; not hearing any noise and seeing only two votive lamps, one in front of the Most Holy Sacrament and one in front of the altar of the Most Blessed Virgin, she remained perplexed for quite a time, not daring to enter lest there be some nun praying in the choir and who, on seeing her, would raise a commotion which might put her in danger of being recognized and therefore severely punished. Notwithstanding this fear, she resolved to follow her first inclination, even at the risk of her life, whereupon she entered boldly.

"Upon passing in front of the Virgin's altar she stumbled over a huge bunch of keys on the floor. Surprised by this, she bent down, visibly disturbed, to look at them and pick them up. She had just started to do this when the very revered image of the Virgin called her name in a rather reproving tone of voice, frightening Doña Luisa so much that she fell half dead to the floor.

"The Holy Virgin continued speaking to her, saying, 'Oh, perverse woman, one of the most evil ever born in this world! How could you have been bold enough to dare appear before my purity when you have so rashly lost yours as a result of the many sacrilegious sins you have committed? Tell me, ungrateful one, in what way will you mend the irreparable breaking of such a precious jewel? With what penance, insolent nun, will you appease my beloved Son whom you have so greatly offended? Oh, daring apostate! What corrective action do you intend to undertake for the sake of again recovering something of the infinite mercies you had deservedly received from my divine Son, on whom you turned your back so thoughtlessly?'

"At this point the sorrowful nun was so intimidated that she dared not nor could she look up or do anything except weep most bitterly. The charitble Virgin, comforting her after the scolding and not unaware of the bitterness and sorrow in her soul which induced her to true repentance, said to her, 'Nevertheless, so that you may realize that my Son is infinitely more merciful than you are evil and knows how to pardon better than everybody knows how to offend him, and does not want sinners to die, but to be converted and live, although you did not deserve it, I pleaded in your behalf (as I was

obliged to do because of the festivals, ceremonies, and recitations of the rosary which you held, celebrated, and prayed in my honor when you were what you should have been.) He, most mercifully, has placed your cause in my hands. To imitate him in showing pity and desiring to confirm by you the title of Mother of Mercies given me by the Church, as he is called the Father because of this great attribute, I have done for you what you would never guess nor be able to repay even though you lived two thousand years and devoted them all to serving me as you did in the first years of your profession. Remember that when you left this house, now four years ago, you told me as you passed before my altar that you were leaving, blind with love for that Don Gregorio, with whom you did go away, and that you entrusted to me the nuns of this house, your daughters, so that I could look after them like a true mother when you were a stepmother; that I should rule over them and govern them, for they belonged to me. After this you threw down in my presence those same convent keys you are now holding. Then understand that I, as a pious mother, was willing to do for you what you asked. So you must know that from that time up to now I have been the Prioress of this convent in your place, assuming your own appearance, aging at the same rate as you have, taking on your speech, name and dress. I have been with the nuns all this time, day and night, in the cloister, choir, church, and refectory, associating with them as if I were you. Consequently, what you have to do now is take those keys, lock the church door, go through the sacristy and follow the same route by which you left your cell, which you will find in the same condition as when you left it. You will even find your folded clothes on the bureau. Put them on as soon as you arrive and put away those pilgrim's garments in the chest. Observe that you will also find on the same table the breviary and the letter you left, unopened and unread by anyone, with a lighted candle beside it. In fact, because of my pious care you will find everything in the same state in which you left it; there is no change in anything; nobody has noticed your absence or that the money you wasted is missing. Therefore, go to bed before the nuns awaken for matins and reform your life as you should, wash away your sins with the tears they demand, for all those who after grave sins have merited the illustrious name of penitents given them by the Church have done the same.'

"Doña Luisa remained in the same state after the celestial Prioress of all the hierarchies had finished speaking; a delicate scent surrounded her, and Doña Luisa was contrite and as consoled in spirit as she was ashamed of having obliged the Mother of God himself to be a mother to her subjects. However, obeying the heavenly order, and fearful lest the hour for matins arrive, she arose from the floor sweaty and fearful, made a deep bow before the lovely image and another before the Holy Sacrament, took the keys, locked the church door, and went to her cell following the same route by which she had gone away. There she found everything as she had left it, just as the Virgin had said.

"After entering she put on her habit and placed the pilgrim's clothing in the chest. No sooner had she done this when the bell rang for matins; wiping her face she picked up the breviary and waited for the nun who usually called her to come and take the candlestick from the table as she was accustomed to doing every night and go before her, lighting the way to the choir. Kneeling, she waited there (quite confused because all she saw seemed to be a dream) for the nuns to gather; when they had, she gave the customary signal, after which the matins began. After this and the usual prayer they all went out again, and at the final signal from the Prioress they went to their cells. She did likewise, with the same nun who had led her from her cell lighting the way back.

"When she found herself alone she began once more to shed tears, partly because of sorrow for her guilt, partly out of gratitude for the unheard-of favor the Most Merciful Mary had shown her. Saying a short prayer filled with fervent vows and heavenly assertions, she took down a heavy scourge she kept on the head of her bed and lashed herself cruelly and bitterly for half an hour, as a beginning of the severe penance she intended to do for the rest of her life on that sacrilegious, unchaste body whose red blood enameled the floor in testimony of her real sorrow for her sins.

"After finishing this act of penance she opened a chest and took out a shirt of harsh horsehair and crushed esparto grass which she used to wear at Lent; it covered her from her neck to her knees and the tight sleeves reached to her wrists. At the same time she put on underneath a small chain from the same chest, wrapped it around three times, and pulled it as tightly about her delicate body as she could, saying, 'Now, traitor, you will pay for the damage you have done my soul. Don't expect any other treatment than this during the short span of life I have left. Thank Mary, Mother of the afflicted and fount of consolation, and her most merciful Son for not sending you to Hell to do this penance, where it would be fruitless, obligatory, and so eternal that it would last as long as God himself, without hope of the pardon and help which you now have at hand although you deserve it so little.'

"Then, leaving her cell, she returned to the choir where until six o'clock in the morning she said the rosary in front of the same image that had spoken to her. When she finished this she sent immediately for the convent confessor, and made a full confession with unparalleled signs of sorrow and remorse, telling him the whole course of her life and the abominable things and sins she had committed against His Divine and Immense Majesty during the four years she had been away from the convent. She likewise told him about the miracle and charitable act that, because of her devotion to the rosary, the Queen of Heaven had done for her by taking her place and attending to all her duties, moved by her virginal piety, saving her honor by not letting her absence be noted. After this she urgently charged the confessor with secrecy about the miracle as long as he should live. He was greatly astonished by her greatness and her soul filled with tenderness and devotion, which assured him of the truth of the matter. He was astounded to think that his unworthiness had merited hearing the confession of and administering communion from his hand, not once but many times, to one with whose purity the purest angels in Heaven cannot compare.

"Nevertheless he tried to see the face of the penitent nun and verify that it was really she and not a devil (as he feared) that was trying to deceive him by taking on her image. Seeing her tears, and informed of the truth, he consoled her as much as he could and encouraged her to continue the penance she had begun and her devotion to the holy rosary. She persevered in everything, improving a thousandfold every day, so that those who saw such a sudden change in her, her privacy in the locutory, her continuous attendance at prayers, her mortification with the usual flow of tears, were astonished, not knowing the reason as did she and the confessor, to whom she confessed nearly every day, very often taking communion. She continued these practices all her life.

"At the end of several months God was pleased to take pity on her ruined lover, as He had in her own case, using as a means to this a sermon he happened to hear delivered by a Dominican monk of great talent in a parish of the Court. Heaven inspiring his tongue, he unexpectedly became absorbed in praise of the Virgin and the mercies she had granted, and continued to grant daily, to damned sinners because of their gentle devotion to her most blessed rosary. In continuation he related the well-known miracle of the desperate man who had given his soul to the devil in a document signed in blood by his own hand, but because of this devotion he was made free and ended his life in this holy fashion, after a well-thought-out and tearful full confession of all the follies he had committed.[1]

"As soon as he heard the inspired sermon the deluded Don Gregorio realized his own mistakes and also remembered how much his Doña Luisa had at different times told him about the heavenly power of the rosary. Pondering the words of the preacher and comparing them to those of his lady which God brought to his memory in this place, he thought that by frequent attendance at such potent worship he would find the arm which would lift him out of the mire of his stupid acts, and a ladder like Jacob's by which he could reach heaven, no matter how deeply he had sunk in the rough wild land of his bestial appetites. Thereupon he decided to go to the convent of the Virgin of Atocha and confess to the holy preacher whose name he had secured from a companion as he came down from the pulpit.

"He did this very thing. He went to the convent, entered the church, knelt before the miraculous image of the Virgin, melted in tears, and there asked God's pardon, mercy from His mother, and help from both in mending past errors and making a full confession. Then he arose, entered the cloister, asked for the preacher, and in his presence his eyes began to reveal what his tongue could not manage to say. However, when his tears permitted, he said, 'Help, Father! Assistance, man of God, for this soul, the most evil of all saved by the charity and immense pity of Jesus Christ!'

---

[1] Allusion to the miracle of Theophilus, which can be read in the *Milagros de Nuestra Señora*, Nº 25, and in the *Cantigas de Santa María* Nº 3, by King Alfonso el Sabio.

"The preacher instantly entered his cell and no sooner was he inside when, kneeling at his feet and weeping bitterly, Don Gregorio began such a full confession of his excesses that the confessor also was sorrowful, perplexed, and relieved to see such a change in so talented a young man. He comforted him as best he could, encouraging him to do as he intended and continue the devotion to the holy rosary, which was responsible for such a happy change. He assured him of pardon for his sins and of the generosity of the everlasting mercifulness which God, to the celestial rejoicing of all the heavens and angels, had shown and shows daily toward sinners newly and sincerely converted. He sent him away absolved, comforted and filled with a thousand saintly and fervent intentions, not the least of which was to go to Rome to visit the holy places, kiss His Holiness' foot and obtain from him the greatest benefit—full absolution.

"Upon leaving the convent he again prayed to the Virgin, demonstrating his gratitude for the great mercy he had just received. He returned to the villa, where he changed into a pilgrim's garb of coarse sackcloth. Without bidding farewell to his master or anyone else, he began to walk toward Rome.

"He arrived there tired but with the fervor with which he had undertaken such a holy pilgrimage not lessened. In that magnificent city he fulfilled all the desires which had taken him there, and having finished, he returned to his native land, wishing to find out about his parents while he was in that disguise and unknown. He was very sure he could not be recognized because he was so thin, emaciated, abject, and disfigured from the hardships of the journey as well as from the penance he had been doing on the way, not the least of which was the tolerance with which he bore the annoyance caused him by some highwaymen in a dangerous incident.

"After several days he arrived in his beloved country tearful, confused, and filled with dread. The first thing he did upon his arrival was to go and ask for alms at the gate of the convent from which he had taken the Prioress, because he wished this to be the scene for his first act of contrition, as it had been for what had brought about his tragic ruin and blind folly. The charitable nuns unhesitatingly gave him alms in good faith; after receiving them he went up to the same messenger-nun who had taken him the first message from Doña Luisa the morning of the day on which their wild love affair began. He inquired who was the Prioress of that house, and she said it was Doña Luisa, who had been so for years because the nuns continued re-electing her because of her great virtue and to the pleasure of her superiors.

" 'Doña Luisa!' he replied, astounded. 'You say that she is the Prioress! How is that possible?'

" 'I say she is and there is no doubt about it,' said the woman.

" 'You are jesting with me,' he insisted. 'Am I to think, since you are trying to persuade me of it, that the Prioress of this community is Doña Luisa, who is very far from fit to be so, according to what I have heard?'

"She replied, 'Doña Luisa is, has been, and will be Prioress many years in spite of all who envy her virtue and high position, for there are many such.'

"Don Gregorio lowered his head, confused and perplexed, as one might expect, and did not dare argue any more with the woman, who was already showing signs of anger in defense of her mistress. On the one hand he feared being recognized by his voice, and on the other hand he was afraid that he might thoughtlessly reveal something of all that had gone on between him and the Prioress. So, leaving there, he walked around different parts of the city, beside himself, begging alms and asking the name of the Prioress of that convent; everyone gave him the same answer as the messenger-nun.

"In order to completely settle his confusion he decided to rush to his parents' home to lay down his burden, so to speak, and make himself known to them and confide to them as he rightly should, the story of that grave event. He went to the door and asked the first servant he met if the owners of the house would give him alms. When the reply was that indeed they would, for both husband and wife were very charitable, he politely inquired their names and whether they had children. From the answer given him he learned that his parents were still living, although they were grief-stricken because of the absence of their only son, who had gone out into the world, they knew not where nor with whom nor why. What saddened them most was not knowing whether he was alive or where he had finally landed, so that they could help him.

"At the reply, tears poured from Don Gregorio's eyes. Turning his head away so he could dry them and conceal them as well as he could, he said again to the servant, 'Perchance was Don Gregorio the name of the son of this couple? Because if that was his name he is undoubtedly the soldier I met in Naples in the Spanish barracks. Indeed he must have been the one, for by the signs he gave of good breeding and the fact that he was an only son, from this town, and heir to his parents' estates (he told me everything because he was such a good crony of mine) this must be their home, and the person of whom I speak must be their son. If he is, it will quickly be apparent if somebody will tell me if he left town with some woman of rank.'

" 'I was not a servant in this house when he left, nor did I know him, but I do know that his name was, as you said, Don Gregorio, and that he did nothing dishonest and there was no complaint about him except that he took away money borrowed from friends, although his parents have now repaid all of it. They have never minded his taking two horses and a large sum of money because, after all, everything would be his in the end.'

" 'Well, friend, for the love of God, I beg you to ask your master and mistress if they will give me alms just because I think I have known their son.'

" 'I should say they will, and most willingly!' said the servant. 'I am sure that not only will they do that for you, but they will also entertain you royally and will consider it a favor if you give them news about the dear one they loved so much. So, please wait for me while I fly upstairs to give the information and the message.'

"Having said this the servant went happily upstairs, not troubling to look closely at the pilgrim. Had he done so he could not have failed to see, from his agitation and tears, that this was his master, the first-born son of the house."

CHAP. XX. IN WHICH THE STORY OF THE HAPPY LOVers comes to an end.

O SOONER had the servant gone upstairs to convey the news to his master and mistress when Don Gregorio repented, because he thought all this might hinder what he planned to do. He had come with the intention only of finding out how they were getting along, then, without making himself known to them, enter the same order as the Prioress, and there, as a monk, do suitable penance which would partially atone for his grave sins.

"Melancholy because of this and desiring to avoid the difficulties which might follow seeing his parents, he turned around to leave the doorway, but he had scarcely moved when the servant came to get him and his parents came to the window to call him, so the troubled pilgrim had to return.

"When he had entered and gone upstairs to a large hall, the venerable old people requested that he sit down. They sat down on either side of him and asked him a thousand questions about the Don Gregorio he had told the servant he had met and been friendly with in Naples, and after each question they expressed their gratitude a million times.

"They told him tearfully, 'Alas, dear brother, what wouldn't we give to have seen, as you have, that beloved only son of ours, absolute master of our estate and the sole cause of the weeping in which we spend our life! Is he well? Does he have enough to eat? Is he a servant or a soldier? Has he married or what sort of life does this person lead who is so pitilessly the hangman of our lives?'

"When Don Gregorio heard these words he remained more dead than alive because of tenderness and emotion, but did his best to conceal it, saying, "Oh, illustrious lord and lady! What I can tell you is that, according to what he told me, he has endured infinite hardships since he left your house and authority. But when did heaven ever fail to give hardships to a son who puts aside his duty to his parents, offends their valor, insults their gray hairs, and impairs his own health, strength, and reputation? I say this because I know Don Gregorio has suffered greatly and I believe he would willingly return to you if the shame which holds him back would permit.'

" 'What does Gregorio have to be ashamed of?' replied the mother. 'Never in his life has he done a base deed nor is there anyone in the city who can complain about him.'

" 'When he talked to me his words didn't indicate that,' the pilgrim went on. 'Instead I always gathered from what he said that he had left because of some fondness he had for some nun or other, whom he called Doña Luisa. Sometimes I suspected that because of her he had broken into the convent or taken her away, for he was so suspicious of anybody who might recognize him.'

" 'The best sign you could give us that the one you knew is our son,' said the father, 'is to tell us that he mentioned Doña Luisa, because she is a very circumspect nun in this town and for years has been Prioress of a certain convent. He often visited her, but you wrong her and her integrity by thinking anything about her that belies her outstanding virtue.'

"When Don Gregorio heard how his parents vouched for the Prioress, confirming what the entire city had said about her, and noted, on the other hand, the tenderness and feeling with which they spoke about him, he was suddenly stricken with a mortal paroxysm that stretched him out in his chair as if he were dead. Taken by surprise, his parents hastened to do something to help him, thinking he was fainting from hunger—taking off his hat, which he had pulled down over his face, and unfastening his jacket with Christian charity. When the mother, who was doing him this kindness and wiping away the sweat, looked in his face, she recognized him and cried out to high heaven saying, 'Oh, my darling son, what a disguise this is by which you attempted to enter your own home!'

"The father, hearing the mother's cries and noting that she was calling the pilgrim 'son', came up to look at him in almost as fainting a condition. Recognizing him, he also helped along with the mother's woeful cries saying, 'What sort of strange idea is this, my dear Gregorio, for you to wish to conceal yourself from us and let us know your identity in such a roundabout way? Could you really have intended to treat your parents as Saint Alexis[1] did his? But I don't believe that because one who for no reason and with no compulsion of marriage has employed such strange cruelty is very far from resembling that saint.'

"The house immediately was in an uproar and the news of Don Gregorio's return spread through the neighborhood; before he could recover from his fainting spell he was surrounded by servants and neighbors. Upon recovering his senses and seeing that his return had been made public, he embraced his parents, knelt at their feet and requested them to let him rest alone and send away the bystanders, for it was enough for them to have witnessed his shame and the forgiveness he had asked for the worry he had caused. All who heard this went away, contented at seeing how happy the parents were, who at once ordered him to go to bed and rest, which he did.

"When he was in bed he asked his mother how long it had been since she saw the Prioress and he learned that it had been only three days. He also learned in the course of their conversation, as she was

---

[1] Saint Alexis was a Roman of the 4th Century who fled on his wedding day only to return years later, in disguise, and live incognito near his parents' house.

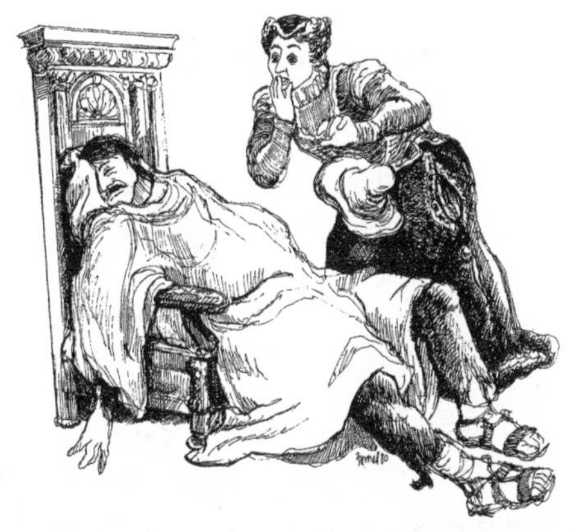

describing how grief-stricken they all were at home because of his absence and not knowing whether he was alive or dead, that the Prioress had shed not a few tears and heaved a few sighs from the depths of her bosom, a clear indication of her sincere love for him and her sorrow for his ruin.

"Don Gregorio's astonishment increased even more when he heard this because, since he did not know about the miracle, and on the other hand was sure about his evil doings and about what had happened between the Prioress and himself, it all seemed like a dream to him, and that his thinking he was in his parents' house, so secure in his native land, was an illusion caused by the devil. So, because of this vivid fancy he became so absent-minded at intervals that he could not answer.

"However, after resting several days he begged his mother to be good enough to go to the convent to see the Prioress and tell her that he had returned wearing a penitent pilgrim's garb after having been in Rome seeking absolution from His Holiness for his youthful recklessness during the years he had been away from home; that he believed he had come to realize this through her prayers and because he had heard a sermon praising the holy rosary and the mercies the Blessed Virgin bestowed on the greatest sinners because of their devotion. He also begged her to urge the Prioress to give him permission in any case to kiss her hand and tell her alone at that time about the things that had happened to him, for his consolation and tranquility depended on his doing this.

"The mother went at once to the visit, deeply anxious to secure the permission her son desired, because she and all the relatives were trying to bring about an improvement in him in view of his serious melancholy state. Arriving at the convent, the mother spoke to the

Prioress, and when she had given her the news reported above and the message, she saw from the tears Doña Luisa shed (Don Gregorio's mother attributed them to joy rather than to confusion and shame) the joy she felt at his return and change of heart.

"After learning from his mother how changed he was, returning from the fount of indulgences and pardon God gives sinners through the hands of his supreme vicar (all of which was clear evidence to Doña Luisa that it was Don Gregorio himself who had sent word to her of his return from Rome) together with the knowledge that he had attained such great mercy by the same means she had, the holy rosary, were sufficient reasons to compel her to grant him unhesitatingly the permission he requested to speak to her the next day, because her heart still told her that the outcome of this second visit would be as happy as the first had been harmful. The mother, glad that permission to speak had been granted at her urging, went home most happily with this answer, and rightly so because she was taking her son, even though she did not know it, the best medicine to comfort and save him.

"He spent the entire night in prayer, imploring His Divine Majesty in the name of the purity of His Holy Mother, whose rosary he never let fall from his hands, to be pleased to grant him on the long-awaited visit the courage one who had been as ill-advised as he would need in such a situation concerning the edification of his soul.

"The saintly Prioress made the same prayer in the choir of the church. Both were preparing themselves to receive the divine sacraments of confession and the Eucharist when morning came. The hour came and they arrived in the locutory where they were to see each other, equally desirous of learning what had happened to each one. Gentlemen, my uncultured tongue has no words to describe adequately the confused words with which the two happy lovers greeted each other at this first meeting. When they saw each other (if their tears allowed them to see each other) he became agitated and she became breathless, so that for quite a long time they forgot who they were and where they were.

"The finery worn by Don Gregorio when he went to see her consisted of a suit of plain cloth without any silken fringe, a hat pulled down over his eyes, no sword, and no companions other than his good intentions and some large rasp-like tin-plate sheets on his breast and back, a cross between his doublet and jacket, a rosary and book of hours in his coat pocket. The Prioress came out arrayed in the same clothing she had put on the first night she came to the convent and in which she began her strict penance, as we have already described.

"Dressed like this, when astonishment and weeping permitted, he began to say to her, 'In the name of the cross on which my eternal God redeemed sinners such as I, and in the name of the tears, insults, and anguish with which He died on it, and in the name of those endured at the foot of the salubrious tree by His most pure Mother, who because of her great purity was the only one who could have produced His omnipotence, I ask you to tell me, oh religious lady! if you are the Prioress Doña Luisa who, with your beauty so blinded, ruined, and enamored me four years ago that I, crazed, foolish, not fearing God, resolved to you take away from here and to Lisbon and Badajoz, committing sacrilegious offenses against heaven, for which I can deserve only hell. If perchance you are who I think you are, tell me also how you went away with me and yet remained here, and if you remained here how you went away with me, because I am certain (would that I were not!) that I saw you, talked to you, loved and courted you, and took you out of the convent with no fear of doing your position and profession the harm that finally followed such an infernal beginning. On the other hand, I find that everybody I ask about you (and this is what is driving me mad) assures me that you have never been absent from this community; instead, they say that you have always governed with outstanding distinction and made a thousand virtuous improvements. I am the evil Don Gregorio, the sacrilegious, the perfidious, the treacherous, in short, the worst of men and Lucifer's equal in thoughts, for I set them on the one who was the spouse of my God Himself, His heaven, and the apple of His eye. I owe the recognition of my errors to the blessed Virgin of the Rosary, because when I left you in Badajoz (if you are who I think you are, and not a ghost) and ended up in Court not thinking about my welfare, I was lucky enough one day by chance to hear a sermon by one of the apostles that Mary has in the world to preach about her holy rosary. He related the mercies her clemency manifests toward those who show such devotion, and he described my blindness and perverse life, at the same time offering a remedy for all my wickedness. He did this by preaching about a miracle and the efficacy of the aforesaid devotion. After his words I felt the power of the Word of divine grace, for I was at once able to confess and leave the court of the Spanish king to seek that of the one who is the Vicar of the One for whom kings rule and where true reigning is only serving Him. I obtained absolution from that Holy See and returned, disguised as a pilgrim, to find out about my parents and to learn the talk and scandal there was about me in this city. I have found out that everybody says you are a modest, exemplary saint and that nobody has ever noted any fault in you, nor have you ever been absent. I alone am the one I have described to you; heaven knows and so do you (if you are who I think you are) and so does my own conscience, which is the sternest prosecutor and which has me skulking along in fear of divine justice from which I can escape only by retiring into the temple of divine mercies through the intercession of the one who is the Mother of them.'

"With these words Don Gregorio stopped speaking and his eyes began again to confess his errors and to reveal his sorrow for them. The Prioress remained greatly satisfied when she had heard from the author of her misfortunes that he recognized them as such, and more so when she learned that he had received such great benefit from the compassionate hands of the one who had returned for the sake of her honor and taken her place governing during the years in which she, leaving God, had recklessly followed her appetites and the paths of damnation.

"Comforting him and giving him an account of what had happened to her and what she owed blessed Mary and how she intended to partially repay her great debt by a genuine perpetual penance for her mistakes and by depriving herself of the sight of him forever, she begged him to do his duty, to look after his soul and to flee from the world, vain conversation, and talk, as much as possible. She gave her word to do the same thing and promised to keep quiet about the event as long as she lived but not after death. Before dying she intended to leave it written down and in the hands of her confessor, commanding that he make it public that very day for the glory of God and in celebration of the celestial aurora of such mercy.

"Don Gregorio promised to proceed in the same fashion and not to remain in the world but to retire to a monastery of her same order where his sensuality would pay for its share of the dissipations, by dint of fasting and flagellation. After praising the Virgin a thousand times and uttering a million expressions of amazement and admiration for the miraculous assistance and unheard-of favor shown by her infinite compassion for the Prioress and for him as well, because of devotion to the rosary, he took his leave of the convent and of her, never more to come to it or to see her. She did as much, each of them tearfully asking the other for forgiveness and to be remembered in prayers.

"The Prioress continued her mortifcations, highly consoled by Don Gregorio's conversion; thanking the Virgin for this as well as for her own, she commended his lifelong care to Her. He went home from there and remained a few days, settling his affairs, after which he informed his parents of his religious leaning and explained that it was their duty to be consoled by having him return alive. He asked their blessing and permission to become a monk, for he owed it to God and His Mother; he implored them to grant this and to be reconciled to his taking such a divine office. After this he also begged them to leave their wealth to the poor at the end of their days, for these are truly recipients who will take the best care of it, for in their possession estates never deteriorate.

"His tears and extraordinary ardor brought him everything he wished and so he left most contentedly to become a monk in the same city. He took the habit with noteworthy manifestations of virtue which led him to become prelate of his monastery, at which time God was pleased to have his life end. Heaven also ordained that the day of his death was the same as that of the Prioress, and so was the hour. Before death each made a devout speech to the community and died with outstanding signs of salvation, having received the divine sacraments.

"After their death the accounts of the love affair, the events of their lives, conversions, miracles, and the help given them by the Virgin were found in the possession of both confessors. Once the case was made public and verified, the entire city hastened to see their saintly bodies which looked very beautiful on their biers. They were given a most magnificent burial, with everybody envying the good fortune of Brother Gregorio's parents who had such an honorable and consoling old age with a happy ending. When the end of their days arrived they divided their estate between the convents of the Prioress and their son, setting an example for everybody, and died burdened with years and good deeds. I say nothing about the years of the parents of the holy Prioress because they, as well as a sister, another nun, died much before she did."

CHAP. XXI. HOW THE CANONS AND CITY OFFICIALS took leave of Don Quixote and his companions, and what happened later to him and to Sancho with them

HE HERMIT had no sooner finished telling his story when one of the canons began praising and extolling it saying, "The events of the story you have related and the fine way in which you have narrated it, Father, leave me astonished as well as enthralled, for your delivery makes it as pleasant as the story is extraordinary. However, I have read one like it in subject matter in Miracle twenty-five of the ninety-nine about the Most Holy Virgin, collected in his volume of *Sermons* by the serious author and master who humbly chose to call himself The Disciple. It is a well-known book and approved by the Church, after scrutiny, on whose testimony the miracle you have narrated will not seem apocryphal to anybody. For this reason, and because so many have been recorded, collected by various serious and pious authors, confirming the holy habit of devotion to the rosary, I solemnly affirm that I shall all my life henceforth be devoted to her Holy Confraternity. After I reach Calatayud I am determined to settle down there and try to be admitted into the hundred and fifty who are engaged in serving and managing the Confraternity, wearing the rosary in full view because of the many indulgences to be won by it, as I have heard preached."

Sancho, in line with his usual absurdities, did not allow the canon to continue his devout praise of the Holy Confraternity of the Rosary and the Holy Virgin; instead he broke in and said, "Sir hermit, you have nicely discussed and sketched the life and death of that blessed nun and the penitent friar; I swear, by God, I would give all I have in my pockets, five or six *cuartos*, if I knew how to tell it, as you have, to the girls at the bakery in my village. I here declare openly that if God gives me some kind of son by Mari-Gutiérrez, I shall send him to Salamanca to study, where he can learn theology like this good Father, and little by little, and point by point, learn how to embellish all the grammar and medicine in the world, because I don't want him to be as big an ass as I am. But the great rascal needn't think he'll waste his father's estate on going to gamble with others like him, for, by the beard on my face, I swear that if he does such a thing I'll give him more lashes with this belt than there are figs in a bushel basket." While he was saying this he was taking off his belt and stamping on the ground with foolish anger, repeating, "Be good, be good; study, study hard; woe to him and to all who defend him and get him away from me."

The bystanders all laughed heartily at his silliness; despite his idiodic cursing they took his arm saying, "That's enough, brother Sancho, no more, for the love of God, because the lad who is to be whipped has not yet been conceived."

At this he left off saying, "Upon my word, he can thank you for this, but another time he'll pay in full. Let this pass as a first offense."

Don Quixote said to him, "Sancho, what foolishness is this? You don't have a son yet, nor is there any hope of your having one, and are you already whipping him because he doesn't go to school?"

"Don't you see," Sancho replied, "that if these boys are not punished when they are small, and molded before they take shape, they will turn out idlers and therefore it is necessary to avoid such difficulties by letting them know from the hour of their birth that learning is acquired at the cost of blood. That's the way my father raised me and if I have any common sense at all he made it sink in my mind by nothing but beatings, so much so that the old priest in my village (may his peace rest in soul) used to put his hand on my head when he met me on the street and say to the bystanders, 'If this boy doesn't die from the beatings with which he is being raised he will grow incessantly.' "

"That's what I would say too, Sancho," responded the hermit.

"Well, for your information," he replied, "that priest was a great man because in the Alcaná he had studied the litterany[1] from A to B."

"You must mean Alcalá," said Don Quixote. "In the Alcaná in Toledo one does not learn letters, but the buying and selling of silks and other merchandise."

"That, or something else," replied Sancho. "What I do know is that he was something of a soothsayer, for he could pick out a good-looking woman from twenty ugly ones. He was so gifted that once he and a student who was passing through my village argued fiercely about the Epistles and Gospels of the Missal, and our priest succeeded in confounding him by asking him about some obscure points, I don't know which ones, about some Church matter, I no longer remember which, and made a fool of him and also made him confess that the priest was a preeminent man."

"Sancho, you certainly have a great imagination," said one canon. "I should like very much, and I believe all these gentlemen would also, for you to tell us some story like those narrated by the soldier and reve-

---

[1] Sancho mixes together *litany*, *Latin* and perhaps *latrine*.

rend hermit. Your memory and skill are so great that the story you tell us will undoubtedly be very unusual."

"I promise you, gentlemen," said Sancho, "that you are touching a note to which more than two dozen flutes will reply, because I know the finest stories imaginable. If you like, I'll tell you one ten times better than those already told, although it's shorter and more truthful."

"Go on, you big animal!" said Don Quixote. "What can you tell, that will be worth hearing? You will vex me and these gentlemen with nonsense just as you vexed me that time in the woods where I encountered six valiant giants in the shape of fulling-mills with the stupid story about Lope Ruiz, a goatherd from Extremadura, and his shepherdess Torralba, a vagabond so in love with his attributes that she followed him from Portugal to the banks of the Guadiana River, after acknowledging her love for him, and tearful because of the sniveling disdain with which he treated her (the usual effect of love on women, who flee when they are sought and seek when they are rejected). There your story, like his goats, got mired, and so did my nose, with the bad odor with which you boldly perfumed it."[2]

"Well, it was a very bad story," said Sancho. "Upon my word, I am delighted that you remember the details so well that by them and those of the story I'll now relate, you will recognize the difference between them, if you'll all grant me a welcome silence."

They all begged Don Quixote to let him tell his story, and permission being granted, he began to speak in an affected tone of voice, "Once upon a time there was, well and good, let the future be good for everybody and the bad be for the abbot's mistress, chills and fever for the curate's lady-friend, a pain in the side for the vicar's housekeeper, and epilepsy for the red-haired sacristan, hunger and pestilence for all who are opponents of the Church."

"Didn't I say so? said Don Quixote. "This jackass is a disgrace to good people and will say nothing but foolish things. Just look at the devilish harangue he has selected for his story, as long as Lent!"

"Well, are herrings bad for it, by the body of my coat?" said Sancho. "Don't stop me and you'll see that I know what I'm talking about. I was engrossed in the best part of my story and now you have driven it out of my head. By Barrabas! Listen, if you will, for I have listened to all of

---

[2] In I, 20, Sancho did tell the story about the goatherd from Extremadura; but there, Sancho's goal was to try to put Don Quixote to sleep by having him count goats (like one counts sheep).

you. As I say, going back to my story, my dear gentlemen, once upon a time there was a king and a queen, and this king and this queen were in their kingdom, and everybody called the male 'king' and the female 'queen.' This king and this queen had a room as large as the one my master Don Quixote has for Rocinante in my village. There the king and queen kept many yellow and white *reales*, so many of them that they reached the ceiling. Days came and went, and the king said to the queen, 'Now you see, queen of this king, how much money we have. How do you think we should use it so that in a short time we could earn much more and buy new kingdoms?' The queen told the king at once, 'King and lord, I think the thing for us to do is buy some sheep.' The king said, 'No, queen, it would be betterr to buy oxen.' 'No, king,' said the queen. 'If you'll think it over thoroughly you'll see that we should buy cloth and take it to the Toboso fair.' They kept on discussing various plans, the queen saying no to everything the king said, and the king saying no to everything the queen said. At the bitter end both agreed that it would be best to take the money to Old Castile or the Tierra de Campos, where there were many geese which they could purchase for two *reales* each and so invest their money. The queen, who had advised this, added, 'And when they are bought we'll take them to Toledo, where they are sold for four *reales*; in a few trips we'll infinitely multiply our money in a short time.' Finally the king and queen took all their money to Castile on carts, carriages, coaches, litters, horses, pack animals, male and female, mules, donkeys and other people of the sort."

"They must all have been of your caliber," said Don Quixote. "God curse you and anyone with patience enough to listen to you!"

"Now that's the second time you've interrupted me," replied Sancho. "I believe it's because of envy of the seriousness of the story and the elegant way I'm relating it; if that's so, consider it finished."[3]

They implored Don Quixote not to allow this and urgently begged Sancho to continue. He did so, and because he was in a good humor said, "Gentlemen, consider how many geese the king and queen must have purchased with so much money. I am certain that there were so many they occupied more than twenty leagues. In short, Spain was as full of geese as the world was with water in Noah's time."

"And if there had been as much fire as at Sodom and Gomorrah and other cities, how would your geese have come out, Señor Panza?" said Bracamonte.

---

[3] This story is virtually the same as the one told in Part I.

"For mine,[4] good and well roasted, Señor Bracamonte. But that wasn't the way it was, nor does it make any difference to me, for I wasn't involved in it. What I do know is that the king and queen went along the road with them until they came to a huge river . . ."

"Doubtless the Manzanares," said the city official. "Its magnificent bridge in Segovia proves that in ancient times it must have carried a great deal of water."

"I only know," replied Sancho, "that when the king and queen reached its banks there was no way to get across, and one said to the other, 'Now how will we get these geese across? If we turn them loose, they'll go swimming down the river and the devil from Palermo couldn't catch them. On the other hand, if we try to get them across in boats we couldn't collect them in a year's time.' 'What I think,' said the king, 'is for us to make a wooden bridge right away, so narrow that only one goose at a time can go across. Thus, following each other, they'll neither stray away nor will we have any trouble getting them all across.' The queen praised the plan, and when it was carried out the geese began to cross over, one by one."

At this point, Sancho grew silent. Don Quixote said to him, "Well, go on with them, devil take you, and let's put an end to the crossing and to your story. Why are you stopping? Have you forgotten?"

---

[4] *Panza* means 'paunch' or 'belly' in Spanish, so when Bracamonte asks, "How would your geese have come out, Señor Panza?" Sancho responds, "For mine [i.e., *belly*], good and well roasted.

Sancho did not say a word to his master in reply. The hermit noticed this and said, "Go on with your story, Sancho, for in truth it is a fine one."

He answered this by saying, "Wait, damn it! How impetuous you are! Let the geese get across and the story will continue."

"Let's take it for granted that they're across," replied one of the canons.

"No, sir," said Sancho. "Geese filling twenty leagues of territory don't get across so fast, so accept the fact that I won't go on with my story, nor could I do so with a clear conscience, until the geese, one by one, have reached the other side of the river, which will be in only a couple of years at the most."

At this they all arose from the ground, laughing like crazy people, except Don Quixote, who tried to curse him but was subdued by everyone. After this, they bade him farewell saying, "Be good enough, Sir Knight-errant, to grant us permission to leave, because the sun is already denying us its light so that it can take it to the Antipodes, and is leaving the earth free of the extreme heat it caused. This is our reason for starting out, for our day's journey is somewhat longer than that of your group. We beg you to command and rely on us, for we shall hasten to your assistance as required by the obligation under which your courtesy and good companionship have placed us."

"I esteem your noble attitude at its face value, in the name of these gentlemen," replied Don Quixote. And for it and in their name I hereby thank you, offering you our services for what they are worth. We should all hasten to accompany you, although I am going to Court because of a compulsory challenge, if this soldier's feet and those of the reverend hermit could keep up with me, but their weariness obliges me to adapt myself to their pace because of their good disposition and my natural piety."

At this point they all very courteously took leave of each other, and Don Quixote put the bridle on Rocinante, mounted him and began to travel slowly with the hermit and the soldier in a different direction toward a hamlet where they had decided to spend that night. They went along slowly, awaiting Sancho, who was putting the packsaddle on his Dapple. On their way to the town, the hermit and the soldier chatted about the stories that had been narrated, and as they were quick-witted and students, they easily got involved in theological points. One of them was more and more amazed at the sinister ending for Japelin and the happy one for the Prioress and Don Gregorio.

At this point they all looked around, especially Don Quixote, who had been listening to them attentively, and they saw Sancho Panza coming along very much at his ease on his donkey. When he drew near, he said, "By the life of Methuselah, I vow that although that Don Gregorio died a very good death, nevertheless, coming along the road I was thinking how badly he bahaved leaving poor Doña Luisa alone in Badajoz, in the hands of those Pharisees who were so in love with her. In this way he gave her the opportunity to be worse than she already was."

"Don't you see, Sancho, that all that happened was by God's permission?" responded the hermit. "He has the habit of getting greater good from very great evil, and He would not have permitted that had it not been for the purpose of showing His omnipotence and mercy toward them because, in short, just as the devil plots to ruin us, so does God seize an opportunity to save us. God and the devil are like the spider and the bee: from the same flower one draws fatal poison and the other smooth sweet honey which soothes and revivifies."

CHAP. XXII. HOW DON QUIXOTE AND HIS GROUP, AS *they were traveling along, encountered a strange and dangerous adventure in a wood, which Sancho sought to go and undertake, as a good squire.*

UR GOOD hidalgo kept traveling along with his group, chatting about what has been related, until, as they were about a quarter of a league from the town where they were to spend the night, they heard coming from a pine grove on their right, a voice, seemingly that of a woman in distress. They all halted, listened again to find out what it could be, and heard the same sorrowful voice saying, "Woe is me! I am the unhappiest woman ever born! Isn't there anyone to help me in this trouble into which Fortune has plunged me because of my great sins? Woe is me! Without a doubt I shall perish here tonight by the teeth, claws, and tusks of one of the many wild animals which usually populate such solitary places. Oh, perverse traitor! Why did you leave me alive when it would have been much better for me if you had cut my throat with the edge of your pitiless sword instead of leaving me like this, so cruelly. Woe is me!"

Don Quixote, who heard these words without seeing who was saying them, said to his companions, "Gentlemen, this is one of the strangest and most dangerous adventures that I have ever seen or experienced since I became a knight. This pine grove is an enchanted forest which can be entered only with the greatest difficulty; in the center of it my old enemy, the sage Frestón,[1] has a cave in which there are many very noble enchanted knights and maidens. Among them, knowing he is doing me a tremendous offense and displeasure, he holds prisoner my intimate friend, the wise Urganda the Unknown. She is laden with chains and tied to the wheel of an oil press turned by two very ferocious demons; every time the poor woman is at the bottom and the stone catches her body, she utters dreadful cries. Therefore, charitable heroes, wait! I am the only one entitled to test this unusual adventure and free the distressed sage or die in the attempt."

When the hermit and Bracamonte heard such nonsense from Don Quixote and considered the faces and expressions with which he uttered them, they held him to be completely mad. However, concealing this opinion of him, they said, "Look, Señor Don Quixote, in this country enchantments are not customary nor is this pine grove enchanted, nor can there be any of the things you mention. The only thing that can be easily deduced from the cries that are heard is that some highwaymen must have robbed some woman and stabbed her and left her in the middle of this pine grove, and she must be lamenting about this."

"In spite of everybody who contradicts me, the person's cries and the reasons for them are as I have said," replied Don Quixote.

When Sancho Panza saw that they were arguing about verifying who was uttering the confused laments they heard, and why, he

[1] Don Quixote believed in I, 7, that Frestón spirited away his library of books of chivalry, and he confessed there that Frestón was "a great enemy of mine."

went up to his master, very comfortable on his donkey, took off his cap which he had been wearing in his presence, and said to him, "My lord Don Quixote, in past days when we were leaving Zaragoza you saw me stand up firmly to Señor Bracamonte, who is present, and had it not been for you and the respect I had for the venerable presence of this hermit, I should not have failed to bring to a happy conclusion or cut short, whatever in the devil the knights errant call it, the adventure or battle I had with him, but a battle which I won hands down. So, in order for me to deserve, by my own efforts as time goes on, being thought a knight-errant like you throughout those worlds, islands, and peninsulas, and leave everybody I run across one-eyed and lame, I ask you humbly to stay here with these gentlemen. I shall go very, very quietly on my donkey, not allowing him to say a good or bad word on the way, and see if the one who is complaining in there is the wise Urganda, or whatever her name is, and if I catch that rascal of a sage you mention unawares you'll see how, after giving him a few punches, I'll drag him here by the collar. But if perchance my faithful donkey and I should die in the attempt I beg you, for the love of Saint Julian, patron saint of hunters,[2] to have us buried together in one grave, because in life we loved each other like foster brothers, so it is appropriate that we should also be so in death. Send me to the Oca Mountains for burial, and if it were my good luck for it to be on the road to Argamesilla de La Mancha, our village, keep us there seven days and nights for the honor and glory of the seven little goats[3] and the seven wise men of Greece. After this is done, we'll go merrily on our way having, however, first lunched elegantly."

Don Quixote laughed saying, "Oh, Sancho, what a great fool you are! If I am to take you and your donkey, dead, how do you expect to rest seven days and nights in Argamesilla and then eat lunch before going on?"

"By God! replied Sancho. "You're right. Excuse me; I hadn't realized I was dead."

"All right, Sancho," Don Quixote said then. "So that you may see that I wish you to gain proficiency in adventures, I give you permission to go and take on this one and win the honor that was due me; I take it from myself to give it to you so that you may start being a novice knight. I promise, if you put your heart into this dangerous exploit you

---

[2] Actually, St. Julian is the patron of travelers.

[3] The seven little goats is the Spanish name for the the Pleiades, a star cluster visible within the constellation Taurus.

are undertaking, as I trust you will, that after we reach the Spanish Court I shall have the Catholic Monarch, by force or of his own free will, make you a knight, so that you may put off your short tunic and cap and in full armor mount my Andalusian horse and go to jousts and tourneys, killing fierce giants and avenging oppressed knights and tyrannized princesses with the edge of your sword, without fearing that the haughty giants and fierce griffins tear you to pieces."

"Señor Don Quixote, leave it to me," said Sancho. "I'll do more in a day with my punches than others do in an hour. If I can just put a little land between us, and stones are plentiful, I'll come out victorious and all the giants will be dead, even though I come across twelve bushels of them. So now, goodby; I am going to see how this adventure turns out. But first give me your blessing."

Don Quixote blessed him saying, 'God grant you in this danger and similar contests the good luck and success Joshua, Gideon, Samson, David, and holy Maccabee had against their opponents, because they belonged to God and His people."

Then Sancho started out. When he had gone a few steps he came back to his master saying, "See here, sir, if I happen to shout, finding myself in danger, come to my rescue right away so we won't give the evil thief something to laugh about, for you might come up so late that when you did arrive Sancho would already have borne half a dozen clubbings by the giants."

"Go on, Sancho," said Don Quixote. "Don't be afraid; I'll come to the rescue in time."

At these words Sancho left and took scarcely six steps when he returned saying, "Look; take this as a signal that things are going badly for me with this wise man, may he be sent to the furies of hell: when you hear me say 'ouch! ouch!' twice, come as fast as thought, because it will be an infallible sign that he already has me on the ground, tied hand and foot, so he can skin me like a Saint Bartholomew."

"You won't distinguish yourself, because you are so afraid," said Don Quixote.

"Well, to the plague with the mother who bore me," said Sancho. "There you are, sitting at ease on your horse and those other two gentlemen are laughing as if it were a joke for me to go unhappily and alone to encounter giants bigger than the Tower of Babylon. And you don't expect me to be afraid! I assure you that if one of you were to come he would do worse. To the devil with them and even the whore-bitch who made me request this permission or try to meddle in these disputes and call a dog with a cowbell."

Hereupon he went into the pine grove; when he had fearfully gone about twenty paces he began to shout for no reason, "Oh, oh! they are killing me!" Hearing the cries, Don Quixote spurred Rocinante, and after him came the hermit and the soldier. When they got to Sancho, who was sitting on his donkey, his master said to him, "What is it, or what has happened to you, my faithful squire? Here I am." "You certainly are!" said Sancho. "I haven't yet seen anything, and I shouted merely to see if you would come at the first clash of shields."

Laughing, they all went back and Sancho went into the woods. Shortly he heard not very far away what sounded like somebody moaning, saying, "Oh, Mother of God! Is it possible there is nobody in the world who will help me?" Sancho, going along with more fear than shame, stretching his neck in this direction and that, again heard near him the same voice coming from among some trees and saying, "Oh, brother peasant! In the name of God, get me out of here."

Alarmed, Sancho looked around and saw a woman in a shift, tied hand and foot to a pine tree. No sooner had he seen her when, uttering a great shout, he threw himself off the donkey and went running and stumbling along the way he had come yelling, "Help! Help, master Don Quixote! Sancho Panza is being killed!"

Don Quixote and the others who heard Sancho went into the pine grove where they came upon him as he was returning extremely upset, looking back from time to time, stumbling over one bush and running headlong into another. Seizing him by the arm and unable to stop him because he was in such a hurry to get out of the pine grove, the soldier said to him, "What's the matter, novice knight? How many giants have you killed with punches? Control yourself, for you are alive and have saved us the trouble of taking you to the Oca Mountains for burial."

"Alas, sir!" responded Sancho. "Don't go over there, in the name of the wounds of Jesus the Nazarene, *Rex Judeorum*! I vow I have seen with these sinful eyes, on which I am not worthy to swear, a soul from purgatory, dressed in white like them, as the priest in my village used to tell. You can take my word it won't be alone, because these souls always go about in flocks, like pigeons. What I can tell you is that the one I have just seen is tied to a pine tree, and if I had not quickly commended myself to blessed Saint Longinus and moved my feet fast she would undoubtedly have swallowed me as she had already swallowed up the luckless donkey and my cap, for I can't find it."

Don Quixote started walking slowly, the others behind him, and Sancho, who could scarcely move because he was so upset, said, "Oh

Señor Don Quixote, for the love of God watch what you're doing, lest we have something to weep over all our lives."

The woman who was tied, hearing the sound of people, now began to lift her voice and say, "Alas, gentlemen! In reverence for the One who died for us all get me out of this torment, and if you are Christians have pity on me."

Don Quixote and the others who saw that woman tied hand and foot to the pine tree, weeping and half disrobed, felt great compassion for her, but Sancho clung to the hermit's robe and got behind him as if he were in ambush. Because of his fear he was moved to say, "Madam soul from purgatory (I hope to see you and all the devils in hell, along with whoever brought you here, purged, because I don't believe it has been for any good purpose), hand over the donkey you have eaten; if you don't, by all the executioners in the *Flas Sanctorum*, my master Don Quixote will drag him out of your maw with lance-thrusts."

The soldier responded, "Hush, Sancho; your donkey is grazing over there, and your cap, which fell off, is near him."

"Oh, praise God!" said Sancho. "How glad I am!" Seizing the donkey, he embraced him and said, "Welcome back from the other world, my darling donkey. Tell me, how did you get along there?" And then, going up to his master, he said, "Watch what you're doing, sir, and don't release her, because this soul looks like the exact image of an aunt of mine who died in my village about two years ago, from the itch and eye-trouble. All those in my family would sooner feel they had a tumor than see her, because she was the wickedest old woman there has ever been in the whole world in all of the Asturias of Oviedo."[4]

Don Quixote paid no attention to the stupid words of his squire. Turning to the hermit and Bracamonte he said, "You must know, gentlemen, that this lady you see here tied so tightly and cruelly is undoubtedly the great Zenobia,[5] queen of the Amazons, if you never heard of her. Dressed in green, she had gone out hunting with a crowd of her most skillful hunters; she was riding a beautiful dapple-gray horse, had a bow in her hand and on her shoulder a rich quiver filled with golden poisoned arrows. Having gone some distance away from her people because she had followed a fierce wild boar, she got lost in these dark woods. She was found by one, or many, wild men of those who roam the world committing two thousand treacherous deeds, and they stole her fine horse, removed her richly embroidered clothing and all her jewels, pearls, bracelets, and rings which she wore about her neck and on her arms and white hands. They left her, as you see, naked except for her shift and tied to that pine tree. Therefore, soldier, untie her immediately and we shall learn her whole story from her lovely lips."

The woman was past fifty and besides having a very wicked face, she had a scar about five inches long on her right cheek which must have been given her when she was a girl, because of her virtuous tongue and saintly life. The soldier went to untie her saying, "I swear to you, sir knight, that this duenna doesn't have the face of Queen Zenobia, although she does have the figure of an Amazon. If I am not mistaken, I think I have seen her in Alcalá de Henares, on Bodegones Street, and her name must be Barbara of the Knife-Slash."

---

[4] Sancho is all mixed up again; Oviedo is a city and Asturias is its region.

[5] Don Quixote is referring to Zenobia, queen of the Amazons, from the romance of chivalry *Don Belianís de Grecia*, and not to Zenobia, Queen of Palmyra in Antiquity.

As he went up to untie her she said that it was the truth, that that was her name. At this the hermit took off his cloak and put it on the poor woman so that she might arrive in the village more decently. When she found herself covered, she went up to Don Quixote and, seeing him in full armor, said, "I give you infinite thanks, sir knight, for what you have just done, for because of it and by your hands I am delivered from the hands of death, in which I doubtless would have found myself tonight, if, through the charity of heaven, you had not passed this way with this noble group."

Don Quixote answered very calmly and gravely, "Sovereign lady and famous Queen Zenobia, whose deeds are already so well known throughout the world, and whose name and courage the famous Greeks knew so well at the cost of their abundant blood, for you and your beautiful as well as fearless Amazons were powerful enough to give the victory to the side you favored of the two splendid armies of the Emperor of Babylon and Constantinople, I consider myself very happy and fortunate to have done you this small service today, the first of those I intend to perform for your royal person from now on at the magnificent court of the Catholic monarch of Spain, where I have an appointment for a dangerous and hazardous battle with the giant Bramidán de Tajayunque, king of Cyprus. I swear to you and promise you right now that I shall crown you queen and lady of that very pleasant island and delightful kingdom, after I have defended your rare and strange beauty against all the knights in the world for forty days."

When they heard such nonsense from Don Quixote the hermit and Bracamonte could not help laughing, but they hid it as much as they could in view of what they owed him for looking after their comfort, seeing how important it was for them to bear with him in order not to lose it. Therefore, they followed his humor like discreet people, although when they were both alone together they laughed about the whole thing.

The good woman, finding herself addressed as queen, did not know what to answer except to say, "My dear sir, although I am a lowly servant, I am not Queen Zenobia, as you call me, unless you do so banteringly because I am so ugly. I give you my word that in my day I wasn't. I have lived in Alcalá de Henares all my life, and when I was a girl I was courted and desired by the most gallant students who at that time were the pride of that famous university. There was nobody but Barbara written on all its courtyards and houses, and my name was on all the doors of convents and schools, written in red and green letters, surmounted by crowns and with palms at the sides and saying 'Hurrah for Barbara!' But because of my misdeeds and after a lazy undergraduate student gave me this mark on my face (may God give him one as bad on his soul) nobody now pays any attention to me. But upon my word, even though I'm ugly, I'm not frightful."

To this Sancho responded, "By my mother's life, may she be in the other world many good years, madam Queen Zenobia, you think you don't frighten anyone but you frightened me before when I saw that bad face of yours, for the rear bee-hive given me by Nature dripped out enough wax to make a half-dozen well-made four-wick tapers."

Don Quixote, who already idolized Barbara, thinking she was Queen Zenobia, said to her as he gave Sancho a push that made him hush, "Fair lady, let's go to the nearby village; on the way you shall tell us how you unfortunately came to be robbed and tied hand and foot to that pine tree." Turning to Sancho he said, "Do you hear, squire? Bring your donkey right away and let the lady Queen Zenobia ride on it to the village."

Sancho brought it, got down on all fours so she could mount, looked around and said, "Mount, queen, put your feet on me." She did so very boldly without making him insist, and when she was mounted they set out for the town. When they had gone a few steps Bracamonte said to her, "Tell us, Señora Barbara, by that life of yours that you thought cost so many lives when you were young, who was that who left you in such a state and who took you from the Calle de los Bodegones in Alcalá, where you lived like a princess and were visited by callow students who filled your desire and pockets full to overflowing?"

"Alas, soldier!" she responded. "Did you know me in those days of my prosperity? Did you ever enter my house? Or did you ever happen to eat the tripe I used to cook? Sometimes I used to make it so good that the students licked their hands after eating it."

"Madam, I never ate in your house because I was in the Trilingual School[6] where they feed the students," he replied. "But I do remember that they highly praised your meat pies and your cleanliness which was so great, they told me, that you used only one kettle of water to wash in a trice two or three intestines, so that what left your hands were greenish-black blood-sausages which were wonderful to look at but, because the street is narrow and dark, one couldn't see the superabundance of dirt which allured the hungriest bruiser in Alcalá.

---

[6] The Trilingual School was a part of the University of Alcalá; the languages involved were Latin, Greek and Hebrew.

"Alas, curse him!" replied Barbara. "What a big rascal and sly fellow I think he is! Upon my word, if I am not mistaken, he has eaten from my hands more than a few times because his figure and clothing are not such as to make me believe that he had been in the Trilingual School as he says. Tell me the truth! Come on!"

Bracamonte pacified her saying, "Before I entered the school, four years ago, I was with six student friends on the Calle Santa Ursula in the lodgings there next to the main church at the market, and I remember that you came up there carrying a rather large pot of tripe. A student named López seized you in his arms without spilling it and took you to his room where all of us friends ate from the pot which you carried around under your filthy skirts, without touching the pot of tripe."

"By my mother's life!" Barbara responded. "I remember that as if it had happened today. Well, upon my word, they were all decent folk, for although it was not right for them to do what they did, I being a woman of my talents, still they had respect enough not to touch my pot. Heavens above! You say you were there? Then you must know that López is now a lawyer and the greatest rascal for falling in love, but despite all that I give you my word that the times I went up to his room he didn't spit on me."

"Well, my dear queen," said Sancho, "if you are such a good hand at preparing tripe, I want you to know that if my master takes you, as he says he will, to the kingdom of Cyprus, you will have plenty of opportunity there to display your skill, because there will be a large amount of tripe from the enemies we kill; you will be able to make meatpies and stews and put in all the vitriol you wish, because that is what gives a stew the best flavor."

"Alas, the worse for me!" Barbara responded. "If vitriol is used to make ink, why are you telling me, brother, to put it in stews?"

"Conscientiously speaking," replied Sancho, "I don't know what they put on top of my wheat-balls at Don Carlos' house in Zaragoza; what I do know is that they tasted exquisite to me."

"You mean meatballs," said Barbara. "That's what they're called anywhere in the world."

"No matter what they're called, what we must try to do is sow a lot of them when we are in Cyprus," answered Sancho.

CHAP. XXIII. IN WHICH BARBARA TELLS THE STORY of her life to Don Quixote and his companions until they reach the village, and what happened to them from the time they entered until they left.

HEY CAME out of the pine grove just as Sancho finished making the simple-minded remarks already set down. Don Quixote joined them on the highway where he had been waiting, thinking of a thousand ways by which he could take the one he considered to be Queen Zenobia to Court. As soon as he saw her approaching the spot where he was waiting for her, he said to her, very respectfully and politely, "I beg Your Majesty, powerful queen, to be good enough to tell us, between this time and the coolness of the day when we arrive at the nearby village, who the rogues were who stole your rich jewels and removed your royal finery and left you tied so tightly and cruelly to that tree."

She answered immediately, "My dear sir, you should know that when I was living in Alcalá de Henares on the street they call Calle de los Bodegones following my honorable and customary trade, Fortune, always contrary to good people, caused a very good-looking and quite discreet young man to come around there, and he came three or four times to eat in my house. As I found him so courteous, prudent, and well-spoken at first, I grew so fond of him (as I should not have) that I could not rest day or night without seeing him, talking to him, or having him with me. Every day I gave him dinner and supper fit for a prince, bought him hosiery, shoes, collars, and all the books he requested, for I took pleasure in doing all I could for him because of my great love. In short, we lived in my house this way for a year and a half, without his spending a penny of his own money but many of mine. At this time it happened that one night when we were in bed he told me that he had decided to go to Zaragoza, where he had very rich relatives. He promised that if I wanted to go with him he would marry me after we arrived there, because he loved me very much. I, who am stupid as an ox, believed his deceitful words and false promises and told him that I was extremely happy to follow him. Then I began to sell my fine things: two sets of good bed-linens, two pairs of outfits of mine, a big chest of linens. Finally I sold everything else I had in my house. It all came to eighty ducats, all in eight-*real* pieces. With them and extraordinary pleasure we left Alcalá together one afternoon, and

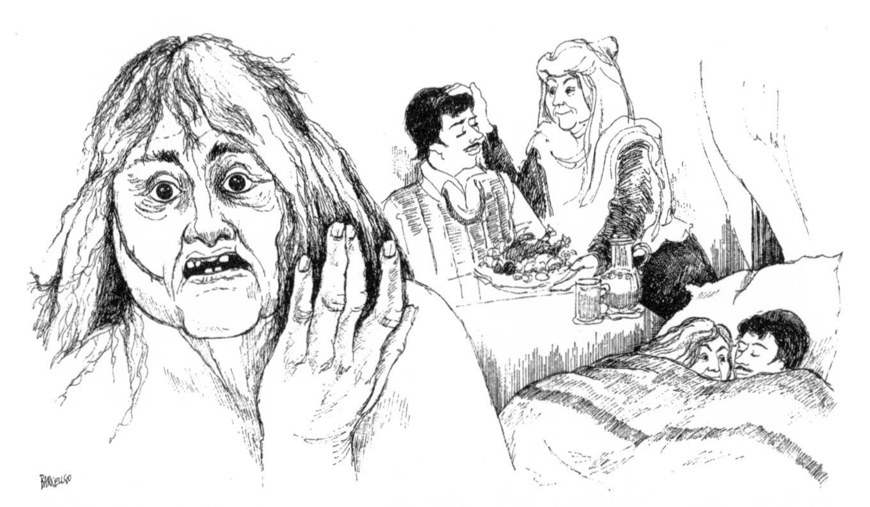

when on the second day we reached the entrance to the woods we have just left, he suggested that we go inside to take a siesta, for he wanted to dally with me (may God give him bad dalliance, in his soul and body!). But I don't want to curse him, because some day we may run into each other and he will beg my pardon for what he has done, and because I love him so much I'll easily forgive him. I followed him, believing what he said (but I should not have done so), and when he saw me alone and in such a secret place he took out a dagger, telling me that if I did not take out all the money I had on me he would take my soul out of my body with that dagger. Seeing such fury in the sweetheart I loved most in the world, I didn't know what to answer except to beg him, weeping, not to do such a treacherous thing. But he began to press me so hard, without heeding my just reasons and tearful words, that when he saw that I was taking a longer time to give him the eighty ducats than his avarice could stand, he began to shout at me angrily, 'Hurry up and hand over the money quickly, you whore, old woman, hag, witch!"

Sancho, attentively listening to Barbara, said to her when he heard her mention so many honorable epithets, "Tell me, queen, was all that string of things the student said to you true, perchance? From his actions I gather that he was such an honest man that not for the world would he say an untrue thing, but only the pure truth."

"What do you mean, truth?" she replied. "At least he lied like a villain when he said I was a witch, for if they once put me on a ladder[1]

[1] A form of public ridicule.

at the main door of the church of San Juste it was because of the testimony given by some envious neighbors of mine who, only because of suspicion, maliciously denounced me; may their hearts fail them, because they caused me to be thrown in jail where I went through God knows what! But it's all right; let them take the consequences, for upon my word I avenged myself on at least one of them: much to my pleasure, taking vengeance for the aforesaid affront, I gave ground glass mixed with poison to a dog she had at home."

They all laughed at Barbara's declaration, but Sancho answered back saying, "Well, by the body of Pontius Pilate, queen! How was the poor dog to blame? Did he perhaps go to the law to complain about you or give the false testimony you mention? The dog probably was very good and harmed nobody and at least he knew how to sniff out a stew pot, no matter how rotten it might be. Unfortunate dog! If my heart doesn't break over his murder . . ."

Don Quixote told him, "Listen, you sheep! Did you happen to see or know that dog? What do you care what happens to him?"

"Well, how do you expect me not to care if I don't know whether the honorable and unfortunate dog and I were first cousins?" replied Sancho. "The devil's clever, and where the hare thinks is safest, he's hunted, so they say, and wherever you go in whatever weather, you'll always find birds of your feather."

Here he began to rattle off proverbs and nobody could make him stop. However, Don Quixote begged Queen Zenobia to proceed and pay no attention to Sancho, for he was an ass. "Well, as I was saying," she continued, "my fine Martín (that was the name of the light of my eyes), a very bitter name to me because it half reminds me of that unlucky day,[2] began to press me for the money, accompanying each insulting word with a sharp prick on this sinful rump of mine that made me cry out to high heaven. So, finding myself in such a tight spot and thinking that if I didn't do what he asked he might give me a worse blow than the one that another like him had given me on the face for much less, I took out my money and gave it to him. But, not content with this, he took my skirt, bodice, and a very nice underskirt I was wearing, and left me in the state in which you found me, may God reward you for the help you have given me."

"Doubtless he would have left you like Adam and Eve if he had taken off another bit of underwear," said Sancho. "Oh, whoreson, sly fellow, villain! Wouldn't it be a good thing, master Don Quixote , for

---

[2] In Spanish, *Martín* sounds like *martes* 'Tuesday'.

me to go out in the world on my donkey in search of that monstrous student and challenge him to open battle, and after cutting off his head bring it spitted on the tip of a lance to enter the jousts and tourneys to the applause of all who saw me? For it is a certainty that they'll say wonderingly, 'Who is this knight-errant?' And I believe I'll be able to answer proudly, 'I am Sancho Panza, squire-errant of the invincible Don Quixote de La Mancha, flower, cream, and foam of the order of Knights-errant.' But I don't want to meddle with students; I leave them to Beelzebub. The other day, when we went to the jousts at Zaragoza, the lame cook and I happened to speak to one of them at the school and some one or other of those devils gave me such an infernal slap on my windpipe that my eyes almost popped out of my head. As I bent down to pick up my cap another landed such a kick on my rear that he made all the wind that should have come out that way issue from above in the form of a belch which, as he said himself, smelled like a spoiled radish. I had no sooner raised my head when such a huge amount of spitballs began to rain on me that if I hadn't known how to swim like Leander or Nero[3]. . . But one lickspittle, I still seem to see him before me, so dexterously threw at me a gob of green mucus which was so coagulated that he must have been holding it back for three days, and it covered my right eye so that I had to run away shouting, 'Help, police! They have done-in the squire of the best knight-errant ever known by those who wear buffalo-skin jackets.' "

At this point their arrival at the little village put a stop to Sancho's words, and when they reached the inn all took lodging there at Don Quixote's order; he stopped at the door to talk to the people who had gathered to see this peculiar person. Not among the last to arrive were two village constables; one of them, apparently more alert, with the authority his staff of office and the conceit he had of himself gave him, looked at them and said, "Tell us, armed sir, where are you headed and how does it happen that you come along here wearing that iron coat and such a big shield? I solomnly swear that for years I haven't seen a man in such a uniform as yours, except on the altarpiece of the Rosario where there is a section showing the resurrection and on it are some terrified Jews of olden times, in trappings like yours, although they are not depicted with leather shields and such as you have nor with lances as long as yours."

Don Quixote turned Rocianante around to face the people who had

---

[3] Leander swam the Hellespont toward *Hero*, a beautiful priestess. *Nero* was a Roman Emperor.

surrounded him and said to all of them in a tranquil, serious voice, ignoring what the constable had said, "Valiant people of León, remnants of that illustrious blood of the Visigoths, who, because Muza entered Spain lost by the treachery of Count Julián in revenge for Rodrigo's lust and to right the wrong done to his daughter Florinda, called La Cava, were forced to withdraw to the inaccessible crannies of the mountains and forests of uncivilized Biscay, Asturias, and Galicia, where they could preserve the very noble, generous blood which was to be, as it has been, the scourge of the African Moors because, urged on by the invincible and most glorious Pelayo[4] and the enlightened Sandoval, his father-in-law, protection and faithful defense to whose zeal Spain owes the line of Catholic kings it enjoys. From him was born the valor with which the edges of your sharp swords did their duty in recovering all that was lost and in conquering new kingdoms and worlds, to the envy of the sun itself which until you stormed them was the only one who knew anything about them. Now you see, distinguished Guzmanes, Quiñones, Lorenzanas, and the rest who hear me, how my uncle, King Alfonso the Chaste, although I am his sister's son and recognized as well as feared by Bernardo, holds prisoner my father, the Lord of Saldaña, and will not turn him over to me. In addition to this he has promised to give to Emperor Charlemagne the kingdoms of Castile and León after his death. It is an affront I will by no means overlook, because he has no other heir except me, by law and by right as his legitimate nephew, the one most closely linked to the royal house. I shall not permit strangers to take possession of anything so clearly mine. Consequently, gentlemen, let us leave immediately for Roncesvalles, and we shall take with us King Marsile of Aragon and Bravonel of Zaragoza. With Ganelon helping us with his wisdom and with the aid he promised we shall easily kill Roland and all the Twelve Peers, and Durandarte, badly wounded in those valleys, will leave the battle. Following the trail of blood he will leave, Montesinos will travel over a rough mountain and a thousand things will happen to him until I meet him and at his insistence take out his heart and carry it to Belerma,[5] who was in his lifetime the object of his solicitude. Observe, famed Leonese and Asturians, that for success in

---

[4] One of the reasons the Moors, who entered Spain at Gibraltar in the year 711, were never able to conquer the northwestern part of Spain was due to the efforts of Pelayo who stopped the drive of the Moors at a place called Covadonga in Asturias.

[5] These are characters celebrated in Spanish ballads (some obviously of French origin). The mention of Montesinos in this Chapter 23 makes us

war I warn you not to quarrel over division of lands or the marking of boundaries."

He turned Rocinante around and, spurring him, furiously entered the inn, shouting, "To arms! To arms! For . . .

> With the best men of Asturias
> From León does Bernardo advance,
> All prepared to go to war
> To stop the passage of France.[o]

Everyone was startled on hearing what the man in armor had said, and did not know to what he was referring. Some said he was crazy; others said he wasn't that but some important knight, and his outfit showed that; then they all wanted to go in to talk to him, but the hermit stationed himself at the door to prevent them saying, "Please leave, gentlemen, for this hidalgo is crazy and we are taking him to the insane asylum in Toledo for treatment. Don't upset him any more than he alredy is."

When they heard these words from the venerable hermit, everyone who was there left at once. Sancho took Rocinante to the stable and Don Quixote and the rest of his group went into a room where Bracamonte and the hermit helped remove his armor. The good Barbara was seated on the floor, covered with the hermit's coarse cloak. When Don Quixote saw her he said, "Sovereign lady, have a little patience, for very shortly you will be taken to your famous empire of Amazons, but first you will be crowned queen of the luxuriant kingdom of Cyprus, which I shall turn over to you after killing its tyrannical owner, the valiant Bramidán de Tajayunque, in the Spanish Court. To do that, tomorrow we shall enter as speedily as possible the strong and heavily walled city of Sigüenza, where I shall buy you some rich clothing in exchange for that which the treacherous prince Don Martín took from you contrary to all laws of reason and courtesy."

"Sir knight, I am grateful for the good deed you are doing me when I have not been of any service to you," she responded. "I wish I were fifteen years old and more beautiful than Lucretia so that I might serve you with all the faculties I have or can ever have. You can believe that if we arrive in Alcalá, I'll serve you there as you will see, a couple of tarts not over fourteen, marvelously good and not very costly."

---

wonder if Avellaneda isn't hinting that he has seen Cervantes' own Chapter 23 of Part II which contains the episode of the cave of Montesinos.

[o] Verses from a ballad about Bernardo del Carpio.

Don Quixote did not understand the tune Barbara was playing and responded, "My dear lady, I am not a man who cares overmuch about eating and drinking; Sancho Panza is good at that. However, if the tarts are good I'll pay for them and we'll take them in the saddlebags to have on the road, although it is a fact that when my squire's mill begins to work it won't leave a single one."

The good lady, seeing that Don Quixote had not understood her, turned to the soldier, who was laughing, and said, "Alas, I'm exasperated! What a tiresome person this knight is! Perhaps he has eaten too much; if he goes to Alcalá he will need to plane down his skull, which is very thick."

"What does your highness mean by thick?" said Don Quixote.

"I was saying, sir, that you are not much so, which surprises me in one of your high rank," she responded.

"Madam, a modern philosopher I used to know complained a great deal about three kinds of people: a doctor with the itch, a deceived lawyer, and a fat man who undertakes long trips and lawsuits," replied Don Quixote. "Because of my profession I have to undertake the two last things I have mentioned, so it is not wise for me to be heavy; that is for lazy men who live without anxieties. Therefore I must not get any thicker than I am, having as many responsibilities as I have."

As they were talking in this vein, Sancho came running in, clapping his hands and saying, "I claim reward for good news, master Don Quixote, good news! Good, good news!"

"I promise to give you that, son Sancho," said Don Quixote. "And I'll give you an even better one if the news is that the student who robbed great Queen Zenobia has put in an appearance."

"It's better news," said Sancho.

"Can it be, perchance, that the giant Bramidán de Tajayunque is in the village seeking me to finish the battle which the two of us have arranged?" added Don Quixote.

"It can't be compared to that," replied Sancho.

"Well then, tell us," said Don Quixote. "If it is as important as you say, you'll certainly get a good reward."

Sancho responded, "You must be aware that the innkeeper says (and he's not joking, because I've seen it with my own eyes) that for our supper he has a very tasty pot of four cows' hooves and a pound of bacon, with sheep's liver and lamb's lungs and turnips; in short, it's so good that by paying five *reales* each, cash on the barrelhead, it will walk here on its own feet to have supper with us."

Don Quixote kicked him saying, "Look at the stupid glutton and the important news he brought me! The reward I'd gladly give him would be a beating with a club, if there were one handy."

As Don Quixote was angrily saying this, the innkeeper entered in a very peaceful frame of mind saying, "What do you wish to have for supper, gentlemen? I'll bring it to you right away."

Don Quixote told him he wanted a couple of pairs of soft-boiled eggs, and the other gentlemen could have what they wished, but to prepare a pheasant for Queen Zenobia, if he had one on hand, because she was a delicate person, used to luxury, and anything else would disagree with her.

The innkeeper looked at the one Don Quixote called a queen and said, "Aren't you the one who ate supper last night with a student and told us you were going to marry him in Zaragoza? Well, how does it happen that yesterday you weren't Zenobia, as this gentleman says, (although you were the sweetheart of that fellow who was as callow as he was shameless), and now you are? To tell the truth, last night you didn't have pheasant for supper, but a dish of tripe you brought with you from Sigüenza, wrapped in a rather dirty napkin, nor did you pretend to be a queen."

"Brother, I'm not asking you for anything," she responded. "Bring the supper, for I'll eat whatever all these gentlemen eat, for this knight is treating all of us."

The innkeeper set the table and they all ate supper, to the great satisfaction of Sancho who served them, his eyes going along with every bite his master took, and his heart following after. When the table was cleared and he went off to eat his supper while the others remained to have an after-dinner chat, the hermit said to Don Quixote, "Sir, on this journey you have been most kind to me and to Señor Bracamonte, and we are both greatly obliged, but because we now have to go in different directions, he to his native Ávila, and I to Cuenca, be good enough to grant us permission to leave, and send word to us in those cities if there is any way in which we can serve you; we shall do our duty with the greatest fervor. We'll do as much for your diligent squire Sancho."

Don Quixote replied that he was very sorry to lose their good companionship, but if there was nothing else to be done, they should leave with God's blessing. He told Sancho to give each of them a ducat for the road, which they very gratefully accepted. Don Quixote said to them, "Indeed, gentlemen, I think it would be hard to find three people like us to travel from Zaragoza to this spot, for each of us is deserving of honor and fame because, as we know, one of three things in this world assures us of them: blood, arms, or letters, virtue being common to all three, making a perfect combination. Because of his blood, Señor Bracamonte is famous, for his name is so well-known throughout Castile; I because of my weapons, with which I have acquired such world renown that my name is known all over the globe; the priest, who is, I think, a very great theologian, for I understand he can give an accounting of himself in any university, whether it be that of Salamanca or Paris or Alcalá."

After finishing his supper Sancho had taken up his place behind Don Quixote to listen to the conversation. Now he burst out with, "And what am I famous for? Am I not also a person like the rest?"

"You are famous for being the biggest glutton that has ever been seen," answered Don Quixote.

"Well, jesting aside, not only do I have one of the titles to fame each of you has, but all three together: blood, arms, and letters," replied Sancho.

Don Quixote laughed, saying, "Oh, you simple-minded man! How or when did you come to deserve one of the claims to fame we have because of our excellence, so that your renown will fly around the globe?"

"I'll tell you, and don't laugh, by golly!" said Sancho. "First, I am famous through blood since, as Don Quixote knows, my father was a butcher in my village and was always covered with the blood of cows, calves, lambs, sheep, goats, and kids he killed, and always had his arms, hands, and apron covered with it. I am also famous for arms, because an uncle of mine, my father's brother, is a blacksmith in my region, and he is now in Valencia, or where only he knows, and always goes around cleaning swords broadswords, daggers, poniards, rapiers, knives, cleavers, lances, halberds, pikes, hatchets, breastplates and helmets and all kinds of armor. As for letters, I also have a brother-in-law in Toledo, a book binder always going around with writings on parchment and loaded down with great books the size of my donkey's packsaddle, covered with Gothic letters,"

They all arose, laughing at Sancho's silliness, and the innkeeper led each one to bed.

CHAP. XXIV. HOW DON QUIXOTE, BARBARA, AND *Sancho reached Sigüenza, and the events that happened to all of them there, especially to Sancho, who found himself in jail.*

AFTER GOD sent the dawn Don Quixote awakened, for the chaos in his mind and the confusion of his faculties with which his fancy was stuffed, served as an inaccurate alarm bell which allowed him to sleep scarcely half an hour at a time. After awakening he got to his feet shouting for Sancho, who could hardly open his eyes, although he had to do so because of his master's haste. He hastily saddled Rocinante and the donkey while Don Quixote paid for the board and lodging of all of them.

When this task was over and they had all left the inn, the hermit and Bracamonte bade Don Quixote farewell, and also said goodby to Sancho, who was quite busy mounting Barbara on an old donkey belonging to the innkeeper, who rented it to Don Quixote for the trip to Sigüenza, along with some clothing, also quite old, belonging to his wife.

After traveling like this most of the day, the four reached the city and went to an inn to which they were guided by the innkeeper, who was their guide. They were well accompanied by boys who went along shouting, "Look at the man in armor, boys! Look at the man in armor!" After dismounting, Don Quixote asked the innkeeper for paper and ink, and, closing himself up in a room, he wrote half a dozen signs to put up on the street corners. They read as follows:

CHALLENGE

> The Loveless Knight, flower and model of the Manchegan people, challenges to singular combat that person, or those persons, who do not admit that the great Zenobia, Queen of the Amazons, who is with me, is the most beautiful and highest ranking female to be found in the whole expanse of the universe. Her rare and singular beauty will be defended by the edge of my sword in the royal plaza of this city, from tomorrow noon to nightfall. Anyone wishing to do battle with the aforesaid Loveless Knight must sign his name at the bottom of this notice.

The copies made, he called Sancho and told him, "Sancho, take these posters, look for a little paste or glue, and put them up at corners in the city so that all may read them. Note most carefully all that is said by the knights who come up to read them: whether they are inflamed with anger in defense of their beloved ladies, whether they say something insulting (because virtue is always envied), or whether they are glad of the honor they will gain by facing me; finally, note whether they ask where I am, or where my lady, the queen, is. Go at top speed, my dear Sancho; observe and note everything with your own eyes so that when you return you can give me a full accounting and report. If it should be necessary, I'll not stop to eat supper but will go immediately to punish their stupid statements and audacity, so that henceforth there won't be others of their sort daring to say such monstrous things about one so well able to punish them."

Sancho remained pensive for a while, holding the papers, because he was very unwilling to perform this errand of putting up posters announcing a challenge, and he would have preferred for Don Quixote to send him for a leg of mutton, because he was hungry enough to eat supper. So, with bent head, he said, "Heaven bless Saint Lawrence's grills, my lord Don Quixote! When we could live in peace in the sight of the holy Roman Catholic Church, is it impossible for us to choose, on our own judgment, not to meddle in quarrels and foolish warring which is none of our business, and do this for no reason? So you want some Barrabas of a knight, refreshed and comfortable along with his horse, to appear wanting to do battle with us when we are tired and Rocinante is so exhausted that he can't eat a mouthful, so that if through God's pity he does defeat us we'll end up in Judas' house with all our mounts? If you plan such a thing wouldn't it be better to seek permission from the magistrate to put up these posters, for I see myself involved in a thousand perils, disasters, and misadventures because of this."

Don Quixote said to him, "Oh, fool! Oh, faint heart! Oh, coward! Are you the one planning to be received into the order of knighthood in Madrid, with public honor, in the presence of his sacred, imperial, royal Majesty, the King, our lord? Well, remember that honey is not for the donkey's mouth, nor is the order of knighthood usually bestowed except on men of spirit, courageous, valiant, and enterprising, and not on gluttons and idlers like you. Go at once and do what I tell you without any more objection."

Seeing his master so angry, Sancho said no more and departed, heartily cursing the one with whom he had cast his lot. At a shoemaker's he bought a *cuarto*'s worth of paste and, carrying it on an old shoe-sole, he went to the plaza where there were some knights and noblemen and many other people enjoying the coolness of the late afternoon with the Corregidor.[1] Sancho went up to the Court House without saying a word to anybody and began to paste one of the posters on its very doors. However, a constable behind the Corregidor saw that peasant affixing a poster with big letters on the Court House, so, thinking the posters were playbills, he went up to Sancho and said, "What are you putting up, brother? Are you a servant of some actors?"

Sancho responded, "What actors or what nonsense? What is being put up, meddler, is not for you; it's much more important business. It is for those who wear black capes, and tomorrow you will see."

The confused constable read the poster and then turned to Sancho who was nearby, putting another poster on a pillar, and said, "Come here, you minion of the devil, who ordered you to put up these posters in this place?"

Sancho answered, "You come over here, minion of Satan, for I don't want to tell you." The Corregidor and those with him turned around at the persistent demands of the constable and Sancho's shouts and inquired what was the matter. The constable came up and said, "Sir, that peasant is going around the plaza putting up posters saying that somebody or other challenges all the knights in this city to battle."

"He's posting up challenges!" said the Corregidor. "Well, is it Carnival now? Go bring us one of those sheets; we'll see what it is. It may be some nonsense which could reach the bishop's ears before we are aware of it."

The constable took down the first poster he found pasted on a pillar, intending to take it to the Corregidor, but when Sancho saw this, he flared up angrily and went after him with a stone in his hand saying, "Oh, you colossally foolish constable! By the order of knighthood my master has received, if it were not that I am afraid of you and the law you carry around, with the first stone I'd throw, I'd make you pay for all the constabularities you've done up to now, so that others like you and the whore who bore you would not dare henceforth to do such crazy things."

When the Corregidor saw that that peasant had a rock in his hand ready to throw at the constable, he ordered him to be arrested and brought before him. Half a dozen bailiffs came up to do this, but with a rock in his hand he would not let anyone seize him. However, when he saw that the affair was serious and that they were unsheathing their

[1] The *corregidor* was the king's magistrate.

swords, he dropped the stone, took his cap in both hands, and began to speak: "Oh, gentlemen! For the love of God let me go tell my master how some rogues and scoundrels won't let me put up the posters about the challenge. You will see that he will come in the shape of an enchanted swan and not leave one pagan alive."

The bailiffs, who did not comprehend that language, were holding Sancho fast in front of the Corregidor while he finished reading the bill. When he had read it he told the bystanders what it was and they applauded him. Turning to Sancho he asked, "Come over here, good man. Who ordered you to put up these posters on the Court House? On my word as an hidalgo, this will cost you and the one who sent you to do it more dearly than you think."

"Oh, unhappy mother who bore me and the woman who suckled me!" said Sancho. "Sir, my master, bad life to him, ordered me to put them up, although I told him frankly we shouldn't go to battling in this region until we had killed that huge giant of a king of Cyprus, where we have to take the lady, Queen Zenobia. Turn me loose; I swear on my word as Sancho Panza that I'll go running to tell him what's up, and you'll see that he will come, walking or on Rocinante, to do such butchery as you have never heard of or seen."

The Corregidor asked, "What is your master's name?" Sancho answered that his right name was Martín Quijada, and the past year he called himself Don Quixote de La Mancha and had as a nickname "The Knight of the Sad Countenance"; however, this year, because he had already left Dulcinea del Toboso (ungrateful cause of the excessive penance he had undergone in Sierra Morena, although later, as a prize for her he won Membrino's precious helmet)[2] he called himself "The Loveless Knight."

"Well, for heaven's sake!" said the Corregidor. "And what is your name?"

He responded, "Sir, speaking with the permission of the honorable elders listening to me, I am named Sancho Panza (if only I weren't) the happy squire of the knight-errant I mentioned, a native of Argamesilla of La Mancha, conceived and born of my father and mother, baptized by the priest."

"How could you have been baptized if, as you said, you were born of a donkey and a mare?" answered the Corregidor, overcome by laughter and ordering the constable and the bailiffs to take him to jail

---

[2] Sancho mixes up *two* things here. First, it is Mambrino's helmet (I, 21), and second, the penance in the Sierra Morena was *after* the episode of Mambrino's helmet.

and put two sets of shackles on him until the whole thing was clarified. When this was done they were to go through every inn in the village in search of that peasant's master and bring him there.

The luckless Sancho was taken to jail at once and no historian, however diligent, could succeed in recording the things he did and said on the way and when they put the shackles on him. Among many silly things they tell about him is the story that when he was shackled he said, "Take off these devilish iron hobbles, gentlemen, because I can't walk with them on, and there was no need to put them on me, for I would consider myself well-fettered without your going to this trouble."

After he was left in jail, three or four rascals who were prisoners there came up with some little tubes of lice in their hands, and seeing that he was a simple person, appearing to them to be an honest man from Old Castile, and also seeing that at every step he fell face down, for he could not walk at all because of the fetters, they threw more than four hundred lice down the open neck of his shirt, which gave him plenty to do, scratching and hunting the whole time he was in jail. They bothered him so much that he did nothing but bemoan his luck and the hour he had met Don Quixote. He tore his beard, saying goodby now to his wife, now to the donkey, now to Rocinante. The great annoyance of the fetters caused him to say to one of those fellows, "Hey, Señor Rascal! May God grant you as much health as the satisfaction you show about my hardship if you'll remove those fetters that don't let me move about, and if I have them on my feet tonight I shan't be able to close an eye."

One of the jailer's servants heard him and said, "Brother, if you'll give my master a *real* he'll take them off you tonight to make you comfortable and do you a good deed."

When he heard this, Sancho took from his coat pocket a leather purse in which he had six or seven *reales* for that night's expenses at the inn. He took out a silver *real* and gave it to the servant, who immediately removed the fetters. Four or five prisoners, who were eagles about finding things before the owners knew they were missing, took careful note of where Sancho put away his purse and made up a scheme among themselves. One came up to Sancho, embraced him and said, "Hey, good man, how glad we are they took off those cursed fetters! I hope it will be for a good long time." Here he guided his hand so skillfully in the direction of the coat pocket that without missing his goal or being felt he took out the purse. But when the catch was made he proceeded to act generously and honorably, for he invited Sancho to have—at his own expense—some wafers, fruit, and wine on which he spent the money.

But returning to Don Quixote—when he saw that Sancho was taking so long to put up the posters on the street corners, he suspected what might have happened and went to the stable, swiftly saddled Rocinante, mounted with his shield and big lance, and set out for the plaza. As he was entering it very slowly, accompanied by boys, the Corregidor, saw him, and all who were with him were astonished to see that phantom in armor with people all about him.

They all came up to find out what he wanted or what he was going to do, and they heard Don Quixote, thinking he was surrounded by princes, begin to address them gravely, resting the butt of his lance on the ground, "Oh, you noblemen who bowed out of battle, you will not bow out of this![3] Do you not know, perchance, that Muza and Don Julián, although one is a Moor and the other a traitor to my royal crown, are laying waste lands that I have owned for a long time, and besides, they are planning to settle on them? They are so swollen with pride over the victories they have won against reason, with us fleeing from their angry faces, not resisting as would be expected from such lesser nobles and good men, not considering the grief of our women, nor the many and violent deeds these wretches will take upon themselves to do for Mohammed and to rebuff our faith, by saying things which should not be said, filled with stupid statements. Lift up, I say, lift up the blades you have thrown down! Let Galindo come forth, let

---

[3] Here Don Quixote starts out by thinking he is Rodrigo, the last of the Visigothic kings, and later King Ferdinand, husband of Queen Isabella. Count Julián, mentioned here, under King Rodrigo's orders, held the ports near the Strait of Gibraltar, but then let the Moors in after learning that his own daughter had been seduced by Rodrigo—according to legend.

Garcilaso come forth, let the good Maestre and Machuca come forth, let Rodrigo de Narváez come forth. Death to Muza, Zegri, Gomel, Almoradi, Abencerraje, Tarfe, Abenamar, Zaide, better at hunting rabbits than battling! I am Ferdinand of Aragón, doña Isabel is my very beautiful wife and queen; mounted on this horse I want to find out if there is among you anyone so valiant,

> That he might bring me the head
> Of that renegade Moor
> Who before my own eyes
> Left four Christians dead.

Speak! Speak! Do not be mute, for I wish to see whether there is among you in this plaza, a man who with blood in his eye is capable of coming out, for the sake of his lady, against the great beauty of Queen Zenobia, who is here with me. She alone, as I know from long experience, can give all of you together, and each alone, plenty to do. Consequently, give me your answer at once, for I am only one man and a Manchegan, which is enough to handle all of you."

When the Corregidor and all those with him heard such words from Don Quixote, they didn't know to what to attribute them nor what to reply. But as they were in this confusion, God willed that two young noblemen of the city should arrive. Seeing the attitude of that man in armor and all those people and the Corregidor gathered about him, one of them came up and said, "I want you to know that the man in armor you are looking at is the same man who, days ago, caused me the same wonder he causes all of you. About a month ago, more or less, he came by here in the same outfit you see, and he stayed at the Sol inn. When I saw him, Don Alonso and I went up to the door to talk to him. From his words we deduced that he is crazy or crack-brained, because he told us so many nonsensical things, making such grimaces and putting on such airs, now about the empire of Trebizond, now about the princess Micomicona, now about the terrible wounds he had received in various battles, and which had been cured by Fierabras'[4] miraculous balsam. We never could quite understand him, but we did get some information from a rather simple-minded peasant he had with him, whom he called his squire. He told us his master was from a village in La Mancha, a very honorable, rich hidalgo who was extremely fond of reading books of chivalry; in order to imitate the

[4] The adventure with Micomicona is in I, 19, and Fierabras' miraculous balsam is concocted in I, 17.

ancient knights-errant he had been wandering about like that for two years. Along with this he related many things which had happened to him and his master in La Mancha and Sierra Morena, which astonished us although we didn't know to what to ascribe it, except that the unhappy man must have lost his wits reading books of chivalry, thinking them authentic and true. Therefore, don't pay any attention to what he says here; instead, if you want to have a little fun with him, let's ask him something and you will see that he speaks as calmly as some great prince of olden times. Lord Corregidor, read what he has written on his shield, which is so ridiculous that it confirms very well indeed what I have said."

Having heard this, the Corregidor looked around and called a constable whom he sent flying to the jail to release that peasant taken there a short time before by his order, and to bring him, unfettered, into his presence. Turning to Don Quixote, who was angrily awaiting the reply, he said, "Sir knight, I, the emperor, and all these dukes, counts, and marquises with me are very pleased by your welcome arrival in this Court, for we are honored to have here today the flower of Manchegan knighthood and the undoer of the wrongs done in the world. Consequently, in reply to your challenge we say that nobody dares to go into battle with you because your courage is recognized and your name well-known in the empire, as well as in all those in the universe, so we surrender and admit the beauty of that queen you mention. We only ask Your Grace to remain in this Court fifteen or twenty days during which you will be served and entertained, not as you deserve but as our means permit. Be assured that all these princes and I will wait upon that queen, kiss her hand, and put our lives and estates at her disposal."

Don Quixote responded, "Lord Emperor, wise and prudent men always rely on the best and soundest advice, so you, being such and recognizing my courage, the strength of my arm, and my reason for defending the great beauty of Queen Zenobia, have hit the nail on the head and realized the truth. You are not like other fierce wild men who, depending on the fury of their indomitable hearts, the strength of their arms, and the sharp edges of the steel of their swords, have presumed like crazy men to enter into battle with me; they have received, as all those who join them will receive, the just payment their stupid acts and mad boldness deserve. Therefore, in answer to what your Highness and those potentates ask of me, that I honor you with my presence for a fortnight, I'll say that I cannot possibly do so now because I have an appointment in the Catholic King's Court for a fierce battle with the arrogant, strong giant Bramidán de Tajayunque, king of Cyprus, and the time set is approaching. But when I finish this, I promise all your Highnesses that I shall visit you again, to add nobility to this magnificent empire, unless I am prevented by some important new adventure, as often happens."

At these words the constable came up with good Sancho who, seeing Don Quixote in the midst of so many people, went up to him and said, "Ah, Señor Don Quixote! For heaven's sake, don't you know that I have just gone through a more terrible adventure than Prester John had in the Indies or than King Cuco of Antiopia had, or than all the knights-errant in the whole province of knighthood can have had? It is true that some uncouth people or rascals who were prisoners there stole my purse by some trick of enchantment and without being seen, and threw down my neck some seven hundred thousand million lice. However, to tell the truth, they got a good susrprise, for I'm leaving them well supplied, as they deserve, so that others like them won't dare henceforth to do such a thing to squires who are as errant and of such quality as I, but instead learn from it and let their beard burn while they drench their neighbor's."

"That's my Sancho!" said Don Quixote. "What has happened and what have you endured at the hands of those scoundrels and thieves you mention? Tell me about it and how you punished them. Did you happen to beat them all with a club?"

"Worse," said Sancho.

"Did you cut off their heads?"

"Worse," he responded.

"Did you cut them in two?"

"I did worse," he answered.

"Did you cut them up into very little pieces to throw to the birds of heaven?"

"Worse," replied Sancho.

"Well, what punishment did you give them?" said Don Quixote.

"The punishment I gave them (poor fellows, what a fix I left them in!)," added Sancho, "Was to get up a game of riddles, and when they had all had their turn I asked, 'What is it, that thing that has the hair, head, ears, teeth, tail, and forefeet and hind feet and, what's more, even the voice of a jackass and really isn't one? And they never could tell me it was a jenny. Now you judge whether I got the best of them, because they are abashed I made monkeys of them without their being aware of it! And if the constable hadn't come to put me in such a hurry, I'd have done the same thing to them again with another question I had on the tip of my tongue."

All those who heard Sancho's simple remarks laughed, but Don Quixote, without paying any attention to them, motioned to them indicating that if they wished to see and kiss the lovely hands of Queen Zenobia they should follow him. They all did so, with the Corregidor still leading the way, talking to Sancho and laughing heartily at the silly things he said.

In due time they all arrived at the Sol inn and Don Quixote dismounted from Rocinante and went in ahead, calling Barbara by the name of the invincible Queen Zenobia. She came out of the kitchen right away, wearing an old cloak of the innkeeper's as a skirt because, as has been said, the poor woman had been left in the woods in her shift and she needed a substitute for the hermit's cloak and later for the innkeeper's wife's old clothing which she had worn this far.

As soon as Don Quixote saw her he said with great civility, "Sovereign lady, these princes wish to kiss your Highness' hand."

As he entered the stable with Sancho to have Rocinante unsaddled and fed, she came to the door of the inn looking as follows: hair disheveled, half of her locks chestnut colored and half gray, full of nits and rather short; at the back, as we said, the innkeeper's cloak was tied about her waist in place of the underskirt; it was very old and full of holes, and above all, so short that it revealed half her leg and a yard and a half long feet covered with dust and stuck in ragged sandals; at the toes there showed quite a bit of toenails; her breasts, displayed between her dirty shift and her aforesaid underskirt, were black and wrinkled and so long and thin that they hung down to a length of two palm-spans; her face was sweaty and not a little dirty from the road dust and the soot from the kitchen she came out of. This beautiful face was embellished by the pleasing beauty spot of the knife-slash which cut across it; in short, it was such that it could have pleased only a galley slave of forty years at sea.

She had just come out of the door in response to the calls of her benefactor Don Quixote when she saw the Corregidor and the knights and constables who were with him, and she was so shocked that she tried to go back inside, but the Corregidor, hiding as best he could the laughter occasioned by the sight of her, prevented her by saying, "Are you perchance the beautiful Queen Zenobia whose extraordinary beauty is defended by master Don Quixote, the Manchegan? If you are, he is very foolish to insist on it, for your appearance is enough in itself to protect you, and I don't mean from the entire world but even from hell. That face, like a mass for the dead, that devilish appearence enhanced by the scar, that mouth so devoid of teeth that it could serve as the gate to the trash pile of any fair-sized city, and those sagging breasts adorned by the scanty, poor finery which covers you, reveal that you resemble a servant of Persephone, queen of the River Styx, more than you do a human being, let alone a queen."

The unhappy Barbara became upset listening to him and suspected that he probably meant to take her to jail, because he might have learned about the vicious trade she had carried on as a witch in Alcalá, which we shall tell below. Therefore she responded, "My lord Corregidor, I am not a queen nor a princess, as this crazy Don Quixote calls me, but a poor woman, a native of Alcalá de Henares, named Barbara. I was seduced by a student and taken from my home, and six or seven leagues from Sigüenza he left me next to naked and stripped as I am, tied hand and foot to a tree, and he took all I had. God willed that when I was in such a predicament this Don Quixote and the peasant who is his squire passed near the pine grove. They untied me and took me with them, promising to return me to my province."

When the mayor heard her say that she was from Alcalá, he called a little page of his who was behind him and told Barbara, "Do you see this boy here who came from there not a month ago?"

The page looked at her closely, recognized her and said, "Bless me! Barbara with the knife-slash! Who brought you to Sigüenza?"

His master asked if he knew her and he replied that he did, that she was a tripe-seller on the Calle de los Bodegones in Alcalá, and quite infamous there, and that it had been two months since they had placed her on a ladder at the door of the church of San Juste, with a pasteboard cone on her head for being a panderer and a witch, and that it was said around Alcalá that she was extremely good, better than Celestina, at passing off as virgins young women who had lost their virginity.

When she heard what the page was saying and saw that they were all laughing, she responded very angrily, "In the name of my mother's memory, the shameless rascal is lying. If they put me on the ladder, as he says, it was because of the envy of some sly neighborwomen of mine. All this and more has happened to me because I did a favor for certain friends who begged me to. But in reality they can't say anything else about me, because I wasn't there as a thief like others they take out daily to be whipped publicly through the streets; praise God for his favors."

After this she began to weep,while the others laughed. Then Don Quixote came out and when he saw her crying that way he took her hand, saying, "Don't grieve, beautiful and powerful Queen Zenobia, for I would be a very bad knight-errant if I didn't avenge you so well for the foolish actions of that student and the treacherous things done to you that you can say without reproof that if you are a beautiful woman, the knight who undid such a wrong is one of the best knights in the world."

Turning to the Corregidor and those accompanying him he said, "Sovereign princes, I am leaving for Court tomorrow; if some time or other, as usually happens, some Tartar or tyrannical king comes to attempt to disturb the peace by besieging that imperial city of yours with his strong army, and he succeeds in keeping you so confined in such straits that because of great hunger and lack of provisions during the hard siege you find yourselves forced to eat men, horses, donkeys, dogs, and mice, and women their beloved children, send for me wherever I am, for I swear and promise in the name of the order of chivalry into which I was received, that I shall come alone and armed as you see me, and by night enter the pagan camp which, after two or three nights, will be ravaged most frightfully. On the last night, by the strength of my arm I shall get through the entire opposing army, and when I enter the city, despite their sentinels, skirmishes, and weapons, you will come out at once to receive me very joyously to the sound of soft music and accompanied by many torches. The window will be full of festival lights and angels marveling at my valor, more beautiful than the three beautiful naked ladies fortunate Paris saw on Mount Ida; they won't be able to hold back their flattering cries and they won't fail to say, 'Welcome to the valiant knight!' I don't know what my distinguishing name will then be: 'of the Sun,' or 'of the Flames,' or 'of the Burning Sword,' or 'The Enchanted Shield.' I cannot state what they will call me, but I do know without a doubt that they will add to whatever name they give me 'Welcome to the favorite of all the ladies, the Phoebus of discretion, the North star of lovers, the scourge of our enemies, the liberator of our native land, and lastly, the fortress of our walls.' After this the king will take me to his royal palace where his grandees will entertain and serve me and where, above all, his daughter, the only one in the line of succession and unique in beauty and prudence, will insist on lying with me. Setting an example of continence, courtesy, and strength for the world and for kinghts-errant who will follow me, I shall use my talents to trample down the nuptial delights offered me by the entire court and the princess herself, because I am under an obligation to some benevolent luminary who will call me to greater and more magnificent enterprises, for the glory of fortunate chroniclers. It will be even more so for my great friend, Alquife, one of the greatest sages in the world; because of what I do he will have the honor, in the golden ages to come, of recording my invincible deeds."[5]

Here Sancho rushed in from the kitchen saying, "Come, sir! To blazes with all the historians of knights-errant from Adam to the Anti-Christ (God curse the whoreson)! It's getting late and the innkeeper says he has a beautiful leg of mutton, roasted with garlic and cinnamon, for you and Queen Zenobia. If you delay I fear it will turn into a leg of charcoal, because it's so tired of waiting for us that it's getting crusty."

The corregidor and all those with him left when they heard the message, some laughing and astonished at the nonsensical remarks of the master and the silliness of the squire, others at the strange kind of mania from which the unfortunate Manchegan suffered, an accursed effect of the harmful and injurious books about fabulous knights and adventures worthy of them, their authors, and even their readers; well-ordered republics will all exile them from their borders. What surprised them most was the ease with which Don Quixote used the style of speech formerly spoken in Castile in the guileless centuries of Count Fernán González, Peranzules, the Cid Ruy Díaz, and the rest of the heroes of old.

Don Quixote, Queen Zenobia, and Sancho ate supper with great pleasure, two of them because of the good food and the hunger with which they faced it, and Don Quixote because of his conceit over the applause he thought he had received from that city's princes. After supper he called the innkeeper and told him to call in a second-hand clothing merchant, because he wished to buy a nice dress for Queen Zenobia right away. After the innkeeper told him it was impossible to do that at the moment, for it was already late, but that he would get up as soon as it was dawn and go after him, each one went to bed in his own room.

Here ends the sixth part of the ingenious hidalgo, Don Quixote de La Mancha.

---

[5] This imitates Don Quixote's speech in I, 21.

SEVENTH
PART OF THE INGE-nious Hidalgo Don Quixote de La Mancha

CHAP. XXV. HOW OUR KNIGHT MET TWO STUdents when he left Sigüenza, and the amusing things that happened as he went with them to Alcalá.

AS SOON as dawn came, the innkeeper went to get a second-hand clothes merchant as Don Quixote had ordered, and he brought back the one who had the best stock in the village. He came laden with two or three women's dresses, so that anyone sending for him could select the one she liked the best. Upon reaching the house they discovered that Don Quixote and Sancho had just gotten out of bed.

When the inkeeper told his guest that the merchant of women's clothes he had sent him after was there, Don Quixote went out to look at the clothes, greeted the merchant courteously, and sent for Queen Zenobia to come and select what she liked. She looked at all of the dresses and finally chose as the best and showiest, the one which Don Quixote preferred. They selected a skirt and blouse of red cloth, embroidered in yellow and green twisted silk thread and piped in blue satin. He paid the merchant twelve ducats for everything and ordered Madam Barbara to put on the clothes there in his presence.

When Sancho saw her dressed all in red he said, overcome with laughter, "Madam Queen Zenobia, by the life of my beloved wife, Mari-Gutiérrez, who is my only consort because our Mother Church doesn't allow anything else, when I look at your roguish face, with that equally evil scar on it, I seem to see the exact image of an old mare just flayed to make sieves and sifters out of her hard hide."

The used-clothing man left, satisfied with the sale; the innkeeper was equally satisfied with the twenty-six ducats he received from the sale of a fairly good mule he kept for hire, on which Don Quixote intended to take Queen Zenobia to Court with the greatest possible pomp. There he expected to do marvelous deeds in defense of her rare loveliness and beauty in that arena.

That morning they all breakfasted, happy with the purchases they had made. When Don Quixote had put on his armor he left the inn, all bills paid, telling Sancho Panza to come along slowly with the Queen, and to look carefully after her pleasure and comfort; he would wait for them and not get too far ahead.

Sancho saddled his donkey and arranged the suitcase containing the money and the rest of the clothing on him; then, calling Barbara, he told her, "Come over here, Madam Queen, by the life of my mother Eve, Your Majesty is so red you might be queen of all the poppies not only in the wheat fields of my village, but even in those of all La Mancha." After this he got down on all fours, as he was accustomed to do, looked around and said, "Climb up! (May I live to see her get up on the gallows, and with her the one who brought us such a fine load of Spanish fly!)"[1]

Barbara mounted saying, "Oh, Sancho, what a great rascal you are! Well, hush; if Fortune gets us safely to Alcalá, I'll entertain you better than you expect."

---

[1] Does Sancho mean he thinks Don Quixote has been given Spanish fly, a strong aphrodisiac, or that at least he acts as though he had been? Sancho may believe he is smitten carnally.

"How will you entertain me?" replied Sancho. "I want you to know that if it isn't with things to eat, and plenty of them, I wouldn't give a gold fig the size of my fist for anything else you can give me."

"You have bad taste, my dear Sancho," said Barbara. "You put your taste on things more fitting for animals than for men. What I'll give you, my friend, if we reach Alcalá with the health I hope for, and if we stay there a few days, will be a girl like a golden pine tree, with whom you can enjoy more than a couple of siestas. I have lots of very fine easy-going girls there and even if your master should want one after another, I'll let him choose as though he were in a shop."

"Well, to tell the truth, Madam Queen Zenobia, I'd be very glad for you to deal me a nice shepherdess," said Sancho. "But if you do, she must be beautiful and have pretty hooves and a mustache, so that nobody will lure her away from me or lead her astray, giving the devil something to laugh at and making some midwife sweat and have some vicar or priest christen some *fructus ventris*."[2]

"You are stupid to want her to have a mustache," said Barbara. "No Barrabas would approach a woman like that. Let me do the choosing. I'll get you one of such soft flesh that it would be as easy to eat her up as eat a partridge."

"The hell you say!" said Sancho. "Not that. Strike over there, overcoat, and not on my lightning bolt,[3] as the sages say, for I am not one of those blacks from the Indies nor one of the Lutherans from Constantinople who, it is said, eat human flesh. That would be the last thing I'd do, for if the law found out about it I'd be sent to the galleys if such a crime were proved on me, in the same way Juan de Mena's *Three Hundred* were."[4]

As the two were chatting in this vein they overtook Don Quixote who, as he was going along waiting for them, had met up with two young students on their way to Alcalá. He had started talking to them in faulty Latin full of solecisms, forgetting, as a result of his dismal readings in his books of chivalry, the good and correct Latin he had studied as a boy. Although the youths were ready to burst

[2] 'Fruit of the womb.'

[3] Here is another place where it looks like Avellaneda has lifted words from Cervantes' Second Part. In II, 10, Sancho says, "The hell you say! [*¡Oxte, puto!* a fairly rare expression—this is its only use in *Don Quixote*—of unknown origin.] Strike over there, thunderbolt!" which is almost a perfect match, and importantly so given the unusualness of the first expression.

[4] *The Three Hundred* was a long poetic work of almost 300 stanzas (therefore the name) which was reprinted, i.e., set in gallies, over a long period of time. Sancho thus indicates that he would be going to row for a long stretch.

with laughter at his nonsensical remarks, nonetheless they didn't dare to contradict him, fearing the hot temper foretold by the weapons they saw he carried.

When Sancho came up and saw them talking like that he said to his master, "Watch out, sir, for these people dressed like thrushes, because they belong to the same class as those at the school in Zaragoza, who spit more than seven hundred gobs of mucus on me. But that's their funeral, for upon my word it almost cost them their lives because, as they say, do ill and feel free, do good and watch out."

"Fool, you'd be expected to get it backwards," said Don Quixote. "But let's see what revenge you took on them and if it was any better than what you did in the Sigüenza jail to those who treated you so badly."

"It's much better," replied Sancho. "Although I give you my word that wasn't bad; but listen to this other, for you'll like my courage. Once upon a time there was, let it be at the opportune time . . . "

When Don Quixote started to hear this he said, laughing, "By heaven, you are a first-class simpleton. You are beginning your account of your revenge like a fairy tale."

"On my life, you are right!" said Sancho. "Correcting myself, I'll say that when those whoreson students, doubtless progenitors of these two beard-sprouting gentlemen, began to spit on me and slap me on the neck, and a great rascal, as I said, cruelly landed a gob that covered this poor eye of mine, I began to thread my way toward the door. But then another of those demons, seeing me running one-eyed, stuck out his foot in front of me and I tripped so hard that I fell headlong outside the door. However, I avenged myself quite to my liking for all that I've told you, because I picked up my cap, which had fallen off, and threw it at another near me and hit him such a blow with it on his black cloak that he was quite lucky the blow I gave him didn't come from a gun."

"You are a devil, Señor Sancho," said one of the students. "If you so mistreat those wearing my robe, although I had nothing to do with them, as you say, I don't want to quarrel with you but to be peaceable and at your service as long as my companion and I are on the same road with you. I know he will agree with me in such a just cause."

"It will be all right," said Don Quixote, "if you will please continue narrating and detailing the curious enigmas you were telling me about as we came along. They must be strange, originating in those fertile minds, because we who belong to the order of knight-errantry and are moved by fervent desires spurred on by the charms of some very beautiful lady, also enjoy poetry; we even speak knowingly about it, and our inclination comes from divine exaltation, for Horace says, '*Est deus in nobis.*' "[5]

"Such as our rough drafts are, we'll be glad to relate them to you," replied the student.

"And it will be," said Don Quixote, "to no small judgment of your abilities that you do it in the presence of the great Queen Zenobia, here present, for her rare discourse will suffice to give eternal value to all that she may praise, and she will do so with the greatest discretion in your affairs."

At this the students looked at Barbara with no little laughter on their part and embarrassment on hers, for she recognized the flavor of muscatel wine in the flattery and praise offered banteringly by both of them. After this, one said, "On condition that Sancho figure out, with his outstanding genius, the following verses; here is the enigma:

ENIGMA

Fastened by harsh chains
I am held, through no fault of mine,
Subject to chance and fortune,
Hanging guiltless and unregretful.

I take my shape from the wind,
Although I am ill treated by it;
Dead, I am not esteemed,
I live and die in a moment.

I am continually around water,
Even though it causes my death;
If perchance I fall to the ground
I change form and die.

I am low and I am high
Near the true God,
And after eating the last bit
I am at once lifeless.

I am bright and clear;
I gladden man's eyes,
And my right name
Ends in *amp*.

---

[5] Don Quixote cites the wrong reference. It was Ovid, not Horace, who said "God is in us."

Don Quixote made him repeat it twice, and the last time said, "Indeed, Señor Student, it is a very fine enigma, and the fact that it is must be the reason that I don't comprehend its meaning. So I beg you to explain it to me, because when we reach the inn tonight I plan to write it down in order to memorize it."

Sancho had been silent all the time, listening very attentively with his finger to his forehead, while the student was repeating it. Now he happily burst out saying, "Aha, my lord Don Quixote, victory! Victory! I know what it is!"

Then the student said, "I certainly suspected it, Señor Sancho, from the first. I considered it impossible that the meaning would slip away from such a keen judgment as yours. I beg you to tell us what you have reasoned out about it."

Sancho was thoughtful for a while, then said, "It's one of two things: it's either a mountain or a latch." They all burst into hearty laughter at Sancho's nonsense, and he, aware that they were laughing at what he had just said, replied, "Since it isn't any of the things I have said, you tell us what it is, by your life. My master and I give up."

The student answered, "Well, gentlemen, you must know that the subject of the enigma propounded is a lamp, which is held blameless in the chains from which it hangs. It is said that it takes its shape from the wind, because the truth is, and one sees through experience, the glass blower forms it with his puffs of his breath. It contains water, which causes its death, for if a lamp is half-filled with water, it is extinguished immediately unless the water is accompanied by oil. As for its breaking when it falls to the ground, there is no other proof needed than experience. The fact that it is either up or down is clear, because during services it is turned up and at night it is turned low. It is true that it is near the true God, because it is usually placed in front of the Holy Sacrament. It is also apparent that after eating the last bit its life ends, because it dies when the oil I have mentioned is used up. In the same way one sees that it is clear and gladdens man; finally, its name ends in *amp*, because it is a lamp."

"By the life of her who bore me!" said Sancho, "you have explained it marvelously. Oh, whoreson, rogue! Only the devil could have guessed it!"

Don Quixote told him it was excellent, and asked the other lad to tell one himself, for he suspeceted it would be no less clever than his companion's. Without making them beg him, he began to speak as follows:

ENIGMA

My point goes always on the highest line,
Because of being, as I am, so light.
In the beginning, I was born of a sheep;
Only the Turk does not care for me.

I have a thousand shapes and aspects:
I am round, with no corners;
I cover more than ten millions,
And among them are animals.

I adorn the poor and the rich,
Without regard to custom or law;
Upon emperor or king
Do I sit, and I am large or small.

If the season of dog days is very hot,
I usually am found in hands,
And courtiers hold me
On my back, at their will.

Then I am again on high;
Hollower than a basin,
Although wind and courtesy
Are enough to bring me down.

No sooner had the discreet student finished when the keen-witted Sancho broke in, saying, "Gentlemen, that fencing term 'point on the high line, ' or whatever it is, is very clear. From the first verse I saw that it couldn't be anything but bacon, because it says "Only the Turk does not esteem me," and it's clear that the Turk doesn't eat it or pay any attention to it, because that's what that ignoramus Mohammad commanded."

Don Quixote begged the student to explain at once, without paying attention to Sancho's silly remarks, because he was most desirous of comprehending it. So the student said, "You must know that the answer to the enigma that I have just said is a hat, because it begins by saying that it always travels with its top at the highest point possible; and that's the plain truth, because it is always put on the head. It originally came from a sheep, because it is usually made of wool. The Turks don't care for it because thet wear turbans. It also says that it has many shapes and aspects, and no corners, because people wear hats that sometimes high, sometimes low, sometimes turned up and sometimes flat, and they all have rounded brims without any corners. The hat covers thousands, which is proven by the hair in which lice breed, the proper forest for that kind of animal. It sits on king and and emperor; at times it is two hands high, as in France, and it is small at other times, as in Savoy. Men hold it in their hands when it's hot, and courtiers hold it upside-down when they politely greet anyone, and afterward put it on their heads again, from where, if the wind is strong, or if he has to show courtesy to a worthy passer-by, it can come tumbling down again."

"I say now that this is more devilish to understand than the other one," responded Sancho. But all the same, let's bet whatever you wish that if you said them again, I'd guess right the first time."

"What an ignoramus," said Don Quixote. "In that way any man in the world would guess right if he were told in advance.

"Well, when did Sancho ever say anything that wasn't told him beforehand?" replied Barbara. "But that's no wonder, because nobody ever was right in what he said unless he had first learned and studied it. If you don't believe this, tell me who can call anything, even the commonest thing, by its name, even the Lord's Prayer, which is the primer of our religion, if it hasn't been said and repeated to him?"

Sancho was infintely pleased with the wise way in which Barbara had made excuses for his answer, and all of them, Sancho above all, praised its cleverness with a thousand compliments. Don Quixote said, "Don't marvel at the cleverness of Her Majesty, because if the edge of my sword were as keen as the conceits of her divine understanding, her royal person would be in peaceful possession of her kingdom and of the Amazons, and I wouldn't have to conquer the kingdom of Cyprus, nor soil my hands on the haughty Bramidán de Tajayunque. But let's put this aside until I find myself in Court, for these are memories that provoke me to such anger that I fear it will make me cause more deaths in the lands where I am going than God caused in the universal flood. Returning to our peaceful conversation, I beg you to be good enough to give me written versions of those enigmas, if you have copies."

One said he would write it at the inn because he didn't have his down on paper. The other put his hand in his coat pocket and took out the one about the lamp, saying, "Take mine, sir, because opportunely I already have it written down."

Don Quixote took it from the student very politely, and as the latter gave it to him, he dropped another piece of paper. When Don Quixote asked him what that paper was, he replied that it contained some verses he had composed in his village to a maiden who was a relative of his and whom he loved very much. Her name was Ana, and he had composed it in such a skillful way that each stanza began with *Ana*. Don Quixote begged him most urgently to read them, sure that since they were by him that they couldn't fail to be exceedingly fine. The student, no little conceited, a trait always found in poets, began reading them, with full attention from those present. I have taken them faithfully from the story of our ingenious hidalgo, which I am translating,[6] in which they are recounted.

STANZAS TO A LADY
NAMED ANA'

Ana, love made me captive
To you, whose name has
Two *a*'s with an *n* between,
Which means two souls yoked together

Ah, not a soul does that yoke tell
That you are in love, except to me alone;
Aware of this, I offered you
The best my soul contains.

Anaxarete was, among wise men,
Famed as a murderess,
And you the same are, of my life,
Ana, by simply moving your lips.

A natty little bird the duck
That swims so gracefully,
So I too, on the sea of Love,
Oh beautiful shore, do swim to you.

Anathema means to the Church
One who has left the faith.
Not so I, for I have loved faithfully
Another Diana of Ephesus in you.

Anastasia was the wife
Of a king who reigns in Heaven,
And, Ana, in this soul you are the queen,
You, who are in every way beautiful.

Ananiah and his companions
Sang inside a furnace;
And you, Ana, like a hot blast,
Set me afire with your north winds.

---

[6] This is the only other time in the whole book that the narrator reminds us he is translating from an Arabic source. See Chapter I, note 2.

Analogy is the name given
  To what means proportion,
  Such as your perfection
  Has with your fame.

Anabaptists teach that
  They are twice baptized;
  And I avow that my troubles,
  Ana, are duplicated carelessly.

An anchorite I do imitate
  By my tears and silence;
  In this way, Ana, I worhip
  Your infinite worth.

Annals, Ana, are history
  Written by some investigator;
  The memory of you lives in me,
  Ana, as though it were in annals.

Ah, Namur was, so they say,
  A rich, strong and beautiful town;
  But you, Ana, are a city
  that anyone must serve.

When the student finished reading the stanzas, Don Quixote said, "Certainly they are rare and fine, in my opinion, from among those of their kind."

After this, Sancho, as usual, broke in, saying, "Señor Student, I swear that in my judgment they are very lovely, although I think they lack the life and death of Annas and Caiaphas, persons whom the four holy Gospels mention copiously.[7] It wouldn't be a bad thing for me to compose some for you also, if only to praise the many honorable descendents they still have in the world. But, leaving this aside, would you be good enough to compose others which will start with *Mari-Gutiérrez* as these do with *Ana*? Begging your pardon, and to my grief, she is my wife and will be as long as God wishes. However, if you decide to compose them, bear in mind that you should by no means call her *queen*, but rather *admiral's wife*, because I don't think that Don Quixote has any intention of making me a king as long as he lives. Therefore, I shall perforce have to end up as an admiral or governor of a province whether I like it or not, when he wins one of those islands or peninsulas[8] he has promised me. In truth, if, though

[7] Annas is mentioned in the Gospels twice and Caiaphas only three times.

[8] In Spanish the words played upon here are *ínsula* 'island' and *península*.

we have both turned to secular things, we had chosen the ecclesiastical line, there, too, we should have prospered since we have gone out in search of adventures, for they have made us cardinals[9] by giving us welts redder than the color used by the cardinals in Rome or Santiago in Galicia. But after all, people are right when they say that one who won't give anything up may up and die."

With this entertainment they reached the inn at nightfall, the two students still with them because Don Quixote traveled so slowly that he went only four or five leagues a day. Not even Rocinante could do any more, because of his skinniness and the years he bore. Consequently, they journeyed more than three days without anything of importance happening to them, although they aroused much notice and amusement in the villages, especially in Hita,[10] because of Don Quixote's treatment of Queen Zenobia, who was quite well-known throughout that region and just as well by the students, who daily recounted her virtues to Don Quixote. However, it was impossible to persuade him about anything contrary to what his fanciful and mad imagination had conceived.

CHAP. XXVI. ABOUT THE AMUSING EVENTS THAT took place between Don Quixote and a company of actors he met at the inn near Alcalá.

As Don Quixote was traveling with his companions and the two students mentioned above, it happened that as they were about two leagues from Alcalá, Sancho and his master thought it was too late to get there by daylight, as they wished. Regretful about this, Don Quixote asked the students if there was any village where they could spend the night before reaching Alcalá. They replied that there wasn't, but perhaps, not wanting to spend the night in the open or without any conveniences, they added that about a quarter of a league away there was an inn where they could spend the night reasonably well.

[9] In Spanish, *cardenal* means both 'cardinal' and 'welt'.

[10] Hita is a village in the hills fairly near Barbara's hometown of Alcalá de Henares. Nowadays, its fame lies in its being the village of the celebrated thirteenth century poet, Juan Ruiz, author of *The Book of Good Love.*

No sooner did Sancho hear the word inn mentioned when he commended himself to all the devils and said, "By the guts of Jonah's whale! I beg my master Don Quixote not to go there for any reason, for what these gentlemen call inns are the enchanted castles you talk about, where giants, hobgoblins, and ghosts, wild men, phantoms or pamphlets, or whatever you call them, have thousands of times given us so much to weep about and to heal, as my squire's bones know, for yours, sir, are luckier with that precious balsam remedy, but its virtue failed with me because I am a not a knight in armor."[1]

Don Quixote paid no attention to his squire's fears and entreaties, but said courageously, "Let come what may; we knights-errant are ready for anything. So let's go there, in God's name."

They had gone scarcely twenty paces when they spotted the inn. When they were within a musket shot from it Don Quixote, who had gone along reflecting on what Sancho had told him, said, "I have just rememebered, my dear Sancho, the great troubles, misfortunes, worries, crises, dangers, and disasters which we went through a year ago in castles like this one we see, where we lodged, because secretly hidden in them was that wise sorceror, my rival, who has always tried and is trying to do me all the damage he has been able and is able to do with his perverse arts. The worst of it is that he has doubtless returned to this castle to do me some serious harm, as he usually does. But in the end his arts will be of no avail against the valor of my person. What can and must be done to avoid this great danger is for you and my lady, the queen, and these worthy students to follow me slowly as a rearguard. I want to go ahead to see if all that I suspect is true."

Sancho replied, "If you had believed me at first, we wouldn't get into these mixups, and please God we won't all cry over it! But go ahead, as you say, and good luck to you. We shall all follow you as far back as we can, although not as much as we'd like."

Don Quixote advanced a little, and when he saw seven or eight people dressed in different outfits near the inn, he was perplexed, turned Rocinante around, went back to his group and said, "Everybody be quiet, gentlemen, and carefully watch the castle door and the horrid monsters there."

They all looked in that direction. When those in the inn saw a man in armor of that kind, with such a large shield, something not very common there, and saw that at one moment he advanced and

---

[1] The episode of Fierabrás' balsam is in I, 17.

the next he went back to speak to a woman dressed all in red, they came out, curious to see the strange sight outside the inn. There were quite a few onlookers from a company of serious actors, among the most famous in Castile, who had decided to stay there that afternoon with their manager to rehearse some plays in order to enter Alcalá well prepared the next day. The theater there is important because of the clever and consummately good creative talents who have made it famous all over Spain.

Accordingly, when Don Quixote saw them standing in a row and that they were able to see him, with their manager, a tall, dark man standing in front of them all, holding a rod in one hand and in the other a playbook which he was reading, he began to speak: "I now realize, friend Sancho, the great favors I receive every day from the wise Urganda, my benevolent, faithful protectress, for today she has clearly given me to understand that my adversary, the wicked sorceror, Frestón is waiting for me in this fortress with some malevolent ploy or deception, among the strong chains of his dark dungeon. However, since I am well informed about the matter, I am determined to put an end to him once and for all, so that henceforth I may go about safe and free in any part of the world I travel. So that you, Sancho, and you, most powerful queen, and you, most virtuous youths, may believe that I am telling the truth, don't you see among those soldiers serving as sentinels at the castle door a tall, dark-complected man with a wand in his right hand and a book in his left? Well, that man is my mortal enemy who has come to prevent my appointed battle with the king of Cyprus, Bramidán de Tajayunque, with the intention of going about the world later insulting me and proclaiming that because of pure cowardice I did not dare to go to Court to face him where he was waiting to fight me. If he should so prevent me with his enchantments, it would be like death for me; consequently, I am determined to go and see if I can rid the world of one who has caused and still causes so much evil and harm in it."

Astonished at Don Quixote's remarks, the students went up to him with their hats off and one said, "If you please, Señor Don Quixote, watch what you say and intend to do, for we know very well that this is an inn and not a fortress nor a castle, nor is there any guard of soldiers as you think. The people at the door are well-known in Spain, for they are actors, and the one you call a sorcerer is the manager, Señor What's-his-Name; the other one, with the cape slung over his shoulder is Señor So-and-So," and in this way he gave the name of each one, because he knew them well.

Angry at this, Don Quixote replied, "What I say stands, in spite of all who try to contradict me. I affirm again that that tall man is the sorcerer I mentioned, my rival, drawing circles, figures and glyphs with that wand he has in his hand to invoke demons, and with that book he has in his other hand he conjures, forces, and lures them to do whatever he desires, whether they want to or not. So that you may clearly see that I am telling the truth, go before him and tell him you are pages of the Loveless Knight, who is coming here, and you will see what happens.

They all very willingly offered to go, and when they did, they told the manager and his company all about who Don Quixote was, what he had done and said on the road and in Sigüenza, how Barbara, the well-known whorehouse-keeper of Alcalá who has a knife slash was called Queen Zenobia by him, and how he had met her on the trip. The manager and his companions laughed uproariously at all this, greatly pleased to have something with which to while away the time that evening.

While this was going on Don Quixote continued approaching the inn slowly. When Sancho saw this, he got off his donkey right away to find out how that affair his master was going to undertake would end. Barbara asked him to lift her off the mule too, because she was so near the inn. He did it by taking her in his arms, and as his face was necessarily close to hers, Barbara said, "Ow! Sancho, what a thick, rough beard you have! Devil take me if its not like the hog-bristles that shoemakers use! Good Lord! What a rough time the wife you sleep with must have every time she kisses it!"

"Well, why in the devil should I have to kiss it?" said Sancho. "Let the mother who made it, or Barrabas, who is no ignoramus, kiss it; I kiss nobody in this world, unless it be a loaf of bread when I pick it up in the morning or the wineskin at any hour of the day."

"Come on, brother, don't play the fool with me," said Barbara. "I'll bet women don't taste bad to you; if you should catch me tonight in the bed I have to sleep in alone and come and get under the sheets very quietly, without anybody hearing you, damned if that would stop me! Only one thing would worry me, and that is that I shouldn't dare to cry out for fear of Don Quixote and the other guests; it's better to endure than to shout. If we did anything, well, we'd better be in the dark and nobody would have to know about it. In short, clearly I, because of modesty, and you, because you are an honorable man, would keep quiet about it."

Sancho, not understanding Barbara's tune, said, "To tell the truth, you're right, for if there's no shouting and we are in the dark, I sleep much better and like a log, so much so that a million bells out of tune wouldn't rouse me."

"Alas! It's a bad day for me!" responded Barbara. "How dull-witted you are! You have to be led along the wagon-road; give me your hand, robber of my soul, for I am so numb that I can't stand on my feet."

Sancho gave her his hand, saying, "What the deuce! Here it is; go slow about that business of 'robber'. You must know that I don't stand for jokes, and some scribe or Pharisee of the many malicious ones there are in the world today might hear it, report me to the law and have me given two hundred lashes."

Turning around, they saw Don Quixote talking loudly. He had gone quite near the inn, and with the butt of his lance resting on the ground he began to address the people at its door in this way: "Oh, wise sorcerer, whoever you are, who have always been my adversary from the day of my birth to this hour, helping (pagan that you are) that knight or those knights you know I have beaten with my strong arm, taking from them the reputation they have in the world and acquiring their fame, proclaiming my deeds and their cowardice in the same way as the Alexanders, Caesars, Hannibals, and Scipios of olden times! Tell me, wicked and devilish magician, why do you do so many and such evil things in the world, contrary to natural and divine law, going out into the highways and their unavoidable cross-roads accompanied by the huge wild men who sereve you in this fortress of yours, humiliating loving knights, who can offer little resistence, by seizing, robbing, and mistreating them, and ravishing women of high rank and maids of honor, who, accompanied by astute dwarfs and watchful squires, travel along the highways with confidential letters and jewels and costly things, seeking the knights whom their ladies tenderly love? Not only are you shameless about doing what I claim you do, but as an inhuman and cruel tyrant, you place them in this castle, not to entertain and welcome them, but to put them in cruel, dark dungeons with many other princesses, knights, pages, squires, carriages, and horses you have in it. Therefore, oh bloody, fierce, and indomitable tyrant, without saying another word, bring out to me right away all the people to whom I refer, giving back to each one the freedom you oppressed and the treasures of which you have robbed them. Prostrate on the ground, in the hands of the beautiful, peerless Queen Zenobia who is with me, swear to emend your past evil life and henceforth aid duennas and maidens and undo the wrongs of needy people. If you do this and turn to merciful ways, I shall spare your life even though I should have taken it many years ago. If you are unwilling to do this, let all those in that fortress of yours come out to do battle with me, on horseback or on foot, with the weapons they prefer, and all together, as is the custom among pagan and barbarous people such as you. Don't think that because you are holding that book and wand like a sorcerer and superstitious magician, no matter how great a one you are, your spells will not protect you from the edge of my sword. I have invisibly with me the wise Alquife, my chronicler and defender in all my hardships, and also the wise Urganda the Unknown; compared to her science, yours is ignorance. Come out quickly, quickly!"

With this he began to make his horse prance back and forth, at which all the actors laughed. When Sancho saw them laughing so heartily after his master had spoken words he thought were capable of frightening them, he called out, "Come now, haughty, monstrous actors, oppressors of the shamefaced princesses there behind you praying humbly to heaven to free them from your tyrannical theatrical life, let's put an end to this. You are to surrender at once to my master Don Quixote de La Mancha, because the Queen of Segovia[2] and I wish to enter the inn, because I vow we are very hungry. If you won't do this, send us out some hunks of bread and Her Majesty and I will busy ourselves massacring them while my master does the same to you in this coming warfare. I'd like to see him fighting at home with all the Greeks in Galicia."

The actors were so astonished that they didn't know what to say in answer to the nonsensical remarks of the one and the silly statements of the other. The manager, however, left the inn with four or five of his companions, went up to Don Quixote and said, "Sir Knight-errant, these worthy students have informed us of your great courage, virtue, and strength, which are not only enough to subdue this fortress or castle in which I have been living for more than seven hundred years, but also the fiercest and wildest giant to be found in the entire nation of giants. Consequently, all these princes and knights and I surrender and submit to being your vassals. We beg you to dismount from that beautiful horse, lay aside the lance and shield, and remove that splendid armor so that it will not be in your way and you can allow these servants to duly serve you, as they wish

[2] Sancho changes Zenobia to the name of the Spanish city Segovia, which is quite familiar to him. This is the first time of many that he does this.

to do. Be assured that although I am a pagan, as my dark face and robust form denote, I still have at hand enchantments to harm anyone I have in mind. Come, enter and eat supper with us and you will see how pleased you will be to have met us. Let your lady, Queen Zenobia, alias Barbara, enter in safety also, for we should all like to find out from her which herb disturbs her most at night, rue or verbena, which is picked the morning of Saint John's Day."

"Oh, false wizard!" said Don Quixote. "Do you plan now to deceive me with your treacherous, flattering words and have me trustingly enter inside your castle, falling into the trap which you, anxious to do what you will with me later, have ready for me at your door? You will not deceive me, because I have known you since Zaragoza, where you fastened me up with handcuffs and a big log on my feet in that dungeon you know about, from which I was taken by the brave man from Granada, Don Álvaro Tarfe."

Sancho, who had been listening to what was going on, took his place at Don Quixote's side, saying as he looked the manager in the eye, "Oh, whoreson, great pagan! Do you think that we don't understand you here? Take your story elsewhere, for by the grace of God we are all Christians here, from head to foot, and we know that three and four make nine, for we are not fools because we were reared in Argamesilla next to El Toboso; if you don't believe us, stick your fist in our mouth and you'll see whether we suck it. I say for him and all those Lutherans with him to surrender if he doesn't want us to lose our temper. Let's become reconciled and this way we'll be as good friends as before."

Don Quixote said angrily, spurring Rocinante, "Get out of my way, Sancho; don't make peace with faithless pagans. The most we Christians can do with them is call a truce."

"Well, sir," said Sancho, standing in front of Rocinante, "if it's true that you are as much a Christian as I am (God knows that) for I have been one since before my birth, and since that time I firmly and truly believe in Jesus Christ and his commandments, and in the holy churches in Rome and in all its streets, plazas, belfries, and corrals, let's call the turuce[3] you talk about, because it seems to be a little late and my insides are spurring my belly from hunger."

"Get out of my sight, you sheep!" said Don Quixote. "I say, get out of the way." With this he lowered the lance, turned Rocinante toward the manager who let him come, and, dodging to the side, he

[3] Sancho garbles the word 'truce' that Don Quixote has just said.

seized the rein of the nag, who immediately became as quiet as though he were made of stone. The other companions came at once to help; one took away the lance, another the shield, and another seized his foot and tipped him over on the other side, after which three or four of those servants called stagehands and grips also came to assist. Some seizing his feet and others his arms, they carried him into the inn, much against his will, where they held him down on the floor for a good while, without his being able to get up.

Let curious people deduce from his nature and ferocity, already comprehended from the first parts of his history, what the unhappy Loveless Knight did and said when he saw himself in such a predicament. This historian won't dare relate them because they are so extraordinary and worthy of the most farfetched exaggerations. What I can say is that the manager ordered the helpers to hold him in that position and not turn him loose for any reason until he returned.

After this he went out with some companions to look for Sancho, whom he found in Barbara's arms, tearing his thick beard and weeping bitterly over what his master was going through. He told Sancho, "Now, rascal, you'll pay for what you've done last year and this year. Get up; tears and prayers are of no avail with me. After I get you to the castle I'll flay you nicely and for supper tonight I'll have your liver, and tomorrow the rest of your body roasted, for I live on nothing but human flesh."

When Sancho heard that cruel sentence he got down on his knees, crossing his hands under his cap, and began saying, "Oh, Señor Pagan, the most honorable one in pagan communities! By the wounds of Saint Lazarus (may he be in glory) I pray you to have pity on me! If you please, before eating me give orders that I be allowed to go and say goodby to Mari-Gutiérrez, my wife, who is quick-tempered. If she learns that you have eaten me without my bidding her farewell she will consider me extremely negligent and will not hold me in high esteem. Enough said; I promise well and truly to return here any day you wish; if I fail to show, may it please God this cap will be missing at the hour of my death, which is when I'll need it most."

"Friend, it can't be helped," responded the manager. Raising his voice he said, "Hey, to whom am I talking? Servants, bring me that three-pronged spit on which I usually skewer whole men, and roast this peasant for me right away."

Upon hearing this, poor Sancho looked around and saw Barbara laughing and talking to one of the actors, and he said to her, incredibly sorrowful in spirit, "Alas, madam Queen Zenobia! Have pity on poor Sancho, your loyal lackey and servant, and see what trouble he is in! And since he is so powerless, request that Moorish lord to take those parts of me he wants most, but not to kill me."

Then Barbara went over, saying, "I beg you, most powerful warden or noble castellan of this castle to spare Sancho's life and limbs this time for love of me, because I am indebted to him for his good services. I'll guarantee his good behavior, and if he fails in this, all his property, furniture, and farms he owns or may own will be forfeited, in addition to whatever punishment you may order given him."

The manager very pompously replied with pretended anger, "You will excuse me, madam Queen of the Calle de los Bodegones in Alcalá; I can by no means fail to put an end to this villain unless he becomes a Moor and follows our Mohammed's Koran."

"Sancho responded, "I say, Señor Turk, that I believe in all the Mohammeds there are from East to West, and in their Corral, in the manner and as you command, and insofar as our Mother the Church, for which I'll give my life and soul and all I can mention, permits and allows."

Well, then, it is necessary to cut off a little of your pluscuamperfectum with my very sharp knife," said the manager.

"What pluscuam are you talking about? I don't understand any of that jargon," responded Sancho.

"I am saying that in order for you to be a true Turk it is first necessary to circumcise you with a very sharp knife," replied the manager.

By Nicomemus'[4] tongs!" said Sancho, "You'll cut off nothing there, for my wife, Mari-Gutiérrez, has it so well measured and accounted for that she often examines it and asks for a report about it; no matter how little was lacking, she'd miss it right away, and it would be robbing her of the apple of her eyes, and she would call me a careless squanderer of Nature's riches. If you please, don't let what you're going to cut off be from there, because, as I say, you are all aware that everything in a house is needed, and sometimes there's even too little. But cut off a piece of my cap, for although it is true that it will be missed, still it can be repaired more easily than that other."

At this, the manager turned his head away because he couldn't hide the laughter Sancho's simplemindedness caused him. After a while, dissimulating to the best of his ability, he said, "Get up, Señor New Moor, and shake hands; bear in mind that from now on you must speak Arabic, as I do, for you will soon be promoted to chief or teacher of the Koran, or a grand vizier."

"For heaven's sake, even if they make me head shepherd," said Sancho, "I should prefer going first to my village to tell two oxen, six sheep, two goats, eight hens, and a little pig I have at home, what has happened to me, and to say good-bye to Mari-Gutiérrez in the Moorish language and to tell her how I have become a Turk. Perhaps she will want to become one too, but I find one problem if she wants to do this: I don't know how we can circumcise her, because there's no place under the sun where it can be done."

The manager replied, "That doesn't matter at all, because we'll cut off the thumb of her right hand, which will suffice."

"Indeed you're very right," said Sancho. "She won't miss that finger as much as I'd miss what you want to cut off. In fact, she is a very poor spinner, but nonetheless I have thought where it would be best to circumcise her so that you won't remove the finger you suggest; it would still be a good thing for her to have five fingers on her hand, as God commands in works of charity."

---

[4] Sancho means Nicodemus.

"Then where shall we circumcise her?" asked the manager.

"Her tongue," responded Sancho. "She has a longer one than the giant Goliath and she is the biggest chatterbox and tattler in all the gossiping groups or lands of parrots."

After this they returned to the door of the inn where the herders had the good hidalgo, Don Quixote, sitting on a chair without his armor and bound hand and foot so he couldn't move. Seeing him, the manager said to Sancho, "Brother, you see what a fix your master is in. You must tell him that now you are a Moor and persuade him to become one also if he wishes to get out of the trouble he is in, because if he doesn't, in two hours we shall be eating him roasted on the spit on which we meant to roast you."

"Leave it to me," he said. "I'll make him become a Moor post-haste."

The manager took his stand in front of Don Quixote and said, "What's the matter, Knight? How are things going? You have finally landed in my hands and before you get out of them your beard will be so long it will drag on the ground, and the nails on your hands and feet will be as long as elephant's tusks; besides this you will be eaten by mice, lizards, bedbugs, lice, fleas, mosquitos, gnats, horseflies, and other repulsive vermin. You will be manacled with a very heavy chain in a dark jail with others of your sort who are handcuffed there, with their feet shackled until they reach the end of their miserable, unhappy days."

Don Quixote answered, saying, "Oh, my wise adversary! Don't think your wild, vain words and injurious acts are enough to cause me to deviate in even the slightest way from my duty as a true knight-errant. Nor will I be intimidated by the suffering to be expected in the forthcoming hardships and tribulations that threaten me, for I am sure that in the course of seven hundred years, at the most, I shall be freed from the cruel enchantment which, contrary to law and reason, and only for your pleasure, you have cast on me. Oh, inhuman wizard! I do not lose hope that before the end of that period of time some Greek prince who wishes to be a knight-errant will get me out of here. There probably is such a one who will leave Constantinople by night, without bidding anyone in Court farewell and without his parent's knowledge, urged on by his honor and encouraged by the counsel of a great and very learned magician, a friend of his. After undergoing very great hardships and dangers, having won much honor in all the kingdoms and provinces of this universe, he will arrive at this well-fortified castle, killing the fierce giants, who, because of your precaution, act as guardians defending its entrance and the drawbridge which protects it. He will also kill the two rampant griffins, inhuman gatekeepers of its first door. Entering the first patio and not hearing any noise or seeing anyone to oppose him, he will sit on the ground a while because of his weariness. Then he will hear a furious voice which will say to him, without his knowing who is speaking, 'Get up, Greek prince, for you entered this castle at an inauspicious hour and to your harm!' No sooner will this be said than there will come out a ferocious dragon spitting fire from its mouth and poison from its eyes, with claws longer than Biscayan daggers, a tail as long and sharp as a polished broadsword, which will knock down whatever it comes across. But the aforesaid prince, aided by the invincible help of his friendly and benevolent sage, will in the end break all this magic spell. Victoriously passing through another door farther inside, he will find himself in a peaceful garden filled with many kinds of flowers, and containing beautiful fruit-bearing aromatic trees whose tops will be full of swans, larks, nightingales, and a thousand different kinds of singing birds. It will be irrigated by a thousand brooks in which it will be difficult to tell whether their waters are crystal or milk. In the center there will appear to him a very lovely nymph clothed in a trailing gown sprinkled with carbuncles, diamonds, emeralds, rubies, topazes, and amethysts. With a kindly expression she will give him a bunch of keys with one hand, and with the other she will place on his head a garland of willow and amaranth, and she will appear to the sound of celestial music. Then the aforesaid prince will go to the dungeons and open them with the golden keys, giving joyous freedom to all the prisoners in them. I shall be the last, and he will ask me to invest him with the armor of a knight-errant with my own hands and accept him as an inseparable companion. I shall grant all he wishes, impelled by his handsomeness, prudence and strength. Afterward we shall go about the world together for innumerable years, happily taking on whatever adventures come our way."

CHAP. XXVII. IN WHICH THE EVENTS OCCURRING to Don Quixote and the actors are continued.

HE ACTORS were highly surprised by Don Quixote's brand of insanity and the foolish remarks he was stringing together, but Sancho, who had been behind the manager, listening to all his master was saying, told him, "Well, Señor Loveless, how goes it? We are all here by the grace of God."

"Oh, Sancho!" said Don Quixote. "What are you doing? Has this enemy of ours done you any harm?"

Sancho responded, "None, although, to tell the truth, I almost found myself sitting on a spit on which this Moorish gentleman wanted to roast me so he could eat me, but he has pardoned me, seeing I have become a Moor."

"What are you saying, Sancho?" said Don Quixote. "You have become a Moor! Is it possible that you have done such a foolish thing?"

"Well, plague take the beard of the sacristan of Argamesilla!" answered Sancho. "Wouldn't it be worse if he had eaten me, for then I couldn't be either a Moor or a Christian? Don't say anything; I know what I'm doing. Just let's get out of here; later on you'll see what happens."

Then the manager, taking pity on the anguish he noted was causing Don Quixote's face to break out in a light perspiration, and seeing that the students, Barbara, and the whole company were now tired of laughing, said, "Hush now, Sir Knight, this is no longer the time to pretend or to conceal what should rightfully be made clear. You must know, Señor Don Quixote, that I am by no means the sage who is your opponent; instead, I am a great and faithful friend of yours, and as such I have always and everywhere looked after and do look after your affairs better than you do yourself. So now I have brought about all you have seen, to test your prudence and endurance. Consequently, all of you leave him alone at once; let him enjoy this castle of mine and rest as long as he wishes, for I have prepared it for such princes and knights. Oh, most famous knight-errant! Embrace me, for I am here to serve you, not to do you any harm, as you thought. Bear in mind that your coming here with the great Queen Zenobia was all brought about by my wizardry, because it is most important for you and your servants to reach the great court of the Catholic king, where a million princes are expecting you every moment, and which you will leave with great applause and victory."

With that the servants let him go and the manager embraced him, as did all his companions. When Don Quixote saw himself free he was astounded, to think that he had believed him to be a necromancer as well as by what he said. Taking it all as truth he arose and with outstretched arms went toward the manager saying, "Oh, wise friend! I was marveling that you failed to help me in the trials and tribulations that I was just experiencing, with your great prudence and efficient cunning. Take me in your arms and come to mine, which have dismembered robust giants and expertly executed your enemies and mine."

Hereupon they all embraced him again with fresh signs of joy. The wife of the manager, coming up to look at the face of that madman who was being embraced by everybody, said to him, considering the ridiculous figure he cut, "Sir Knight, I am the daughter of this great sage who is your friend. Take care so that if some time I need your help, or some giant or magician carries me off under a spell, you won't fail to help me; in any event, my father here will pay you."

Another one of the actresses (a woman who was standing to one side, laughing) said, "He'll even let you see the performance for free, if you'll only put a half *real* in his hand."

Don Quixote responded, "It is not necessary, sovereign lady, to request of me anything requiring sevice to you when I am under such obligation to your sage father. Believe me, even if the entire universe should plot against your beauty, and all the sages and magicians born in Egypt should come to Spain to touch even a hair of your head, I alone, not relying on the great power of your father, would be able not only to defend you and get you out of their hands despite all they could do, but also to lay their treacherous false heads in your hands."

At this point the manager called him, saying, "Sir Knight, supper is ready and the tables are set, so will you please come and honor me and these gentlemen with your company, because we have important business to do later." He said this because after supper he intended to rehearse a play they had prepared for Alcalá and the Court.

Sancho was surprised to see his master freed from imprisonment. He was so happy he went up to the manager to say, "Oh, wise sage! About this matter of becoming a Moor: now that you have made me see how worthwhile it is, does it have to continue? Because, for God's sake and my conscience, I think I cannot be one under any circumstances."

The manager answered, "Well, why can't you?"

"Because every day I'd break Mohammed's law that commands one not to eat bacon or drink wine. I am such a devilish guardian of such things that when I find them at hand I don't fail to eat and drink even under threat of torture," he said.

A clergyman who happened to be in the inn answered this by saying, "If you, Señor Sancho, have promised this wise magician that you will become a Moor, disregard your promise, for I, by virtue of the papal bull of compensation, absolve you of it as well as of the act. By virtue of this I can do so by only giving you the penance of not eating or drinking for three whole days. Be advised that only by doing this light penance will you be as much a Christian as you were before."

"Don't order me to do that, licentiate," responded Sancho. "Not for three days, not even for three hours, would I dare do that penance, even though I knew I'd burn for not doing it. What you can prescribe for me, if you'd like, is for me not to sleep with my eyes open, not drink with my teeth clenched, not wear my jacket under my shirt, nor relieve myself with my pants on. Even though these things are difficult, I give you my word that I'll do them, before God and my conscience."

After these words they went to the table to sit down and eat supper, but before doing so, while they were all standing around the table, hats off, the clergyman began to say grace in Latin, and they began to eat supper. The manager said, "You must realize, gentlemen, that the reason Sancho did not take off his cap while grace was being said is that he still has the habits of the time he was a Moor, although he has yet to be circumcised. I have delayed doing it because he begged me in tears to circumcise his cap, if it had to be done, instead of the part where circumcision is usually done, because that was what his wife was most zealous of and for which she held him most accountable."

After this he continued relating all that had happened, and finished at the same time the supper was over and the table cleared. He turned to Don Quixote and proceeded to tell him that in order to entertain him in that castle of his he had ordered a play to be performed in which he would take part also, and so would the one who said she was his daughter.

Don Quixote thanked him very politely and, sitting down in the patio with Barbara, the clergyman, the two students, and Sancho, and the people at the inn, they began to rehearse the serious play

called *The Testimony Avenged*, by the outstanding Lope de Vega Carpio, in which a son accuses the queen, his mother, of having committed adultery with a certain servant, in the king's absence. He was moved by the devil and angry because on a certain occasion, following the express order given her by her husband, the king, she had refused him a Cordovan horse to which he had taken a liking.[1]

As the play reached this point and Don Quixote saw the manager's wife, whom he thought to be his daughter, so grieved (because she was playing the role of the accused queen) and noted that there was nobody to defend her cause, he arose in sudden anger, saying, "This is the greatest iniquity, treachery, and perfidy, violating God and every law, committed against the innocent and very chaste queen. That knight who thus accuses her is a false and deceitful traitor, and as such I challenge him to singular combat with no weapons except what I now have, one single sword."[2]

Saying this, he seized it with incredible fury and began to call for the accuser, who was a good actor. He, laughing with all the rest at Don Quixote's foolish anger, took his stand in the center with his sword unsheathed, saying that he agreed to the fight, to take place in

---

[1] *The Testimony Avenged* is indeed a play by Lope de Vega, and was first published in a rather defective edition in 1604. Its story is based on a medieval historical occurance.

[2] Was Avellaneda here copying yet another episode from Cervantes' Part II? In Cervantes' Chapter 26, Don Quixote interrupts a puppet play, this time to save Don Gaiferos and Doña Melisendra, who are being pursued by

the Court before the king, within only twenty days. Looking around to see if he could find anything to give him as a pledge he saw a packsaddle propped against one of the inn's posts, and on it there was a broad crupper. Half-laughing, he threw it at Don Quixote saying, "Cowardly knight, pick up that rich and precious garter of mine as a pledge and sign that our battle will take place before His Majesty at the time I have set."

Don Quixote bent down and picked it up. Seeing that they all laughed as he did so, he said, "It is not suitable for valiant princes to laugh because a deceitful traitor like this has the courage to fight me. Instead, they should weep, seeing the queen so sorrowful, although she had had the very good fortune to find me here in such a crisis, so that such treachery may not continue." Turning to Sancho, he said, "Oh, faithful squire! Take this precious garter which belongs to the king's son and put it in the suitcase for the twenty days until I kill this deceitful prince who has given such false testimony against my lady, the queen."

Sancho took it and said to his master, "Why do you want us to put this crupper in the suitcase with our linen when it is so dirty? To the devil with it; I'll tie it to my donkey's cinch and it will stay there until we find out to whom it belongs."

"Oh, fool, you call that a crupper?" said Don Quixote

"Well, what in the devil is it but a crupper strap?" said Sancho.

"Don't you see, jackass, that it is an exquisitely fine garter belonging to the king's son, which has what they call fringes of gold, and from each cord there hangs an emerald or a ruby or a diamond?" replied Don Quixote.

"What I see here, if I'm not drunk, is a plaited length of esparto grass with two cords at the ends, each quite dirty; it is used as a rump strap on the packsaddle of some donkey," responded Sancho.

"Did anybody ever see such madness as that of this squire, which causes him to call a scarlet garter of folded taffeta a crupper?" said Don Quixote

"I say once and two hundred times that it is a crupper as surely as I know my grandfather; there is no need to be obstinate," Sancho answered.[3]

Moors; he destroys the whole production, including props and puppets, trying to save the two lovers.

[3] Here Avellaneda imitates the episodes in Cervantes' *Don Quixote* (I, 21 and 45) where Don Quixote swears that the barber's basin is, in fact, Mambrino's helmet.

They were all astonished at the stubbornness of the master and servant about the crupper. The manager came up and took it, saying, "Señor Sancho, watch what you're saying and open your eyes: to this world it is a garter and exceedingly valuable; I'll say nothing about the other world."

"It must be what I say it is," responded Sancho. "I am not blind and I have worn out more cruppers like this than there are stars in Limbo."

At this point there came out a stable-hand to whom the packsaddle and crupper belonged. Coming up to Sancho he said, "Brother, hand over my crupper, for it isn't there for you to carry off."

Sancho was greatly pleased to hear this and turned around laughing to say to the bystanders, "God be praised, gentlemen, you must be satisfied! In truth, now you'll have to acknowledge my good judgment, whether you like it or not, for you see that I was right from the first about this being a crupper, something which so many and such good minds never before failed to recognize."

Saying this, he gave the crupper to the peasant. When Don Quixote saw this he went up to him and with a yank took it away from him, saying, "Oh, filthy country bumpkin! Since when have you and your ignorant race been worthy to wear such a fine garter as this?" He was going to put it in his coat pocket, but the peasant, who didn't understand jokes, prevented it by seizing his arm, with Don Quixote stubbornly resisting.

Finally the peasant, a man of muscle and strength, which Don Quixote lacked, being so skinny, was able to give him such a shove in the chest that he knocked him over backwards and jumped on him forcibly taking the crupper from his hand. At this Sancho came up to help his master and landed two or three cruel blows on the peasant's face with his fist, whereupon he turned on Sancho like a lion and cinched him about the face two or three times with the crupper.

The actors' laughter was unrestrained, the students were in great haste to separate them, and Barbara was notably diligent in helping Don Quixote get up. He was infinitely angered and Sancho was suffering even more: he held his hand to his nose, which was bleeding profusely because the peasant had struck it with the crupper. He started furiously to go to the stable after him saying, "Wait, wait, you big muleteer! You'll see whether I'll make you admit, like it or not, that you are better than I am, being a great knave, a sodomizer, and the son of one like yourself.

Don Quixote called to him, "Come back son Sancho; let him go, for he is taking with him quite a bit of dishonor since he fled infamously from the fight without daring to wait for us. But how could one expect a fool like him to dare wait? I have already told you many times to furnish a silver bridge for the enemy who is fleeing. If he takes the precious garter from us there is no need to fear, because I have read that many thieves have robbed knights-errant, taking not only their prized horses, but also their rich armor, clothing, and jewels."

"I am not afraid of being robbed," said Sancho. "You are used to having thieves dare to steal rare jewels from you. Once in Zaragoza one such stole, by clawing them out of my hands, the royal suspenders made from the Phoetrix bird, or whatever you call it, which you won with your good lance in the ring-lancing contest."

Don Quixote grew angry at this news and said, "Well, villain, if such a thing occurred, how did you happen not to tell me right then and there, so that I could tear the bold thief to bits?"

"To save you sorrow," responded Sancho. "I kept silent from fear that your anger would cause you to have a fit of cholera. But let's say no more about my irritation and the tears the damned suspenders cost me."

Saying this, he began to weep, repeating, "Alas, my beloved suspenders! Woe to the mother who bore you, for having seen such a misfortune happen to you! Don't forget this faithful and loyal servant of yours, I beg you, in Christ's name, for as long as I live I shall not forget you, nor your excellent quality. May your sweetness and flavor bring bad luck to the thief!" Don Quixote quieted him, saying he was recompensed by his tears and the forgiveness he asked for the loss.

The manager rose from his chair, laughing heartily, shook his hand and told him, "Sir Knight, you have come out very well in this battle, and now we ought to go to bed, for it's already late and you are tired. Let the play stay at this point." He led him and Sancho to a barren room he had ready for them and would not leave until he had them both in bed and locked in, fearing that the servants would give poor Sancho a dousing of cold water, as he knew they planned to do.

In the morning the manager and his entire company left the inn without saying anything to them, on the advice of the students, and went to Alcalá. The innkeeper opened the door and Don Quixote got up, rather late because of the fatigue caused by the recent frays. The first thing he did upon awakening was to ask Sancho about Queen Zenobia, if they had given her a bed and all the necessary equipment the night before, with all the propriety due her royal person.

"Sir, I was so busy with the bloody battle we had with that fellow who stole the crupper or the garter, or whatever you please, that I did not think about her any more than if she weren't a queen, but I understood that two of the actors' servants were good enough to take her with them, and much to her pleasure, so as not to give any reason for evil tongues to talk."

Here Barbara came upstairs with the students to Don Quixote's and Sancho's room and said, "A very good morning to the flower of knights-errant. How did you get along last night?"

Don Quixote responded, "Oh, my lady, pardon my neglect of your royal person last night, but the negligent Sancho is to blame. I ordered him to walk continually in front of you and by looking at your face see if you took a fancy to something, and he grew careless because he was so exhausted by the recent battles undertaken, as he just now said."

To this Sancho replied, "Sir, I look at her face often enough, but since she has such a devilish one, every time I look at her and see that scar, I am tempted to tell her, 'Boo to you, Marta!' from an old song the children used to say to an old monkey that the priest in our village used to keep at the door of his house."

"I hope your days will be evil, great knave, and that you won't live as long as I, may it please Christ!" answered Barbara. "But hush; in truth, don't go to the other world to do penance, for I know how to cause quite a lot of afflictions by night to others sharper than you; the tambourine is in the hands of one who knows how to play it well."

The students said to Sancho, "Señor Sancho, don't bother the queen, for she knows better how to do what she says in deeds rather than in words. Tell us, why do you want to find yourself some night flying about the chimney place in the midst of kitchen shelves, plates, and spits, and everything in sight and weep over not having wanted to obey her?"

"Well, if she makes me fly about the kitchen shelves I shall complain to one who will make her spend all her life rowing in the galleys," said Sancho.

"But don't you know that women don't row?" replied one of the students.

"What difference is it to me if they don't row?" responded Sancho. "It may even be that if she doesn't row she will at least be good at doling out refreshments to the crew and galley-slaves. I know that she won't lack cleverness for that, and if she is more comfortable there she will really be like the clouds in every way, because, being a woman, she should resemble them somewhat."

"Well, in what way is she supposed to resemble them, or how does she resemble them in any way?" asked the student.

Sancho responded, "In that the clouds load up on the sea with what they will later unload as rain on the earth, by dint of thunder and lightning. She will do the same: if she should become pregnant on the seas, she will later have to unload her cargo by dint of cries and sighs. Besides, it is apparent that all women are like clouds: we know by expreience where and how they unload, just the same as we don't know where and how it got into them."

The students laughed, and so did Barbara herself, at the astronomical application made by Sancho, but Don Quixote, who had nothing more laughable than the remoteness of his uprooted mental powers, told Barbara with asperity and a frown, "Don't pay any attention to what this fool says, because he is so stupid that he never says anything but idle talk. What is important now is for us to try to leave here, because I intend to enter the Court today unless some necessary business and dangerous adventure comes up to detain us in Alcalá."

Calling the innkeeper, he paid the bill by merely thanking him for the lodging. It was easy for him and his group to leave the inn after such a light payment, because the manager of the aforementioned company had already settled the account for everybody, out of pity for Don Quixote's madness and his squire's simplemindedness and because he considered himself well repaid with the bad times he had put them through and the good and amusing times he and his company had received.

Don Quixote, in armor as usual, mounted Rocinante, Sancho his donkey, and Barbara her mule; the students remained behind because they were now near Alcalá, which they did not wish to enter, for the sake of their honor, in the company of a group so provocative of catcalls, raillery, and bad jokes as that of Don Quixote. As they set out, Barbara said to him, "Sir Knight, you have done me a great kindness by bringing me here from Sigüenza, giving me clothes, food, and a mount as if I were your sister. However, if you do not order otherwise, I have already decided to remain here in Alcalá, my native town, which I shall serve in any way I can, governing my actions by whatever the circumstances require."

"My lady, Queen Zenobia, I marvel to hear such a decision from so discreet a person who has taken as many long and dangerous trips through unknown kingdoms just to find me, impelled by the fame of my valor and person. How is it possible that, having my companionship, which you have desired so much and which you have secured, you should say now that you want to give it up, not considering how much I have done and plan to do in your service, nor the misfortunes that may happen to you when your enemies and rebellious vassals grow bold without due respect for your worth and seeing you away from my help and side? To avoid these and greater obstacles which may come up, I beg you as earnestly as I can to come with me to Court. We shall not come away from it for many days, because when the grandees learn of my arrival they will certainly detain me, insisting on lavishing attention on me in order to be honored by being at my side and learning about military matters. There you will see what I'll do to serve you, and after I have killed the King of Cyprus, Bramidán de Tajayunque, with whom I have a battle that has been postponed, and the other son of the King of Cordova, who yesterday brought a serious false accusation against his mother, you shall choose whether to go to Cyprus or remain in the Spanish Court. Therefore, for the love of me you must do what I implore."

Sancho, who heard what Don Quixote had said to Barbara, went up to him in great anger saying, "For heaven's sake, sir, I don't know why you want to take along the lady queen. It will be much better for her to stay here in her village; we shall spare ourselves a great deal. Why do we want to take her with us at no profit? A fine load of trash to be carrying when we enter the Court with her! Send her to Lucifer and don't beg her any more, for when one implores the low person he assumes an air of importance. God's mercy will not fail us without her. To Judas with her and the one who bore her and made her known to us! Well, I vow that if my temper flares up and I begin rant and rave, it won't take much for me to make her hawk and spit and sniffle more than a hanged man does in the noose. Here you are, giving the prattling woman a thousand luxuries and services, calling her queen and princess when she is what she knows she is, as those students said. And now she has to be coaxed! Let her pay us for the skirt and little red frock and the mule and what she has cost us, and goodby, I'm on my way; or, as Aristotle says, "*Allons*, for the grapes are getting ripe." In truth, if I were my master, I'd beat it all out of her since she doesn't know me well."

"Oh, villain!" said Don Quixote. "What right have you to pick a quarrel with the queen? Are you worthy, perchance, to take off her little shoe?"

"Little!" answered Sancho. "In Sigüenza she told me to beg you to buy her a pair of shoes, and when I asked the size she wore she replied that it was between fifteen and nineteen, maybe more."

"Well, don't you see, fool, that Amazons are manly people, and as they are always in fights they don't have feet as delicate and beautiful as those of the ladies at Court, who sit on a dais, pampered and idle, and therefore are more tender and feminine than the valorous Amazons."

Barbara replied with no little resolve to Sancho's offensive malicious remarks, and said, "I didn't plan, Señor Don Quixote, to go beyond here. However, to satisfy you and make this knave Sancho rave, I'm willing to go to Madrid, and there I'll do whatever you command, in spite of this garlic-stuffed rustic."

"Rustic!" answered Sancho. "I may be a rustic in God's sight, but as far as the world is concerned it matters little if I am one or not. But it is a big lie to say what you did, that I am stuffed with garlic, for this morning at the inn I ate only five cloves that the thieving innkeeper gave me for a *cuarto*. Imagine how stuffed that would make me! However, putting this aside, tell me truly, madam Queen, which is worse: to have been with those two servants of the actors last night and this morning breakfasted with them on fine fried tripe with four liters of wine, as the innkeeper reported you did, or for me to have eaten five cloves of raw garlic?"

"Brother, if I was with them I harmed no one," responded Barbara. "I am free as the cuckoo and have no husband to whom I have to report, thanks to *Domino Dio, et vivit Domine.*[4] I did it more because the weather was a little cool than because of roguery, as you suspect because you are very malicious."

"Do you call me malicious?" replied Sancho. "Upon my word, you wouldn't dare say it behind my back as you do to my face. But go on! There are more sausages than there are days; there's no hurry, and we know here how to suck our thumbs and not be deceived, even if we are dolts."

[4] "Thanks to the Lord, and as the Lord liveth."

CHAP. XXVIII. HOW DON QUIXOTE AND HIS GROUP reached Alcalá, where he escaped death in a strange fashion, and the danger he incurred by trying a perilous adventure.

DON QUIXOTE was taking great care that Queen Zenobia should wish to do him honor at the entrance he planned to make into Court, and so, having her disregard the impertinent remarks of his squire, he said to her, "I beg you, high-born lady, not to take notice of anything this animal says to you, but to tolerate him as I do, suffering him for what he is, if only because we need him on the roads. Now that we are in Alcalá, I think we should proceed little by little behind these walls and not go through the center of town, which is large and has people of quality. I also think it will be wise for you to cover your face with that lovely gauze headdress until we get to the other side, because you are known to everybody. Once there, we can secretly stay tonight, if you like, at some inn, and in the coolness of the morning enter Madrid."

That procedure was followed, and as they began to circle the wall Barbara turned towards Sancho and said, "Now, Señor suitor, let's be friends and don't be cross with me, for your life's sake, for I forgive all that has happened."

"Friends?" responded Sancho. "I'd rather be a friend of the devil in hell than you, although it's all one and the same thing."

"By the life of my mother, we must become friends before we reach Madrid," said Barbara.

"In the name of my donkey, I'd rather become Pontius Pilate than your friend," replied Sancho.

Barbara said to him, "Come on now, you lion!" and Sancho responded, "Go on now, you serpent!"

However, Don Quixote noted the enmity between Sancho and Barbara and the gallantries they were exchanging as they went along, and he said, "Now cheer up, Sancho! Aren't you my squire and don't I have to pay you a salary, as we agreed between the two of us, for serving me well and thoroughly in every way? Well, by virtue of the aforesaid agreement I wish, and it is my will, that you now, without argument, become friendly with my lady Queen Zenobia. I'll see that a fine banquet is prepared tonight for her and for you as a sign of the stability of your future and perpetual friendship, for it is not right for us three to be on bad terms."

"Of course, master," replied Sancho. "I'll have to do as you say, if for no other reason than that banquet you mention, although, maintaining my stand, it would be right for me to wait for persons of importance, such as half a dozen canons from Toledo, or at least a few cardinals, to be appointed to ask me to do this. But all right, since you order it. Come on, madam Queen, give me those hands of yours, although I'd prefer them to be cows' heels, well cooked and with parsley, for I'm sure they'd be of more benefit to me."

Barbara laughed and held out her hand, saying as she did so, "My love, take this queen's hand; I am sure that more than two ecclesiastical princes of the Court of Alcalá, where we are to sleep tonight, would greatly value receiving this favor."

When Don Quixote saw them shaking hands he went ahead a short distance, dreaming up in his mind what he would do at Court with Queen Zenobia,and the battles with the giant and the treacherous son of the King of Cordova, and how he would make himself known to the kings and grandees. He was so absorbed and absent-minded because of all this that he was not aware of what Barbara was saying to Sancho as they went along.

"From here on, friend Sancho, we must love each other to the utmost as a married couple does, for master Don Quixote has been the godfather of our peacemaking. To confirm it, I want us to sleep together in the inn where we will be tonight. My heart tells me that it will surely be so cool that I'll be obliged to cover myself comfortably with a blanket such as one made of your hair, my lord Sancho. To tell the truth, I don't believe I'll have to beg you very much, for you are more a knave than a fool."

Sancho did not understand Barbara at all, so he responded, "Let's reach the inn safely and eat supper as a sign of our friendship, fulfilling my master's promise to us. As for that matter of the blanket, there are sure to be two or even three; I'll get some from the innkeeper so you can put them on your bed, but it's not cold enough now to fetch them."

Barbara saw that he had not understood her, so she spoke more clearly: "Well, Sancho, if your master has to rent two beds, one for me and another for you, wouldn't it be better for us to save the *real* for the one bed so we could buy a nice dish of tripe and a quarter of a loaf of bread so you could stuff yourself and devil take the consequences?"

"On my faith, you're right!" responded Sancho. "Let's save that *real* for the one bed without my master's knowledge, for I'll sleep on a stone bench at the inn; as far as I'm concerned, I'll sleep as well in one place as in another. In exchange, we'll give ourselves, as you say, a bellyful with that *real*."

Seeing Sancho's dim-wittedness, Barbara did not try to pursue that subject and they hurried on after Don Quixote until they overtook him. When he saw them near him he said, "It seems to me it's too late for us to be able to reach Madrid today. It won't be a bad thing for us to stay in Alcalá tonight and continue our journey tomorrow, for you, Señora Queen, can be well concealed, closed up in a room, with your face covered so you won't be recognized when you are served at table."

She told him to do whatever suited him, for she would comply with his decision. Just then they reached an inn outside what was called the Madrid Gate, and after they entered, Don Quixote told Sancho to take the mounts to the stable and provide them the necessities, and he asked the innkeeper for a secret and well-appointed room, where he immediately ordered Queen Zenobia be taken. He stayed behind and was strolling about the patio, without removing his armor, when he heard four well-tuned trumpets suddenly ring out, and after them the hoarse sound of kettle-drums. Hearing this caused our good knight to be visibly startled, so he kept listening attentively, not knowing what it could be. In a short time, after having wandered about in his fantasies, he called Sancho and said to him, "Oh, my good squire Sancho! Do you happen to hear that tuneful music of trumpets and kettle-drums? Well, you must know it is a sign that some famous jousts or tourneys are doubtless being held at this university to enliven the marriage festivities of some renowned princess who must have been married here, and a foreign knight, as yet unknown because he is a novice, is probably attending. Despite his youth, as a beginning for his famous deeds he has already overcome all the knights in this city and from the Court who have come here for the festivals, unless he has come to take part in them, which seems the likeliest thing. Or he may be some fearless wild man who, having conquered and overcome all the presidents of the tourneys and the adventurers, has remained absolute owner of the prizes of the jousts, and now there is not a knight, however valiant he may be, who dares enter the arena with him a second time. Hence, the princes are so sorrowful that they would give anything in the world if God would present them with any good knight who would humble this cruel pagan's pride and thus leave the whole country happy, and the festivities would be completed to perfection. Therefore, my dear

Sancho, saddle Rocinante for me right away, for I have to go there and enter the plaza bravely and benevolently. Then all those occupying the golden balconies, high belvederes, and canopied grandstands will be surprised by my presence. A joyful murmur will arise from them, saying, 'Hurrah, God has decreed that this gallant foreign knight should come to save the honor of the natives, seeing that not one of them has been able to withstand the incomparable courage of this fierce wild man. At this point all the trumpets, flageolets, sackbuts, and kettle-drums will ring out, and at their sound my good, strong horse will begin to get excited and whinny, desirous of entering the fray. All will grow silent, and I shall slowly approach the stand on which are the judges and knights. Making my trained horse kneel two or three times in front of them, I shall give them a formal courteous greeting, afterward making my horse give great leaps and bucks around the wide plaza, finally arriving at the place where the fierce wild man is. After acknowledging his presence, I shall go up to the hard ash lances, take the one I like best, draw near that wild man without giving him any courteous greeting whatsoever, and say to him, 'Knight, if you see fit I should like to enter into combat with you, but on condition that it be at all costs, which means that one of us two will remain as supreme winner of the jousts and take off the other's head to present it to the lady of his choice.' Of course, since he is proud he will have to answer that it will be done that way. After this, turning Rocinante around so that the sun will be where I want it, the trumpets will ring out. At their sound both of us, valiant warriors, will dash forward like the wind. He will not miss his aim, but will hit me in the middle of the shield without piercing it but twisting my body around with the force of the blow, and the lance will go flying in bits through the air. However, I, more skillful, will strike the center of his visor such a heavy blow that it will be torn from his head, and its force will cause him to fall backward from his horse to the ground. Since he is agile he will get to his feet again and will come at me sword in hand; I, not wishing to have the advantage in this fight, will dismount in mid air, although many will judge this foolhardiness, seize my short sword, and we shall begin the dogged battle. However, unable to withstand my blows, he will beg to rest a little because he is somewhat fatigued, but I, not heeding his pleas, will take the sword in both hands, raise it in heroic wrath and let it fall with such fury on his unprotected head that, hitting it full, I'll split it down to his breast and the cruel blow will make him fall to the ground with such a horrible crash that it will make the entire plaza shake and more than a few barricades and grandstands collapse. The cries of the people will be many, the joy of the judges great, the contentment of the vanquished knights extreme, the applause of the crowd extraordinary, and unheard-of music will ring out in praise of my fine success. From then on the things I shall do will cause future historians a great deal of work in writing them up and describing them in their entirety. Consequently, Sancho, bring out Rocinante at once."

Deeply grieved because he saw the longed-for supper delayed, Sancho went to saddle up. While he was doing so the innkeeper came up to Don Quixote, to whose long, rambling discourse he had been listening, and said, "Sir Knight, you may take off your armor, for you are tired; tell me what you wish for supper, because this young fellow here will bring goodly provision."

"For heaven's sake!" said Don Quixote. "You're well in the know, aren't you! Just you see what is happening in the plaza, the dishonor of your native land, the insult to your knights, and that I am going to help them; and you talk to me about supper! I say that I don't want to have supper nor eat a bite until I honor this university with my presence and I'll kill all those who contradict me. It is a shame, a very great one, for one single wild man to overcome and subjugate a city such as this; therefore, go with God's blessing and see if my squire is coming with the horse."

The innkeeper said, "Excuse me. I thought that what you were just now telling your servant was some story about Mari-Castaña or from the books of chivalry about Amadís de Gaula. But if you wish to go in your armor to honor the university professor, everybody will be very grateful."

"What university professor or what trifling nonsense?" responded Don Quixote. Three or four who had halted at the door, seeing that man in armor, said to him, "If you plan to go to the parade you can, because it's time now; the professor is probably arriving at the market now. Here there are no jousts or wild men such as you have talked about, but there is a parade the university is having for a doctor who has just been elected to the chair of medicine by a plurality of more than fifty. To make it more festive they are having a triumphal float go ahead of him, with the seven virtues and heavenly music from within. Its like has never been seen except for the one last year in the parade given for the professor who took the principal chair of theology. The trumpets and kettle-drums you hear mean that they are already going along the main streets, with more than two thousand students carrying branches and shouting 'Hurrah for So-and-So!' "

"In spite of everybody, the whole world, and in spite of you and all who may want to contradict me, things are just as I have said," replied Don Quixote.

Sancho now came out with the horse and Don Quixote mounted. The horse was in such a condition and so tired that he could scarcely move, even when Don Quixote pricked him with the hard spur, and there wasn't a house which he failed to try to enter. Sancho stayed in a room with Barbara who, as we said before, was trying not to be recognized by anybody in Alcalá.

Our knight rode slowly along the street, always going towards the place from where he heard the sound of trumpets, until he found the crowd in the middle of the main street. When they saw that man in armor, looking as we have said, they thought he was some student who came arrayed like that to enliven the festival. When he took his place in front of the triumphal float which preceded the professor and saw the imposing structure moving without being drawn by mules, horses, or other animals, he was greatly surprised and began to listen quietly to the sweet music sounding inside.

In front of the musicians, on the same float, were two masked students in women's clothes and adornment; one, representing Wisdom, was richly clothed and wore a laurel wreath on his head. In his left hand he carried a book, and in the right a small but very lovely castle made of cardboard and bearing the inscription: *Sapientia aedificavit sibi domum.*[1]

At his feet was Ignorance, naked and laden with tin chains; under his feet were two or three books with this inscription: *Qui ignorat, ignorabitur.*[2]

On the other side of Wisdom came Prudence, dressed in pale blue, carrying in one hand a serpent and this inscription: *Prudens sicut serpentes.*[3] With the other he seemed to be throttling a blind old woman to whom there clung a blind man. Between the two was this inscription: *Ambo in foveam cadunt.*[4]

Don Quixote stationed himself in front of this float, mentally concocting one of the wildest speeches he had ever made, and said

---

[1] "Wisdom built its own house," after Proverbs 14: 1: "The wisest women built up their homes."

[2] "He who ignores will be ignored," after I Corinthians 14: 38: "If he does not acknowledge this, God does not acknowledge him."

[3] "As prudent as serpents," after Matthew 10: 16: "Be wary of serpents ."

[4] Luke 6: 39. "Will they not both fall into the ditch?"

loudly, "Oh, you magus and enchanter, whoever you are! You are guiding this enchanted float by means of your evil and perverse arts, carrying imprisoned in it these ladies and the two duennas, one naked and chained, the other eyeless, with her husband trying forcibly not to let her go. The ladies' beauty denotes they are undoubtedly heiresses of some great princes or lords of some islands, and you are taking them to place them in your cruel fetters. Turn them loose here and now, safe and sound, returning all their jewels you have stolen. If you will not, release here on me all the powers of hell, for I shall get them all away from you by force of arms, because it is common knowledge that demons, with whom those of your profession consort, cannot go against Christian Greek knights, such as I am."

Don Quixote would have proceeded with his peroration, but the university people, seeing that that man in armor was delaying the float and hindering its advance, made four or five of the retinue go up to him, thinking he was a student who had come with that clever disguise. They said to him, "Hey there, Señor Licentiate! Stand aside, if you please, and let the people pass, because it's very late."

However, Don Quixote responded, "Vile rabble! Without a doubt you are servants of this wicked magician who is carrying off these beautiful princesses. If that is so, watch out! Choose the lesser of two enemies."

With this he seized his sword and aimed such a terrible slash at one of the students who was approaching on mule-back that if he had not had the wise foresight of dodging and of being helped by the mule's quickness, he would have come out very badly. Don Quixote then turned on another who was coming along behind, and with a back-slash he hit the mule's head such a heavy blow that he opened a gash six inches long.

Everybody began to scream and get excited; the music stopped; some ran, others rode toward the spot where Don Quixote was, sword in hand, but when they saw him so furious, scarcely anybody dared go near him because he was slashing back and forth, to right and left, so forcefully that if the horse had helped him a little more the following misfortune would not have happened to him.

It occurred in this way: when everybody saw that in reality he was not joking as they had at first thought, they began to surround him, some on foot, others riding closer, some throwing rocks, others sticks, others the branches they were carrying, and they even struck him on the helmet with two or three bricks. If he had not been wearing it he would not have come out of the Calle Mayor alive. Although

Although there were many people, excessive shouting, and the rocks were raining down, nevertheless ten or twelve of the crowd got to him and one seized his foot, another Rocinante's rein, and they pulled him off the horse and took away the shield and the sword he was holding. After this they unloaded on him some good blows and would have throttled him there if Fortune had not saved him for greater perils. He owed his life to the manager of the company of actors he had met at the inn the night before. Strolling by chance under the porticos of the Calle Mayor, he came up at the cries and shouts of the people, and when he saw that man in armor being dragged along by six or seven men he suspected that it was Don Quixote, as it really was. At the moment he had been shoved into a big house, where he was putting up as much resistance as he could but to no avail.

Seeing him like that, the manager and some of his company who were with him felt sorry for him, and by much pleading, made all the students who were mistreating him leave the house. They all stayed alone with him, and when the university professor had gone on with his triumphal parade and the street was empty of the people following it, the manager went up to Don Quixote and said, "What's all this, Señor Loveless Knight? What unfortunate adventure has this been, and what necromancer has placed you in such a predicament? Is it possible that spells can be cast on your valor? But patience and be of good heart, for there is another and wiser magician here, your great friend, who, if he didn't stand by you, would be acting contrary to the law of good friendship, but I have shown you the greatest amity, for if I had not come to the rescue with my magical power you undoubtedly would have been finished this time with all knight-errantry. Arise, as I am a sinner! Your teeth are bathed in blood, you have no shield, no sword, and no horse, for the students have taken everything."

Don Quixote got up, recognized the manager and said happily, "Oh, wise Alquife, my good historian and friend! I was surprised that you failed to help me in this great trouble and hardship in which I find myself because of the great slowness of my horse, confound him! Consequently, oh, faithful wise man! make them give him back to me or give me another, so that I may pursue those knaves and challenge all of them as traitors and sons of traitors, and take the vengeance on them that their arrogant and vicious life deserves."

After the manager heard this he requested one of his companions to go at all costs and bring Don Quixote's horse, shield, and sword, redeeming them all at any price wherever they might be. The actor went about inquiring; he got the horse from an inn, and the shield and sword from a pastry shop, where everything had been pawned. He returned it all to the manager, who gave everything to Don Quixote, who thanked him fervently, attributing everything to the power of his magical wisdom. When the manager on his part inquired where his squire, Sancho Panza, and Barbara were, he replied that he had left them at an inn next to the Madrid Gate. "Well, let's go there right away," said the manager. "I'm in charge now and you must obey me, for it's very important."

Don Quixote responded that not for the whole world would he fail to obey him as a very wise person in whose hands he had for two days already placed his affairs. The manager had Don Quixote's horse, lance, and shield taken ahead by a boy, and told Don Quixote to walk hand-in-hand with him as far as the inn, where he left him in the care of the innkeeper, with orders that he by no means be allowed to travel on foot or on horseback that afternoon. The innkeeper punctiliously carried out the orders.

When Sancho saw his master's bloody teeth he said, "By the body of Saint Quentin, Señor Loveless! Haven't I told you four hundred thousand dozen of millions times that we shouldn't meddle with what doesn't concern us, the more so when students are involved? I'll bet that they've covered you with spit as they did me in Zaragoza. Wash yourself, for as sure as I'm a sinner in God's eyes, your nose is covered with blood."

"Oh, Sancho, Sancho!" responded Don Quixote. "How grateful those knaves who left me in such a state can be to the wise Alquife, my friend. If it had not been for him I would have slaughtered them so that their old parents would have much to bury and their wives to weep over the rest of their lives; but the time will come when they will pay in a lump sum for what they have done last year and this year."

Hearing him, the innkeeper replied, "As you value your life, Sir Knight, don't meddle with students! There are more than four thousand in this university and they are such that when they gather together and unite they make everybody in the land tremble. Thank God that they have left you alive, which is no small thing."

"Oh, cowardly chicken, one of the basest knights who ever wore a sword!" said Don Quixote. "Do you believe that my personal valor, the strength of my arm, the swiftness of my feet, and above all, my strength of spirit are as craven as yours? I swear by the life of Queen Zenobia, who is the one I most prize, that only because of what you have said, I have a mind to mount my horse again and once more enter the city and not leave a living person in it, destroying even dogs and cats, men and women, and all rational and irrational beings that dwell in it, and afterwards raze it with fire until it remains like Troy, a warning of Greek fury to all nations. Sancho, bring Rocinante at once, for I want this knight or innkeeper, or whatever he is, to see that I know how to put my words into action better than I know how to say them."

"You won't carry out your plan about the horse this time, Sir Knight," answered the innkeeper, "because the manager of the company of actors left me strict orders not to let you have him for any reason, and I have locked up the stable."

"What actors or nonsense!" replied Don Quixote. "Can there be anybody in the world who goes against my wishes? I assure you that you can be grateful to that sage and friend of mine who brought me here, for it is not right for me to violate his command for any cause. Otherwise, today I should have done such a deed that it would be remembered for many centuries!"

"Yes, you would," said the innkeeper. "But now come in and eat supper, for you are making all the people at the door laugh and the house is getting so full of boys that there's no room for us."

Whereupon he seized Don Quixote's hand and led him up to where Barbara was, with whom he had a very pleasant conversation, interspersed with quite a few silly remarks from Sancho. Together they enjoyably ate a good supper and went to bed afterwards, for Don Quixote especially needed to do so because of the rough treatment he had undergone at the inn and on the Calle Mayor. Upon going to bed he still stubbornly wanted to make more of the potion or precious balsam that he said came from Fierabrás, to cure the mortal wounds he felt in his teeth. However, it was impossible for him to do this, because the innkeeper, knowing about his madness, persisted in saying that not one of all the things he required was to be found in the town.

CHAP. XXIX. HOW THE VALIANT DON QUIXOTE REAched Madrid with Sancho and Barbara and his encounter with a nobleman.

HE FOLLOWING morning the valiant Don Quixote de La Mancha arose refreshed, for he had rested all night. He called Sancho and ordered him to saddle Rocinante, the queen's palfrey, and his own donkey; he was to feed and saddle them while the innkeeper was preparing the breakfast they had agreed upon the night before. Everything was done as ordered; they ate a good breakfast of pastry and chicken, and the bill was added up and paid.

Don Quixote mounted Rocinante as usual, and Queen Barbara (her face concealed very carefully from the people at the inn who tried in vain to see it) mounted her mule, assisted by Sancho, who then reclined at ease on his donkey as he followed his master and the queen as they very hurriedly left the inn and the town. They traveled in such haste that, leaving at half-past nine o'clock, it was after three in the afternoon when they were almost at Madrid, at the fountain called the Caños de Alcalá.

On Barbara's advice, in view of the heat, Don Quixote decided to dismount in St. Hieronymus' Meadow to rest and enjoy the coolness of the poplar trees next to what they call the Gilded Fountain. They remained there until after six o'clock, resting the animals which grazed while their masters alternately slept or chatted. But at six o'clock, hearing people on their way to the customary outing in the Prado, they decided to ride into Court.

As they were crossing the street Don Quixote saw the great number of people, horses and carriages, and ladies and gentlemen who usually go there; he halted a little, turned Rocinante, and took it into his head to ride along the Prado without saying anything to anything to anybody. Barbara and Sancho, worried by his mood, followed him to see if they could reason with him, and cursed when they saw that after the first turn they already had more than fifty people behind them. Many of the gentlemen strolling about kept coming up, astonished and laughing at that man armed with lance and shield, and at the shield's inscriptions and figures, for they did not know why he was carrying it.

As more and more people came up, Don Quixote grew prouder and kept stopping on purpose, so that they could read the mottoes on his emblem without his having to say a word. Others scoffed when they saw him looking as he did and accompanied only by Sancho and that veiled woman dressed in red, thinking it was a disguise and that they were coming from a masked ball.

It so happened that as Don Quixote was continuing his ride with his retinue, without his companions being able to make him see reason, he saw approaching a rich carriage drawn by four fine white horses, accompanied by more than thirty mounted knights and many lackeys and pages on foot. As soon as he saw this Don Quixote stopped in the middle of the road along which it was to pass, rested the tip of his lance on the ground, and waited with genteel visage.

When those approaching saw so many people covering half the street, together with that man in full armor with his great shield, they went up to the person inside the carriage, a grave nobleman who had come out to enjoy a ride in the cool air, and said to him, "Sir, a great crowd of people can be seen down there, and in their midst is a man in armor with a shield as large as a mill stone. We don't know, nor does anybody, who he is or for what reason he is coming."

Upon hearing this the nobleman leaned out and when he saw that Don Quixote was already quite near, he told a court constable who had been talking to him to be good enough to find out what it all meant. He had no sooner left the carriage to investigate when one of the gentleman's own lackeys approached him and said, "For your information, Your Lordship, about a month ago in Zaragoza I saw that man in armor who is approaching when I went to deliver to Don Carlos the news about your marriage. I ate dinner in his house one day with his squire after a famous ring-lancing contest which was held there and to which this armed man was invited. He is half-crazy, or I don't know what else you could call it; they did say he is a rich and honorable hidalgo of some village or other in La Mancha, but because of having taken to reading too many of the deceitful books of chivalry which are being printed, and believing them to be true, he

has become so addled that he has left his home, fancying he is a knight-errant, and is wandering other regions the way you see him. On a donkey, at his side, he has as his squire a poor peasant from the same village, who is one of a kind, very witty and a huge eater."

After this he continued telling him all that Don Quixote had done in Zaragoza: about the man being flogged, the ring contest, and how Don Carlos' secretary had played the part of the giant Bramidán de Tajayunque. There was no doubt that he was coming to Court to seek him out for battle, because the lackey was more than well-informed about everything from what Don Carlos' servants had told him.

The gentleman was greatly astonished by what he was being told about that man and he immediately suggested taking him and his group home with him that night to have some amusement. The constable came up and said, "Well, sir, that man is one of the oddest individuals Your Lordship has seen. His name is, he says, the Loveless Knight, and he has painted on his shield certain ridiculous writings and images. There is a woman dressed entirely in red with him and he says she is the great Zenobia, Queen of the Amazons."

"Well, drive the carriage over there and we'll see what he says," said the nobleman. As they were approaching him, Don Quixote pulled on Rocinante's rein and rode up to one side of the carriage to face the gentleman. He told him arrogantly, so that the bystanders heard it, "Illustrious sovereign and prince Perianeo of Persia whose valor and strength were severely felt (and to his cost) by the never-vanquished Don Belianís of Greece, your mortal enemy and rival for the love of the peerless Florisbella, daughter of the Emperor of Babylon whom you forced to recognize you by going into singular combat with him, but neither one had any advantage over the other,

although the very prudent sage Fristón, my adversary, was on your side; as a knight-errant addicted to seeking adventures throughout the world and testing the strength of fierce, strong wild men and knights, I have come today to the Catholic King's court, the news of your great courage having reached my ears. Since you are one of those I have often read about in that authentic book, I thought it would be held against me if I failed to test my fortune against your invincible strength today, here in this Prado, before all these knights of yours and the other people watching us. I do this solely because for many reasons I am a unique and particular friend and devotee of Prince Don Belianís of Greece: first, he is a Christian and the son of a Christian emperor, and you are a pagan, of the families and race of the Emperor Oton, Grand Turk and Sultan of Persia; second, to rid that close friend of mine of the great obstacle facing him, you, in order that he may thus more freely enjoy his delightful love affair with the princess Florisbella. It is apparent and well-known to everybody that he deserves her more than you do; there will be other Turkish beauties whom you can marry, for it is impossible for there not to be many in your country. Leave Florisbella for my friend Don Belianís of Greece. If you do not get out of your carriage at once, mount your fine horse after putting on your enchanted armor to fight me tomorrow, after I have killed the giant Bramidán de Tajayunque, King of Cyprus, and the treacherous son of the King of Cordova, I shall proclaim your cowardice and lack of spirit before this entire court and its king. Therefore, answer me at once, and concisely; if you won't, admit yourself conquered and I shall leave for other adventures."

Everybody was astonished to hear Don Quixote's nonsensical remarks and began to talk about them among themselves, laughing at him and the figure he cut. Sancho, however, who had been listening very attentively to what his master said, rode up to the carriage on his donkey saying, "Lord Perineo, you don't know my master like I do, but bear in mind that he is a man who has waged war with others better than you, Biscayans, Yangueses, goatherds, melongrowers, and students. He has won the Membrillo's helmet[1] and is known even to the Queen Micomicona, Ginesillo de Pasamonte and, what's more, to my lady, the Queen of Segovia, who is present. Besides, he is the man who attacked more than two hundred who were flogging a man in Zaragoza, which must be a matter of knowledge around here. Look, we have a lot to do, our mounts are tired, and the Queen and I are a bit hungry. So for God's sake admit that you are conquered, as my master begs you to do, and be as friendly as you were before. Don't look for three feet on a snake,[2] because those in this country are like the ones in mine and have less than that. Confound it! Let's go to our inn; to the devil with you and these heretics from Persia, your native land."

The gentleman told the constable who was with him to reply in his stead and take the man to his house that night. The constable did so, saying to Don Quixote, "Sir Loveless Knight, all we bystanders are very glad to have seen and met you today, as you are one of the best knights-errant who were found in Greece in the happy time of Amadís and Phoebus, and I thank the gods, since we are pagans, as you said before, that we have the right to see in this Court the one who has so much fame and renown in the world and far exceeds all those we have heard of or have seen who wear solid armor and ride powerful horses. Hence, illustrious Prince, Lord Perineo here willingly accepts your battle-challenge, not because he expects to come out victorious, but in order to be able to boast, wherever he may be (assuming you leave him alive) that he has done battle with the best knight in the world, and because being conquered will result in infinite glory for him and splendor for his lineage. If you like, the battle will take place on the day we agree upon tonight in his house, where he and I shall be honored to lodge you and all your companions, where he will entertain and attentively serve you and Queen Zenobia, whom he very much desires to meet. But, in order for everybody to thank the gods for seeing her rare beauty, he requests that she be kind enough to uncover her face by removing the cloud over those two beautiful suns of hers, so that their splendor may light up the face of the earth and make golden Apollo halt in his luminous sphere, astonished to see such beauty which can

[1] *Mambrino's* helmet, Sancho means.

[2] "Don't look for three feet on a cat" is the proverb that Sancho mixes up here.

furnish him with new light, for it will truly be greater than that of his lovely Daphne."

Don Quixote went to her, saying that by all means she should uncover her face before Prince Perianeo of Persia, because it was very necessary to do so. She discreetly refused as much as she could. However, Sancho, who had been lolling on his donkey without ever taking off his cap, went to the carriage-step and said, "Pagan Lord, my master Don Quixote de La Mancha, the Loveless Knight on sea and land, kisses your hand for your kindness in inviting us to have supper in your house as Don Carlos did in Zaragoza, long life to him. I say that we'll all three go very willingly in body and soul, just as we are. But Queen Segovia over there is telling me by her glances that she can't uncover her face now, until she puts on the one she uses for parties, better than the one she now has, so please excuse her."

Hereupon Don Quixote moved closer to the other side of the carriage, pulling Barbara's mule by the reins. She had already unwillingly uncovered her ugly face, which was more calculated to make children fall silent than it was to be seen by people. When all those around saw it, so ugly and wrinkled besides having a badly healed and worse stitched-up slash, they could not restrain their laughter. Seeing the gentleman in the carriage looking at her carefully and crossing himself because of her ugliness and Don Quixote's madness, Sancho said, "You are right to cross yourself, because there is no better way to drive off devils, according to the priest in my village. Although the Queen is not one now, she could be if God granted her ten more years of life, for she is almost one now."

The gentleman, holding back his laughter as best he could, said to Barbara, "Indeed, my lady Queen Zenobia, I now say sincerely that all the Loveless Knight told us about you is true, and he can consider himself fortunate in taking such nobility about the world with him, to affront and disconcert all the ladies in it, especially those in this Court. So now, tell us, if you please, where you are from and where you are going with this valiant knight, for tonight he and you and this good man who speaks the naked truth will be my invited guests."

Barbara answered, "If you please, sir, I am not Queen Zenobia, as this knight says, but a poor woman from Alcalá, and I make a living working at my honest trade as a tripe-seller. To my misfortune a knave of a student took me, or rather, enticed me from my home. As he was taking me to that of his parents with the promise of wanting to marry me, he stole everything I had and left me in my shift tied to a tree in a pine grove. This knight was passing by with some people and they untied me and took me to Sigüenza. Señor Don Quixote, the one in armor" (during all this Don Quixote was displaying to any and all the paintings on his shield, proud that so many would look at them) "secured this dress for me and bought me this mule on which I could ride to Alcalá. In all the villages, on the roads and at the inns, he called me Queen Zenobia and sometimes took me to the plazas to defend what he calls my beauty, it being, as a reward for my sins, such as you see it, and now, although I wished to remain in my land, he persuaded me to come to Court, where he says he must kill a son of the King of Cordova and a giant who is King of Cyprus, and he will make me queen of that kingdom. Not to be ungrateful for all his kindness I have come with him, intending to return as quickly as possible to my home. Now, Your Lordship, see whether you wish anything more from me, because I want to leave. I believe these gentlemen are laughing too much and their laughter could cause Don Quixote, since he is unbalanced, to do something foolish."

With these remarks she turned her mule and went to Don Quixote. Sancho said to the gentleman, "Now you see, my dear sir, what a good person my lady the Queen is if God puts her where her talents are most useful. Excuse us if she doesn't have as nice a muzzle as my master says and you expect. She's to blame, and very much so, because I've often told her that she should have had that *per signum crucis*[3] on her face given her on some other place, because it would be better where it was not so visible. She says that one who receives does not do the choosing. So come along right away; night and supper-time are approaching, and truly, by God's mercy, with my present appetite I don't need any mustard or parsley to eat magnificently well."

With no more courtesy than this he began to whip his donkey and went to Barbara and Don Quixote, who were among all those people enthralled by his long, detailed account of Rasura and Laín Calvos. He said that he had known them, that they were very honorable, outstanding people, but that none of them could equal him, because he was Rodrigo de Vivar, otherwise known as the Cid Campeador.

Hearing these last remarks, Sancho said, "Curses on all the Cids there are in Cid-Land! Come on, sir! As I'm a sinner, these poor mounts are in such a condition that they can't utter a word because they are so tired and dead of hunger."

"Oh, Sancho, how badly you know this horse!" responded Don

---

[3] 'By the sign of the cross' refers to a slash on the face.

Quixote. "I vow that if you asked him which he likes best—to listen to what I say about wars, battles, and matters of chivalry, or half a bushel of barley—he would say, if he could answer, that there is no question that, rather than eat or drink, he prefers for me to talk from now to Judgment Day. Unquestionably, he would listen to me very attentively for days and nights."

At this juncture, one of the nobleman's servants went up to Don Quixote saying, "Lord Loveless Knight, my master begs you to come to his home, because he wants you, Queen Zenobia, and your faithful squire to be his invited guests tonight and as many days as you like until the time for the appointed challenge arrives."

"Sir Knight," responded Don Quixote, "we shall go with greatest pleasure to serve Prince Perianeo; you have only to lead the way and we shall all follow."

CHAP. XXX. ABOUT THE DANGEROUS AND DUBIOUS *battle our knight had with one of the nobleman's pages and a constable.*

HE SERVANT, Don Quixote, and Barbara started toward the house of the nobleman who had invited them, to the great wonder of all they met on the streets and no less trouble on the part of the servant, who had to tell one and all the disposition and the name of the man in armor, the nature of the lady, and where and why he was escorting them. With this nuisance, he got them into his master's house; ordering the animals to be fed, he immediately took the three upstairs to a rich apartment, saying to Don Quixote, "Here, Sir Knight, you may rest, remove your armor, and sit in this chair until my master comes, for he won't be long."

To this, Don Quixote responded that he was not in the habit of removing his armor for any reason, even less in pagan territory, where a man does not know whom to trust nor what can easily happen to knights-errant to dishonor their bravery. "Sir, we are all friends here," replied the servant. "We desire to be of service to knights of your quality, so you can rest easy in this house without fear of adverse fortune."

However, seeing that he insisted on refusing to remove his armor, the servant left, telling him to suit himself and wait until the master arrived. He left a page on guard for greater security in keeping Don Quixote from leaving the house.

Don Quixote began to pace about the room, and when Barbara saw that it was a good time to talk to him alone, she said, "Señor Don Quixote, I have kept my word in coming to Court with you, and now that we are here I beg you to send me back as soon as you can, because I have to return to my home to attend to some important business. Besides, I fear that that constable who was with the gentleman in the carriage, whom you called a prince of Persia, has had us brought to this house, God forbid, to find out who you are and who I am. It is certain that when he sees I am going around with you, he will believe that we are living in concubinage, and they will have us taken to jail, where I'm afraid we shall be severely punished and insulted. Believe me; watch out that they don't put you in a position there to spend the little money you have left, so that afterwards, when you may wish, having come back to your senses, to return to your home, you will be forced to beg. For that reason, think carefully what we ought to do about this affair; I shall very willingly agree with your opinion."

"My Lady, Queen Zenobia, I am very sure that the gentleman in the carriage is Prince Perianeo of Persia and that the one he calls a constable is an honorable squire of his," said Don Quixote. "So don't be afraid; to please me, stay with me in this Court, even if only for six days. Afterwards I myself will take you back to your home with more honor than you expect."

"By heaven, Señor Don Quixote!" said Sancho. "I heard I don't know how many people say that the man in the carriage, whom we called a pagan, was Somebody-or-Other, I don't know who, but a very good and Christian man. Indeed he seems so to me—first, because of his charity, for he has invited us to such a good and liberal supper; the other reason is that if he were a pagan he would certainly be dressed like a Moor in red, green, or yellow, with his cutlass and turban, but he is as God made him and his mother bore him and you have seen him, dressed all in black, and all who accompanied him were dressed the same way. Besides, nobody spoke in the pagan language, but in Spanish, as we do."

At this Don Quixote angrily insisted, "Well, you and the Queen may say what you like, but there is no doubt whatsoever that he is what I have said he is."

Then Barbara called the page who was at the door and said to him, "Tell us, young man, that gentleman who was driving along the Prado accompanied by so many people, the one to whom this knight and I talked, who is he?"

The page told who he was, his rank, and how he had explicitly ordered them taken to his house. "And what does he want to do with us?" replied Sancho. "Let's not find ourselves in another calamity like the one in which I found myself in the Sigüenza jail, so covered with lice that I still have enough of them to fill up half a dozen pillows."

"My master doesn't want anything except to be entertained by you and to entertain you for a little while," answered the page.

"Come here, page," said Don Quixote. "Isn't your master's name Perianeo of Persia, son of the Grand Sultan of Persia, brother of Princess Imperia, and rival of the never-conquered Belianís of Greece?"

The page laughed quite openly when he heard such foolish remarks, and answered, "My master is not a prince of Persia, nor a Turk, nor was he ever in his life these, nor did he see Don Belianís of Greece, whose lying book I have in my room."

"Oh, base page of an infamous breed!" said Don Quixote. "You call one of the best books written by the famous Greeks[1] untruthful! You and that barbarous Turk of a master of yours are the liars, and tomorrow, before the king, I shall make him admit it with the edge of my sword, no matter how he objects."

"I say that my master is a very good Christian, the best of knights and renowned in Spain. Whoever says the contrary lies and is a knave," responded the page.

Hearing this, Don Quixote seized his sword and went in a flash toward the page who, seeing this, went down the broad stairway to the street and began to shout as he came out of the door, "Let the devil who slanders my master come out, for I'll see to it that it costs him dearly."

No sooner said than done; he picked up a rock from the street to use it against Don Quixote, who also came out into the street, in his armor. Sword in hand, protected by his shield, he attacked the page who, getting in the first blow, threw the stone at him with such fury it would have endangered his life if it had not struck him a glancing blow on his armored breast.

Many people came up at the noise and shouts and did not know what to say when they saw that man with a sword and shield threatening and even attacking the page of the well-known nobleman. Then two constables arrived with their bailiffs, saw what was going on, and one approached Don Quixote, tried to take his sword, and said, "What are you doing, man of Barrabas? Are you crazy? In such a place you'd

---

[1] Supposedly, the Spanish *Don Belianís de Grecia* was originally written in Greek by Fristón

lay a hand on the page of a person of such importance as his master, the owner of this house? Hand over the sword immediately and come on to jail, for you'll really remember the jest more than four pairs of days."

Don Quixote did not answer a word, but stepped back, raised his sword and dealt the constable such a genteel slash on the head that it began to stream blood. When the wounded constable saw this he began to shout, "Help in the name of the law! This man has killed me!"

At the noise, a thousand bailiffs and constables and other people came up, grasping their swords to use them against Don Quixote, who was saying very happily, "Let Perianeo of Persia come forth with all his allies, for I'll make them understand that he and all who live in this house are dogs, enemies of the faith of Jesus Christ." At the same time he kept slashing in all directions with both hands.

Poor Sancho was standing at the door watching what his master was doing, and he said in a loud voice, "That's it, Señor Don Quixote! Don't let yourself be overcome by those rascally Turks who would take you to the Koran and circumcise you whether you liked it or not, and then would put hobbles on your feet as they did me in Sigüenza."

At this point so many people fell upon our good hidalgo that in spite of him they took away his sword. Half a dozen bailiffs seized him and tied his hands behind his back. While this fray was going on at nightfall, a court peace officer happened to ride by. When he saw so many people gathered together he inquired as to the cause. One of the bystanders told him, "A very great insult. A man in full armor entered this house where a certain titled man lives, as you know, and tried to kill a page of his. When some constables tried to arrest him for it, he offered such resistance that he boldly gave one of them a severe slash."

"A bad affair!" said the court peace officer, and going up to where the bailiffs were holding Don Quixote, unable to take him away because of his resistance, he ordered him to be turned loose. They lifted him from the ground and when he stood up, hands tied behind his back, the peace officer, surprised to see him in that condition and so angry, said to him, "Come here, you devil; where are you from and what is your name, for you have a lot of nerve in entering the house of a man of such illustrious qualities?"

Don Quixote replied, "And you, you Lucifer who ask that, who are you? What you must do is go on your way and not meddle with what is none of your business. Whoever I may be, I am a hundred times better than you and the vile whore who bore you, and I shall make you admit it here and aloud if I mount my proud horse and take the lance and shield that stupid, base rabble took away from me. But I will give them the punishment their boldness deserves after I kill the King of Cyprus Bramidán de Tajayunque, whom I have agreed to fight before the Catholic King. I shall likewise take vengeance on Prince Perianeo of Persia to whom this estate belongs, if he doesn't punish the discourtesy done me by those of his royal palace, since I am Fernán González, first Count of Castile."

The peace officer marveled to hear that man's nonsensical remarks, but one of the bailiffs said, "My lord, believe me: this man is more of a rogue than he is a dunce. Now that he has done this foolish act and recognizes it as such, he pretends to be crazy so that we won't take him to jail."

"Go on, now!" said the peace officer. "Take him to jail and keep him under good security until tomorrow when the high court will hear his case." At this the bailiffs began to take hold of him and he resisted as much as he could.

It was already nearly nine o'clock and the nobleman happened to come home at this hour with some people. Seeing so many gathered in the street he inquired the reason, and the peace officer went up to him to tell him all that the man in armor had done and said. After hearing it, the nobleman laughed heartily and told the peace officer what Don Quixote was, and that he had ordered him brought to his house. He requested that Don Quixote be released and offered to stand bail for him, promising to hand him over whenever he was summoned or until it was evident that he was not what he was said to be. He would also be responsible for all the damages and the cost of the constable's medical treatment, and make full amends to him. All those present likewise begged the same thing, wishing to spend the night with the entertainment promised by the prisoner's nature and that of those who were with him.

In view of the pleas and surety given him by such important people, the peace officer was forced to yield to their wishes, so he ordered the bailiffs to release Don Quixote and turn him over to the nobleman, who said to him when he saw him free, "What is this, Sir Loveless Knight? What adventure has happened to you?"

Don Quixote replied, "Oh, my lord Perianeo of Persia! It's nothing. Because all these people are base, I did not want to do battle with them, although I believe that one of them has already carried away the payment for his madness."

Sancho, who had been far off watching what his master had suffered, now came up, took off his cap and said, "Oh, Sir Prince! You are welcome, since you come to free my master from these great constable knaves, worse than those in my land, for they have dared to try to take him to jail, trussed up, as if he were not as good as the king, the Pope, and the one who has no cloak.[2] I have watched the affair and know that if it had not been for you they would have carried out their plan; even I, if I hadn't feared them, would have given them two thousand punches."

"You may well believe, friend, that if I had not been as close as I am to the court peace officer, and if he had not had respect for me because of this, things would have gone badly with Señor Don Quixote," said the gentleman. And then he told Don Quixote, shaking hands with him, "Come, Sir Prince of Greece; enter my house, for in it all will go well, and your rascally opponents will be punished as they deserve."

Very politely he took leave of some of those with him, as he already had of the justice of the peace, and went upstairs with Don Quixote and Sancho. The bailiffs were left in the street like buffoons without their prey, astounded to see the nobleman taking that man away with him and calling him "prince."

[2] There is a Spanish saying, "You can ask that of everyone from the Pope to the man who has no cloak."

CHAP. XXXI. ABOUT WHAT HAPPENED TO OUR *invincible knight in the house of the nobleman, and about the arrival of the latter's brother-in-law Don Carlos, accompanied by Don Álvaro Tarfe.*

FTER THEY went upstairs the gentleman ordered his steward to take Don Quixote, Barbara, and Sancho to a certain apartment and give them a good, plentiful supper. After this was done and the nobleman had eaten also, he ordered the same steward to bring Barbara to him in order to begin the entertainment he and those knights who had had supper with him planned to have. Don Quixote's nonsensical remarks were to furnish this and he relied on Barbara to give them an account of how it began and the cause.

She came down, quite a bit uneasy and fearful when she saw that she alone had been summoned. When she faced the knights the one who had given them lodging said to her, "Tell us the naked truth, madam Queen Zenobia, about your life and that of the gallant, valiant knight-errant who is so watchful of you and protects you."

"Illustrious gentlemen, my life is as I told it in the Prado, short and filled with high and low spots like the land in Galicia. My name is Barbara de Villalobos, a name inherited from a grandmother who brought me up in Guadalajara, God rest her soul! I am old, but I used to be young and when I was I had the same experiences as other girls, for I didn't lack for someone to entreat and praise me, nor did I lack the usual pride of all women, believing my figure and charm were even greater than what was said by the poet who praised me, for he was the knave who carries the responsibility for my chastity: I gave it to him and I gave myself to him, loving him and lying to the persons who rightfully asked me to account for my comings and goings. Where I was going and coming quickly became known in Guadalajara, for there is nothing more talkative than a woman who has lost her modesty, because her tongue, hands, feet, eyes, movements, clothing, and adornments publish her own dishonor. My grandmother grieved over it very deeply and soon died because of her sorrow. I regretted it very much, especially because my Escamarrán[1] had already left me. I was her heir; I sold the furniture, getting all I could for it, and with the money I went down to Alcalá where I have lived

[1] He was a famous ruffian, popularized in ballads.

for more than twenty-six years, busying myself by being of service to everybody, especially the people who wear the black cape and long robes.[2] In fact, I am inclined by nature to learning, although mine is only knowing how to make and thoroughly unmake a bed, cook a good tripe stew of any size, and especially give the finishing touch to that meat and vegetable stew they call *olla podrida*[3] and steam a bowlful of cabbage, soaked bread and broth with reckless abandon.[4] I have already told Your Lordship in the Prado about the rest of the misfortune which took me away from that *vita buona*, and I have already recounted how I believed the crafty Aragonese who led me to think he would marry me if I sold my furniture and followed him to his home. I hope misfortune will follow him better than he fulfilled his promise. I was certainly stupid, but it's right for the one who does as I did to pay for it. He put me in a pine grove and stole everything I had, leaving me beaten, with my hands tied, and in my shift. This crazy crack-brained Manchegan with the fool Sancho Panza and some others, passed that way and, hearing my laments, untied and helped me, bringing me with them to Sigüenza, where Don Quixote bought me the clothes I am wearing. So now I am obliged to accompany him until he tires of calling me Queen Zenobia and suffering, with his squire, the blows and insults I have seen him endure in Sigüenza and in the inn near Alcalá, where the manager of some

[2] Refers to students, priests and professors.

[3] The Spanish *olla podrida*, lit. 'rotten pot', is a stew.

[4] This speech is loaded with sexual innuendo, only *some* of which comes over in translation.

company of actors annoyed them so much that they almost put an end to their adventurous misadventures."

After this she related, with a wit and ease that made them all marvel and provoked them to laughter, all that had happened to them in the inn and Alcalá until they had arrived at the Prado. To top off the farce, they sent for Don Quixote and Sancho to come downstairs. When both faced them, one in armor and the other wearing a cap, the nobleman said to Don Quixote, "Welcome, never-conquered Loveless Knight, defender of the needy, undoer of wrongs, procurer of equity."

Making Don Quixote sit down next to him, with Barbara at his side, for he would have it no other way, and with the room full of the members of the household, dying with laughter, he continued, "How have things gone with you in this Court since you have been here? Tell us what you think about its grandeur, and pardon my boldness in offering lodging in my house to persons of such outstanding worth as you and the lady, Queen of the Amazons; receive the willingness with which I serve you as a substitute for more tangible acts."

Don Quixote responded, "I'll accept that, illustrious Prince Perianeo, and so will the powerful Queen Zenobia who is honoring this drawing-room. The time will come when I shall repay such great kindness with interest, and it will be when I go with the Persian Duke Alfirón to the great city of Persepolis and make him marry your lovely sister in spite of everybody. Then I shall call myself the Knight of the Exquisite Face because I shall have the lifelike face of the Princess Florisbella of Babylon painted on my shield."

"I beg you not to touch on the subject of the Princess Florisbella, because you know that I am passionately fond of her," said the nobleman who was a man of lively wit. "Please let this subject drop. The merits of my claim in this matter will quickly be apparent when I go into field battle with you, as I have arranged."

"I urge it to be done, and with no deception," replied Don Quixote.

After hearing this, Sancho burst out, "For heaven's sake, Sir Pagan, you are the most upright man whose likes have never been seen in Pagan Land, leaving aside the fact that you are a bad Christian, because you are, as everybody knows, a Turk. Therefore you shouldn't want to put your life in jeopardy by going into battle with my master. It would be a bad thing for one who has done us such a good turn in his house by feeding us a supper fit for parrots, consisting of so many and such stews they were enough to bring a stone to life. Do you know whom I wish my master Don Quixote would fight? These demons of constables and doormen who at every turn cause us terrible calamities such as the one we just had, for they put master and servant in the tightest spot we've been in since we've been roaming about those worlds hunting for adventures. If you had not come in the nick of time my master would have found himself half scourged, as he was in Zaragoza. But I swear to you by the lives of the three kings of the Orient and all there are in the West, that if I catch one of them in the open where I can handle him in safety, I'll slap him around, giving him a punch here, a punch there, this one above, this other one below, until I'm satisfied."

Sancho was saying this so angrily, hitting at the air as if he were really fighting the constable, whirling around a thousand times, that his cap fell to the floor. He picked it up saying, "He can truly be grateful that my cap fell off, because if it hadn't the big beggar would have received his just deserts, so that another time he, or another like him, wouldn't dare pick a quarrel with a squire-errant as honorable as I am, with such a valiant master as my lord Don Quixote."

Everybody in the drawing-room laughed at Sancho's silly anger, and the nobleman told him, "Señor Sancho, I cannot refuse to go into battle with the Loveless Knight, and there is no doubt I shall come out victorious, because my courage is known and I have the extraordinary help a certain magician on my side always gives me."

"That remains to be seen from the deeds which I will offer," replied Don Quixote

It now appeared to everybody that it was time to stop for the night and the nobleman rose from his chair and said to Don Quixote, "Sir Loveless, ponder very carefully what you are attempting when you undertake to fight me, so sleep on it."

"My master will sleep better on a very good bed, and my lady, the queen, and I on another such," responded Sancho.

"You'll certainly have them," said the nobleman. He gave the order and they all went off to bed.

They had these and even better periods of diversion for two or three days, at all hours and with all three guests, whom they never allowed to leave the house, knowing their disposition and how easily they could raise a ruckus at Court.

At the end of this time it was God's will that Don Carlos should arrive with his friend Don Alvaro, whom he did not wish to leave until he recovered from an ailment that had come upon him in Zaragoza. This was the reason he had not come much earlier. The whole house was excited and joyous about their arrival, which they all desired for the celebration and the ceremony of the marriage of the owner of the house. A while after the guests arrived the nobleman told them he would offer them some interludes of entertainment with three interlocutors he had there, who had a fine sense of humor for making up farces extemporaneously. When he told them who they were and the way he had found them and brought them to his house and what had occurred there, Don Carlos and Don Álvaro were extremely happy at the news. They had come anxious as well as curious about Don Quixote, whom they ordered to appear as usual, in the drawing-room after supper, with Sancho and Barbara.

The nobleman had already told the story of her life to Don Carlos and to Don Álvaro, as they had told him all that had happened to them at the inn in Zaragoza with Don Quixote and his squire Sancho. Don Álvaro in particular had told him about the events in Argamesilla.

The two decided not to let themselves be known at first and sat down beside the nobleman with their hats pulled down. As the three—queen, master, and servant—entered the room, the pretended Perianeo began to speak in the following tenor:

"Soon, valiant Manchegan, I shall measure my sword against yours if you persist in your intention not to surrender to me and do not cease helping Don Belianís of Greece. It is a certainty you will be infamously vanquished in the battle, for here at my side is the wise Fristón, my very diligent historian and great promoter of my talents."

Saying this, he pointed to Don Álvaro who, concealing himself as much as he could, took his stand at once between Don Quixote and Sancho (for Barbara was already occupying her usual place) and said in a hollow, arrogant voice, "Loveless Knight of the Princess Dulcinea del Toboso whom you once adored, served, wrote to, and respected so much, and because of whose disdain you did harsh penance in Sierra Morena, as is related in I know not what annals which are scattered about, written in commonplace language by the hand of an unknown Alquife, are you perchance Don Quixote de La Mancha whose fame is spread throughout the four corners of the world? If you are, how does it happen that you are as cowardly as you are idle in this place?"

When Don Quixote heard this he looked around saying, "Sancho, you answer this wizard Fristón, because he isn't worthy of hearing the reply he expects from my mouth. I don't deal with people who have nothing but words, like these magicians and necromancers."

Sancho was very glad to hear what his master was ordering him to do, so, facing Don Álvaro with his arms crossed he spoke furiously as follows: "Haughty and extraordinary wizard, we are those from the four parts of the world about whom you inquire, just as you are the son of your mother and the grandson of your grandparents."

"Well, tonight I shall cast such a strong spell to harm you that I shall take Queen Zenobia through the air and put her on a peak in the Pyrenees Mountains," replied Don Álvaro. "There I'll eat her fried in an omelet, and then come back after you and your squire Sancho Panza to do the same thing with both of you."

"As far as we're concerned, we don't want to go there, and it hasn't even entered our minds," responded Sancho. "If you want to take Queen Segovia you're welcome to do so. We'll be very glad, and to the devil with anyone who says otherwise. On the road she is of no more use to us than to increase our expenses, for we have already spent more than forty ducats on a mule and clothes for her, not counting what she has eaten; even worse, the servants of the actors are the ones who get the best part afterwards. I give you only one piece of advice, as a friend: if you do take her, be careful how you eat her, because she is a little old and must be tough as the devil. What you can do is put her in a big pot (if you have one) with cabbage, turnips, garlic, onions, and bacon. If you let her cook three or four days she will be somewhat more palatable and eating her will be like eating a piece of beef, although I don't envy you the meal."

When Don Álvaro heard this he was unable to pretend any longer, seeing that everybody was laughing, so he went up to Don Quixote with outstretched arms saying, "Oh, my dear Loveless Knight! Embrace me and look me in the face, for it will tell you that the one before you, speaking to you, is Don Álvaro Tarfe, your host and great friend."

Don Quixote recognized him at once and said, embracing him, "Oh, my dear Don Álvaro, welcome! I was startled by hearing the wise Fristón speak to me so insolently, but the joke you have played on my sevant Sancho and me hasn't been a bad one."

Upon hearing what his master was saying to Don Álvaro, Sancho recognized him at once and knelt at his feet, cap in hand saying, "Oh, my dear Señor Don Tarfe! You are as welcome in this room as would be a stew such as one I have cooked up with Queen Segovia. Excuse my anger, but since you said you were that accursed wizard who wanted to take us to the Pyrenees Mountains, I have been tempted a thousand times to land blows on you with these closed fists, even if they are sinful, before you left the room. I was confident that at the first clash of battle my master Don Quixote would help me."

Don Álvaro answered, "I am very grateful, Señor Sancho, for the good turn you wanted to do me. Truly I have not done such bad things to you in my house at Zaragoza and in Don Carlos' house, where we gave you those delicious dishes, as you know."

"Where is Señor Don Carlos?" asked Sancho.

"Here, at your service," he responded, rising from his seat to embrace Don Quixote, who returned his embrace, as did his servant. Then he said, "I wouldn't have come to this Court, Señor Don Quixote, except to sponsor you in the battle you are to have with the King of Cyprus, Bramidán, ridding the world of him. I am told that he is in the center of the main plaza daily, challenging all the knights who ride there and overcoming all of them. Nobody can stand up to him, which has the king and the grandees of the kingdom no little abashed. They are waiting for God to send them at any moment a knight who will be excellent enough to overcome such an infernal monster and cut off his head."

Don Quixote responded, "I do believe, Señor Don Carlos, that the sins and iniquities of the King of Cyprus have reached their highest peak and are calling aloud to God. This afternoon, without fail, he will be given the punishment his evil deeds demand."

"Bear in mind, Señor Don Carlos, that today we will put an end to that devilish giant who has harrassed us so much," said Sancho. "However, so that my master Don Quixote may understand that I have not received the order of squiredom for nothing, I say that I, too, and before everybody, want to battle the black squire that giant has with him, whom I saw in Zaragoza at Señor Don Álvaro's house. I think he has no sword or other weapons at all, and is just like I am. Therefore I want to put up a bold front and have a bloody fight with kicks, punches, pinches, and bites, for if he is the squire of a pagan giant, I am the squire of a Christian Manchegan knight-errant, and squire against squire, Valladolid in Castile,[5] master against master,

[5] "Valladolid in Castile' is part of a Spanish proverb.

Lisbon in Portugal. Damn him and his black mother! Well, let him watch out for me as he would the devil for before getting into the fight I'll eat half a dozen raw garlic cloves, and I'll take another six glugs of Villarobledo red wine, and I'll give him a punch that would knock down a cliff. Oh, poor black squire! What a villainous afternoon is being prepared for you! It would have been better for you to have stayed in Monicongo with the other sooty brothers who are there than to come to die at Sancho's hands from pounding. Farewell, goodby; I am going to do it!"

Don Carlos stopped him saying, "Wait, friend, it isn't time to fight yet. Rest easy and leave things in my hands."

"I'll do that very willingly," replied Sancho. "I'm very grateful for your favor, for the man who wanted to see your hands cut off now wants to kiss them."

"Oh Sancho!" said Don Carlos. "Have I done you so much harm that you would want to see my hands cut off?"

"I don't mean it in that way," he responded. "But that proverb came to my lips, as others do, and please God I'd rather see such honorable hands busy with those blessed dishes of meatballs and that creamed chicken, as in Zaragoza, for I confess that in those other matters things would go badly for me."

After these remarks Don Quixote turned to the nobleman saying, "Prince, here is the flower of my friends, who will inform you adequately about my valor and exploits and will make clear to you how rash it is for you not to surrender to me by waiving your courtship of the Princess Florisbella in favor of Don Belianís, my close bosom friend."

"Then does this prince intend to enter into battle with you, Señor Don Quixote?" responded Don Álvaro.

"His daring is so great that he wants to defy and confront me," he replied. "I regret it deeply, because I should not like to find myself forced to execute one who has been so honorable and courteous a host, but what I can do for him, so that he may have more time to deliberate on what is best for him, will be to battle with King Bramidán de Tajayunque first, then the treacherous son of the King of Cordova, in defense of his queen mother's honor."

"By postponing this battle you are doing all of us a great favor," Don Carlos told him. "In fact it is important to all of us that disputes between two princes as powerful as Perianeo and you be avoided. In the end I trust your claims will be settled without offense to either party."

"The pagan prince's claims are such that I am compelled to wish to serve him even in the fight," responded Sancho. "I'll do so as of now, by advising him not to go out unless he has eaten heartily, for after all, the afternoon is long. It will be even better for them to take along a cold lunch to eat while they rest, in case weariness makes them hungry. I'll offer now to take everything on my donkey in some big saddlebags I have, if you wish. Besides, I offer to tell my master, when he has overcome you and has you down on the ground, ready to cut off your head, to cut it off slowly so that it will hurt you less."

Prince Perianeo thanked him for his proffered good help and accepted from Don Quixote the postponement of the fight, proving he greatly desired his friendship and feared entering the field with him, in view of the way Don Carlos and Don Álvaro vouched for his valor. The latter told them all, "I think, gentlemen, that these affairs are at a good stage, so we should go to bed, for we shall have plenty to do tomorrow advising the entire Court of Señor Don Quixote's arrival, his objective in coming, which is his great desire to liberate it from the annoyance caused by the insolent King Bramidán.

Everybody thought well of the clever plan to cut short the lengthy conversation and they all left the drawing-room, each going to his own room. No sooner was poor Sancho outside when he was caught by the servants of Don Carlos and Don Álvaro, whom he knew well. After he inquired about the lame cook, and they greeted each other, one of them said, "In truth, Señor Sancho, you are prospering in a fine fashion; I am not displeased that in your later days you have taken to being a pimp. Upon my word, the girl isn't bad; you've picked a plump one, which is a sign of good taste. However, keep her away from the young hawks of the Court and be on your guard lest some Court bailiff catch you red-handed; they'd really give you no less than two hundred lashes and the galleys, for in the Court they give out those benefits most liberally."

"The girl doesn't belong to me," said Sancho, "but to the devil, who thrust her upon us in her shift in the middle of a wood, and in that condition and for that reason you may take her whenever you wish, for the clothes she is now wearing cost us money. By God! I swear that if they'd give me not two hundred lashes and the galleys for her, but four thousand bishoprics, I'd send her and all her lineage to Barrabas and make her remember me as long as she lives."

After this they took him up to their rooms to sleep, causing him to exclaim two thousand absurdities about leftovers from their supper.

CHAP. XXXII. IN WHICH THE GRANDIOSE DEMONSTRATIONS *of their valor given by our hidalgo Don Quixote and his most faithful squire Sancho at Court are continued.*

HE NOBLEMAN and Don Carlos thought that the first thing they should do, after leaving the house and hearing mass, was to kiss the hands of His Majesty and other high-born gentlemen and members of the Council, and inform them of the marriage arrangements. They did this, accompanied by Don Álvaro and other friends who had come to visit Don Carlos.

His guests, Don Quixote, Barbara, and Sancho, were already up when they left, and the gentlemen had quite a little difficulty making the guests understand that they were to remain in the house. Nothing would suit Don Quixote except being allowed to honor them with his company, riding Rocinante. By dint of promises that they would send for him after informing the grandees about his arrival they made him stay, although not unguarded, so neither he nor his group could leave the house for any reason.

As the gentlemen were leaving, Sancho went hastily to the window, calling out, "Señor Don Carlos, if you happen to run across that black squire, my adversary, tell him that I present my compliments and that he should prepare for this afternoon or tomorrow to finish that battle he knows about with one of the best squires who ever sprouted a whisker. Besides, after the fight I challenge him to see which one can reap faster, and I'll even give him a handicap of three sheaves, on condition that we first eat a fine young rabbit cooked with garlic, for I know how to fix it wonderfully well."

At this Don Quixote tugged angrily at his smock saying, "Is it possible, Sancho, that for you there can't be a war, a conversation, or a pastime unless there are things to eat? Let the black squire alone. Let the blame be upon me if he does not come into your hands with more than enough strength left over; indeed, I can understand that you will have your hands full with him."

"No, I won't," replied Sancho. "I intend to go into the fight forearmed with a big ball of that soft pitch used by shoemakers in my left hand, so that when the black fellow gets ready to give me a hard punch on my nose, I'll parry it with this ball; in his fury he'll be sure to hit me so hard that his hand will get stuck and he won't be able to get it loose. So then I, seeing he is minus his right hand and can't use it, will in safety hit him so many and such fierce blows on the nose that it will turn from black to red just from blood."

The nobleman, Don Carlos, and Don Álvaro paid their visits and were fortunate in being able to present their compliments to His Majesty unhurriedly and discuss their affairs with him and the other gentlemen whom they were obliged to inform first about the marriage. The last visit they made was to a person of their own rank, a very intimate friend married to a lovely lady. They told them about their guests and the good times they had had with them, the best that any man in the world could have. They praised their guests' drollery so highly that the husband and wife begged them very earnestly to bring them to their house so they could spend a delightful afternoon.

They offered to do so on condition that the husband pretend to be the great Archipámpano[1] from Seville with his wife, the Archipampanesa. They said that Don Quixote was fond only of princes with resounding titles, because in his madness he believed that he was a knight-errant, righter of wrongs, defender of kingdoms, kings, and queens, and as a result he had taken it into his head that a very ugly tripe-seller from Alcalá whom he forcibly brought with him was Queen Zenobia. He was set in this belief because the habitual reading of books about fabulous knightly deeds to which he had become addicted caused him to accept as true all the fanciful tales in them.

Having agreed upon this they went home to dine and after dinner they gave Don Quixote a message from the great Archipámpano saying they were all to go at sundown for Don Quixote and Sancho to kiss His Lordship's hand. They were to go by coach, because during that season it was customary for princes to take their outings by carriage and not on horseback. Don Quixote accepted the invitation and so did Sancho.

When the gentlemen thought it was time they sent for the carriages and all got in with Don Quixote, wearing his armor and shield, and Sancho. They made their way to the home of the feigned Archipámpano, who was immediately advised by the pages that visitors were arriving. Upon hearing this, he took his place under a canopy in a large reception hall to receive them, and when the nobleman, Don Carlos, and Don Álvaro entered they greeted him with extraordinary courtesy and pomposity, and at his command sat down beside

---

[1] *Archipámpano* is a high-falutin sounding title indeed, meaning 'self-styled dignitary', but its literal meaning is 'Arch Grapevine-shoot'.

him. The hall was filled with the people who accompanied them and the members of the household, and at the other end, on a handsome dais, was the wife with some duennas and maid-servants.

Don Álvaro rose, took Don Quixote's hand and presented him with great courtesy to the Archipámpano saying, "Your Highness, lord of the rise and fall of the sea, most powerful ruling Archipámpano of the Oceanic and Mediterranean Indies, of Hellespont and great Arcadia, here is the cream and flower of the entire Manchegan knighthood, a friend to Your Highness and the great defender of all your kingdoms, islands, and peninsulas."

Having said this, he sat down again and a man-servant brought Don Quixote his lance, the butt of which the knight then grounded on the floor there in the center of the hall where he remained as he had been placed, looking all around most gravely. He kept silence until he saw that everybody had seen the images and read the epigrams on his shield. When he saw that they were silent and waiting for him to speak he began talking in a calm, serious voice: "Magnanimous, powerful, and ever-august Archipámpano of the Indies, descendant of the Heliogabalus, Sarganapalus,[2] and the other ancient emperors, the Loveless Knight has come today into your royal presence. If you have never heard of him, he has come after traveling over most of our hemisphere, killing and conquering an infinite

[2] Elagabalus, sometimes erroneously known as Heliogabalus, was a Roman emperor of the early third century century A.D. Sarganapalus may refer to Sargon I of Mesopotamia (ca. 2276-2221 B.C.) or Sargon II of Assyria who reigned from 721 to 705 B.C.)

number of barbarians and huge giants, disenchanting castles, and freeing maidens, in addition to having righted wrongs, avenged kings, conquered kingdoms, subdued provinces, liberated empires, and brought the peace desired by the most remote islands. Looking thoughtfully at the rest of the world, I have noted that on its face there is not a king nor an emperor more worthy and deserving of my friendship, association, and intimacy than Your Highness, because of your valor, the pride of your progenitors, the grandeur of your empire and patrimony, and principally because of the strength manifest in your handsome, robust body. Consequently, I have come, magnanimous monarch, not to be honored by you, for I have acquired enough honor; not to secure wealth or kingdoms from you, for I have yonder empires of Greece, Babylon, and Trebizond whenever I want them; not to learn courtesy or any other pleasing manners or virtues from your knights, for one known to all knowledgeable princes as the mirror and model of virtue, breeding, and everything pertaining to prudence and good military discipline has very little to learn. Instead I come so that from this day on you may consider me a true friend; from it there will result not only honor but also the greatest contentment and joy. It is clear that all the emperors in the world, seeing me on your side, will have to be your vassals whether they want to or not, send tribute, increase the number of ambassadors, only with the objective of maintaining an inviolable and perpetual truce, while I am in your house. They will be compelled to do this because of their fear when the thunder of my name and the glory of my exploits enters their ears and pierces the depths of their hearts. So you may see that the fame of my deeds, of which you have heard, is not merely a voice carried away on the wind, but heroic bravery and famous conquests accomplished with the greatest good fortune and to the glory of the Order of Knighthood, I desire that in your presence that haughty giant, Bramidán de Tajayunque, King of Cyprus, with whom I have had an appointed battle for more than a month, come to blows with me, before you and all your grandees, in whose presence I shall cut off his monstrous head and offer it to the great Zenobia, most beautiful Queen of the Amazons who honors me with her presence and to whom I intend to give the aforesaid kingdom of Cyprus, until such time as this arm restores her to her own, usurped by the Grand Turk. With this victory behind me I hope to attain another one over a certain son of the King of Cordova, so treacherous that in my presence he falsely accused a queen to whom he was stepson. As a finishing touch, I'll make Prince Perianeo of

Persia give up his life or his courtship of Princess Florisbella, because my great friend, Belianís of Greece pursues her love and I would not fulfill the obligations I owe to what I am if I left her without such an important suitor in such a serious courtship. Consequently, Your Highness, order the three to come at once to this royal hall, for I defy, challenge and summon them."

Having said this, he remained silent and everybody in the hall was so surprised by that man's well-structured nonsensical remarks and his gravity and grimaces as he made them that they didn't know who could answer him or what could be said. But after a while the Archimpámpano himself said, "I am infinitely happy, invincible and gallant Manchegan, that you have chosen to select my court and the services I mean to do for your benefit and glory, and to increase my holdings. I am more so because you have come at a time when that barbarous prince of Tajayunque you mention is oppressing my dominions. However, because the duel you have arranged with him is an arduous one and so that I may deliberate on it more wisely, I wish you to delay until I consult my grandees. Those challenges issued to Prince Perianeo and to the Prince of Cordova are of less significance, for after you triumph over the King of Cyprus they will easily come to terms or surrender. Therefore I request, first, that you consent to a delay in your battle, and second, I beg you to keep away from the ladies in my home and court as much as you can, for when you, the Loveless Knight so gallant, attractive, well-spoken, and valiant, are present they will all certainly be on the watch and there will even be rivalry over which will be the happy and fortunate one to deserve you. I do not intend for you to marry any of them because I plan to marry you to my daughter, the princess you see over there, as soon as I see you crowned emperor of Greece, Babylon, and Trebizond. From now on I shall receive you as a son-in-law in waiting, so you may consider this house yours, availing yourself of it and my own knights and servants."

At this point Don Carlos called Sancho over to one side of his chair to say to him, "Now it's time, friend Sancho, for the powerful Archipámpano to know you and see what a good mind you have, so don't miss your opportunity. Rather, tell him very eloquently to be good enough to grant you permission to battle that black squire you know about. If you triumph he will be sure to receive you into the Order of Chivalry and you will be as much a knight and as famous as Don Quixote all your life."

No sooner did Sancho hear such advice when he went to the center of the hall, knelt before his master, cap in hand, and said loudly, "My lord Don Quixote de La Mancha, if I have ever done you a favor in this world, I beg you in the name of the good services of Rocinante, who is the person having the most influence on you, to give me, in payment for all this, permission to say half a dozen words to this lord, the Arcadepámpanos,[3] for when he sees my cleverness he will, in the course of time, give me the order of knighthood with all the doings and undoings that you have."

Don Quixote told him, "Sancho, I grant it, but on condition that you not say any of the silly things you usually do."

"I have a good remedy for that," said Sancho. "You stand behind me, and if you see one is getting away from me, pull on the skirt of my tunic, and you'll see how I'll deny all that I may have said."

Immediately Don Quixote went up to the gentleman he thought was the Archipámpano and said, "My dear sir, so that you may see that as a knight-errant I have with me a talented squire, most reliable for carrying messages back and forth to princesses and knights with whom I need to communicate, I beg you to listen to the one whom I now present to you, named Sancho Panza, a native of Argamesilla de La Mancha, a man of very good talent and humility. He has an important matter to discuss with Your Highness if you will grant him permission." The Archipámpano replied that he gave him full permission, for he had realized from his bearing, outfit, and face that he could not be less circumspect than his master.

Then Sancho got between them, and looking around at Don Quixote he said, "Give me that lance so that I may look as you did when you were talking to the Arcapámpanos." Don Quixote responded, "Why the devil do you want it? Don't you see that you are not in armor as I am? You are already starting to do silly things."

"Well, keep count," replied Sancho. "I already have one." Steepling his hands to make a point and not taking off his cap, which caused no little laughter from those watching him, he remained quite a while not saying a word until he saw they were quiet, when he began to speak, trying to begin like his master Don Quixote, to whose words he had been very attentive: "Magnanimous, powerful, and harvest-time grape-vine shoots . . . "[4] Don Quixote gave his cloak a yank,

---

[3] Sancho's first transformation of *Archipámpano*—this version means 'chest of vine-shoots'.

[4] Sancho first mixes up *august* 'royal' with *August* 'harvest-time', then he reverts to the real meaning of *pámpanos*, 'grapevine-shoots'.

saying "Say, 'august Archipámpano' and be careful what you say."

Sancho looked around and said, "What's wrong with August or harvest-time in that business of pámpanos or vine-shoots? Doesn't it all go off in the same direction?" And he continued, "For your information, sir, as a descendant of the emperor Ellgobbler and Sarganápalos, my name is Sancho Panza the squire, husband of Mari-Gutiérrez, from in front and behind, if you never heard of him; by the grace of God and the Holy Apostolic See, I am a Christian and not a pagan like Prince Perianeo and the devilish black squire, and for days now I have been roaming about on my donkey with my master throughout most of this . . . " and, turning to his master he said, "What the devil is the name of that hum-thingy?"

"Curse you!" replied Don Quixote, " 'Hemisphere,' you fool!"

"Well, what do you want now?" answered Sancho. "Put down two silly things on my side; do you think that man's memory should be as long as the missal? Tell me its name and be patient, for my judgment has already gotten all twisted up again."

"I've told you its name is 'hemisphere,' " responded Don Quixote.

"Then I'll say, going back to my story, Sir King of Hemisphere, up to now I have not killed or torn asunder those great giants my master talks about; instead, I flee from them as from damnation, because the one I saw in Zaragoza in Señor Don Carlos' house was such that the Tower of Babylon would have a terrible time trying to measure up to him! So I don't want to have anything to do with him; let him have it out with my master. The one I want to test my talons on is the black squire he has, God curse him! After all, he is my mortal enemy and I won't stop until I wash my hands in his black blood in this hall, in the presence of all of you. By doing so, I am confident that Your Highness will make me a knight, although it is true that when I am on my donkey I am as much one as anybody. I only stipulate that in the fight neither my master, nor Don Carlos, nor Don Álvaro should fail to be at my side in case anything comes up. Besides this, we are not to fight with sticks or swords, for we could hurt each other with them and have to be treated afterward; the fight must be with hard punches or slaps on the face or head, and Saint Peter bless the one who can manage to throw in a hoof or bite. But it's true that even this way the devilish black fellow will have quite an advantage, because for more than two and a half years I haven't been going around exchanging blows with anybody, and if that isn't practiced it's forgotten like the Hail Mary. But the decision lies in Señor Don Álvaro's hands. Who am I talking to? Come over here, and here comes a tug at my tunic!"

"Speak, Señor Sancho, for I can hear you clearly," responded Don Álvaro. "I shall do whatever you like."

"Well, what you must do is put some blinders on him when he comes out to fight, so that he can't see me and will miss his aim, and I will go up very quietly and hit him a thousand blows first on one side, then on the other, until I make him go to kneel before my wife Mari-Gutiérrez and beg her to forgive him. So now, Lord King Harvest, you have the battle ended and the black squire vanquished, and so there is nothing else to be done except dub me a knight, for I don't stand for jests and you can't fool an old dog."

"Indeed, Sancho, you deserve the rank of knight you request," said the Archipámpano. "I shall grant it to you, with other favors, the day on which the battle with the King of Cyprus ends. But just to please me tell me about Señor Don Quixote's exploits and the adventures he ran into in those hemispheres, for the Archipampanesa and I and my daughter, the princess, and all these gentlemen will be very glad to hear about it."

No sooner did they give Sancho an opportunity to speak when he so expertly got ahead of his master in telling all that had happened to them that he never let him stick in a word, however much Don Quixote angrily insisted, contradicted, and dissented. Sancho kept on telling all about Ateca, their arrival and departure, what had happened to them in Zaragoza, about Queen Segovia in the woods, Sigüenza, the inn, Alcalá, and even the Court itself.

His master gave him a bad scolding when he'd finished telling that, and some fine stories were told about the identification of the crupper, at which the listeners laughed so heartily that Don Quixote felt obliged to tell them, "Certainly, gentlemen, I am greatly astonished that such circumspect people should be so quick to laugh about things that happen or can happen daily to knights-errant, for the strong Amadís de Gaula was as honored as I, and yet I remember reading that a magician took him prisoner by tricking him, put him in a dark dungeon and invisibly pumped into him a concoction of sand and cold water, with the result that he almost died from it."[5]

After these words, the Archipámpano rose from his place, afraid that Don Quixote would follow them up with a deluge of sword-slashes aimed at everybody (which really was to be feared from the way that he was working himself into a fit of anger). Going up to his wife he asked her what she thought of the bravery of master and servant. When she praised them as worthy to be kings, Don Carlos said to her, "But Your Highness has yet to see the best one, Queen Zenobia; if you don't believe it, let Sancho decide."

He replied, looking at the ladies present, "By heavens, ladies! You may be whatever you command, but I swear before God and my conscience that Queen Segovia excels all of you in a thousand ways: first, her hair is as white as a snowflake, and yours is as dark as the black squire, my adversary. As for her face, she's ahead of you there, for I swear, by God, that it's bigger than a shield, more wrinkled than a soldier's breeches, and redder than cow's blood; her mouth is no less than three inches larger than yours and more spacious, for inside it she doesn't have so many bones and snags for whatever she may hide in its darker corners. She can be recognized even in Babylon by the equinoctial line on her face; her hands are wide, short, and covered with warts; her breasts fall as long as young summer squashes. Suffice it to say that she has more in one foot than all of you together, counting all your feet. In short, she looks just prettily perfect to my master Don Quixote, and he even says she is more beautiful than the star Venus at sunset, although I don't think she's so much like that."

Since it was midnight, the cocks wanted to crow,[6] and everybody praised the picture of Queen Zenobia drawn by Sancho, and they

---

[5] In Part I, 15, Don Quixote recounts how a somewhat similar enema was administered to the Knight of Pheobus, but the incident is not recorded either in *Amadís of Gaul* or in the book of the *Knight of Phoebus*.

[6] "It was exactly midnight, the cocks wanted to crow," is the beginning of the ballad of Gaiferos.

urged Don Carlos to bring her there at the same time next day. He promised to do so and, calling his brother-in-law the nobleman, who was standing a short distance away, they begged both of them to leave Sancho in the house that night. They all yielded to the request of the Archimpámpano, particularly Don Quixote, who was told by the nobleman, Don Carlos, and by Don Álvaro that he couldn't refuse. After this they all took leave of Their Highnesses and returned to the house with the companions who had come with them, Don Quixote quite comforted by seeing that he was now beginning to be known and feared by those in Court.

CHAP. XXXIII. IN WHICH THE HEROIC FEATS OF OUR Don Quixote are continued, and the battle between our spirited Sancho and the black squire of the King of Cyprus, together with Barbara's visit to the Archimpámpano are recounted.

HAT NIGHT the Archipámpano and his wife were very pleased with Sancho because of his witty, foolish remarks, not the least of which was to say, when he saw supper brought up and they told him to sit down at a small table next to theirs at which sat with them a very beautiful little girl, their daughter, "Well, in heaven's name! why do you seat that youngster, the size of my fist, at that big table and put in front of her big plates larger than Mari-Gutiérrez' dough trough, and leave me at this little table, smaller than a sieve, when I am as big as a Corpus Christi dragon of Toledo, and as bearded as Adam and Eve? Well, if you're doing it to be paid, the two and a half *reales* I have in my coat pocket are as good to pay for what I'll eat as all those the king has and the ones the Jews gave Judas for Jesus Christ. And if not, look at them anyway."

Upon this he rose and took out as many as three *reales* worth of dirty, greasy *cuartos* and threw them down on the lady's napkin. He had scarcely done so when he saw that she was going to push them away; thinking she meant to take them he picked them up again furiously saying, "By God! You won't grab them, for I haven't had a very good supper. My faith, I bet you already fattened your eye on them, like the other fat Galician girl at the inn whom my master called a princess. If it weren't that she was not wearing as good clothes as yours and didn't have a ruff like that you are wearing about your windpipe, I'd swear by God and this cross that you're one and the same."

All gave the appropriate responses to the litany of foolish remarks strung together like a rosary by Sancho, then the steward said to him, "Be quiet, Sancho; so that you may eat supper more pleasurably, we have set up a separate table for you."

"The more that table with those bloated birds on it over there falls to my lot, the more to my pleasure will I dine," replied Sancho.

"Well, begin with this dish of them," the steward said at once, handing him a fine dish of squabs in brown gravy. He ate that and the other things they brought him so without scruple of conscience that it was a blessing from God and an entertainment for those present to watch him.

When he saw that supper was over and the lady was loosening her ruff or collar, he said to her, "Won't you tell me, in the name of the one who misbegot you, what is your object in wearing those spiked watch-dog's collars about your neck? They look exactly like the ones worn by the shepherds' mastiffs in my region. But all these house hounds must bother you so much that you need that to keep anything from happening and even more to protect yourself from them."

Having said this, he again took out the money saying, "Now take it and pay yourself for whatever the supper cost, because I don't want to go to bed without settling bills; that's the way my master Don Quixote and I always used to do on the road. The priest used to tell me this is what the commandments of the church command when they demand payment of tithes and first fruits . . . "

The gentleman took the money saying, "I am satisfied that what is here pays what you owe for supper and bed, and tomorrow I'll also give you the noon-day meal for it, without further pay."

"I kiss your hands for your kindness," responded Sancho. "I accept your promise and I'll be as quiet about it as a weather-vane upon a roof. For although I know my master needs me very much, I shall make my excuses by saying I couldn't find the house. Considering that when a man suffers half a dozen blows in exchange for a good meal the cost is not so great that it won't turn out to be excessively cheap; and on other occasions we were given them free, and without any meal at all."

The order was given for him to be taken off to bed and the rest went also. The nobleman, Don Carlos, Don Álvaro, Don Quixote, and Barbara did likewise, after a good supper at their house. However, after the meal they had a bit of a quarrel because when the nobleman told them to prepare to go the next day to visit the Archipámpano and the Archipampanesa, who were expecting them, Barbara answered with the excuse that she should not be ordered to appear in public in front of people because this meant shaming her too much and upsetting her a great deal, for she was well-known, as she had told them, as an abject tripe-seller, Barbara by name, and in civil record. She implored them to be content with the patience with which up to now she had gone along with the tiresome jests and bantering that Señor Don Quixote did and wanted them all to do.

Don Quixote had no sooner heard this when he said to her, "Whatever may happen in the world, Your Majesty, my lady Queen Zenobia, don't deny your grandeur nor conceal it by saying such a very blasphemous thing as what you have just said. I am weary from having heard you repeat it on other occasions, and we won't accept from your lips that business of being a tripe-seller. As far as I am concerned, I know without any doubt who you are and your worth; however it is necessary for everybody to know it. Your Highness, go and talk to whatever person Prince Perianeo and these knights request you to, for among ladies such as the Archipampanesa and her daughter, the princess, your beauty must be outstanding. I guarantee that after they see you they will esteem and respect you as you deserve and we all wish."

Wisely, she did not make any more difficulties, knowing how indebted she was to Don Quixote and that up to then nothing but good had come to her from complying with his crazy ideas; at least she was leading an easy life, so she agreed to go.

When morning came the Archipámpano went to hear mass, taking Sancho with him. On the way he inquired if he knew how to assist in mass. Sancho responded, "Yes, sir, although it is true that for some days now, as we are always involved in this devil of an adventure, confession and all the rest has flown from my head and I remember only about lighting the tapers and draining wine vessels for the Eucharist. To tell the truth, in my village I used to play the organ divinely from the back where I couldn't be seen,[1] and when I wasn't working them, the whole village missed me."

They all laughed in earnest, and when mass was over they went

[1] This obviously means that Sancho used to work the bellows of the organ, which were pumped from the back.

home to eat, and after this, not without some very amusing interludes with Sancho, the Archimpámpano said to him, "Señor Sancho, having thought it over I want you to stay in my house henceforth and serve me, and I offer you a larger salary than the Loveless Knight gives you, for I, too, am a knight-errant like him and need a squire like you for any adventures that may come my way. Therefore, to seal the bargain at once I promise you a fine outfit for you as your first payment. But tell me, how much does master Don Quixote pay you yearly?"

To this Sancho answered, "Sir, my master gives me nine *reales* and my keep each month, and some shoes each year, and in addition he has promised me all the spoils of the wars and battles we win, although up to now the spoils we have taken, may it be for the good, have been nothing but hard knocks with a club, such as the melon-grower in Ateca gave us. But despite all that, even though you added one more *real* a month, I wouldn't leave the Loveless Knight because he is, in truth, very valiant, at least according to what I hear him say daily. The best thing about it is that he is courageous without hurt or injury to anybody, for up to now I have never seen him kill a fly."

The Archipámpano responded, "Is it possible, Sancho, that if I gave you more than your master does, and gave you an oufit and a pair of shoes every month, with a ducat as your salary, you would not serve me?"

He replied, "That isn't bad. But withal, I wouldn't serve you except on one condition: that you buy me a fine dappled donkey to ride along those roads, for you must know that I am not much good as a foot-traveler. Besides, we have to take along a suitcase of money so we won't find ourselves in the predicament we were in a year ago in those inns in La Mancha. Besides this, you would have to swear and promise to make me, in due time, king or admiral of some island or peninsula, as my master Don Quixote has promised from the first day I served him. Although I may not have very good expedience in governing, Mari-Gutiérrez and I together would be able to clear up nicely the injusticeness in those islands. It is true that she is somewhat stupid, but I believe that since I have been wandering about here she won't have failed to learn something more."

"Well, Sancho, I bind myself to fulfill all those conditions, provided you stay in my house," said the pretended Archipámpano. "You may bring your wife with you as well so she can serve the great Archipampanesa, for I am told she knows how to string pearls beautifully."

"You'd better say 'string liters of wine,' for upon my word she lines them up as well as Queen Segovia, and that's the highest compliment I can give her."

Here the gentlemen put an end to the conversation so they could take a short siesta, having sent word to some gentlemen, friends of theirs, to come that afternoon to enjoy the entertainment that was awaiting them with the knight-errant, his lady, and his squire. The nobleman, Don Carlos, and his brother-in-law, Don Álvaro, did the same.

The hour duly arrived and the carriages were made ready. They got in with Barbara who insisted on having Don Quixote at her side. With this little farce and quite a bit of laughter from those who saw them in the carriage, they arrived at the house of the Archipámpano. When the ladies and gentlemen had taken their usual seats, Don Quixote, in full armor, entered through the hall, leading Queen Zenobia in a courtly manner. Upon seeing them enter, Don Álvaro Tarfe rose and said, kneeling before the Archipámpano, "Powerful Lord, the Loveless Knight and the peerless Queen Zenobia come to visit Your Highness."

No sooner did Sancho hear his master's name when he got up from the floor where he was sitting and ran toward his master to kneel before him and say, "Be most welcome, my Lord; thank God we are all here. But tell me, did you remember to feed the donkey last night? The poor ass must be grieving very much because he hasn't seen me since yesterday, so I beg you to tell him for me, when you see him, that I send very best regards to him and to my good friend Rocinante, and that I haven't gone to see them because I was invited by Señor Arcapámpanos to eat supper, stay overnight, and dine today for only two and a half *reales*. I'll be hanged if that wasn't a bargain, may it please the Mother of God! But for when I do go I'm keeping in my bosom a couple of legs of certain little pea-owls."

Don Quixote paid no attention to these foolish remarks, but continued walking sedately with Queen Zenobia, just as he had entered, until he was in the presence of the Archipámpano, whence, once he was presented, he said, "Powerful Lord and respected monarch, here in your presence is the Loveless Knight with the most excellent Queen Zenobia, whose virtues, charms, and beauty, with your august permission, I shall defend as extraordinary and peerless, against all knights, beginning tomorrow afternoon in the public plaza."

Here he dropped her hand, and while those present, in astonishment, were nodding to one another in pleasure over his madness and her ugliness, the master turned to the squire to ask how it had gone with him that night at the house of the Archipámpano, and what His Highness had said to him about Don Quixote's courage, strength, and appearance.

At this point Barbara arrived, summoned before the gentlemen and ladies. She knelt, shamefacedly silent, waiting to see what they would say to her. They were so occupied in marveling at the ugliness they saw in her, more so because she was dressed in red, that they couldn't manage to say a word to her because of their laughter. However, humiliating her as much as he could, the Archipámpano told her, "Arise, my lady Queen Zenobia, for now I realize the good taste of the Loveless Knight who brings you here, because, being loveless and hating women as much as I am told he hates them, he is right to bring you with him so that by looking at your face he can more easily keep up his claim, although in his case it could be said, as in the proverb, that *qui amat ranam, credit se amare Dianam*.[2] However, I am of the opinion that if all the women in the world were like you, all the gentlemen in it would have the highest degree of aversion toward loving them."

The man who was nearest his wife asked her what she thought of Queen Zenobia whom the Loveless Knight brought along as a model of beauty. She responded, "I am sure the rivals for her beauty will give him few occasions for quarrels."

The Archipámpano then continued his conversation with the Queen, asking about her life, and when he learned from her lips that her name was Barbara, and everything else concerning her status and her trade, and the reason she was following the crazy Don Quixote, he inquired whether she would venture to remain as his wife's maid, because she needed somebody to guide the footsteps of a little girl they were bringing up, a task he believed she could do better than anybody. She apologized and declined, saying she had little training and experience in palace work. Sancho was immediately at her side as her champion and took up the cause saying, "Sir, you don't have to ask her because this devil of a queen will not leave the mean calling of preparing a sheep's entrails and cooking cows' heels, for she knows nothing else."

Going up to her and pulling on her red skirt, which was more

---

[2] "He who loves a frog thinks he loves Diana." A medieval proverb found earliest in *El libro de los gatos*, a book rendered into Spanish from Odo of Cheriton's *Narrationes*.

than a span and a half too short, he said, "Madam Segovia, in the name of all the Satans, pull down that skirt, for your legs can be seen almost up to the knees. Tell me, how do you expect them to take you for such a beautiful queen if you show those legs and broken shoes and your muddy red hose?"

Turning to the Archipámpano he said, "Why do you think my master has ordered Queen Segovia to wear short skirts and reveal her feet? For your information, he does so because she has such a bad countenance and in addition that blemish on her face which takes in the entire right side of her mustache. In this way he tries to make a *noverint universi*[3] which will declare to all who look her in the face that she is not a devil, for her feet are not those of a rooster but of a person;[4] therefore they will be disabused by looking at her feet which, by God's mercy, she has somewhat shamefully exposed, but nevertheless, God help us."

Don Quixote said, "I'll bet, Sancho, that you have a full belly and a loaded stomach, from the way you talk. Watch out that I don't lose my temper and give you another load and that one right on your back to help distribute your blood a little better."

Sancho responded, "If my stomach is full, it's costing me a full two and a half *reales*."

As they were engaged in this give and take, Don Álvaro made Sancho and Don Quixote stand aside and said to the Archipámpano, respectfully bowing as he gestured toward the entrance of the royal hall, "Illustrious monarch, here is a black squire, a servant of the King of Cyprus, Bramidán de Tajayunque, who comes with a message for Your Highness and also to fight some sort of duel with the squire of the Loveless Knight."

When he heard this Sancho turned pale and hastily replied, "Well, tell him right away, in the name of Christ's mercy, that I am not here and I am in no mood to fight now . . . But, by the soul of the anti-Christ! Go tell him to enter, for I'm waiting for him here, and damn the hour that he and his black whore of a mother come. If my master

[3] A Latin phrase which has come to mean knife slash.

[4] According to legend, the devil has the feet of a rooster. Such feet are seen in many of the miniatures in King Alfonso's *Cantigas de Santa Maria* as well as in numerous medieval pictures.

and Señor Don Carlos, who loves me dearly, will help me, I'll dare make him remember me and the day his black father begot him as long as he lives."

It must be explained here that Don Álvaro and Don Carlos had ordered their secretary to blacken his face as he did in Zaragoza and enter the hall to present himself to Sancho in the same way he had appeared back there before him and his master, continuing the hoax of the challenge. So the aforesaid secretary entered, face and hands smudged, wearing a long garment of black velvet, a great gold chain about his neck; his fingers were be-ringed and heavy hoops were fastened to his ears.

When Sancho saw him, since he already knew him from Zaragoza, he said, "You are most welcome, smoke mountain. What do you wish? My master and I are here. Protect yourself against the devil and watch what you say, by the life of my Dapple, because you look like nothing but the mounds of pitch used in El Toboso to line the big jars."

The secretary took his stand in the center of the hall, without showing any courtesy to anybody. After a short silence he turned to Don Quixote and spoke as follows: "Loveless Knight, my master, the giant Bramidán de Tajayunque, King of Cyprus, sends me to you so that you may inform him when you wish to conclude the battle you have agreed to have with him in this Court. He has just now arrived from Valladolid where he happily terminated a dangerous adventure in which he alone, with no weapons except his steel mace, killed more than two hundred knights. Consequently, give me your answer at once so that I may return to my master, the giant."

Before Don Quixote could reply Don Carlos went up to his disguised servant saying, "Señor squire, with Don Quixote's permission I wish to answer as one who also has reason to be avenged for your master's haughty words. So I say, for both of us, that the contest will be waged Sunday afternoon, in the place designated by Their Highnesses, in whose presence it must be fought, and it is to be with the weapons he thinks most appropriate. And with this you may leave and go with God, unless something else should be offered you."

The secretary answered, "Well, before I go I wish to take vengeance here in this hall on an enormously arrogant squire of the Loveless Knight, named Sancho Panza, who has taken it on himself to say that he is better and braver than I. Therefore, if he is among you, let him step forth so that I may chew him up into the tiniest pieces and throw him to birds of prey to be eaten."

All were silent. When Sancho became aware of such a universal silence he said, "Isn't there a devil here, now that he's needed, to speak in my behalf out of gratitude and in payment for all that I have said at times for everybody?" Going up to the secretary he said, "Señor black squire, Sancho Panza, that's me, is not here now, but you'll find him at the Puerta del Sol in a pastry shop where he is happily concluding a great and dangerous adventure with a batch of pastries. Consequently, tell him for me that I say for him to come at once to fight you."

"Well, since you are Sancho Panza, my adversary, how can you say he is not here?" replied the secretary. "You are a big chicken."

"And you are a great rooster," responded Sancho, "if you expect me to be here in spite of my not wanting to be, no matter how much I may be Sancho Panza, squire of the Loveless Knight and husband of Mari-Gutiérrez. If I'm denying who I am, Saint Peter was more honorable and he denied Jesus Christ, who was better than you and the whore who bore you, whether you like it or not. If you don't think so, speak to the contrary."

The onlookers could not restrain their laughter at this nonsense. Gathering new courage, he continued, "If you don't know it, know now that I am slowly waiting to get angry in order to quarrel with you. You may believe well and clearly that if with your face looking like a cook from hell you expect to chew me into the tiniest pieces and cast me to the sparrows, I, with my cheerful face, expect to slice you up like a melon with these fingernails, in order to feed you to the pigs. Consequently, let's get to it. But how do you want us to fight?"

"How should we, except with our sharp swords?" replied the secretary.

"Shut your face, whoreson," said Sancho. "Not that, because the devil is clever and a misfortune can easily occur when one least expects it, and we might stick the point of a sword in an eye without wanting to and then have to be doctored for many days. What we can do, if you like, is to have our fight consist of nothing but blows with our caps, you with that red bonnet you're wearing, and I with my cap, for they are soft things and when one man throws one at the other and hits him he can't hurt him very much. If we don't do it that way let's fight with punches; if not that, let's wait until winter when there's snow and we can rain snowballs on each other at musket-shot range."

"I am satisfied for the fist-fight to take place in this hall, as you say," said the secretary.

"Well, wait a while; you are too hasty and I haven't fully decided to fight with you." responded Sancho.

Don Quixote became angry and said, "It certainly seems you are too afraid of that black man and I believe it is impossible for you to come out of this at all well."

"Oh, curses on the one who bore me and on the one who gets me to battle with anybody!" replied Sancho. "Don't you know that I am not accompanying you to fight with men or women, but only to serve you and feed Rocinante and my donkey, for which you give me the salary we agreed upon? I'd just as soon leave the fighting to Judas and to the one who brought me here. In God's name, look what a spectacle you're making! There is the Lord Arcapámpanos with his wife and his whole tribe and Prince Perianeo and Señor Don Carlos and Don Álvaro and the rest, splitting their sides laughing, and you armed like Saint George, contemplating your Queen Segovia. And you don't expect me to be afraid when I am waiting for my enemy with a candle in my hand, as they say! I wouldn't object if they all got between us and reconciled us, for they know they would be doing the seven acts of mercy."

"You are right, Sancho," said Don Álvaro. "Therefore, out of respect for me, Señor Squire, you must make peace with him and desist from your intention and duel, for the one your master has arranged with his is enough, for by virtue of it the squire of the lord who is his opponent is vanquished."

"That would be a great mercy for me," responded the secretary. "To tell the truth, my soul was quivering in my body from fear of valiant Sancho. However I shall not consider it a definite truce unless we give each other a foot-shake.

"My feet already shake!" said Sancho. "And I'd give everything I have never to set eyes on you again." Saying this, he raised a foot to give it to him, but no sooner had he done so than the secretary seized it and made him fall heavily.

They all laughed, and the secretary went out running, after which Don Quixote went to lift Sancho up saying to him, "I greatly regret your misfortune, Sancho, but you can flatter yourself that you have come out the victor, for by trickery and after a truce has been declared and, still worse, by fleeing, your adversary has done you perfidy. However, if you wish him to be brought here so you can avenge yourself, say so; I'll go after him like a flash of lightning."

"No, by God," said Sancho. "I would come out worse if we

fought on equal terms. As you say, make a silver bridge for the fleeing enemy."

After this they were informed that it was the supper-hour, because the time had passed unnoticed as they were seeing and hearing these and an infinity of even more foolish things. The Archipámpano insisted that they all stay for supper, which they did with great pleasure, exchanging clever jokes during the meal. Afterward they all retired, some to their rooms, others to their homes, except Sancho, who half-unwillingly had to stay in the Archipámpano's room.

CHAP. XXXIV. ABOUT THE OUTCOME OF THE BATtle arranged between Don Quixote and Bramidán de Tajayunque, King of Cyprus, and how Barbara was taken into the Order of Penitent Women.

NOT ONLY did those gentlemen enjoy many happy days with Don Quixote, Sancho, and Barbara, but so did many others with whom they shared their good natures, the nonsense of the one and the stupidities of the other. The affair came to the point that they were already the Court's universal pastime. As a greater diversion the Archipámpano had a fine outfit made for Sancho; it had tightly fitting trousers he called breeches from the Indies, which became him extremely well. In addition he had a sword at his side and a new cap. In order to persuade him to gird the sword they had to tell him one afternoon that he was being dubbed a knight because of his victory over the black squire, and he was taken into the Order of Chivalry with much rejoicing and gaiety.

But, Don Quixote was so rapidly becoming ill-humored because of the praise he saw Sancho's exploits were getting from the nobles, and even more since he saw his squire dubbed a knight, that the Archipámpano and Prince Perianeo, moved by their doubts, were forced to stop plaguing him. With the intention of curing him, they ordered him removed from Barbara's company and kept him from talking with outsiders; Sancho, although he was a simpleton, was in no danger from this decision.

They told Don Álvaro their resolution and, thinking well of it, he said that he would take on the responsibility (enlisting the ingenuity of Don Carlos' secretary, who had to leave within the week for Cordova, where his friends probably were by now, having gone by way of Valencia) of taking Don Quixote personally to Toledo, and giving him a well cared for cure, with all expenses paid, in the Casa del Nuncio,[1] since he had many friends in that city to whom Don Quixote could be entrusted.

He added that he felt obligated to do this because of his qualms about being responsible for Don Quixote's leaving Argamesilla for Zaragoza, since he had informed him about the jousts being held

---

[1] Tha Casa del Nuncio was a famous insane asylum in Toledo, founded in the late fifteenth century by a *nuncio* 'Pope's ambassador.'

there and had left his armor with him and praised his courage. However, Don Álvaro was of the opinion that he should not be told anything until he had been allowed to fight Tajayunque, because this was so firmly fixed in Don Quixote's mind that he deemed it impossible to persuade him to any new adventure until that one which had him so befuddled was finished. What should be done was to order it postponed until the next day, and that for greater acclaim, it take place in the Casa del Campo,[2] where for more entertainment they could invite many friends for supper. He was sure the end of the adventure would be most comical, for he did not expect less from the secretary's cleverness.

Don Álvaro's opinion pleased them all, especially the Archipámpano, who took it upon himself to provide the supper and get the place ready. The only thing he requested Don Carlos to be good enough to do was try to persuade Sancho to stay at his house and send for Mari-Gutiérrez, for the Archipámpano would be responsible for helping and protecting them as long as they lived. He and his wife liked Sancho's disposition and were positive they would find Mari-Gutiérrez no less pleasing. In order that not one of the protectors of Don Quixote and his group should remain without a responsibility with regard to securing their welfare, he made Prince Perianeo responsible for getting Barbara to accept the retirement into a house for penitent women that he was trying to get for her, and he also offered to provide her with the dowry and income needed to live there honorably.

When they had all been made responsible and each one had been individually charged to do all he could for the person entrusted to him, the time had come for the battle with Bramidán. The aforementioned gentlemen went with many others of their rank to the Casa del Campo, where other people were already conversing with the ladies who had gone with the wife of the Archipámpano.

The gentlemen took Don Quixote with them, in full armor, and even fuller of courage. They took with him Queen Zenobia and Sancho, a lackey leading Rocinante, glossier as a result of his idleness and good food, and a page carrying the lance. Don Carlos' secretary was already provided with one of the giant figures used in the Corpus Christi procession in Court.

They reached the theater of the jest, and the seats prepared inside

---

[2] The Casa de Campo (as it is known today) was a former royal park in Madrid, now open to the public.

the house were occupied (after a long while spent in conversation and walking about the garden), and Don Quixote was in his place when Sancho came up to him saying, "What's up, Señor Loveless Knight? How are you getting along? Are the honorable Rocinante and my discreet Dapple well? Haven't they told you anything to tell me? I'm sure you haven't given them my messages, for they wouldn't have failed to reply. However, I know the remedy, which is for me to get rid of all this palace business, get ink and paper, and write them half a dozen lines, for there'll be a page or a purge, or whatever they call them, to take them."

Don Quixote responded, "Rocinante is well and soon you will see him over there doing marvelous things as soon as he faces Bramidán's indomitable horse. I'll not talk about the donkey, son, except to say that he likes the Court very much because he doesn't work and it suits him fine."

To that Sancho replied, "That makes me realize that we are half related, for we have the same disposition. I swear to you, my lord, that never in my life have I eaten better or had a better time than since I have been with the Arcapámpanos,for he doesn't mind spending eight or nine *reales* a day on food any more than I mind eating it up. He has given me a bed on which to sleep, and I swear to God the souls in Limbo don't have a better one, no matter if they are children of kings. The only drawback about it is that with so much luxury I am forgetting the business of adventures and fights. But what do you say about these breeches from the Indies? They are the worst you can imagine: on the one hand, if you don't put thirty laces on them they'll fall off you on the sides; on the other hand, if you put on as many as they require they won't be obliging enough to come down in case of necessity unless you untie them one at a time, even if you implore them, bonnet in hand, and no matter how much they see your heart knocking at your back teeth. Besides, a man can't move with them on or bend over to pick up his own nose from the ground, however much it may fall with the weight of mucus. Oh, whoreson, what wretched things they are for reaping! With them on, not for the whole world would I bet on reaping twelve sheaves a day; I don't know how Indians can reap with them on or swing to and fro without falling flat at every swing. Judging from the way they hop and jump about I believe the Arcapámpanos' pages must be born there in the Indies of Seville with these devilish tights on. I don't know whether knights-errant wore them in former times; what I can say is that every time I have to make water I have to remove one lace from in front, and even after that, whatever I do, half of it goes inside. Breeches in my region are fine things, for if diarrhea hits you when you're wearing them, you have only to untie one bow knot and they're down. I have asked the Arcapámpanos a thousand times to have some like mine made for himself, as wide at the bottom as they are at the top, of good heavy cloth; at the most they wouldn't cost him more than twenty *reales,* and wearing them he will be somebody. Although he tells me he will, I never see that he has done so."

While they were talking in this fashion they heard the pages at the door making a great commotion. Don Álvaro quieted them down and ordered Sancho to sit down on the floor at the Archipámpano's feet, and then Don Carlos' secretary entered the hall inside the giant, who carried a sword of dyed wood three yards long and a span wide. As soon as Sancho saw him appear he shouted, "You see here, gentlemen, one of the most enormous beasts to be found in all beastdom: this is the devil Tajayunque, who more than four months ago has come from the end of the world only to pursue my master. His weapons are so formidable that he needs ten pairs of oxen just to transport them. If you don't believe me, look at the sword with which people say he is accustomed to splitting a blacksmith's anvil in half. Now see what he'll do to my poor master Don Quixote! By God's wounds! Order everybody to be good enough to throw him out of here to join Barrabas so that he can go and carry on war there with his filthy mother. Don't think we have no interest in this, for with one back-slash he will split ten or twelve of us as I would split the soul of Judas with a flick of my finger if he came before me."

Don Quixote ordered him to be silent until they saw what he wanted, for an answer would be given accordingly. The tall giant took his stand in the center and said very deliberately, after enforcing silence on everybody by looking around for some time, "From my presence you must have clearly realized, Loveless Knight, Don Quixote de La Mancha, that I have kept the promise I made you in Zaragoza, to come to the Court of the Catholic King to effect, before his grandees, the singular combat we arranged between us. Today then, is the day on which the days of your life will end on the edges of this fearful sword of mine, because today I shall triumph over you and make myself lord of all your victories, cut off your head and take it with me to the kingdom of Cyprus, where I intend to fasten it above the door of my house with a sign reading 'The Manchegan flower died at the hands of Bramidán.' Today is the day on which, by removing you from the world, I shall be peaceably crowned king of the whole earth, for there will not be power enough to prevent it. Today, in short, is the day on which I shall take away to Cyprus all the ladies in this hall and Court, to do as I please with them in my rich and great kingdom, for today Bramidán will begin and Don Quixote de La Mancha will come to an end. Consequently, if you are a knight as valiant as the whole world says, attack me at once. I have no offensive or defensive weapons other than this single sword made on the forge of Vulcan, hell's blacksmith, whom I adore and revere as a god, together with Neptune, Mars, Jupiter, Mercury, Pallas, and Proserpine."

Having said this he fell silent, but not Sancho, who got up saying, "Well, upon my word, Don Great Giant, if you are joking when you call all those drunkards you mention 'gods,' and if the Holy Inquisition finds out about it, you came to Spain at a bad time."

However, Don Quixote, full of fury and his sense of honor, stood up before him gripping his sword, and very deliberately and solemnly began to speak: "Oh, haughty giant! Don't think that the arrogant words with which you are accustomed to frighten knights of little vigor and courage will suffice to put one hair's breadth of fear in my indomitable heart, for I am the one the entire world knows and you have heard mentioned in all the kingdoms and provinces through which you have passed. You will observe that I have come to this Court only to seek you, with the aim of giving you the punishment which your evil deeds have richly deserved for so many years. But it seems to me that now is not the time for words, but for deeds, for they are usually witnesses and proof of the purity of heart and the courage of knights. However, so that you will not boast that I had some advantage when I went into battle with you, since I am in full armor and you have only your sword, I wish, as a further demonstration of the little worth I place on you, to remove my armor and fight you in shirt sleeves, also with only one sword, for although yours, as one can see, is longer and wider than mine, for that very reason this one is manipulated and governed by a better and braver hand than yours."

After this he turned to Sancho, saying, "Arise, my faithful squire, and help me take off my armor. You will soon see the destruction of this giant, your enemy and mine."

Sancho got up saying, "Wouldn't it be better, sir, for all of us in this hall, since there are more than two hundred of us, to attack him together, some seizing his garments, others his legs, others his head, and others his arms, until we land him on the floor with a great gigantic crash? Afterwards we'll stick all the swords we have in his belly, cut off his head, then his arms, and after this his legs. I assure you that if they leave me alone with him afterward, I'll give him more kicks than can fit in his coat pockets, and I'll wash my hands in his treacherous blood."

"Do as I tell you, Sancho," replied Don Quixote. "The affair is not going to be as you think."

Finally Sancho removed his armor and the good hidalgo remained in his shirt sleeves, exceedingly ugly because he was tall and withered and so skinny. Wearing armor every day, and even some nights, had so wasted him away and destroyed him that he looked like nothing but one of those figures of Death made of a framework of bones and usually placed in the charnel houses at the entrances to hospitals for the incurable. On his black tunic were the marks of his breastplate, backplate, and gorget, and the rest of his garments, such as his doublet and shirt, were half rotted with sweat, for nothing else could be expected from one who so seldom removed his clothing.

When Sancho saw his master looking like that, with everybody surprised at his appearance and skinniness, he said to him, "Upon my soul, I swear to you, Señor Loveless Knight, that when I look at you, so thin and tall, you seem like one of those old nags they turn out into the pasture to die."

At this point Don Quixote turned to the giant saying, "Now, tyrant and arrogant King of Cyprus, grasp your sword and sample the taste of the sharp edges of mine."

Having made these remarks he took two steps back, and unsheathing his half-rusty sword kept slowly approaching the giant who, seeing him coming, was swift to shake from his shoulders the cardboard structure he bore, and the secretary, who had been supporting it, elegantly dressed as a woman, stood there in the center of the hall. Because he was young and had a pretty face he looked the part so well that anybody who didn't know him could easily be deceived.

All those who did not know about the plan were frightened, but Don Quixote, without moving in the slightest, remained quiet, the tip of his sword on the floor, waiting to hear what that maiden he thought was a giant was saying. Having scrutinized the persons present, the maiden said to Don Quixote without moving, "Valiant Loveless Knight, honor and pride of the Manchegan nation, doubtless you are surprised to see such a terrible giant turned into so

tender and beautiful a maiden such as I today, but you need not be astonished for you must understand that I am the Princess Burlerina.[3] If you have never heard of her, I am the daughter of the luckless King of Toledo who is being persecuted and besieged by the deceitful Prince of Cordova, raiser of false testimony against his own stepmother. He has sent word many times these past days that he would lift the siege and give back all her father's land, which the aforesaid prince rules as a general, only if he sent him his daughter Burlerina, me, to use in any way he pleased, on condition that I was to be accompanied by twelve of the most beautiful maidens in the kingdom, together with twelve millions in pure gold, the finest produced in Arabia, to help with the costs of the war and the siege. He vowed by the immortal gods that if this were not done he would not leave one person alive in Toledo nor one stone on another. When my grieving father saw himself reduced to such a necessity and that his forces could not resist those of his adversary, and that he and all his vassals had to die at the cruel hands of such a powerful enemy or accede to his only condition, he sent a request that he be given forty days of grace in order to seek the twelve maidens and that great sum of money. If at the end of the designated time he did not come with the specified demands, the severe action with which he was threatened should be carried out in his kingdom. Oh, invincible Manchegan! When the great danger my father, his brother, and I, his niece, were in was told to an uncle of mine, the sage named Alquife, a great wizard and necromancer who is very fond of you, he cast a very strong spell, placing me in this simulated giant lying here, and sent me hidden in it, to protect my chastity, to look for you throughout the world, leaving no kingdom, island, or peninsula unsearched. My luck was such that I found you in Zaragoza, and I saw no better way to get you away from there and bring you to this Court, only twelve leagues from Toledo, than to invent the deferred challenge. Consequently, oh magnanimous prince! if there is in you a trace of pity or the shadow of the infinite love you had for the ungrateful princess Dulcinea del Toboso, even though you are now the Loveless Knight, for the sake of the laws of friendship you owe my uncle Alquife and because of what my hopes placed on you merit, I implore you to set aside all the adventures which may come your way in this Court, and all the honors which its princes offer you, and immediately hasten with me to the defense and help of that distressed kingdom. By going

---

[3] *Burlerina* has as its root *burla* 'joke'.

into singular combat with him you will overcome the accursed Prince of Cordova and free my venerable father from his tyranny. I vow and promise, by the god Mars, I myself will be the reward for your hardships."

Having said these words she remained silent, waiting for Don Quixote to answer. Sancho, however, completely astounded, said before his master replied, "My lady, Queen of Toledo, you don't have to swear in the name of Mars, for my master will surely go to kill that arrogant rogue, the Prince of Cordova, and I shall go with him without fail. Therefore, you go a little in advance and tell your noble father that we are already on our way and to have a good supper for us and keep that no-account prince tied to a post and naked until we arrive. I assure you that if you do it, I'll make him remember, with this belt, your name and even the names of his father and mother, as long as he lives."

Sancho's foolish reply visibly delighted everybody, but his simplemindedness was outweighed by what Don Quixote said to the lady: "Indeed, my lady, Princess Burlerina, one who makes you wander about in this way neither loves nor respects you, even though he be the sage Alquife, my great friend and your uncle, but obligated by what I owe him, with less hesitation would I defend the kingdom of his brother, your father, King of Toledo. Moreover, since danger to the freedom of your noble and very lovely self comes into the picture, the obligations moving me to hasten willingly to help in the need mentioned will be greater. Therefore, my reply is that I shall go in person to assist and aid your father. What remains to be done is for you to decide when and how we leave. For my part, I am ready and prepared to go with you at once to avenge you on that tyrannical prince you mention, for we already know each other. I even desire this opportunity for him to feel the touch of my hands, for I have challenged him, but he fled like a coward."

Prince Perianeo, seeing the new adventure which had come to Don Quixote, and how quickly and well Don Álvaro had arranged with the secretary or Don Carlos an easy way to transport Don Quixote to the Casa del Nuncio in Toledo, told him, "From now on, Señor Loveless Knight, I relinquish my suit of the Princess Florisbella of Greece, not wishing to engage in battle with one who can assure entire kingdoms of being victorious even when he is absent. Therefore, I publicly admit being vanquished by that valor, to your not insignificant glory and my shame, and the satisfaction of Prince Belianís of Greece."

These remarks made Don Quixote very happy and he thanked him, declaring himself a friend, and so did Sancho, who wanted to get out of that quarrel. By order of the Archipámpano, he got up and went very respectfully to the Princess Burlerina, taking her hand, at the sight of which all the gentlemen as well as the ladies laughed heartily, knowing it was Don Carlos' secretary and not a woman, as Don Quixote and his squire thought.

Sancho could not bear seeing everybody laughing and said, "What are you laughing at, in the name of her who bore you? Haven't you ever seen a king's daughter in trouble! Well, for your information, my master and I come across them every day on these roads; if you don't believe it, talk to the great Queen Segovia. What you must do, ladies, is to see to it that this princess sleeps with one of you tonight; if not, my bed is at her service, for I kiss her hand."

At these words everybody rose to eat supper and the secretary disappeared. There was a big supper with much talk about the nonsensical actions of Don Quixote and Sancho. They all praised the Archipámpano's decision when they learned he was planning to send Don Quixote to Toledo to receive treatment in the Casa del Nuncio. They returned home by carriage, as they had come but Sancho remained at the house of the Archipámpano, as usual, and Barbara and Don Quixote went with Don Carlos and Don Álvaro to Prince Perianeo's house.

As soon as he got there, the latter undertook zealously to persuade Barbara to retire to a house for women of her condition, since it was so much to her advantage and the Archipámpano wished it, for he was offering to pay for her admission and give her enough income to take care of her for the rest of her life. Convinced by his good reasoning, and knowing how bad it would be for her to return to Alcalá where everybody already knew her behavior and where she would find herself without anything to eat and no endowments with which to earn a living, she consented with no little joy to do as he wished and stay wherever they put her. So within two days her retirement was effected without Don Quixote finding out about it. When they found her so amenable they persuaded him that due to their efforts her vassals had been able to take her away from the Court and return her secretly to her kingdom.

CHAP. XXXV. ABOUT THE WORDS THAT PASSED *between Don Carlos and Sancho Panza concerning his desire to return to his land or write a letter to his wife.*

ON CARLOS was already on the eve of celebrating his sister's marriage to the nobleman, and he wanted Sancho to settle down in Madrid for the pleasure of the Archipámpano and to add to the greater solemnity of the occasion. Thus, to force him to bring his wife and to forget about his home, he said to him one day when he found him in the Archipámpano's house, "You already know, my good Sancho, that ever since I saw you in Zaragoza I have always desired your welfare and I myself personally entertained you at my table the first night you entered my house, and the servants in my house have always shown you favor, especially the lame cook. Therefore you must be aware that what has always motivated me in this has been to see you a respectable man of good character. I was sorry to see a person of your age and good qualities suffer, more so because you were in the company of a man like Don Quixote, so crazed that you couldn't fail to undergo a thousand misfortunes, because his mad, nonsensical acts and sudden spells of anger can't promise success for him nor for anybody who accompanies him, and I'll not mention what you may have experienced since last year. If this isn't so, tell me, what did you get out of the old adventures except drubbings, cudgelings, bad nights and worse days, in addition to much hunger, thirst, and weariness, besides finding yourself, at your age, tossed in a blanket by four villainous peasants? Tell me, have you suffered any less in this last sally? In it the islands, peninsulas, provinces, and governments you and your master have conquered have turned out to be misfortunes in Ateca, the interlude of misery in Zaragoza, amusement for the rascals in the Sigüenza jail, ridicule in Alcalá, and finally, mockery and jeering in this Court. However, since it was the will of God for you to enter it at the end of your pilgrimage, be grateful to him, because he has undoubtedly permitted it so that your troubles will end here, as have those of Barbara who, having retired into a house of virtuous and penitent women, is now separated from Don Quixote and spending a life of ease, lacking for nothing because of the alms that the charity of the Archipámpano has given her. His benevolence is so great that, not content with helping only her, he is now attempting to do the same with your master. So you will soon lose him, for in a few days he is being sent to Toledo with orders that he undergo treatment at the Casa del Nuncio, a hospital reserved for those who are mentally disturbed, as he is. His generosity is not satisfied with helping those mentioned; he is trying more earnestly and with greater affection to help you by having you closer, inside his house, where he is keeping you with all the luxury, abundance, and comfort you have been experiencing for so many days. What remains to be done is for you to try to keep the protection you have, which is noteworthy, as is the fact that he, his wife, and the household love you. You and your wife, Mari-Gutiérrez, will not leave here as long as you live, and my advice is that you bring her by having her sent for. I shall give you a reliable messenger and pay the expenses, for the Archipámpano will be pleased to have you in this palace and will give both of you a room and a salary and a very decent allowance every day of your lives; with this you will lead a happy and untroubled existence in one of the best places in the world. Meanwhile, what you must do is consent to what I ask of you and presently give me the answer my zeal for your welfare deserves."

Don Carlos remained silent after these remarks. Sancho remained perplexed for a good while after hearing them, and then he responded, "Indeed, Señor Don Carlos, the favor you and the Arcadepámpanos have shown me these days, although I beg your pardon for it, just in case it hasn't been as much as I deserve, for the way I see it, all the money all the old clothes dealers have couldn't repay me. Nevertheless, I thank you, and in Argamesilla I have at your disposal twenty-six head of cattle, two oxen, and a pig as big as those around here. We are going to kill it, God willing, for Saint Martin's Day, by which time it will be the size of a cow. So I say in reply, give me, if you like, a few months' time, because this thing of changing locations is not to be done all of a sudden. What I shall do is discuss it with my Mari-Gutiérrez, or at least write her all you have said. If she is halfway in accord, I'll very willingly be more so, so get me ink and paper, if you please, and let's write a letter right away to tell her all that as clearly as a Hail Mary. I say 'Let's write' because the one who gets things done does plenty, although I don't know how to write any more than a dead man, even though I had an uncle who wrote beautifully. I was such a big rogue that when they sent me to school as a boy I used to go to the fig trees and vines and stuff myself with figs and grapes, and so I turned out to be a better eater than a writer."

Don Carlos was satisfied with the reply, and they put off writing the letter until after dinner, which Don Carlos ate with the Archipámpano. In the course of the after-dinner conversation Don Carlos told him that he had already secured Sancho's consent to bring his wife to the Court, if it suited her, and all that was needed now was to write to her and for ink and paper to be brought so he could act as secretary to write the letter Sancho would dictate.

Everything was brought at once, and Don Carlos had just started to fold the paper when Sancho said, "Do you know, gentlemen, what I think? Believe me, it would be a lot better and wiser for me to return home and stop beating about the bush, for it's been nearly six months since I left, wandering about like a loafer, following my master Don Quixote for a miserable salary of nine *reales* a month, although up to now he hasn't given me a cent; in the first place, he says he will include the donkey in the account, and in the next place, he will be paying me quite a lot, for he will give me the governorship of the first island or peninsula, kingdom, or province he wins. But if you are taking him, as Don Carlos said, to be a Nuncio in Toledo,[1] and I can't belong to the church, I now renounce all the rights and privileges that may belong to me by inheritance or legal decree over whatever he may conquer. I have decided to return to my home now that planting time has come. In my village I can earn two and a half *reales* and my keep every day, not counting grouse-hunting. Consequently, joking aside, your lordship Señor Arcapámpanos, order my dark breeches to be given back to me at once, and take these of yours from the Indies (I hope they'll burn them!). Likewise give me my smock and the other cap, and goodby, for I'm on my way. I know that my Mari-Gutiérrez and everybody in my village will be waiting for me, because they love me and I am the light of their eyes. Who tells me I should meddle with pages that don't leave me alone all day long, not to speak of some damned gentlemen who do nothing but bother me with 'Over here, Sancho,' 'Over there, Sancho'? Even though the food here is always appetizing, if not always to the mouth at least always to the eyes, still the salary is very poor. Often I see them pretending to cast the blame on the servants so they can refuse or take away their ration allowance or dismiss them underpaid. If that doesn't happen when they're well, it's a sure thing that when they're sick no master will order, nor will any steward perform a charitable deed for the poor servants. In short, the rascals in the kitchen are right when they say that palace life is bestial life where one lives on

[1] Sancho has misunderstood, and thinks that Don Quixote is to be *made* a *nuncio*, a Pope's ambassador.

hopes and dies in some poorhouse. It's all over, master Don Carlos; there is no room for argument. In short, tomorrow I intend to take to my heels. It is true that if the Arcapámpanos would provide me a ducat every month and two or three pairs of shoes every year, with a slip of paper stating that there would be no dispute later, and if you vouched for it, you would undoubtedly have in me a servant for many days. Therefore, if you decide to do it there is nothing to do except carry it out, hand over your pair of mules, and tell me every night what I have to do in the morning and where I must go to plow or take a look at some stubblefield or other; as for the rest, leave it to me, for you won't be dissatisfied with my work. It is true I have two faults: one is that I am somewhat of an eater, and the other is that to awaken me in the mornings the master has to come sometimes to my bed and hit me with a shoe. With that I wake up right away like a buck deer, and after feeding my belly and the mules I go to the blacksmith's to get the plowshare and work the bellows while he pounds it. I return home an hour before dawn, singing seven or eight *seguidillas*,[2] for I know some fine ones. Then I roast a few cloves of garlic to freshen my breath, eating them with two or three pulls at the wineskin which I also take to the plowing, and at dawn, thus prepared, I mount the stoutest chestnut mule . . . "

He was going to go on from there, but Don Carlos cut him short, surprised by his ingenuous speech, and said to him, "What I have advised you to do must be done faithfully, for all the conditions you have requested will be granted."

Sancho replied, "I truly doubt it, coming from one who was not ashamed to take two and a half *reales* from a squire like me for the first supper he gave me, so I don't want to have anything more to do with him except for God to send him to those places where He can make better use of him."

The Archipámpano, seeing the words were directed at him, said, "Sancho, I shall do all that Don Carlos has promised you in my name, better than you could wish. Be assured that in my house God's grace will not be lacking."

"God's grace, where I come from, means a fine omelet of eggs and rashers of bacon[3] which I know how to prepare most perfectly," said

[2] *Seguidillas* are very emotional songs.

[3] "Eggs and bacon, the grace of God," was a saying referring to the two kinds of food universally available in Spanish homes—there was always bacon hanging from a rafter and a daily supply of eggs—therefore an unexpected guest always could be fed, by the 'grace of God', even when the cupboard seemingly was bare.

Sancho. "With the first money God sends me I'll make such a one for me and for Señor Don Carlos that we won't leave the least bit of it."

"I'll be very glad to eat it, but it must be on the condition that for love of me you will put on a hat such as we wear in Court, and leave off the cap," responded Don Carlos.

"In all my born days I haven't worn a hat, nor do I know what they're like, because my cap fits my head, which is a blessing from God," replied Sancho. "In short, it's an excellent protection, for if it's cold a man can pull it down to his ears; if it's windy he covers his face with the front fold as if he were wearing a winter cap, and goes on as sure it won't fall off as the mill wheel is that it will turn, and it doesn't blow off like hats, which roll around over the fields as if a curse were on them when a gust of wind strikes them. Besides, a dozen of them cost twice as much as half a dozen caps, for each one costs two and a half *reales*, counting workmanship and all."

"It's very clear, Sancho, that you know how I need you, and that I don't need to offer anything in return for your staying in my house, since you ask for so many delicacies," said the Archipámpano. "But so that you will realize my generosity, tomorrow I'll order that you and your wife be paid two years' salary in advance, and when she arrives I'll clothe both of you very handsomely."

"I am most grateful to you for that favor," said Sancho. "Now we only have to know if your fields which I am to sow this fall are far away. After that, since I am not familiar with them, I shall have to go there next Sunday, and I also need to know the mules and their bad habits and if their yoking straps and the rest of the harness are good. I don't want you to say later that I am careless."

"Everything will be as you wish, Sancho," replied Don Carlos. "What we need to do is write the letter to your wife."

"Of course, let's write, with God's blessing," he responded. "But I warn you that she is a little deaf, and we'll have to write a little heavily for her to hear. Make the cross and say, LETTER TO MARI-GUTIÉRREZ, MY WIFE, IN ARGAMESILLA DE LA MANCHA, NEXT TO EL TOBOSO. Now then, tell her that I end here but I don't stop praying for her soul."

"What are you saying, Sancho?" said Don Carlos. "We haven't told her anything and you are already saying 'I'll stop with this.' "

"Be quiet, because you don't understand," he responded. "Do you want to know better than I what I must say? Devil take me if you haven't made me break my thread of the finest astrological thought anyone could think of. But say, for I remember now, 'You must know

that up to now we haven't seen each other since I left Argamesilla; everybody says my health is very good; my eyes hurt just from looking at things of the other world; please God the same will be true of yours. Notify me about how you are getting along with your drinking and if there is enough wine in La Mancha to cure that thirst my presence causes you; upon your life, root out the weeds which usually trouble the little garden. Send me the dark old woolen breeches which are on the chicken coop, because the Arcapámpanos here has given me some breeches from the Indies in which I can't move; I'll put them away for you, for perhaps they'll fit you better. Besides, if it isn't too much trouble, bring the glass knob, carefully packed, for they have a front door which is opened and closed by just a strap. If you want to come, I have already told you what salary the Arcapámpanos will give us every month; so I order you to come to serve the Arcapampanesa before this letter leaves here, and to bring with you all our household goods and rootstock which is there, and don't leave one span of earth or one leaf in the orchard and don't be argumentative, for I'm already getting tired of your peevishness. It will all turn out for the best; don't make me have to tell you, as I usually do, with a stick in my hand, 'Whoa! or I'll give a rub-down to my father-in-law's jenny.' "

When these remarks were written down he turned to Don Carlos saying, "You must know, sir, that today's women are devils and if you don't whack them on the noggin they won't do anything right if they get burned up. Upon my word she'll do this or if not, look out, my dark darling!"

He said this taking off his belt and angrily holding it in his hand, and added that he knew how to handle Mari-Gutiérrez better than the Pope. The Archipámpano and everybody present were astonished to see such innate stupidity and expected to see him hit Don Carlos with the belt. However, not doing so, he continued, "Write this, 'I've already told you, Mari-Gutiérrez, that we shall get along fine here, for even if you are opposed to being in the house with these ceremonious nobles, still the Arcapámpanos is an honest man and has sworn that after you arrive here he will clothe both of us and give us two years' salary in advance, which is one ducat for each animal each month, one for me and the other for you. Therefore, bear in mind that we can live a thousand months at least if we have a good supply of money. About Señor Don Quixote, I'll tell you only that he has been made Nuncio of Toledo; if you need him, you'll find him, when you pass through there, in the appropriate houses, accompanied by quite a few people. The Arcapampanesa, the mistress you are to serve, kisses your hands and is more interested in writing you than in seeing you. She is a very honorable woman, so her husband says, although I don't think she is. I see that she is lazy, because since I have been here I have never seen her hitch her skirts up into her belt. I am told Rocinante is well and has become quite a person and a courtier. I don't believe the donkey is as much so, or at least his few remarks don't indicate it, unless he is silent because he is bored with being at Court such a long time.' I think there's nothing more to write because she's been told all that she needs to know as well as the best apothecary in the world would tell her, and I am sweating merely from digging letters out of my mind."

"See whether you want to tell her anything else, Sancho, because I'm here to write it down and there's plenty of paper, glory be to God," said Don Carlos.

"Close it up," responded Sancho. "And I'm free Mohammed."[4]

"One can scarcely close a letter without signing it," replied Don Carlos. "Tell me how you usually sign."

"Now there you have a fine trapping!" responded Sancho. "For your information, Mari-Gutiérrez is not fond of so much rhetoric and there is no need to sign for her, because she believes very firmly and steadfastly everything the holy mother church of Rome teaches and believes, and so she doesn't need any sort of signature, nor do I sign my name."

---

[4] An exclamation indicating that one has finished with one's obligation.

When it was finished, the letter was read aloud to him, to the incredible laughter of those present and attention on Sancho's part. Then the Archipámpano said to him, "How will Don Quixote take the news of your remaining in my house, Sancho? I shouldn't want him to become angry and then come here to challenge me to singular combat, so that I should unwillingly be obliged to make you return with him."

"Don't fear," responded Sancho. "I shall speak plainly to him before he goes to Toledo and I'll return the donkey and the suitcase together with the giant Bramidán's huge glove which I put away in it the night he attacked and challenged him at Don Carlos' house. I'll give it back to him so he can return it to the Princess Burlerina or give it as a gift to the archbishop when he enters Toledo as Nuncio, for I don't want anything from anybody. The most I'll say to him is that he go with God, for from now on to Judgment Day I curse fights and want nothing to do with them, for I have come out of his claws so stripped and beaten, as my poor back knows, and I fared so badly in an inn about two months ago that some actors almost turned me into a Moor and would even have circumcised me if I hadn't begged them, weeping bitterly, not to touch those outlying neighborhoods because it would mean touching the apple of Mari-Gutiérrez' eyes. Later, the defense of a mule's rump strap which my master called a lovely garter, cost me some very fine thwacks. Even though he cares so much for me that I understand he will give me what he promised, which is the governorship of some kingdom, province, island, or peninsula, I still will say tomorrow that I can't go with him because I have an agreement with you, and what he can do is send it to me, because I am man enough to govern it from here as well as there. But do you know what I think? That since no reliable messenger between here and Argamesilla will be found, it will be wiser for me, knowing the road, to take the letter myself, because I assure you that I shall only put it faithfully in my wife's hands and return immediately."

"Well, as for that, Sancho, was it necessary to write her if you were going there in person?" said the Archipámpano. "Don't worry about it, for I shall look for somebody who will take it very soon and bring back the reply at once, although I doubt it will be as elegant as your letter in which you show that you have studied all the literary knowledge they teach in Salamanca, judging from the way you have embellished it with wise statements."

"I haven't studied at Salamanca," responded Sancho. "But I have an uncle in El Toboso who is now, for the second time, steward of the Rosary Guild. He writes as well as the barber, so the priest says. As I have often gone to his house, I have always benefited somewhat from his good skill because, as people say: 'Who is your enemy? The one in your profession'; 'the evil man sins in a chest which is always open;' finally, 'the one who steals from a thief deserves to be pardoned.'[5] So, due to him, I know how to write letters; if I have stolen from him something of what he knows along this line, as this note reveals, it doesn't matter. He more than owed it to me because I went with him a day and a half to harvest, and may the devil take me if he gave me more than a four-*real* piece. And my wife went for twelve days in the month of March to clear up his land, and he gave her nothing but a yellow *real* whose value we don't know. Consequently I am better off with the *cuartos* and *ochavos*, which are the coin of the realm and which have to be accepted by the king himself and the Pope, whether they like it or not."

At this point they arose from the table to go for a walk, leaving the Archipámpano to order the secretary and the steward to send two servants to Argamesilla at once with that letter, with the command that for no reason should they return without Sancho's wife, but that they should bring her comfortably without delay.

It was so done. Mari-Gutiérrez arrived in Court with them within two weeks and Sancho received her with comical compliments, and the Archipámpano was the best entertained man in Court during those days. Not only he, but also many people there and his entire household for many months spent some merry intervals of conversation and amusement with Sancho and his Mari-Gutiérrez, for she was no less stupid than he. I shall leave the events that happened to this good, innocent married couple for the story that will be made of them in time, for they are such that they alone require a large book.

[5] Sancho cites three proverbs and mixes up two of them; it is the *righteous* man who sins when the chest is open, and the man who steals from a thief earns a *hundred years* of pardon.

CHAP. XXXVI AND LAST, HOW OUR GOOD KNIGHT, Don Quixote de La Mancha was taken to Toledo by Don Álvaro Tarfe and placed there in fetters in the Casa del Nuncio so that he might be cured.

WHEN DON ÁLVARO was ready to return to Cordova and had bidden farewell to all those at Court that his obligation required, he contrived on the eve of his departure that, in order to take Don Quixote away, one of the Archipámpano's servants, dressed in traveling clothes, should enter just after they finished supper. He was to be fancily dressed as if he came from Toledo in the name of the Princess Burlerina to get him to go with them as hastily as possible to lift the city's siege and free it from annoyance by the treacherous Prince of Cordova. He was as well instructed about what he was to do and say to Don Quixote when he gave him the message as though he were fresh off the road from Toledo as to where, by order of the Archipámpano, he was to accompany him in order to conceal the stratagem better and to bring back news of Don Quixote and the state in which he was left.

When the appointed night and hour arrived Don Carlos, Don Quixote, and Don Álvaro had just finished supper at Prince Perianeo's house. Don Álvaro had just informed Don Quixote that he was leaving the next day for Cordova, and asked if he had anything to send to Toledo, through which he was to pass, when the aforesaid page of the Archipámpano entered, handsomely attired, by way of the drawing-room. After courteously greeting all those present, he turned to Don Quixote and said, "Loveless Knight, the Princess Burlerina of Toledo, whose page I am, humbly kisses your hands and implores as earnestly as she can that you be good enough to leave with me tomorrow without fail, swiftly and quietly, for the great city of Toledo where she and her sorrowful father and the best and most splendid of the kingdom are waiting for you from moment to moment, for it is only three days until the end of the forty-day period of grace given them by the Prince of Cordova to deliberate on whether to surrender the city or deliver the inhuman tribute he demanded. If you do not help them with your brave arm they will doubtless all be miserably killed, the city sacked, the temples and the foundations of towers and battlements will fill the happy streets and their stones will serve them as a highway and pavement. My lady the

the Princess, and the King are waiting for you with the best knights of their court at a certain rear gate unknown to the enemy, so that the next day, before dawn, at the sudden call to arms, with shouts of 'Santiago' and help from him we shall attack, catching them unawares, so that the enemy will be conquered, as it undoubtedly must be, with you the conqueror. After this, if you like, though it be a small prize for your unheard-of greatness, you will be married to the very beautiful Princess who has rejected many other sons of kings and princes just to marry you. Consequently, valiant knight, go to rest at once so that by leaving early in the morning we may at a timely hour reach the imperial city of Toledo where they are expecting you at any moment."

Don Quixote answered very deliberately, "You have come at a very good time, fortunate page, for I can go this time accompanying Don Álvaro, who has just told me that he is also leaving for Toledo in the morning. Therefore we have only to prepare what is necessary so we can leave together at dawn and I can arrive with such a distinguished company to help your lord, the King, and the Princess Burlerina, niece of the sage Alquife, my good friend. In truth, I do not think I should be rewarded as you said, and marry the Princess after killing the treacherous Prince of Cordova, her adversary, and sacking their field of battle. In fact, being known around the world as the Loveless Knight it will not be right for me to be engaged in love affairs until several dozens of years have passed, for it could happen, as it has happened to other knights-errant, that as I roamed about such a multitude of varied kingdoms and provinces I would find and even fall in love with some princess of Babylon, Transylvania, Trebizond, the Ptolomaic kingdom, Greece, or Constantinople. If this happens to me, as I trust it will, from that day on I shall have to call myself the Knight of Love, for I shall undergo extraordinary hardships, dangers, and difficulties for the sake of such a princess until, after freeing her kingdom or empire from the very strong enemy besieging it, I shall reveal my love to this certain princess in her very own apartment which I shall enter in full armor one dark night, stepping noiselessly through a large garden, guided by a wily maid of hers. Although at first, being a pagan, she will be terrified to hear I am a Christian, still she will be smitten with my endowments and, impelled by the reasons with which I shall persuade her of the truth of our holy religion, she will marry me with public festivities, and she and her whole kingdom will be baptized. But such notable wars, and so many of them, have happened to me because of certain insurrections by envious vassals that they will supply future historians with much to relate."

When Don Álvaro saw that he was now beginning to rave he got up saying, "Let's retire, Señor Don Quixote, because we must get up early in order to reach Toledo in time, for it is dangerous to delay." With this remark he turned to the page to tell him, "You, discreet ambassador of the wise Princess Burlerina, go now to eat your supper and then retire in the bed the steward will show you."

The page left the room with the others and they all went to their beds, Don Quixote paying no more attention to Sancho than if he had never seen him, which was a special favor from God. It is true that when he got up in the morning, as Don Álvaro's servants and the Archipámpano's page were saddling up, he asked for his squire, but Don Álvaro diverted his attention by telling him not to worry about him, because he was already preparing to follow them and would come along slowly behind them, as he often did. After a good breakfast they took leave of Prince Perianeo and Don Carlos and left the Court in the direction of Toledo. Along the road they had some very amusing opportunities to laugh, especially in Getafe and Illescas.

When they arrived in sight of Toledo Don Quixote said to Princess Burlerina's page, "I think, friend, that before entering the city it would be good to make a nice foray into the enemy's camp, for I am well-armed and the camp seems to be unprepared for the blow which, by my effort, is so close to falling on it and its arrogance. It would be a start toward lowering its crest, which is so proudly raised."

The page responded, "Sir, the order I bring from the King and the Princess is for us to go without any noise whatsoever to the place where they are awaiting us."

"That is a very prudent order," added Don Álvaro. "There is no doubt it would put the victory in jeopardy if you gave them the slightest opportunity in the world to prepare themselves. They would have a great chance to do so, with the disturbance we would create, for it is certain that upon hearing the noise we would make, the alert sentries would give the warning that there were enemies around."

Don Quixote replied, "I mean to follow that opinion as the wisest one, for at least it assures me that I shall catch them unaware. Therefore, you, page of Princess Burlerina, guide us to where we are to enter without being heard, but be forewarned that if we are alone before entering the city I must cause the bloody destruction of these pagan Andalusians who have dared come up to the sacred walls of Toledo."

The page walked ahead straight toward the gate they call El Cambrón, leaving the Visagra Gate to the left. But as Don Quixote did not notice any noise of armed persons about the city, and on the other hand saw people going in and out of the Visagra Gate at will, he said wonderingly to the page, "Tell me, friend, where has the Prince of Cordova encamped, since I don't see any war material around here?"

"Sir, the enemy is astute," he responded. "Consequently they have taken their position on the other side of the river where our artillery cannot harm or bother them."

"Certainly they know little about military science," said Don Quixote. "Don't the fools see that by leaving these two gates open and unprotected those inside can easily get the help and provisions they desire, as indeed my entrance today shows; not everybody knows everything."

As I say, they entered through the Cambrón Gate, and Don Quixote went along the streets looking on all sides to see when and where the King, the Princess, and the grandees of the court would come out to receive them. At the entrance to the town Don Álvaro pretended he wanted to stay and wait for Sancho, so he could enter the inn where he was to stay, not accompanied by the boys following Don Quixote. In fact, he did this, sending two or three servants of his to be with the Archipámpano's page and Don Quixote. With them and an unbelievable crowd of urchins following him because he wore armor, the unhappy man arrived unwittingly at the doors of the Casa del Nuncio. Don Álvaro's servants remained there on guard and Don Quixote entered alone with the page and a muleteer who held Rocinante for him. Upon dismounting, the Archipámpano's page said to Don Quixote, "Sir Knight, stay here while I go upstairs to report your secret and longed-for arrival to the Princess." Then he went upstairs.

Don Quixote remained in the center of the courtyard, looking all around. He saw four or six rooms with iron bars, and inside were many men, some chained, others fettered, and others handcuffed; some were singing, others weeping, many laughing, and not a few were preaching. In short, every insane man there sang his own song.

Wondering about them, Don Quixote asked the muleteer, "Friend, what is this house? Or tell me, why are these men held prisoner here, and why are some so happy?"

The muleteer, who had already been instructed by Don Álvaro and the Archipámpano's page how he was to deal with Don Quixote, responded, Sir Knight, for your information, all who are here are enemy spies whom we have caught at night in the city, and we are holding them prisoner to punish them at our leisure."

Don Quixote continued questioning, "Well, why are they so happy?"

The servant responded, "They are so happy because they have been told that three days from now the city will surrender to the enemy; therefore, the expected victory and freedom make them unaware of the present hardships."

As they were talking like this a young man came out of a room with a bucket in his hand; he was one of the madmen who was already somewhat regaining his senses. When he heard what the muleteer had said to Don Quixote he gave a great burst of laughter, saying, "Señor armed man, this servant is deceiving you; know that this house is the insane asylum, called El Nuncio, and all those in it are as lacking in wits as you are. If you don't believe it, wait a bit and you will see how quickly you'll be put in with them. Your face and appearance and your arrival in armor promise nothing except that these thieving guardians are bringing you to throw a heavy chain on you and give you a thorough trouncing until you recover some sanity whether you like it or not. They've done the same thing to me."

The servant told him to hush, that he was a drunkard and was lying. "In good faith," the crazy man replied, "if you don't believe I am telling the truth, I'll wager you have come for the same reason as this poor man in armor."

At this Don Quixote stepped aside, laughing, drew close to one of those barred windows, looked carefully at the person inside and saw squatting on the floor a man dressed in black and wearing a filthy bonnet; he had a heavy chain on his foot and on both hands were light fetters which served as handcuffs. He was staring so unblinkingly at the floor that he seemed to be in a profound dream. When Don Quixote saw him he said, "Ah there, good man! What are you doing here?" Raising his head very deliberately and seeing Don Quixote in full armor, the jailed man slowly went up to the barred window, leaned against it and remained without saying a word, very carefully inspecting him.

The good knight was astonished at this, and was more so when he saw that out of twenty questions he asked, not one was answered, nor did the man do anything except look him up and down. However, after a long while he suddenly laughed with signs of much enjoyment and then began to weep most bitterly saying, "Oh, Sir Knight! If you knew who I am you would undoubtedly be moved to the greatest pity. For your information, I am a theologian, an ordained priest, an Aristotle in philosophy, a Galen in medicine, an Ezpiculeta in canons, a Ptolemy in astronomy, a Curcio in law, a Tully in rhetoric, a Homer in poetry, an Amphyon in music,[1] in short, I am of noble blood, unique in bravery, unusual in love, unequaled at arms, and first in everything; I am first among the unfortunate and last among the fortunate. Doctors persecute me because, with Mantuano,[2] I tell them:

His etsi tenebras palpent, est data potestas
excruciandi aegros hominesque impune necandi.[3]

The powerful torment me because I tell them with Cassaneo:

Omnia sunt hominum, tenui pendencia filo,
et subito casu quae valuere ruunt.[4]

The timorous, the hateful, and the greedy would like to see me burned because I always have on my lips:

Quatuor ista timor, odium, dilectio, census,
saepe solent hominum rectos pervertere sensus.[5]

Detractors worry me to death because I tell them that anybody who smirches a reputation must restore it:

Imponens, augens, manifestans, in mala vertens
qui negat aut minuit, tacuit, laudatve remisse.[6]

---

[1] Ezpiculeta was a famous Spanish theologian and lawyer (1491-1586), and Amphyon was a figure in Greek mythology who was given a four-stringed lyre to which he added three more strings (thus seemingly inventing the basis for Western music).

[2] Juan Bautista Mantuano (born 1436) was a commentator of Virgil and Petrarch.

[3] "To them has been given the power—though they may touch the shadows of death—of tormenting the sick and of killing men with impunity." *Eclogue VI.*

[4] "All the affairs of men hang by a thin thread, and those things which were strong collapse with a sudden fall." These verses by Ovid must have been cited by Bartolomé Cassaneo.

[5] "These four things—fear, hatred, love, fortune—often corrupt the upright spirit of men." A medieval proverb cited by Cassaneo in his *Catalogus gloria mundi.*

[6] ". . . deceiving, exaggerating, revealing, perverting: he who denies, diminishes, suppresses, or praises faintly."

Poets consider me a heretic because I tell them what Horace says about their fondness for reading his verses:

Indoctum, doctumque fugat recitator acerbus,
quem vero arripuit tenet, occiditque legendo,
non missura cutem nisi plena cruoris hirudo.[7]

And together with them I am hated by historians because I tell them:

Exit in immensum fecunda lecentia vatum,
obligat historica nec sua verba fide.[8]

Soldiers can't bear for me to place letters ahead of them and tell them this by Alcibiades:

Cedunt arma togae, et quamvis durissima corda
eloquio pollens ad sua vota trahit.[9]

Lawyers who are seen talking about legal matters, when they don't keep the laws of God, cannot tolerate being faced with the prudence of their wise predecessors who said:

Erubescimus dum sine lege loquimur.[10]

Ladies lay a thousand traps for me because I proclaim about them:

Sydera non tot habet caelum, nec flumina pisces
quot celerata gerit faemina mente dolos.[11]

Married women deny that anyone can say of them:

Pessima res uxor, poterit tamen utilis esse
si propere moriens det tibi quidquid habet.[12]

---

[7] "The harsh reciter drives away the ignorant and the learned, and he holds on to the man he catches and kills him by reading: the leech will not release the skin until it is full of blood." These are the last verses of Horace's *Ars Poetica*.

[8] "The poet rises to great heights with the fertile license given him, and his words are not restrained by the exactitude that history requires." Verses cited from Ovid.

[9] "Arms retreat before the scholar's gown; a man learned in eloquence attracts the hardest hearts to his bidding." Verses by Andrea Alciato (1492-1550), inspired by Cicero.

[10] "We blush while we speak without law."

[11] "Heaven has not so many stars nor rivers fish as the wicked female mind has deceptions."

[12] "A wife is a very bad thing; but she may be useful, nevertheless, if by dying she leaves you whatever she has." Medieval Latin verses.

Girls don't tolerate hearing:

Verba puellarum foliis leviora caducis
irrita, qua visum est, ventus et unda ferunt.[13]

And also:

Ut corpus, teneris sic mens infirma puellis.[14]

Beautiful women make faces upon hearing:

Formosis levitas semper amica fuit;[15]

although it is true that of all of them it can be said:

Quid sinet inausum faeminae praeceps furor?[16]

Idle lovers would like for my tongue to be exiled, for it repeats to them:

Otia si tollas periere Cupidinis arcus,
contemptaeque jacent et sine luce faces.[17]

Priests are ashamed to have repeated to them what Judith said about their old law: *Et nunc, fratres, quoniam vos estis presbiteri in populo Dei, et ex vobis pendet anima illorum, ad eloquium vestrum corda eorum erigite.*[18] Royal power which, like love, admits no companionship,

Non bene cum sociis regna Venusque manent,[19]

is such that it is well verified by what Ovid said in an epistle about a queen who, when she was besought by her lover, responded to him:

---

[13] "Girls' words are lighter than the falling leaves, and breath and wind carry away the useless sounds." This and the following quotation are from Ovid.

[14] "A girl is weak-minded as her body is tender."

[15] "Vanity was ever a friend of beautiful women."

[16] "What will the rash fury of a woman leave unattempted?" From Seneca.

[17] "If you take leisure away, Cupid's bow will perish, and torches will lie neglected and without light." A quotation from Ovid's *Remedia Amoris.*

[18] And now, brothers, since you are priests among God's people, and their souls hang upon your eloquence, stir up their hearts." From the Apocrypha—II Judith 8:21.

[19] "Kingship and love do not suffer companions." From Ovid's *Ars amandi.*

Sic meus hinc vir abest, ut me custodiat absens.
An nescis longas regibus esse manus?[20]

Oh, most valiant Prince! Such are the people who have me here because I reproach the regard for public opinion based on the conservation of possessions of fortune, which the Apostle calls dung, with the breaking of God's law, as if, by keeping it, David had not risen from a humble beginning to become a powerful king, and the great Judas Maccabeus an invincible captain, or as if we did not know that all kingdoms, nations, and provinces of this century which, with moderation of carnal desires and wisdom of their natives, have tried to improve their condition, have destroyed it miserably."

The crazed man pursued his theme, to the great amazement of Don Quixote who, seeing he did not allow him to speak, shouted at him, "Wise friend, I don't know you and I have never seen you in my life. However, the imprisonment of such a talented person has caused me such grief that I don't intend to leave here until I give you precious freedom, even though it be contrary to the King's will and that of his daughter, the Princess Burlerina, who dwell in this royal palace. Therefore, you with the bucket in your hand, bring me the keys to this room here and now, and let this great wise man come out free, safe, and sound, because this is my will."

As soon as the madman with the bucket heard this he began to laugh, saying, "Well now, the bulls are out and running. Upon my word, you have come to a fine place to purge yourself of your sins; how unfortunate it is you've come here!"

Having made these remarks he went upstaris and the insane clergyman said to Don Quixote, "Sir, don't believe a person in this house, for there is no more truth in any of them than in something printed in Calvinist Geneva. But if you want me to tell your fortune in exchange for the good deed you will do for me by freeing me as you offer to do, put your hand through this grille. I'll tell you all that has happened to you and will happen, because I know a great deal about palmistry."

Innocently believing him, Don Quixote removed his gauntlet and stuck his hand through the grille. No sooner had he done so when a sudden rage came over the lunatic and he bit him viciously two or

---

[20] "My husband is away from here in such a way that though absent he watches over me. Do you not know that kings have long arms?" Again from Ovid; this time taken from Helen's letter to Paris in *Heroidas*.

three times, ending by seizing his thumb between his teeth in such a way that he almost lopped it off. Because of the pain, Don Quixote began to shout, at which the muleteer and three or four more of the household hastened up and pulled on him so hard that they made the madman turn loose and left him laughing very contentedly in his cage.

When Don Quixote realized he was wounded and loose he drew back a little and grasped his sword, saying, "False enchanter! I swear that if it were not because it is beneath me to lay hands on such people as you, I would very quickly take revenge for such boldness and madness."

At this remark five or six of those who took care of the house came downstairs with the Archipámpano's page. When they saw Don Quixote, sword in hand and dripping a great deal of blood, they suspected what it might be and went up to him, saying, "Don't kill any more people, Sir Knight in armor."

After this one seized his sword, others his arms, and the rest began to remove his armor while he resisted as much as he could; but it did him no good. In a short time they put him, well-tied, in one of those cells, where there was a clean bed and a bucket. When he was somewhat calmed down, after the Archipámpano's page had very solemnly put him under the protection of the superintendents of the house and described to them his type of madness, his characteristics, where he was from, who he was, and had given them a quantity of *reales* to put them under further obligation, he said to Don Quixote, "Señor Martín Quijada, you are in a place where they will look after your health and person with all possible care and kindness. Bear in mind that others as good as you and just as sick with the same illness enter this house. God grant that shortly they will all come out cured and with the clear judgment they lacked on entering. I trust the same will be true of you, that you will return to your senses and forget the readings and wild fancies in the insane books of chivalry that have reduced you to such a state. Take care of your soul and realize God's mercy in not permitting you to die on those roads in the disastrous situations in which your madness placed you so many times."

Having said this he left with Don Álvaro's servant for the inn in which he was staying and gave him his report about everything, which he passed on to the Archipámpano when he returned to Court. Don Álvaro stayed in Toledo several days and even visited and cheered Don Quixote and tried to quiet him down as much as possible. By means of giving quite a few gratuities he bound the overseers

of the house to do the same and he charged some reliable friends of his in Toledo to look after that sick man, for this would mean doing a great service to God and a very special favor to him. After this he returned happily to his city and home.

It has been no little work to collect from Manchegan archives[21] these accounts about the third sally made by Don Quixote de La Mancha: they are all as true as those collected by the author of the first part, which has been printed. What has to do with his imprisonment and his life and the hardships he endured until then is not known for certain, but there are conjectures and traditions of some very old Manchegans to the effect that he was cured and left the aforesaid Casa del Nuncio, and that as he passed through the Court he saw the now prosperous Sancho who, seeing him now apparently well-adjusted, gave him some money so that he could return to his home. The Archipámpano and Prince Perianeo did the same so he could buy a horse on which he could travel more comfortably. Don Álvaro had left Rocinante to work at the Casa del Nuncio, and there he ended his honorable days, no matter what you hear to the contrary.

However, as it is rare to cure insanity, people say that when he left the Court he went back to his mania, bought another and better horse, and returned to Old Castile. Stupendous and unheard-of adventures happened to him there, for he took as his squire a "working girl" he found by the Tower of Lodones. She was dressed like a man and was fleeing from her master because in his house she became, or they made her become pregnant unwittingly, although not because she didn't give plenty of cause for it. She was roaming around in fear, and the good knight took her without knowing she was a woman until she gave birth in the middle of the road and in his presence, leaving him highly astonished at the birth and imagining the wildest fancies about it.

He turned her over to an innkeeper in Valdestillas to take care of her until his return, and without a squire he went through Salamanca, Ávila, and Valladolid, calling himself the Knight of Hardships, for the celebration of which hardships a better pen will surely not be lacking.[22]

Here ends the second part of the History of the ingenious hidalgo Don Quixote de la Mancha

---

[21] The Manchegan Archives are just as fictional in Avellaneda as they were in Cervantes.

[22] At the end of *Don Quixote*, Part I, Cervantes dares someone else to write about his hero's third sally when he transcribes (badly) this verse from *Orlando Furioso*: "Forsi altro canterà con miglior plectio." 'Perhaps someone else will sing with a better plectrum" (or *pen*, as Cervantes later stated). Here Avellaneda invites yet another author to continue Don Quixote's exploits in his fourth sally. No one took up the dare.

TABLE OF THE CHAPTERS of the present book

Fifth Part

Sixth Part

Seventh Part